THE LARKS DON'T SING
IN THE
VALLEY

ROY DAVIDSON

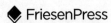 FriesenPress

Suite 300 - 990 Fort St
Victoria, BC, V8V 3K2
Canada

www.friesenpress.com

ISBN
978-1-5255-7374-3 (Hardcover)
978-1-5255-7375-0 (Paperback)
978-1-5255-7376-7 (eBook)

1. *FICTION, ACTION & ADVENTURE*

Distributed to the trade by The Ingram Book Company

THE LARKS DON'T SING
IN THE
VALLEY

AUTHOR'S NOTE

This is a story about the Blackfoot Indians—the *Niitsitapi* they call themselves—the real people. Beginning in 1834, the story is written in English, but the Blackfoot spoke their own language— a language common to the three tribes of the Blackfoot—the Piikani, the Kainai, and the Siksika. Some of the characters in the book speak English, but most speak Blackfoot. When you read conversation in *italics*, it is meant to designate that the speaker is speaking in a language other than English—mostly Blackfoot, but the context will indicate if it is otherwise. Sometimes, Blackfoot names or words have been utilized, in which case, they also appear in *italics*.

At one point, the home range of the Piikani covered an area that now comprises northern Montana, in the United States, and southwestern Alberta, in Canada. This home range was divided, north and south, when the Canadian and American governments agreed on a boundary between their two nations, running along the 49th parallel. The Piikani called this imaginary line across their land "the medicine line." Probably at the behest of the intruding whites, the Piikani began calling themselves the North Piikani, or *Aapátohsipikáni* and the South Piikani, or *Amsskaapipikani*. In America, the South Piikani are called the Blackfeet or the Blackfeet Nation, while in Canada, they are the Blackfoot. I have yet to discover a verifiable reason for this anomaly.

At the end of the book, the reader will find a Glossary, which will help give meaning to most of the words, terms, or expressions that may not otherwise be obvious.

Let me also note that throughout this book, I use the word 'Indian' rather than the more modern terminology of Native, Native American, Aboriginal, Indigenous, First Nations, or maybe others. Such people are governed by the *Indian Act*. In education, they are referred to as FNMI—First Nations, Metis, and Inuit. Which is proper? When I ask Aboriginal friends what they prefer to be called, they typically say, "I don't care—Indian, I guess." Perhaps, that is because we are friends. With others, I know they prefer something else. I do not wish to be offensive to those who are the subject of this book, but I must call you something. To be authentic to the time at which this story takes place, I have used the terminology of that day, including the pejorative. It was how they spoke back then. Know, however, that I respect you and honour you! And, because I do, I dedicate this book to you, the Piikani, who have been my neighbours and friends for many years.

1

The sound of the shots startled a young Blackfoot hopeful who his people called Badger. Even though he had seen fourteen winters, it was his first raid, and he had been unsure what to expect. The sight of the *Liars* carrying fire-sticks had unnerved him, for his party had none. He was unsure how he and his companions would fare armed with just bows and arrows. He had heard many stories that set his imagination on a dark course.

Wishing he still had a father to guide him on such a significant venture, Badger had been forced to accompany Eagle Head, an older cousin, on his first war party. Rather than a rite of passage, the trip had become an ordeal. There had never been a day when Eagle Head had given him any respect or treated him kindly. The youngest on the raid, Badger had thought about leaving and going home many times. But for fear of humiliation, he might have done so. And, he had paid such a very high price to come along: his treasured horse. How he regretted his foolish bargain!

Eagle Head and Rides Alone had sprung the ambush, but that was not what had been agreed upon. They were supposed to have waited until the *Liars* came in front of them all, but seeking glory for themselves, they had loosed their first volley of arrows with their enemy yet out of range for the rest of the group.

One of the *Liars* had been struck with an arrow from Eagle Head's bow and stumbled to the ground. Almost simultaneously, another pair of arrows flew toward the remaining figures. It all happened so fast, as Black Plume and Little Dog now raced to join the action, singing their war songs. Gunshots and smoke filled the air, arrows were flying, and clubs were swinging. Badger had not even loosed an arrow when suddenly, it was over. It was his comrade's noisy, victory celebration which jarred him to his senses. With uninhibited frenzy, all but Little Dog set upon their vanquished foes.

Only a little older than Badger and having been on a few war parties, Little Dog had never seen anything like this before. Stepping away from the triumphant warriors, he waited for Badger to emerge from his cover and join him. Together, they stood and watched in amazement as the others slashed at the bodies with knives and clubbed them with rock hammers. Their wrath quickly spent, the exultant victors set to stripping their victims, yelping and shouting victory cries.

"*Hai! This one is a napikawan!*" a suddenly subdued Black Plume exclaimed soberly, standing over one of the bodies. The others left what they were doing and gathered around him.

"*Let me see!*" Eagle Head blurted. Breathing heavily from their exertion, they all gawked at the pale figure lying in the tall grass. None of them had ever seen a white before.

Black Plume had stopped short of bludgeoning the fellow, and as soon as he saw Eagle Head raise his club to do so, he intervened, grasping him by the arm. "*No! Not this one! We have no quarrel with the napikawan!*"

"What do you mean? He was with the Liars!" the younger hothead protested, trying to pull away from his leader's grasp.

"They are not our enemy! Leave him!" the older one commanded, glaring into the other's eyes until he relented.

"Look at his clothing!" Rides Alone observed, and the onlookers leaned in. Bending over Matthew Preston's body, Rides Alone poked at it with the end of his bow before stooping further to examine the unfamiliar manner in which his shirt was fastened. Eagle Head tugged at the buttons at the front of the trousers. Once they figured out the buttons, they stripped the body.

"Look at the colour of him!" Black Plume pointed out, as Rides Alone put on the shirt and Eagle Head examined the trousers. Curious, Little Dog and Badger gawked morbidly at the now naked form.

"Look at his thing!" exclaimed Eagle Head, poking at it with the tip of his bow. *"Míisinsski! Touch it!"* he teased his cousin.

"No!" Badger responded with disgust.

"Are you afraid?" Eagle Head goaded him.

"No! I do not want to!" Badger insisted.

"Girl!" his cousin mocked. *"Touch it! You are afraid!"*

"No! I just do not—"

"I told you to touch it!"

"No!"

"Do it!" the older one hissed. The others were used to seeing him provoke his cousin, never missing an opportunity to make life miserable for the younger boy. *"You are afraid!"* he taunted, seeing Badger's reluctance. No Indian boy wanted to be accused of being afraid.

"I am not!" the boy insisted.

"You are afraid!" Turning to the others, he announced, *"He is afraid!"*

"No! I just do not want to!" the rattled boy protested.

Eagle Head took a step toward his cousin, but at once, the younger one turned away and announced that he was going to get the horses. *"Yes! That is a good job for a girl!"* the antagonist sneered. *"Hai! Nothing one!"* his cruel relative continued, trying to get him to stop and face him. Badger was fearful of what his cousin might make him do. He did not stop, but his relative would not let up. *"Where were you, nothing one? Where were you when we were going after these Liars?"* he spewed. Ignoring his cousin's questioning, Badger kept walking, while the others stood by and watched to see how it was going to end this time. The elder one was not about to relent. *"Hai, nothing one! I am talking to you!"* Still, the boy ignored him and kept walking.

Little Dog had been Badger's best friend growing up, and he now tried to intervene. *"Why not let him just—"*

"You stay out of this!" Eagle Head snapped at him. *"He is my cousin! He lives in my lodge, and he does what I say!"* The riled warrior was not about to let his younger cousin disgrace him with his insolence. Trotting after the boy, he grabbed him by the shoulder and was as surprised as the others when the smaller figure turned and gave him a shove. Enraged by such unexpected temerity, he grabbed Badger by the shoulders and threw him to the ground, falling on him with a knee to the stomach. Winded, the boy squirmed onto his side, ready to ward off any further attack with his feet. *"You really did it this time!"* his assailant railed between clenched teeth. *"You should never have done that, you nothing one! Go and bring me my horse, girl!"* he demanded, turning away angrily. *"I will make you sorry for this!"* he snarled over his shoulder.

With the altercation apparently over, Little Dog hurried over to his friend. Reaching out a hand, he asked, *"Are you all right?"* The stricken boy only groaned and tried not to let his friend see his tears as he got painfully to his feet, ignoring the hand that had been offered. Not wishing to show his face, he lurched off in the direction of the horses without giving his friend any response.

Relieved to be alone, he choked back tears and hurried to get out of sight. Humiliated, he sought the horses hidden in deep cover. As he struggled through the clawing brush, he wished for a way to avenge himself. How could he prove himself a man. Maybe, he should just leave and end the abuse before it got any worse? He thought about taking all the horses and leaving—it would be impossible for them to catch up to him on foot! But no.

He could never have imagined what his cousin had in store for him.

* * *

"Hey, Andy!" Matthew Preston hollered, seeing his mop-headed, younger brother seated with a couple of the rowers of the same age. They had found a spot out of sight from the men and were sitting together. "Hey, I must tell you something," he cried as he got a little closer. His brother quickly handed something off to one of his companions, who shoved it behind the log they were sitting on. Seeing what it was, Matthew scolded him, "What are you doing?" But having something else on his mind, he did not await his brother's response. "Do you wish to know what I'm doing tomorrow?" he asked, ignoring the others. Matthew had refused to give up the proper English he had brought with him from their home in England. His younger brother had been working hard to leave everything English behind. Much more outgoing than the older one, Andy was strong-willed and adventurous, while Matthew was cautious and reserved in demeanour. Both were strapping and fit, darkly tanned where their skin had been exposed to the summer sun.

"What?" Andy replied sheepishly, feeling foolish for having been caught smoking a pipe and hoping his brother was distracted enough not to care.

"Do you remember those Indians that showed up a short time past?" His brother nodded, and still, without waiting for a response, the older one continued. "They are Cree, and I shall be accompanying them on the hunt tomorrow!"

"Ain't we rowin'?" one of the other boys inquired, using a vernacular more aspired to by the younger brother. These boys were the youngest of the crew and usually hung around together—not one of them being old enough to shave yet. A few others on the crew were in their late teens and early twenties; the rest were men. Only the two brothers and a few of the others had joined the boats at the Red River settlement. Many of the crew had made the arduous trip up the North Saskatchewan River to Edmonton House before. Even a few of the younger ones could boast that they had done it before, too. The 13-year-old, a half-breed, born at Edmonton House, had made the trip out in the spring with his father, and they were now returning for the fall.

"No, you fellows are going to gum the bottoms of the vessels tomorrow," Matthew continued with excitement in his voice. "It will be a day off from rowing for you, lads! The Cree say they knew where they will find buffaloes, right by the river. And, Mr. McConnell has invited me to accompany them. When the rest of you get underway, we should have fresh meat waiting for you!" The whole crew had been anticipating the rich, red meat of the buffalo—everyone was sick of eating fish.

"Where? How come you get to go?" Andy asked. "Can I come?"

"Yeah, can we come?" a couple of the others piled on.

"I doubt it!" the older boy responded. "I already inquired on my brother's behalf. Mr. McConnell is thinking about it. He will decide."

"Aww!" Andy pouted, clearly expecting disappointment.

"Shucks!" another said with a frown.

"You must possess a suitable weapon—none of you have such a thing," Matthew reminded them. "I have that which was left us by my father."

"That's not much of a gun!" one of the youngsters observed. "You can barely even knock over a deer with it!" he reminded the eager hunter.

"I recognize that," Matthew agreed. Giving the youngsters a bit of a sneer, he continued, "That is why Mr. McConnell will be allowing me the use of one of his weapons!" Turning to his brother with a grin, he told him, "And that means you may use mine! Come! Let us speak with Mr. McConnell!"

Andy's companions groaned their disappointment as their friend scrambled to his feet to accompany his brother. Jealous, the one who had been concealing the pipe brought it out and put it to his lips, knowing it would earn Andy a scolding from his brother.

"'T' ain't but a squirrel gun!" the proprietor, McConnell, bellowed when Andy said he could use his brother's weapon, begging to go along.

"Might do fer dem Blackfoots, ifn dey runs inta dem," one of the French half-breeds offered, with a cackle.

"Are there Blackfoot around here?" Matthew asked, suddenly alarmed. They had heard the men on the boats speak of the Blackfoot and how they were at war with all the other Indians. They were rumoured to be the fiercest warriors on the western plains. Many were afraid of them.

"That's who our pa's supposed to be with!" Andy exclaimed, recalling his father's colourful descriptions of the Blackfoot in his infrequent letters.

"Naw! We're a little too far east to start runnin' into them. Mostly Cree 'round here," McConnell assured them. "I just don't know if I wanna spare 'im—you know any Cree, boy?"

"*I am a friend!*" Andy replied in Cree. He had picked up a little Cree from their periodic visitations, looking for handouts. "*We want sex; where are your women?"* he continued awkwardly, trying out something the older men had taught him.

McConnell and the others chuckled, and he asked, "Where'd you get that one?"

"From Etienne. Why?" Andy wondered. "You say it when you first meet them—it means something like, 'It is good to see you,' or something like that," the young one said eagerly.

"Yup, that's what it means all right!" one of the other men assured him, smirking. "You should have a big bunch of 'baccy with you to give 'em when you say that. Say that, an' offer 'em the 'baccy—they really like that! You'll be their friend right away!" the man said. The toothless grin on his grizzled face directed toward his friends let the two boys know that something was not right about it.

"Uh, Andy, you better just stay with what you know," Matthew cautioned his brother. Turning to McConnell, he urged him to let the younger one go along. "He is a perfect shot! He has dispatched a number of deer for his family. And, he brought down a moose once with that small weapon! A moose is no small animal!"

With a chuckle, McConnell agreed to let the younger boy go along. "Maybe just watch and see how it's done, this time," he warned. "In fact, I'd rather you didn't take that little pea shooter along at all—might get yourself into a heap o' trouble. You just go along an' see how it's done for now," he said to Andy.

It did not matter to Andy that he could not take the gun along; he was just glad to be able to go. He hated feeling left out of things that his brother got to do.

Before everyone turned in for the night, the boys were introduced to the three Cree hunters and learned that the plan was to leave before first light, which came early at that latitude.

Neither one slept much, and the eastern sky had just begun to lighten when the hunting party left camp, heading upstream on foot. The Indians knew the terrain well and moved quickly. But the brothers were in good shape from a summer of rowing and had no difficulty keeping up.

At mid-morning, the Cree indicated that the buffalo were near. Dropping to their hands and knees, they approached the valley rim overlooking the great river, where Andy and Matthew got their first look at buffalo. "They're huge!" Andy exclaimed. "There's no way our gun woulda done anything to them at all!" But he was disappointed when he learned the plan.

"You gotta stay here," his brother told him, after speaking with the Indian hunters. He had learned a little more Cree than Andy.

"How come? You said I got to go with you!" the headstrong boy protested.

"Listen! They wish you to stay here!" Matthew responded impatiently. Andy knew it was because his brother was nervous; he was always edgy about trying new things. "I will be accompanying them downstream in order to get across the river. They wish you to stay on this side while we make our way around behind them, on the other side. You see that ravine, going up from the river, where the buffaloes are?" Matthew asked his brother, pointing it out to him. The boy nodded. "Well, they say we will cross the river and work our way to that ravine," he said, pointing out the route that had been indicated to him. "Our quarry apparently come down that ravine to the water where we see them now. The Indians will find a place just up from them, and when we hail you with a high-hand, they wish you to charge down the draw, raising Cain. That will frighten the beasts in our direction, and you should hear our barrage!" he told his brother excitedly. "The meat will be very near the river, so we do not have to carry it very far."

"Why do I have to be the one to stay behind?" the younger one asked, disappointed. It did not seem like much of a job, and he would miss out on the shooting. "I thought I was gonna see how it's done!"

"Andy, that is the way they wish to do it! I cannot argue with them! Just do it, please! We shall just be over there, see?" He tried to point out, again, the route the Cree had pointed out to him.

Andy could see that their intended route would take them across the river, some distance, before circling back to where the buffalo lazed by the river. "What if a Blackfoot comes along? I'll be all alone!" Andy was still protesting when one of the Cree hunters approached them. By sign, something Andy had come to understand only a little, he pointed out where Andy should be watching for their signal. When he saw one of them raise his bow above his head, Andy was to count to ten twice for each one of his fingers. "What? What does that mean?" he asked his brother, not caring to understand.

"I wish you had paid a little more attention, rather than spending so much time with your friends smoking! You would know what they are saying!" Matthew responded exasperatedly. "Count to two hundred—you know, ten times ten fingers, twice—two hundred."

Scowling, the disappointed boy watched until his brother and the Cree hunters had disappeared, headed in the direction of the river.

Once they were gone, he crept up to where he could look down on the buffalo. Lying on his stomach, he watched them, shifting his gaze between the dark animals and the spot where the hunters had indicated they would cross the river.

The buffalo seemed content to stay by the water. Andy couldn't blame them—it was already a hot day. He wished he was in the water too. He and his friends had spent long summer days swimming, back home. His thoughts evoked a pang of longing for the friends he missed and all their fun in the water. His departure had been so sudden that he had not had a chance to say good-bye. Matthew had discovered that boats were leaving for Edmonton House and looking for anyone who could man an oar. Worried that they might be sent back to England to live with an uncle they hardly remembered, they had left the very next day—rowing toward the big lake and filled with the hope of finding their father.

"Gosh, that sun's hot!" Andy muttered, regretting that he had forgotten to bring his hat along. "Sure gonna take my time crossing that river!"

Being careful that the dark beasts would not see him, he took off his shirt and tried to prop it up on a small shrub to give himself some shade. "Oops, better not do that!" he murmured when the shirt began to flap in the breeze. "You might see it!" he said, more to himself than the oblivious beasts across the river. He moved cautiously to a different position, where he could hang his shirt for shade. Unable to see the buffalo, he had a good view of where the hunters were to cross the river.

Moments later, movement caught his attention. Surprised how quickly the hunting party had reached the river, he whispered to himself, "You guys must really be moving!" He saw Matthew turn and wave in his direction when he reached the other shore. Andy waved back, neither of them having any idea what was about to come. And once the hunters were out of the water, they quickly disappeared into the dense bush that grew along the south side of the river valley.

Andy waited impatiently, wondering how long it would be before he would have to start watching for the signal. The hunters had to go uphill, and there were a few ravines they had to go through. "Then again," he murmured, "It didn't take you long to get down there."

Looking at the terrain around him, he saw how the big river had carved a broad valley out of the endless rolling plain. The sky was a pale blue, dotted with high, wispy clouds. A breeze, for which he was thankful, cooled him little. Checking on the buffalo from time to time, he watched a spider patrolling the dry grass beside him. Intrigued by its darting movements, he picked it up and put it onto a flower that was being visited by a bee, disappointed when they seemed to ignore each other. Bored and hot, he grew tired of waiting.

"Where are you going?" he said softly. He had noticed a cow buffalo that seemed to have set a deliberate course up the ravine and away from the river. Its calf scampered along ahead of it, and both were shortly out of sight. "Uh-oh! Where are you going? You can't do that!" he whispered, seeing others beginning to move in the same direction. Anxiously, he looked for some sign of the hunters and began to worry that the buffalo might be gone before they were in place. What if they didn't get a shot? "No, wait! Wait!" he urged a little louder, hoping the animals would tarry. A few of them, yearlings Andy reckoned, stayed behind a little longer than the rest, but before long, they too had disappeared up the ravine.

Unsure of what to do now, Andy took his shirt off the small tree. Did he still need to stay out of sight? Would it be all right for him to wander down to the river and maybe cool off a bit while he waited for the others to show up? He did not wish to miss their signal, though, and he might not be able to see it if he was down at the river. Beginning to fret, suddenly, he thought he heard something. Was that a shot, he wondered. There it was again. Yes! They're shooting! And, another! Were they really shots? Or, was the sizzling summer breeze playing tricks with his ears? He listened carefully but heard nothing more. "Just three lousy shots! They're gonna be really disappointed in you!" he scolded.

When the buffalo were long gone, Andy could see no reason to remain hidden, and he got to his feet, giving a mighty stretch. "So, what am I supposed to do now?" he sighed, still keeping an eye out for his signal. Restless, he began pacing, stooping from time to time to pick up a stone and throw it down the hill. Finally, he sat down and fussed. It was getting hotter, and he wished he could get off that darned hill and find some shade. His shirt offered little shelter from the relentless sun, which would soon be overhead.

The shore where the buffalo had languished was deserted. There had been no signal—no sign of anything from the other side of the river. And nobody had reappeared where the hunters had crossed the river. What was going on? Up on his feet again, throwing rocks, Andy searched anxiously for any sign of his brother. "What're you doing?" he hollered into the empty valley. It was so broad that there was not even an echo, and suddenly he felt alone. Spooked, he looked around, checking over his shoulder as if there might be something stalking him. "All right! That's it! I'm coming over there!" he hollered and began his charge down the hill, setting a course that would bring him out where the others would have expected him. If the hunters were not there by the time he arrived, he decided, he would walk down the river to the place where they had crossed.

With one eye watching for any sign from across the river, he made his way down the hill, eventually reaching the brush that grew along the river. There, he worried that he might have missed something from the other side while trudging through the bush. He stopped and scoured the other side with anxious eyes. Nothing! "The heck with you then!" he exclaimed, doffing his moccasins and his trousers. Rolling them up in his shirt, which he had been carrying over his shoulder, he tucked everything under his arm and waded into the refreshing water.

Andy loved being in the water. He had always liked those stretches of river where they would get out of the heavy boats and trudge through the water, some pushing the craft and others pulling with ropes. At first, it had been a surprise to see that many of the crew stripped for such a task. A few wore a breechclout on days when they would be in and out of the water all day, but most went naked—especially the boys, who had no such garment. Soon he and his brother had done the same. It was better than wet clothing.

The anxious boy trudged along, making his way to the other side, where he intended to toss his clothes onto the shore and wait for the others in the refreshing waters of the river. Why not? They would come back, eventually. But by the time he reached the other shore, he had begun to doubt his own plan. He could not see very much from the river's edge. Maybe it would be better to go back to the side he had started from; there, he would be able to keep a better watch for the hunters—whenever they showed up. So, with no sign of them at the place of the buffalo, he returned to the north side of the river. The current persistently nudged him some distance downstream, where he was delighted to find a spot where he could see the place of the buffalo, as well as the crossing and the signal place.

Tossing his clothes onto the shore, he returned to the water to claim the reward he had promised himself. He could not imagine that it would take them very much longer to show up, so he determined to enjoy himself while he had the opportunity to be alone, for such moments of solitude had been rare. Maybe he would escape having to butcher and haul the meat.

The water was clear and warm, the sun was hot, and he tried to entertain himself in the water until he'd had enough. Returning to shore, Andy found the sand was hot under his feet, and he laid down in it, using his clothes for a pillow.

He had not intended to sleep, but nerves and excitement had kept him up the night before; fatigue had an easy time catching up to him.

Andy awoke with a start. "Damn!" he cursed, scrambling to his feet and looking anxiously for any sign of the hunters, trying to ignore the guilt he felt for using such language. Although his brother and their preacher father would not have approved, it was the language of so many of the boatmen. Even the 13-year-olds used language worse than that. Still, he felt bad about it and apologized under his breath, wondering how long he had dozed.

"Where the heck are you?" he muttered in frustration, scouring the opposite bank for any movement. "Matty!" he hollered. Framing his mouth with his hands, he hollered again, "Matthew! Where are you?" No response. Fretting for a while, he decided to cross the river a third time to check for footprints or anything that might indicate that the hunting party had maybe returned while he dozed. But before leaving his spot, he hung his shirt, so anyone would see it and know where to look for him.

Knowing the current would carry him downstream, he marched up the shoreline until he was beyond the place of the buffalo. Purposefully this time, he entered the current. Only in one spot was the water so deep that he had to swim. When he reached the other side, he found nothing but buffalo tracks. At once, he started down the shore, intending to make his way to the place of crossing.

"The heck with this!" he eventually said to himself, plunging back into the water to let the river take him there. It was a pleasant ride! Getting to where the water was at his chest so that he could drift with the current, he kept a constant lookout and had a much easier time than if he had been walking.

When he reached his destination, tracks made it clear that the hunters had not been back since their initial crossing. He pondered his next move, filled with indecision. To stay meant he would miss seeing them if they came back to the river anywhere upstream. Same, if he followed the tracks. All he could do was go back to where he had left his clothes; surely, they would show up by the time he got back there. But upon returning to his pile of clothes, and seeing no one, a knot of worry formed in his stomach. What could have happened? Someone ought to have come back to the river to summon him! At the thought, his anger turned to fear; Matthew ought to have known that he would be worried! For the first time, he wondered if something had gone wrong.

Pacing back and forth along the beach, stopping from time to time to throw rocks into the current, by mid-afternoon, he could stand it no longer; he had to do something! Repositioning his shirt to make sure that nobody could miss it, he etched a message in the wet sand at the river's edge, saying he was on the other side, looking for them. Once again, he crossed to the south side, this time finding little pleasure in the coolness of the water.

At the place of crossing, he etched an angry message to his brother: 'Wait here!!!' Donning trousers and moccasins, he followed the tracks away from the river and up a game trail leading up the ravine.

The trail turned hard and dry as he moved away from the water, and he eventually gave up trying to follow any track. The brush was thick enough that they would inevitably have stuck to the trail. Picking handfuls of ripe saskatoon berries along the way and munching on them as he trod, he tried to keep his gnawing fear at bay as he continued up the ravine. He was uncertain what he would do if he reached the top and did not find them.

At a fork in the trail, it took him some time to determine which to follow. Scouring each route for quite a distance, he thought he could make out a faint track on one and followed it, all the while crossly planning what he was going say to his brother.

Near the top of the ravine, he came upon a place where he could turn and look back toward the river. Happy to get a good look at it, he saw no sign of the boats and pressed on.

The trail eventually petered out in a meadow, but he knew enough about tracking to know that he would probably pick up a trail on the other side. He trudged on, but before long, he spotted a place where the long grass had been trampled; someone had obviously been there. It gave him a sense of reassurance, but then a dark shape drew his attention. Not recognizing what it was, the grass flattened around it, he drew closer to investigate. An animal, he wondered. Or a rock—what is it? Is someone sleeping? It was someone's back! An Indian! "What the heck!" he exclaimed aloud, stopping dead in his tracks.

Not sure what he was looking at, he moved cautiously forward, trying to figure out what he was seeing. "Oh shit! O God!" he shrieked when he saw the pale skin of someone white, sandwiched beneath two darker, obviously Indian bodies. "O God! O God!" he cried, racing toward the gruesome pile.

There was a fourth body—another Indian—sprawled near the others. Its head was gone; its hands and feet had been hacked off. "Matty!" he screamed desperately, throwing himself to his knees where bodies had been piled one on top of the other. "Matty!" he shrieked, recognizing the back of his brother's head. Why didn't he move or say something? "I'm here!"

"Wha?" he exclaimed, detecting movement beneath his brother's body. The air went out of his lungs as he tried to figure out what was going on. Someone was alive underneath that pile— hands and feet bound to stakes in the ground—underneath Matty and the other two! An Indian! What was going on? Glancing away from his brother's form, he looked into the terrified eyes of an Indian boy, staked out at the bottom of the pile.

"Matty, what happened?" Andy fought tears as he clawed at the ropes that bound the victims together. The Indian boy's eyes were riveted upon his as he worked frantically at the leather cord. Unable to hold them back, tears began streaming down Andy's face, making it difficult to see what he was doing. Fully sobbing by the time he had undone three of the ropes, he dragged his brother's body from the pile. Everyone was naked—even the boy on the bottom. But Andy was in too much shock to give it much thought. "Matty!" he whimpered, searching for some sign of life in his brother. "Matty, no!" the terrified boy cried, finding none. "O God!" he moaned loudly. Reeling with shock, he sat on his heels, buried in his face in his hands and cried. He cried as hard as he had the day his mother died.

Penetrating his grief came a terrifying thought: whoever did this might still be around! At once on guard, tearing his face from his hands, he looked around desperately. He fully expected to find himself surrounded by the savages about whom he had been warned. But there was nothing, just the peaceful meadow, the tall grass shimmering in the breeze, and the mercilessly hot sun, witness to it all.

The Indian boy had managed to get onto his side and was picking at the binding that held him to the last stake. He was working feebly with fingers that would not do the job. A deep impression on his wrist told how tightly he had been tied. Believing the Indian boy must be in the same mortal danger as he, Andy dove to his side, and brushing aside his feeble effort, quickly untied the remaining knot.

The instant he was free, the Indian boy made an awkward getaway. Scrambling on hands and knees then stumbling to his feet, he lurched toward the bush at the edge of the meadow where he disappeared.

Figuring the boy could be no threat to him—and was probably a victim, just like his brother—Andy's attention once again returned to the lifeless form of his brother. There were two small wounds on his torso, but neither one showed enough blood to have been very serious. He supposed them to have been made by arrows, but he had never seen such a thing before—or were they gunshot wounds? Rolling his brother's body to one side, he observed a similar hole on the lower back where some kind of a projectile must have completely penetrated his body.

Taking a quick look around him, Andy noticed that the dead Indians had been mutilated and murmured, "Why'd they do that?" Their hands and feet had been removed, leaving bloody stumps, with the gleaming white of an ankle joint showing on one. But not Matthew—how come?

Every fibre of Andy's being was on edge, as he knelt over his brother's body. Glancing around him, he had no idea what to expect from the Indian boy, wherever he had gone. Were there others? Would he be next?

His fear of a fate similar to that of his brother kept the full extent of his grief from overtaking him when a sudden movement caught his eye. The Indian boy was watching him from the low brush, not a stone's throw away, making no effort to conceal himself. Feeling uncertain, Andy rose and faced the silent figure. Without any weapon and entirely naked, how dangerous could he be?

The two stared at each other for a long moment until Andy broke the gaze to look again for any sign that the killers might be returning. When he glanced back, the Indian was gone. "What're you doin'?" Andy whispered nervously. On edge, he took another look around, to see if he could figure out what had happened and figured he ought to get out of there. Suddenly aware of how terribly alone he was, he longed for the men on the boats and the safety of their numbers.

Matty's gun! The whole hunting party had been carrying firearms. Where are they, he wondered. And, there was no clothing—the bag Matty had been carrying over his shoulder was missing. "They got your stuff!" he exclaimed aloud, his mind racing.

Suddenly, he knew he had to get back to the river! "I gotta get outta here!" he mumbled to himself, beginning to think more clearly. But he was reluctant to leave Matty. He looked at the dead Indians. They had been scalped, too. He had heard of such a thing, but he had never seen it, and the sight of it shocked him! He had always thought the whole scalp would be removed, but there was just a small patch of the scalp missing, where there had apparently once been a braid. Matty's head was untouched. Why? What if he left and the murderers returned to finish their job? Should he try to carry his brother to the river? It would be a challenging task, and it would take too long. What if he missed the boats? His mind in turmoil, suddenly, the arrival of the boats loomed as the matter of greatest urgency. "I'll be back!" he whispered and turned toward the river.

He did not waste any time—his body and his mind both raced the whole way back to the river's edge, where he hoped he might encounter the boats. "O, Jesus, please don't let them be gone!" he pleaded into the wind. "You gotta help me!"

When he reached the river, his fear and anxiety had numbed his grief. Impatiently, he paced up and down the shore. Alternately, he kept watch for any sign of the boats and scouring the ravines for danger. When a movement on the other side caught his eye, he looked closer and realized with a start that his shirt was declaring his location like a beacon, potentially signaling his whereabouts to his brother's killers. He could not risk being found by anyone until he could hail those boats! Whipping off his moccasins and trousers, he dropped them on the shore and wasted no time getting to the other side.

2

From the bushes where he had taken refuge, Badger had watched his rescuer depart. He was grateful for the stranger's timely arrival, frustrating his cousin's hateful vengeance. Rubbing his wrists and ankles where the vicious ropes had carved into his flesh, he felt— almost choked on—his immense regret over going on the raid in the first place. The hatred he felt for the Crow warrior who had slain his father was now matched by the hatred he felt for Eagle Head. From the day his uncle had taken Badger's family in, Eagle Head had made the boy's life miserable, constantly humiliating him in front of others and abusing him terribly. Badger had never been able to find anything that could make any difference. Alone, without a father or an older brother, he had been so desperate to make a name for himself and end the constant humiliation that he had risked everything to come along on the raid. And now it had cost him everything.

With feeling beginning to come back into his limbs, Badger watched the white boy disappear down the same trail the *Liars* had used, before the ambush. *"I thank you, great Sun! Thank you!"* he breathed a prayer of thanksgiving, recalling how he had fought for every breath under the gruesome weight from which he had been delivered. Relieved to have escaped his intended fate, he took a deep breath, and feeling a sense of gratitude and curiosity, he set out to follow the stranger.

Stumbling frequently, from legs that still felt weak, he pondered his future as he made his way down the ravine. He knew that Eagle Head would be sure to come up with some disgraceful story about him so that if he ever got back to camp, he would certainly be put to shame. *"Dogs!"* he cursed them all. *"Female dogs!"* Even his mother and sister would be ashamed of him; how could he ever face them? Deeply troubled, he shuffled after the stranger, gaining more and more feeling in his hands and feet until they were almost back to normal when he reached the river.

Not knowing what to expect, he approached with great caution, leaving the trail and making his way stealthily through the thick underbrush. Peering out, he was surprised to discover the white boy mid-river, having left his leggings and moccasins on the shore. Sure the boy would come back for them, Badger determined to wait, finding a place where he could sit and watch without being seen.

Shaken by shock and fear, Andy was feeling weak by the time he set foot on the north shore. He had planned to grab his shirt and return to the other side as quickly as possible, to await the boats. But his mind was racing, and before he reached the garment, he changed his mind. What if his brother's murderers were still nearby? What if they had seen him crossing the broad river? Better to wait right where he was, where he would have the advantage of taking flight while the murderers crossed the river. It might give him a bit of an edge. He eased himself a few steps into the bushes and dropped to the ground. Once under cover of the bush, the full weight of his loss consumed him, and he buried his face in his hands and wept violently. Filled with despair, he was overcome with profound loneliness and fell forward, where he sobbed until he was exhausted.

The pale one's actions were a puzzle to Badger, who had risen to his feet and was trying to figure out what was going on across the river. When it became apparent that his rescuer was not coming back, the young Indian decided to go over to him and take the leggings to him.

It was a risky thing to do; he would be totally exposed crossing the wide river and would be an easy target. Thinking that his life was no longer worth much anyway, he stepped out into the open to retrieve the leggings. They were a peculiar-looking garment; he had never held leggings such as these. He looked them over before tossing them around his neck, scooping up the moccasins, and heading for the river. All the way across, he kept his eyes locked on the spot where his saviour had hidden. Emerging from the water, he stalked silently along the river's edge until he caught sight of the strange figure.

Andy had his face in his hands, periodically sobbing and trying to pray to his god. It wasn't easy. His mother's sudden death had shaken his faith. After her death, the minister had said that he might have to send him and his brother back to England if they did not soon hear from their father. Neither boy had wanted to return to England! Since that time, there had been all sorts of distractions on the boats to keep him from his faith. Now, Matthew! Not knowing what to do, and with nobody to turn to, he begged his god for help.

Badger approached within about five paces, to where he could see the strange-looking figure more clearly. The pale boy had no idea he was being watched. Sitting with his face to the ground, he was naked. His hair was the colour of the sun. Watching him for a long moment, finally, Badger took a deep breath and ventured softly, *"Hai! I am a friend!"*

"O shit!" Andy screeched in fright, leaping to his feet, stumbling and almost falling over in his panic. He skittered backward, about to bolt when he recognized the Indian boy he had set free. Wide-eyed, he shrieked, "What are you doing? You scared the crap outta me!"

"I am sorry!" the Indian uttered, seeing his fright. But the stranger's reaction had amused him, and he could not keep from grinning. *"I did not mean to scare you,"* he smirked, holding up the trousers. *"I brought your leggings to you. And your moccasins. Are you all right?"*

Andy was not amused as he wiped his face with his hand, his entire body vibrating from the sudden adrenalin surge. He had not understood the Indian's words but took his gesture as one of peaceful intent. "You scared me!" he blurted.

Both naked, they gave each other a thorough looking-over before Badger looked the other in the eye and muttered, *"I brought your leggings,"* trying to sound cheerful. Holding them up, he added, *"I have not seen anything like them. Maybe you would let me try them sometime."*

"Thanks," Andy replied, not understanding the words, understanding only that his clothing was being returned to him. He took his trousers back and immediately stooped to put them on. Unfamiliar with buttons, Badger watched with great interest as his companion skillfully buttoned the fly, noting the boy's strange skin colour. His upper body, well-muscled, was a dark, golden-brown colour—the colour of a buffalo calf, unlike anything he had seen before.

Having donned his pants, Andy looked up and observed a friendly look on the Indian's face. Feeling a bond with him, he assumed they had to be on the same side—given the state in which he had found him. Surely, his own kinsman would not have left him to die in such a manner. Perhaps the Indian boy had somehow been connected to the Cree hunters.

Still feeling entirely raw inside, Andy tried to pull himself together. "I'm Andy—Andrew, really, Andrew Preston. My friends call me Andy," he announced. His eyes and nose red from crying, he straightened up and stuck out a hand to the Indian. Badger took hold of it; not shaking it, he held it briefly before letting go.

Looking around, as if to make sure nobody would hear him, Badger introduced himself. "*I am*"—he announced, hesitating to look around again— "*I am Míísinsski.*" Not understanding the Blackfoot taboo against saying one's name, Andy looked around to see what he might have been looking for. "*Míísinsski,*" the Indian repeated his name, pointing a finger to his chest.

"*Míísinsski?*" Andy repeated with a wisp of a grin, pointing at Badger, who nodded approvingly. "Andy!" he said his own name, placing a finger on his own chest. "I'm Andy!"

"I-mandy," the Indian repeated the sound awkwardly.

"No! Just Andy. I mean, Andy!" Again, placing his finger to his chest, he repeated his name. While the Indian struggled to form the word, Andy looked him over and saw that he was handsome. Very dark-skinned, his features were sharp. And looking extremely fit and muscular, his eyes were black, yet seemed warm.

"An-dy!" When Badger got it, he repeated it a couple of times to Andy's nodding approval. He went on to try to explain that he had had nothing to do with the death of that other *napikawan*, but Andy held up his hand and interrupted him.

"I don't understand."

After several minutes of futile signing and gesture by the Indian, Andy realized he must be trying to tell him what had happened, but he could make no sense of it, no matter how hard the Indian tried. Giving up, they stood in awkward silence.

Badger had his eyes on the ground, and Andy gazed across the water for a moment. He was glad for the Indian's companionship

and invited him to sit. There was comfort in having an ally—
someone beside him. Similarly, the Indian felt good about his
companion and a sense of loyalty to the one who had saved his life.

Eventually, by gesture, Badger asked if he could try on Andy's
shirt. "Sure," the white boy responded, reaching for it and passing
it to him. Nearly the same size, he slid the shirt over his arms and
shoulders, though he had to be shown how to fasten the buttons.

"*I like it!*" the Indian commented with a smile, rising to peer
down at himself. "*Can I try on those leggings?*" he asked, pointing
toward what he wanted.

Andy shrugged. "I guess so." And, getting to his feet, he doffed
his trousers and handed them over to his curious companion.

"*This is so strange!*" Badger observed, clumsily trying to fasten
the buttons at the front. "*What is it made of? It is not any kind of
skin, is it?*"

Though the words were foreign to Andy's ears, he heard the
question in the Indian boy's voice and gave what he guessed
might be the answer. "I dunno. Trousers! They're called trousers!"
Feeling a little better now, at least temporarily distracted, Andy
attempted some of the Cree expressions he had learned. His companion did not indicate any comprehension. "I guess you're not
Cree, then. How about this: *We want sex, where are your women?*"
Getting another blank stare, Andy concluded, "Nope, not Cree. I
hope you're not the other. Are you Black Something? Blackfoot? I
don't reckon you know what I just said, do you?" The same blank
expression gave him his answer.

After the darker boy had admired himself in the other's unfamiliar clothing, he peeled it off and handed it back to its owner.
Feeling self-conscious about being fully dressed while the Indian
remained naked, Andy just laid it aside and sat down again, thinking his companion might feel better about it that way.

Without the benefit of conversation, Andy busied himself
scraping back the dry sand, scooping out the moist sand beneath

it to fashion cabins and castles with his hands. After watching him for a while, and not understanding what he was making, Badger got up to break off a branch from a willow that stood nearby. Andy took the opportunity to furtively examine the other's nakedness, looking away when he spun around and returned to sit once more. Pulling several strands of long, black hair from his head, the Indian twisted them together and began to fashion a tiny bow. By the time he had completed it and fetched some bits of driftwood, from which to make little arrows, Andy was watching him with open curiosity. "Hey! You made a little bow!" he exclaimed when the Indian shot his first arrow with it.

The Indian offered the toy to him and handed him one of the arrows. *"You try it!"*

"You try it!" Andy repeated the sounds.

"Yes! You try and shoot it!" The Indian used gestures to give meaning to his words, and Andy gave it a try, breaking the makeshift bowstring when he pulled too hard. Its maker just laughed good-naturedly and began to fashion another. Intrigued, Andy fetched the materials to make a bow of his own, and when his teacher saw him making an attempt, he pulled more of his long hair out his head and offered it to him. Soon, Andy was grinning with satisfaction when his arrow made it to the water.

"Ha!" he blurted with a grin because Badger's attempt had failed to reach as far. The Indian returned his smile. So comforting was the small gesture that it made Andy break into tears again. Embarrassed by it, he covered his face with his hands, causing Badger to move closer and put a hand on his shoulder. In a moment, Andy was able to look up and breathe, "Thanks!"

Badger had no idea why they were waiting around on that side of the river. It seemed to him that they should be on the other side, doing something with the body of the other *napikawan*. There was a good chance that predators would find the bodies before morning. *"Who is that other fellow back there—the napikawan—like you? Do you understand me?"* A blank look was all he got. Making another attempt by sign, he tried to indicate that he could help him place the body into the trees, which was how his people treated the dead. Andy figured that he was probably saying something about Matty, but failed to grasp his meaning, and eventually, Badger gave up.

All evening, Andy was not ready to give up on the boats. He knew they might keep rowing until there was hardly enough light to find a place to land, and he did not wish to risk missing them in the failing light. Pacing and fidgeting from time to time, and at other times sitting together, they tried to talk, naming parts of their bodies and things around them. When he grew tired, Badger put his head on his hands and closed his eyes to indicate they should sleep, but Andy kept shaking his head.

After a time, when he judged it too late for the boats, it was Andy who made the gesture to Badger, who promptly lay down and patted the soft sand beside him, gesturing for Andy to join him. Andy was not so sure about sleeping that close together and pretended not to see. Settling on a place of his own, he draped his shirt and trousers over him. He was surprised when, after he had laid down and gotten himself comfortable, the Indian crawled over and laid alongside him.

3

The sun had not yet cleared the valley when a strange sound caused Badger to stir. Sometime in the night, they had moved closer together, and by the time the chilly morning broke, there was no space between them. He had been awake for some time, lying motionless, not willing to forsake the white boy's warmth and not wishing to disturb his sleep by moving. But the rhythmic sound in the distance alarmed him, and he lifted himself on an elbow and looked in the direction of the river. In the cool stillness of the morning, he could hear an occasional, dull thud with which he was unfamiliar; and he made out rhythmic chanting growing nearer. Getting to his feet to see what it was, he disturbed Andy, who looked around groggily.

"*There is something there!*" Badger whispered, looking intently in the direction of the river, where he could see something on the water.

"What?" his companion replied, startled. Sensing the Indian's concern, Andy sat up. At once, he recognized the familiar sound of the oars bumping the sides of the boats and the men calling out the strokes. "It's them!" he shouted, startling the Indian, who had begun looking for cover so as not to be seen.

"*What are you doing?*" he blurted, whirling toward Andy, who had scrambled to his feet. "*Quiet!*" He had no idea what they were looking at.

Andy paid no attention. Hurrying for the shore, he hollered in the direction of the boats, "Hey! Over here! We're over here!" Waving his hands over his head, he shouted, "Francois! Francois! Over here! It's Andy! I'm over here!" There was no response at all from the boats, which were yet too far away for their occupants to be able to hear him. Racing along the shore, he hollered at the top of his voice, running downstream until a cut bank impeded his progress. Badger followed, suspicious of what he saw on the water. As soon as he recognized that they held people, he feared who they must be.

"*They are Liars!*" he cautioned. "*We need to get out of here!*" But his companion ignored him, not understanding what he had said—focused entirely on the boats.

It took a while for the boats to get close enough for Andy to recognize anyone. The men were rowing hard against the current. He first spotted Francois, standing at the front of the lead boat, peering ahead with his glass. Beside him was Mr. McConnell, the proprietor; in those following, most of the bowmen were standing, craning to see. He could make out the American's distinctive slouch hat in the second boat, but it seemed to take forever for them to come within shouting distance.

"You got dat meat, boy?" cried Francois when they came close enough for him to be heard, recognizing who it was. "W'ere dem others?"

"I need help!" Andy shouted back, anxiously. "They killed my brother—Indians! Killed 'em—all of them!" His voice was quavering. "Matthew's dead!" He choked on his words.

"What you say?" came the reply.

"Mr. McConnell, we need help!" Andy hollered to the proprietor, as they drew closer. "Indians attacked—Matthew and the others—an' killed 'em. They're all dead!"

"Oo's dat you's got wit you," interrupted Francois. "*Arrêtez! Arrêtez!*" he commanded the bowmen while scrutinizing Badger carefully. The oarsmen held the lead boat some distance from shore, many of them scanning the shoreline for any sign of an ambush.

Andy was already in the water and waded still deeper to get to them. "We need help!" he begged the men on the boats, plodding toward them. "They got my brother! He's dead!"

"Who got your brother? Who yuh got with yuh, boy?" hollered Mr. McConnell, studying the boy's companion. "What's happened?"

Seeing that they were more interested in the Indian than his plight, he wanted to reassure them. "He's a friend! I helped him an' he helped me!" Then, he continued, "Please! Matthew's dead! I need help!" he pleaded, as the second boat drew abreast of the first, holding fast. The American was in the nearer boat and was speaking quietly with McConnell.

"What happened, boy?" Mr. McConnell shouted, barely taking his eyes off Badger.

"Indians, sir," Andy repeated, again. "Indians...musta ambushed 'em. It's awful, they're scalped an' everything! An' this guy"—he gestured toward Badger, who was poised to dart for cover in the nearby bushes— "was all tied up—they all were. Please! We need help!"

"What kinda injuns?" interjected the American.

"I don't know, sir," Andy replied. "Can you help me?" All the boats were now holding some distance from shore, and the oarsmen were speaking animatedly among themselves. It was clear they were not coming any closer, so Andy moved toward them, deeper.

"When?" Mr. McConnell asked.

"Where?" the American interjected.

"'Ow many was dem?" Francois asked, almost simultaneously.

"Over there," Andy pointed toward the ravine across the river. "I don't know!" he continued, urgency rising in his voice. "We need help!"

"Were they Blackfoot?" the American inquired insistently. Nodding his head toward Badger, he asked, "Is he one o' them?" The Indian was acutely aware that he was the centre of their attention.

Blackfoot? Andy could not believe the Indian might be one of the dreaded Blackfoot. "I don't think so—no! They were after him, too! We need to help him!"

The men in the boats were not paying any attention to what he was saying. The American brought the musket he had been holding to his shoulder, giving a signal to the others. "No!" Andy screamed, his voice breaking in panic at the sight of the weapon pointed at his companion. "What're you doing? You don't need that! He's all right! He's my friend!" he shouted. "He's not one of those other kind! He helped me!" he cried, retreating now toward the shore and the one whose life he had saved.

"If he's one o' Bug's Boys, we need to get rid of 'im," Andy heard the American pressing Mr. McConnell.

"Oui!" agreed Francois. "Shoot! Shoot!"

Hearing it, Andy screamed, "No!" He raised his arms overhead and struggled toward his companion without taking his eyes off the intimidating weapons.

Although Badger did not understand what was being said, the sight of the fire-sticks and the white boy's reaction to these strangers was alarming. When others in the boats raised their weapons, all pointed at him, he turned quickly and dove for the bush. In the same instant, the startled Indian heard the voice of a fire-stick and the *whish* of its projectile zinging over his head. With Andy screaming something behind him, he heard the roar of more shots and the balls tearing into the leaves around him as he plunged further into the bush. The Indian scrambled into the depths of its cover.

Getting himself into the line of fire, Andy shrieked at the men in the boats, "No! Stop!"

"Get outta the way, boy!" shouted the American angrily, but Andy bravely stood his ground. Turning to McConnell, the man urged, "If them're Blackfoot, we're sittin' ducks! We need to get the hell outta here!"

"Get over here, boy!" McConnell shouted to Andy. "We gotta get outta here!" Some of the oarsmen who were Andy's friends joined the chorus of voices urging him to come out to them.

"Yo har!" cried Francois. The other bowmen repeated his command to their crews, guns now visible in every boat.

"Hold fast!" McConnell ordered his men and turned back to Andy. "Get over here, boy! Now!" he demanded.

Andy plunged back into the water, looking anxiously over his shoulder for any sign of the frightened Indian. "What about Matty?" he cried, "I don't wanna leave Matty!" he pleaded, his voice breaking. "We gotta go get him! We gotta do something!"

"No!" shouted the American, believing their gunfire would surely draw a horde of Blackfoot he imagined were concealed in the bushes. Paying no heed to the boy's plea, he warned those in the boat, "They'll be all over us! If we didn't get 'im, he'll bring 'em back!"

Andy slowed his effort, stunned by what was happening. The water was at his waist, the current pushing him insistently. He could not understand the men's reaction to the Indian boy, who he knew to be harmless.

The oarsmen in McConnell's boat were intent upon catching up with the other boats that had begun to move toward the middle of the river. The proprietor again ordered them to hold off before turning back to Andy. "Andrew, I'm responsible for this whole goddamn outfit! We're not gonna stop! Now get over here!" McConnell commanded fiercely. "Or, we're leavin' yuh behind!" McConnell's oarsmen kept the boat moving away from the frustrated boy. "That injun's Blackfoot, and they'll get us all," he shouted, holding his hand out to Andy, who was struggling to stand against the current.

"No, he's not! He helped me! Please, we gotta get Matty!" Andy begged.

"Get over here"—McConnell commanded him— "or, we're leavin' yuh behind!" The oarsmen had begun to move the boat away again. "Stop that!" McConnell turned and shouted at them. "Get over to 'im!" he commanded. The bowman whispered something to McConnell, and the boats held their position.

"Help me! Ple-ease!" Andy cried again, tears starting to stream down his face. "I can't leave Matty behind!"

"Allons! Allons!" cried the bowman. *"M'sieur,* we be dead if we be wait 'ere. We join dem udders, yeah?"

"Damn you, boy! Get over here, or I can't help you!" shouted the frustrated proprietor. "This is your last chance, or I'm leavin' you behind!"

The boat had now moved far enough upstream that Andy would be hard-pressed to reach it against the current. "I can't leave 'im! I'm staying!" he yelled defiantly, quite certain they would not leave him behind. "I'm not leavin'!" he whimpered, giving up and letting the current take him. He heard McConnell arguing with his bowman, as the oarsmen now hastened to rejoin the others. The other vessels had already reached the centre of the river and were pulling away, the crews rowing mightily. McConnell was still standing, watching him; guns bristled from all the boats.

Shocked by the callous reaction of men he had thought would react differently, Andy could not keep from sobbing. He allowed the current to carry him, pushing with his feet toward shore, where he crawled out of the water on hands and knees before collapsing into the welcoming sand. Suddenly cold, deep sobbing overtook his body. "O God, O God, what are you doing?" he cried through his tears. "Help me! Please help me! Don't let them leave me!" he uttered in despair. "I got no one!" he whimpered, certain they had killed the Indian boy. His body was wracked with anguish and disappointment.

At that moment, the sun came over the ridge and shone on him. Feeling its warmth, he let it swaddle him.

Badger had fled through the bush, all the way to the top of the river valley, where the bush gave way to short grass on the steep hillside. From the last remaining cover, he peered down at the boats, watching them depart. He wondered the reason for the whites' hostility. Not until he was sure they were gone, did he look around and spot the white boy, face down on the shore. It appeared that the boy's own people had shot him!

Bewildered, Badger made his way back to the river, keeping out of sight as much possible, until he reached the place where the white boy's body lay. With great caution, the puzzled Indian ventured into the open and approached the solitary figure lying prone in the sand. Not having seen what happened, he could not understand why the others would have killed him. Dropping to one knee, he could see no indication of any injury. "*Hai!*" he whispered hopefully, wondering if his rescuer might still be alive.

Andy lifted his head at the sound of his voice and was greatly relieved to see his companion alive. "Sons of bitches!" he cursed, his grief and fear suddenly yielding to anger. Lifting himself up, the sand that had dried to his skin now rained down. "They got all our stuff, too!" he exclaimed angrily. "Where's our stuff?" he yelled angrily at the bare river, already missing their gear which had been on the boats. The Indian did not say anything but observed the boy carefully as he stood gazing up the river. "You can't do that! You can't just leave me here!" Andy raged, feeling some relief in voicing his internal anguish. "Bastards!"

Turning to Badger, he sighed, "I dunno what I'm gonna do!" He was ready to cry. His lower lip quivered, and he turned away. Burying his face in his hands, he struggled to keep control of his emotions.

"*We can be friends!*" Badger reminded him, his tone friendly. Andy turned toward him, and the Indian stuck out a hand. He grasped it but wished for someone who would embrace him and erase his nightmare. They stood looking into each other's eyes, and the first shadows of trust began to form.

Badger did not know what to make of the white boy. It was clear he was in a desperate situation—a situation he did not altogether understand. But it was evident that he needed help.

Andy was feeling so lost and vulnerable that he was determined to hang onto this new friend, now his only friend. But he had to get back to Matthew. "Do you wanna go get my brother?" he asked, pointing across the river. "I gotta do something. I guess I gotta—" His voice tapered off. He could not bring himself to give words to what he was thinking. Badger had a hunch what he was talking about and helped Andy gather his clothing, before turning toward the river.

Andy followed him, and in silence, the pair crossed to the other side where Andy got himself dressed. Badger watched him, and then sombrely headed up the path, leading the way in silence.

Just before reaching the scene of the slaughter, he stopped and turned to the white boy. He had heard the coyotes in the night, from across the river. "*You might not want to go any further. The coyotes have probably been around, and you might not want to see it,*" he said kindly. Knowing his companion would not understand, he tried to indicate his concerns using gestures, sounds and facial

36

expressions. Andy picked up on what he was trying to say. He had been thinking of the same possibility and had been dreading it.

Making a face, he said, "Yeah. That's what I'm worried about." However, moving forward to show he had no intention of turning back, he said, "I gotta do it, though. He's my brother!" Badger quickened his pace, not wishing to let the other get ahead of him, and they closed the distance together.

It was worse than Andy could have imagined. Seeing what was left of his brother, he fell to his hands and knees, and his empty stomach heaved, interrupting his shriek of horror. Badger stood beside him and felt sorry for him. *"I can do this,"* he volunteered. *"I will get him into a tree and cover him with branches."* He spoke softly, compassion in his voice, but Andy was too shaken to answer. Moving to sit on his heels, he just moaned and looked away, tears streaming down his face.

Eventually, he regained control of his emotion, and with a deep sigh, he rose slowly to his feet. "I gotta do this," he said with determination. He retched again when he got close enough to see that there was not much left of any of them. Removing his shirt, he laid it over what was left of his dear brother, looking around for something with which to dig a hole.

Badger was not sure what the white boy was doing as he began tearing at the soil with a stick. He was used to seeing his people put the bodies of their loved ones on the branches of a tree, that their spirits might more readily depart. But he helped get the remains of the *napikawan* into the ground—somewhat wrapped in Andy's shirt, finally covering it with what rocks they could gather. Neither spoke a word.

When they had finished, Andy stood over his brother's final resting place and thought for a long moment. "I got somethin' else I gotta do," he said, determination in his voice. Digging in his pocket, he pulled out a small, folding knife. Badger watched him, wondering what he was doing as he cut one of the legs off his last piece of clothing and tore it into strips. Using the strips, he tied two sticks together to fashion a cross, planting it at the head of the fresh grave. Standing for a long time looking at it, Andy had tears streaming down his ashen face.

Badger wondered about the cross and figured it must be a charm to keep the spirits away. He was growing impatient and wanted to get away from this place of death, always having heard that it was a dangerous thing to be around the dead for fear of their spirits. Believing it now more than ever, the young Indian did not wish to stick around. As soon as he could, he suggested they make for the river.

When they reached it, neither one knew what to do, so they eventually sat down on the shore. Andy, clad in what remained of his trousers, did not say a word and stared at the water. Badger left him to his thoughts until after Sun had passed overhead when he managed to get him to try to talk.

Rehearsing each other's names, they practised some of the words they had learned the day before. After his new friend lost enthusiasm for it, Badger stood up and took Andy by the arm, pulling him to his feet. *"Come,"* he said, giving a nod to indicate he should go along, not releasing his grip. Andy was puzzled but followed him out of curiosity.

A short distance up the trail, Badger cut off and headed across a meadow, where he pointed out a badger hole, with its mound of dirt. *"Míísinsski,"* he announced, pointing down the hole. *"That is me, Míísinsski."*

Andy looked at him quizzically. "A badger hole?"

Pointing down the hole, Badger repeated, *"That is me— Míísinsski,"* pointing back and forth between himself and the hole.

Andy was puzzled. *"Míísinsski* means badger?"

Grinning, Badger gave a good impression of how a badger moves along the ground. *"Míísinsski,"* he said again, pointing alternately at the hole and at himself.

"You're a badger?" Andy was still not quite sure what he was saying, but suddenly, it dawned on him. He had learned that many Indians carried the name of an animal or its characteristics. "Okay! I get it. You're *Míisinsski! Míisinsski* is a badger—your name is a badger!" He was delighted to have figured it out. *"Míisinsski,"* he repeated, pointing to Badger. Next, pointing at the hole, he said, *míisinsski.* The Indian nodded his head and smiled at their success. Andy grinned with satisfaction. "Hey"—he said— *"Míisinsski,* let's go to the river," for he had taught the Indian the word for river, and they ambled back to it.

When they returned to their spot, Badger decided he wanted to go swimming and went straight to the water. Turning to Andy, he urged, *"Come! It is too hot! Get out of those ugly leggings! Let us go swimming."* Andy gathered what was being suggested but did not feel much like it. *"Come,"* Badger repeated, *"Swim!"* diving in and swimming a few strokes to make sure he was understood.

"I dunno!" his companion sighed. But the Indian was insistent, coming ashore to cajole him. Even though he was still feeling blue, Andy relented, saying, "Okay, what the heck!" Getting to his feet, he hesitated for a second then reached for the buttons at the front of his trousers.

Andy tried to enjoy the water, but his grief would not allow him to join in his companion's fun. Still, the water was a pleasant, if temporary distraction. Feeling raw inside, he was labouring over what was going to happen to them. Finally, he went along with the Indian who goaded him into a wrestling, dunking, test of strength. They were evenly matched, and although Badger managed to upend him a couple of times, Andy figured he could take him if he really tried.

Badger was delighted when his new friend finally cracked a smile. No stranger to loss, he assumed Andy and the dead *napikawan* had been brothers and knew it would take some time before he felt happy again. He was glad to play around and distract his new friend.

Before long, though, Andy lost his playfulness and started back toward shore. Badger followed him out of the water and flopped down beside him in the warm sand.

"I am getting hungry!" he said after they had fallen silent for a while. Getting to his feet, he rubbed his stomach, and using gesture, he tried to indicate that he was going to look for something to eat.

Seeing his companion get up and leave, Andy was curious about what he was doing. Quickly scrambling to his feet and pulling what was left of his trousers back on, he followed his friend up the ravine, taking one of the forks that Andy had turned away from the day before. Sombrely, he followed the Indian, watching his long black hair, long enough to reach his backside, swing from side to side as he strode.

It was early evening, and they had covered some distance when Badger spotted a rabbit. It had been a long time since he had done such a thing, but he managed to send a stick flying at it, stunning it long enough for him to pounce and snap its neck. He used Andy's knife to cut it apart and was ready to eat it raw when Andy saw what he was doing and intervened. "Hey! No, I got something," he blurted, pulling something else from his pocket. Badger had no idea what it was as his friend showed it to him. "It's a flint," Andy announced. Puzzled, the Indian took it and examined it.

Giving his head a shake, he handed it back. *"What is it?"* he asked.

Hearing the question in his voice, Andy replied, "Look!" Giving the flint a slash, it sent forth a shower of sparks.

"Hi-yah!" Badger exclaimed in surprise. *"I wonder if we could light a fire with that!"*

Giving the instrument a couple more swipes, to show how it worked, the white boy stooped and gathered some dry grass into a pile. In a moment, he had it smouldering, and his companion rushed to find twigs. They had fire.

After devouring the crudely cooked rabbit, they returned once again to the river. Along the way, Badger tried to teach his companion a few more words, but found him deep in thought and not very communicative.

As darkness consumed the twilight, a near-full moon illuminated the river valley. Not ready for sleep, Andy wandered to the shore by himself. The water shone in the moonlight, and he heard an owl, up the ravine. Mourning silently, how he wished he could go back and change the events of the past two days! Sitting down to pray that his god would care for him, he was startled by Badger's voice, close behind him, *"Did you hear the owl?"*

"Hi," Andy managed to say. "You scared me a little!"

"They are the spirits of the dead," his companion continued. *"Let us hope they do not bother us tonight—we should make sure we stay together."*

"Yeah," Andy responded forlornly, not understanding him. "I can't sleep. I can't stop thinking about Matty. I really miss him!" His voice broke as he once again fought back tears. Badger sat beside him and remained silent until Andy asked, "Have you got a brother?"

"I do not know what you are saying. I wish I could understand you—I could probably help you!" They continued in silence, both gazing across the water. *"My father died when I was a boy. I still miss him!"* the Indian boy volunteered eventually. *"I wish I was like him!"*

Andy wondered what he was saying. "I wish I could talk to you!" he sighed. "I'm so lonely!" Adjusting the way he had been sitting and trying not to let the other notice what he was doing, he wriggled himself a little closer, seeking what comfort he could eke out of their closeness. "I think I like you," Andy murmured finally. "I hope we can be friends." After another long silence, he asked, "Are you getting tired?" The look Badger gave him in the moonlight said he had not understood. "Sleep?" Andy said and imitated his companion's actions from the previous night.

"Sleep?" Badger recognized the word he had learned the night before. *"Yes!"* he agreed and clambered to his feet. Andy got up and let his friend decide where they would sleep. Once he had selected a suitable location, which was little more than a place where there was some grass, Andy was glad when Badger had finished squirming and wrapped his arm around his chest, pulling himself up tightly to him. Unaccustomed to the skin to skin contact, Andy was nonetheless thankful for the warmth and gave a wriggle to signal his approval. He was much too exhausted to think about it and was soon fast asleep.

4

Before the sun rose, Badger awakened with a sense of worry. He was confident he could find his way home, but he was just as confident that his cousin and the others would have arrived long before him. Doubtless, they would have told some disgraceful story explaining his disappearance. It would be humiliating, of that he was certain. On the other hand, he reasoned as he laid awake, they would probably be telling everyone that he had been killed, for that would surely have been his fate had it not been for the white boy's intervention. Perhaps he would be able to the tables on his cousin for once and embarrass him for a change, telling some story about the intervention of the spirits. The idea held some appeal, but in the meantime, there was the white boy to look after.

As soon as Andy was awake, Badger was itching to get underway and led the way up a ridge. From there, he spotted a long ravine leaving the river in a southwesterly direction. Filled with bush, it would provide good cover. He knew the ravines were always interlaced with game trails, which would make travel easy, so he led the way up the first one he encountered. Andy was content to trail along behind him, seeing they were headed west. In his mind, it was the right direction—his father was to the west. But leaving his brother behind was almost too much for him to bear. His heart ached as he trudged along behind the Indian.

The sun was high when they reached the brink of the river valley. *"I have a bad feeling about travelling out in the open,"* Badger muttered to himself, knowing his companion would not understand him. *"I think we will wait here until dark."* Giving Andy a shrug, he turned around to retreat into the cover of the ravine. Before long, he found a spot where they could wait out of sight until darkness, but he could not make Andy understand the reason for their delay.

Communication was difficult. Andy wished he had paid more attention to the sign language which his brother had taken to so readily. Searching for ways to make the other understand what they were trying to say, they rehearsed what they had already learned—their body parts and objects nearby—but without much more than that, they spent prolonged periods in silence. It was a long day, especially for Andy, whose mind was in a turmoil with all that had happened. Both were hungry, but neither said anything about it. In the evening, knowing what lay ahead for them, Badger suggested they rest.

The Indian seemed able to go right to sleep, but for Andy, sleep was next to impossible. As his troubled mind processed his loss, there were simply too many questions and things going on in his mind. He cried—quietly to himself—and tried to pray, which made him feel little better. He had just begun to doze off when Badger stirred, and it was time to leave.

Dusk was beginning to give way to darkness when the young Indian led the way out into the open. Not sure why they were leaving just as it was starting to get dark, Andy followed his companion loyally from the ravine.

They had not travelled far when the full moon broke over the eastern horizon. Knowing Moon would light their way, Badger kept up his steady pace across the open landscape. As far as Andy could tell, he did not seem to be following any particular path. Sometimes he would pick up a buffalo trail and follow it a while, but eventually, he would step off it and strike out in a new direction, for no apparent reason. Crossing open, rolling prairie, checkered with patches of dark, foreboding brush, the Indian walked with a confidence Andy did not share.

The land had begun to rise steadily as they moved away from the river valley until they found themselves standing on a low ridge with a commanding view of the surrounding terrain. Rolling out before them, illuminated by the brilliant moonlight, the parkland reached the horizon, and to the southeast, a vast, open prairie. Behind them, from its dark valley, the river that had brought the white boy to this new world painted a silver ribbon in the distance.

Summer nights being short, dawn's first light caught them out in the open. Not wishing to risk being seen, Badger urged his friend to hurry and began jogging for a thicket he could see in the distance. His sudden haste caused Andy alarm, who tried to keep up while looking around for the cause of the unexpected hurry.

The Indian reached the thicket ahead of his companion and was waiting there when Andy caught up before leading them into its cover. Not the type of bushes in which they had rested the day before, these wore silvery leaves—the tallest, over their heads, while the lowest did not reach their knees. They found a clearing large enough that they could stretch out among the tallest bushes. Sitting cross-legged at first and trying to converse, each was learning more and more of the other's language.

"Sleep!" Badger eventually announced. He had been rehearsing the word and had been anxious to use it. *"Now, we sleep,"* he said, giving the sign for sleep.

Andy recognized what he had said and was more than ready to oblige—he was exhausted. *"Yes, sleep,"* he agreed, his friend's unfamiliar words awkward on his lips. At least it would not be cold. The sun was going to be blazing hot again.

They passed the coming days repeating their nightly marches and sun-drenched repose. Some evenings, a thunderstorm would wrack the prairie and cool the temperature, offering a temporary respite from the heat. Even the prairie nights were hot, so whenever they encountered a suitable body of water, they would spend the day holed up nearby, jumping in anytime they grew too warm.

The pair regularly sighted buffalo and other large game, but Badger could only lament the fact that he had absolutely nothing to hunt them. Instead, killing grouse and rabbits when he could, and having Andy gather berries, he managed to keep them fed.

Reminding them of their need for constant vigilance, one day, as they rested during the heat of the day, they were awakened by shouts and the sound of dogs barking. A large band of Indians was passing by the small lake near which they had stopped. *"It is a good thing we were not out there in the water!"* Badger whispered. It was something they might have been doing on such a sweltering day.

The sizeable contingent brought their horses to water, and soon the lake was ringed with people letting thirsty animals drink, or getting water themselves, and children playing along the muddy shore. The two hidden travellers were relieved when some of the young men, who had been keeping watch, ushered the people on.

When the place was once more deserted, Andy breathed a sigh of relief. *"I am not sure!"* the Indian said. *"I am quite certain they were our friends—Atsíína. And, that would have been all right—they are our allies. Maybe I should have let them know we were here!"*

Andy did not understand him but voiced his relief that the apparent danger had passed. "That was close!" he exclaimed.

Wide-awake now, neither one of them was capable of sleep. "Swim?" the Indian suggested after their unexpected company was out of sight.

"Sure, why not?" Andy agreed and stood up.

Anytime they swam, Badger remained highly cautious, not wishing anyone to catch them by surprise. But with a whole camp having just passed them by, it seemed unlikely that anyone else would be in the area to disturb them, so he raced to the water with abandon.

Wading out until he had found the deepest spot, he turned, and with the water at chest level, waited for his friend. *"Hai!"* he said as Andy approached. *"Put your feet on my shoulders,"* he said, patting his shoulders with his hands, *"and I will duck under the water and throw you!"* Bending his knees and ducking beneath the water, he lunged upward to demonstrate his intent. Andy had played similar games with his friends and was pleased to have understood his friend's suggestion.

"Okay, and then I'll do it to you—get down!" he said, feeling eager for a change. The grin on his face told Badger he was ready to participate.

They were trying to see who could launch the other the farthest when they were surprised by the sudden appearance of horseback riders. A group of boys from the recently passed camp had decided to return to the watering spot for some fun of their own, but they were surprised to find their swimming hole occupied. Play changed instantly to war, as the band of intruders raced toward the two startled figures. Too far from shore to be able to make their escape, the careless pair was quickly surrounded by the group of mounted boys, come warriors, all of whom now held a bow and arrow pointed directly at them.

Andy was petrified, anticipating the same treatment Matty's party had received. Crouching in the water, he was certain he was about to die when he heard Badger exclaim, *"Hai-ya!"*

Badger, too, had crouched at the onslaught, but following his earlier hunch, he looked for the one that seemed to be the leader and began to sign. The leader had a giant claw hanging from his neck and looked about the age of Badger and Andy.

Claw Boy was sitting confidently astride his horse, bow fully drawn, ready to use it. Observing Badger's signing, the young warrior suddenly relaxed his bow and gave a hearty grin, before turning to speak to his companions. At once, he dropped his aim and removed the arrow. Returning it to its quiver, he slung the bow over his back so he could respond in sign.

To Andy's enormous relief, the others lowered their weapons too. They clamoured to see what was being signed and look over Andy's pale figure. When he saw Badger reach up to shake the leader's hand, Andy felt relieved. Friends, he thought, figuring they must be Badger's people. But he wondered why they would be signing if that was the case. Who were they then?

The intruders' aggressive demeanour vanished as suddenly as it had manifested. They became so friendly that Andy wondered if they somehow knew and recognized his companion. One of them, maybe 13 or 14 years old, hopped off his horse into the water and strode up to face the white boy with outstretched hand. Feeling self-conscious about his nakedness, Andy nonetheless stood up out of the water to take the hand that had been offered, and at once, the rest followed suit, all wanting to shake his hand and get a good look at him. Andy had no idea who these Indian boys might be.

Wasting no time with formalities, the carefree bunch doffed their garments and treated the two strangers like long-lost friends. Intent on play, everything became a contest: wrestling, rough-housing to see who could upend the other, who could un-horse his opponent and who could hold his breath and swim under-water to surprise an opponent from below. They even let Badger ride one of their horses, but Andy declined when the offer was made to him for fear they would see that he was not a very accomplished horseman.

Andy was the focus of much of their attention. They seemed to want to test him more than Badger. Very quickly, he forgot his woes and enjoyed the attention he was being given, having nearly as much fun as he would have had back home among his friends.

Afterward, the cheerful boys lounged and rough-housed in the long grass beside the water. Apparently, nobody was in a hurry to leave. While Badger could sign and was kept busy doing so, Andy had nothing other than gesture and facial expression by which to communicate. Consequently, he mostly watched and grinned at the antics of the Indian boys, many of whom seemed to be trying to impress him and win his friendship. It amazed him how quickly these once-deadly warriors had turned into playful boys!

He had been trying to figure out how old they might be. Claw Boy was definitely the eldest and looked to be the same age as he and Badger. He had a slender, well-muscled build. Fine-featured, he had long black hair hanging to his backside. Two were twins—perhaps the leader's younger brothers, for they all stuck together. Another, 14 or so, bore a long scar across his chest that was still red and healing. There was some discussion with Badger about the wound, which Andy could not understand, but it was apparent the boy considered it a badge of honour. Two others were young enough that they were not yet displaying the curly black pubic hair of the others. Nevertheless, they seemed well-accepted by the rest. The last boy, also looking about 14 years old, was a clown and was doing anything he could to make the two strangers laugh.

All found an opportunity to come over and try to communicate with Andy. A couple of them made comment about the colour of his hair, pointing at the golden sheen on his limbs. None of the intruders had any hair on their bodies, other than what grew at their groin. All were lithe and muscular.

Eventually, Claw Boy got up and retrieved his breechclout, letting the others know it was time to leave. They all began to get themselves ready. As Andy got up to retrieve his ragged trousers, Badger approached him, *"We are going with them,"* he gestured. *"They are friends!"* But before leaving, he had one of the boys cut a piece of hide from what had served as his saddle. Using the boy's knife, he quickly crafted a belt and breechclout out of it, donning the simple garment as a covering.

When each *Atsíína* boy was mounted, Claw Boy rode over to Andy and held out a hand to him. The white boy let himself be hauled up, and Badger easily hopped on behind another. With a shout, they were off at full speed, forcing Andy to wrap his arms around his rider's waist to stay on. Still in the dark as to who these Indian boys were, and where they were being taken, he had little choice but to trust in Badger's judgement.

5

It was an exuberant gang of excited boys that raced into their camp, singing and shouting to draw attention to themselves. After charging boisterously through the camp a couple of times, they stopped near its centre to show off what they had found. Andy's strange appearance drew the attention of many, and he was very quickly surrounded by a curious swarm. He enjoyed being the centre of everyone's attention, but Claw Boy soon wanted him to go along with him.

He took the newcomers to a big lodge, where two women were finishing its assembly. Both stopped to stare at the pale boy. Badger's rider paused his horse just long enough to let him dismount before taking off with the others, who apparently had somewhere else to go. With great excitement, Claw Boy and his brothers leapt to the ground and shouted excitedly to the occupants of the lodge. The twins disappeared inside and shortly emerged, followed by a man who looked the two strangers over warily. The boys were jabbering with the curious man, as he strode toward their new friends.

Claw Boy had just begun to introduce them to his father when he spotted another man approaching. Interrupting himself, he hailed the man who walked over briskly. He was introduced to Badger, and the two began to converse. *"He speaks my tongue!"* Badger blurted to Andy, with delight.

No one else seemed to comprehend anything of their conversation, and Claw Boy turned to show Andy to his father. Names had not been figured out yet, by the time three women and an older girl approached. Andy was paraded before them too. It turned out that, besides his two younger brothers—the twins—Claw Boy had a sister, who looked to be older than he was, and—Andy could not figure this one out—did they have three mothers? He was left wondering about the three women, because at that moment, Badger and the other man re-joined the conversation. The man appeared to be a fluent speaker of Badger's language, as well as whatever it was that Claw Boy and his people spoke. But nobody had any understanding of Andy's English.

Through sign and gesture and help from the Blackfoot speaker, Andy began to understand that Claw Boy's real name had something to do with a howling dog and a tail—no, not a dog, a wolf. And, no, not a wolf and a tail, but the tail itself—Wolf Tail. Struggling to master the boy's name, Andy tried to teach them his own name, while Badger was readily introduced by the man who spoke Blackfoot. They were still working on names when one of the women called them to the lodge for something to eat.

Inside the newly erected structure, Wolf Tail's father took a seat opposite the door. Wolf Tail sat at his left and Andy and Badger were invited to sit beside him. The Blackfoot speaker sat to their left, and Andy observed that there existed a definite order and a protocol for seating. Before long, one of the women, aided by Wolf Tail's sister, began to serve meat. Offered first to the man, he deferred to his guests, who helped themselves. *"Ki-yah! Nitapi waksin! This is good!"* Badger exclaimed as it was passed to him, cramming a large piece into his mouth and grabbing another. "Buffo," he announced to Andy with his mouth full.

"Buff - a - lo," his friend corrected him. "Buff - a - lo."

Holding up a piece of meat to the man, Badger repeated, "Buff - a - lo."

"No, no," and Andy corrected his pronunciation. Everyone tried the word; even the girl attempted it timidly. Catching Badger's eye, Andy said, *"Iinii,"* bringing a grin to his friend's face, and both ate hungrily.

There was not much conversation during the meal. But once it was finished, Badger was kept busy explaining the circumstances which had led them there. With one eye watching the signs and listening to the stories, the girl aided one of the women in making a place for the boys to sleep. They had already been given a warm welcome, but once he understood that they would be staying as guests, Andy was even more delighted. He had grown weary of the night travel.

For the rest of the day, Wolf Tail took his guests around the camp to meet his many friends. At some of the lodges, they were invited inside to sit beside the man of the lodge and were served more and more food. By early evening Andy thought they must have met every boy and young man in the camp. They had been shown horses, bows, arrows, knives, scars, and injuries, each of which seemed to have a long story attached to it, little of which was understood by Andy. Several girls had been pointed out to them, and from the amount of laughter, he assumed there had been lots of joking, too.

The evening was little cooler than the day, and one of Wolf Tail's friends suggested they go swimming. *"They want us to go swimming with them,"* Badger told Andy, who recognized the word for a swim. Soon, many boys were ready to go. A few fell in beside

Andy and jostled each other to be able to walk beside him, trying to converse with him. They were a rowdy bunch, and there was much laughter.

It was a long walk downstream before those in the lead stopped on a sandy beach beside one of the few deep holes in the river to wait for the rest to catch up. *"This must be where they swim,"* Badger observed as they walked out onto the warm sand. "Swim— here," he added, making sure his friend had understood him.

Nobody waited for anyone after that! Rushing the final few steps to the beach, each boy hastily doffed his covering and plunged wildly into the water. The general confusion and splashing halted only briefly when everyone paused to watch Andy remove his garment and enter the water.

"What?" he said when he noticed that every eye was on him, but in the next instant, Badger leapt onto his back, and they tumbled into the water.

They did not return to the camp until after dark.

6

The sleeping arrangement became another entirely new experience for the white boy. The rest of Wolf Tail's family were already in their beds when the boys entered the lodge. The twins bounded for the buffalo robes that were their beds. Andy looked to Wolf Tail for direction just as one of the women sat up and reminded him where his guests were to sleep. Andy was surprised when all the boys simply stripped off their breechclouts in full view of the women and tumbled onto the robes that had been set out for them. More conscious of the girl than the women, he chose to sit down to remove his tattered trousers with his back toward them. There was excited talk in hushed voices and some rough-housing among the boys before they were told to be quiet.

The next morning was another very new experience for Andy. He had awakened early and was alert when the women got up. Apparently, everybody slept naked. And he saw everything as the women rose and moved about the lodge, before getting into their leather dresses—even the daughter. Andy watched her wide-eyed as she moved about, naked, before donning a one-piece leather dress. He had never seen a woman naked before and could not keep from gaping.

The women were still fussing at the back of the lodge when Wolf Tail's father roused himself and got the boys stirring. *"Hai, you lazy cubs! Get out of there!"* he said, standing over his sons and poking at them with his toe. None of the women seemed to pay any attention to the boys' nakedness as they slowly clambered to their feet, standing around sleepily, waiting for a more reluctant Andy to get up.

"Don't you guys care if they see you?" he muttered uncomfortably, not venturing from his robe. "What are we doing?" he asked.

His friend heard only the question in his voice. *"We are going for a morning bath!"* Badger replied grumpily, not ready to be up yet. "Swim!" he growled, giving the motions of washing oneself. *"Get up!"*

With Andy showing no signs of movement, the rest abandoned him to follow the man, who had already headed out the door. Not wishing to be left behind, he took a deep breath and stood up, hurrying after them. Casting a nervous glance in the girl's direction as he ducked out, he saw her watching him closely and felt himself blushing as he joined the others.

All the way to the river, Andy felt like every eye in the camp was upon him. None of his companions seemed the least bit uncomfortable with their nakedness as they all strode purposefully toward the placid water. There, they joined men and boys who were already bathing. A sleepy affair for most, greetings were grunted back and forth among friends. But to Andy's alarm, it was all taking place in plain view of the women and girls who were bathing just downstream, where Andy gaped at their nakedness. Others were coming, getting water, and going. A few paused to observe when they noticed his pale form but most paid little heed when the bathing was done and the boys left the water.

Wolf Tail became an instant friend, and with his family, embraced the newcomers as their own. But their closeness with one another made Andy miss his own family, and he hung back, quiet, while the rest were boisterous.

It was not long before Wolf Tail's mother began looking them over for size, directing his *almost mothers* to begin making clothes for them. In the meantime, she scrounged through her eldest son's things to find them something to wear.

Other boys and young men in the camp were all anxious to befriend the pair but gave special attention to Andy. He was taken by their sense of humour. They were always kidding around and joking, and he wished he understood their language so he could join in their fun. Sometimes, the Indians would take the time to sign; they all seemed as fluent at sign as they were their own tongue, often signing as they spoke. Taking it all in, he just smiled and enjoyed their laughter, which helped him feel better.

A reasonable match for them in the physical things—the tests of strength and wrestling—when it came to the use of a bow and arrow, Andy was a complete novice. Everyone clamoured to be the one to show him how to use a bow and give lots of noisy advice, but Wolf Tail insisted that he be the teacher. To that end, he had promised to take his guests with him when checking on his father's horses. Without the others around shouting their advice, he could better show Andy.

Sometimes accompanied by his little brothers, Wolf Tail was responsible for checking on the horse herd, chasing them to water before leaving them for the day. Finding a suitable bow and arrows for Badger, who already knew what to do with them, he also found something that would suit Andy. So, after their morning bath, they were ready to leave.

From horses tethered in the trees behind the camp, Wolf Tail selected two to ride. The white boy envied the ease with which Badger mounted. Andy had not ridden very much; his family had

had an old workhorse, which they had seldom ridden. On those rare occasions, he had usually led the docile beast to a fence from which he would struggle onto its broad back.

Neither of these horses had a saddle. Wolf Tail gestured for Andy to get onto the one he was holding. Giving the white boy a boost to get on, he handed up a coil of leather rope attached to a leather bundle before hopping on effortlessly in front of him. Before Andy could examine what he was holding, the Indian swung the horse around and headed for the river. Badger followed.

The ascent out of the valley was steep! Andy was forced to wrap both arms around Wolf Tail, pulling himself up tightly to his host's bare back as the horses pushed for the top. Once on the rolling prairie, he tried to follow the conversation as the two Indians signed, but it was a difficult task, sitting behind them. Quickly, he tired of it and paid more attention to his surroundings.

They had ridden for some distance when Wolf Tail adjusted their course toward a patch of dense bush, standing like an island in a sea of grass. It was the sort of place Badger would have chosen for cover while they had been marching across the prairie only days earlier. Coming around one end of it, they encountered the herd. Wolf Tail's horse let out a whinny which jarred both riders, and all the horses that were within view lifted their heads to watch their approach.

Wolf Tail gave a gesture to Badger, who seemed to know what was required. He had already begun to move his horse in the direction indicated. As the two riders separated, the herd started to bunch up. Knowingly, the animals began to move off in the direction of the river. The riders eventually fell in behind them, following them down a well-used trail into the river valley. Passing through trees and the dense bush that grew near the river, the herd filed out onto the muddy shore and spread out to drink, many not stopping until the water was at their bellies. Andy tossed the leather bundle to the ground and slipped off to let his companions water their mounts. He was waiting for them when they finished up and tethered their horses in the shade.

"Come!" Wolf Tail urged his pale friend. *"I will show you!"* He gestured as he spoke, helping Andy understand him. He scooped up the leather bundle, which turned out to be something of a target, setting it a short distance away. Between Wolf Tail's demonstration and both boys attempting to explain what to do, it did not take long before their student began hitting the target. He was doing well until his teachers attached the target to the leather rope Andy had carried and suspended it from a branch. The swinging target was much more difficult for him to hit. Still, he was disappointed when it was time to go.

Likewise, the herd did not seem to want to leave, with most of the animals unwilling to quit the cool of the river valley. Wolf Tail asked Andy to wait while he and Badger worked their way through the bush, driving the animals out of the valley and onto the prairie. Eventually, it was Badger who returned and helped Andy on behind him. Joining their friend at the top of the valley, they pushed the horses to leave them beyond the spot where they had initially found them.

The return trip did not seem to take as long as the trip out, and when they arrived at the encampment, Andy slipped backward over the horse's rump, letting the others tie the mounts.

"We need food!" Wolf Tail announced hungrily when he was done. At his mother's lodge, they found that she and her daughter had food waiting for them. Helping themselves with just their fingers, Andy smiled at the sister and tried to get a reaction from her. Giving a nervous glance in her mother's direction, she flashed him a smile and returned to her duties.

Before the boys had eaten their fill, two others joined them. These two were soon followed by others, and before long, several boys were buzzing around the fire. Badger and Andy recognized most of them, as they began helping themselves to the meat and chattering. A couple of them tried to engage Wolf Tail's sister in conversation while the rest swaggered about, meaning to distract her, but before long, all the boys headed for the river.

At the swimming hole were a couple of older boys who had not yet met Andy and who looked him over carefully. Because they were older, Andy found himself somewhat intimidated by them, especially when they sought to wrestle him and try to beat him at a match of strength. He fared well enough, though and seemed to win their respect. Most of the others cheered for him, and soon everyone headed for the water.

When the boys returned to camp at sundown, Wolf Tail's father was entertaining four strangers at his fire. The man who spoke Badger's tongue was among them. Looking the strangers over carefully, Badger took Andy by the arm and pointed something out to him, exclaiming excitedly. Unable to make his friend understand him, he was much too intent on the newcomers to try and explain.

Leaving his companions, Badger approached the fire and silently sat on the ground across from the strangers. The young Indian gazed into the flames, stealing occasional glimpses at the four, who paid little attention to him. Curious as to what was going on, Wolf Tail and Andy joined him.

Andy was unable to understand what was being communicated and soon lost interest. Spotting Wolf Tail's sister working at something outside her mother's lodge, he got up and joined her there, finding her busy with the garments she had been working on earlier. He squatted across from her.

As he did, he spotted the girl's mother eyeing him. Even though the woman was busily occupied with meal preparation, moving between her lodge and the fire, she made it evident that she was keeping a mother's eye on him.

Trying to ignore her, Andy studied the girl's face as she looked down at her work, seeming to ignore his presence. She had a well-defined nose and dark, piercing eyes that were almost black. Her full-length skin dress, belted at the waist, was decorated colourfully. She wore braids that were even longer than those of her brother. Admiring her good looks, Andy wished for something to say. Stuck for words, he could only watch her work.

Suddenly coming up with an idea, he grabbed a handful of his long and unkempt hair announcing, "Blonde! My hair is blonde!" The girl flashed him a grin and looked down again at her work. The long silence ended when she stood up in front of him, holding up the shirt she had been working on. Saying something to Andy, she gestured for him to stand up, too. As he complied with her wish, she lifted the leather garment to his bare chest, looking its fit over carefully. While she did so, Andy continued to admire her good looks—until she indicated that she wanted him to hold the shirt. Taking over from her and holding the garment up to his chest, he felt the tips of her fingers brush his skin as she ran her hands down the sides. Giving a nervous glance in her mother's direction, she took the shirt from him, openly looking him over. Andy watched her eyes cover every inch of his body. Hesitantly, keeping an eye on her mother, she ran her hand across his smooth chest, and with the back of her finger, brushed the train of golden hair, which descended from his navel into the remnant of his trousers. Saying something he could not understand, the lovely girl's smile was inviting. He returned it, but at that moment, the woman came toward them, and the girl suddenly fell to her knees and returned to her toil. She had been working on stitching a design of coloured porcupine quills onto the shirt. Andy was about to sit down with her and continue to watch her work when Badger raced over with a grin across his face.

"*Hai! They are my people! They are Káínaa!*" he blurted to a puzzled Andy. "*These men—they are my people!*" he exclaimed, pointing to the strangers. "*Niitsitapi—the same as me! They are my people!*" Continuing to point at them then himself, he repeated, "*Niitsitapi.*"

Andy understood that they were somehow the same, but his excited friend was giving him no opportunity to respond. Getting to his feet, Andy nodded his head and said, "Yeah, yeah, same as you," pointing to Badger and pointing to the men.

"*Yes! Niitsitapi—Káínaa.* Friends!" Badger continued, before turning to rejoin the men. Curious, Andy followed him, giving a shy wave to the girl as he left her. He found Badger exchanging words with the men, revealing their common tongue and wondered if Badger somehow knew them. As the curious white boy approached, his friend took him by the arm, bringing him forward to stand with him. He heard his name mentioned as Badger spoke, still holding him by the arm. Finished, he draped his arm around Andy's shoulder and pulled him close while the *Káínaa* looked him over.

The white boy scrutinized the *Káínaa* as carefully as they did him. They looked much older—three of them appeared to be in their twenties, and the fourth was older still, with a hint of grey running through his coal-black hair. They were tall and strong, leaner than their hosts. The oldest was a huge man, noticeably taller than the others—taller even than Wolf Tail's father, who was a big man. They all had prominent noses, but this man's nose was much bigger than the rest, dominating his face. Their hair was styled differently.

Before he could gain any greater understanding of who they might be, two others, friends of the host, approached the fire and were introduced. The newcomers then signed to the *Káínaa* and took a seat on the ground. Shortly after that, by ones and twos, other men from the camp joined them. Without being able to understand what they were signing, Andy once again lost interest and looked around for something else to do.

Seeing his restlessness, Wolf Tail got up and nodded for him to follow. They walked around the camp and found a couple of boys Andy recognized from earlier. At first casual, their conversation became increasingly excited, and before long, they all scattered. Wolf Tail grabbed Andy by the arm and dragged him to his lodge. There, he retrieved their bows and arrows before returning to meet up with the others, who were all now carrying similar equipment in their hands or on their backs. Leaving the camp, shortly, they reached a clearing where there was a single, large tree from which was suspended a tightly bound bundle of grass and twigs. The bundle was about the size of a man's torso. The boys began placing arrows in their bows while one of the youngest ran forward and gave the bundle a mighty heave to set it swinging.

Wolf Tail blurted something to the others, and they all turned to Andy. He was to go first. Nervous, he tried to remember what his friends had taught him earlier, as he reached for an arrow. He and Matthew had made bows and arrows to play with back at the settlement, but they were nothing like the one he held in his hands. Made from a branch or slender tree stalk, it was wrapped with rawhide, where he gripped it. The string certainly was not the twine his mother had given them to use but some kind of fine leather or gut material. The arrow had been expertly fashioned from something, perhaps a branch, Andy thought. It had a small, sharply pointed stone tip at one end and three feather vanes at the other.

Andy's clumsy handling of the weapon brought a barrage of advice from the boys until Wolf Tail silenced them. Standing quietly, they watched Andy arm his weapon with an arrow and pull back on the bowstring. The grass target had almost stopped swinging by the time his arrow flew, grazing the target slightly before fluttering off into the grass. His earlier practice had helped. There was a clamour from the others, and the young boy was sent to get the target swinging again. Andy's second shot hinted that the first had been pure luck, and a third arrow proved it.

Having had enough of his efforts, the others were all anxious to take their shots. Andy was surprised how quickly Wolf Tail pulled an arrow from his quiver and put it through the very centre of the target. The others all groaned and sent the youngster to keep the target swinging once more. He was kept busy as they all took turns shooting at it. Some hit it most of the time, but Wolf Tail hit it every time.

When most were out of arrows, someone called a halt, and

everyone hurried forward to gather them. All the arrows looked alike to Andy, but each boy seemed to know exactly which were his own, and there were no arguments. Observing the next round, he noted the rippling muscles on the boys' arms and on their backs and figured he was probably not pulling hard enough. He felt better about his subsequent efforts, but he could see it would take a lot of practice to achieve the skill exhibited by every one of his hosts.

The approaching darkness brought an end to the target practice. Slowly, disappointed to be done so soon, everyone sauntered back to the camp, each boasting of his skill. Encountering a group of girls, they exchanged looks and comments unknown to Andy as they passed each other.

At Wolf Tail's lodge, the men were still engaged in a celebration around the outside fire, eating and laughing, activities which seemed to mark these peoples' lives. And, Badger was right there among the *Káínaa,* having as good a time as anyone. But as soon as he spotted his friend, he got up and hurried over to tell him something. Speaking excitedly, he paused to think about how he could tell his friend what was happening. Using the little English he knew, signing as he spoke, he tried to make Andy understand that they would be leaving with the *Káínaa.*

"Where are we going? *"Where?"* Andy asked. The Indian was evasive and quickly turned to go back to the fire, leaving his friend in wonder. What he did not tell his friend was that the *Káínaa* were out to make war on an enemy—apparently the *Liars.* Intent on finding trouble, there was certain to be killing. But Badger was hoping that it would end up being a way to get home with them.

7

Awakening early the next morning, Andy could not get back to sleep. As so often happened, he would lie awake and think of his family and all that had happened. In such quiet moments, he missed them terribly and wished he knew what had happened the day his brother died.

Reminiscing about his younger years, his eyes filled with tears remembering how he used to sit with his mother and chat with her while she worked in her kitchen, the others off somewhere. How he missed her and longed to go back to the way they had been—with Matty and their father, all together. Often, he asked God why, never sensing any response. It made him sometimes question his faith in a god who allowed such things, wondering if God paid any attention to him at all. The suddenness of his mother's death and the horror of losing his brother, all with his father so far away, not infrequently made him wonder if God had abandoned him. Other times, he baselessly blamed himself for his family's misfortune.

"God," he whispered this morning, "there's gotta be some reason. I dunno, I guess your ways higher than mine." Remembering how his father had prayed those words, he smiled fondly and ended his prayer as his father had always done. "I accept your will. So, let it be."

Morning came, and things followed the same pattern as they had the day before. As Andy approached the river to bathe, he wondered again why nobody seemed concerned about their nakedness. At home, it had been only the boys who saw one another naked, so long as there were no adults around—or girls. But these people seemed oblivious to the eyes of others; nobody seemed to pay any attention to it. His father had warned him and his brother not to let anyone see them naked, and he had never understood why. But it made him especially conscious when a couple of girls eyed only him as he strode with the others. "Take a good look!" he muttered to himself.

Clouds filled the sky, and it was cooler this morning as the boys readied themselves to ride out and check on the horses. The twins wanted to come along and would be riding double, but Andy was given his own horse to ride. He felt awkward, seeing how easily the others mounted and rode, even the twins.

When they returned to camp later, Wolf Tail's father was entertaining his guests again. But when he saw his sons returning with their friends, he excused himself to go and greet them.

The big man tried awkwardly to say their names as he approached, but not doing a very good job of it, he switched to sign. Seeing what was being signed, Badger grinned a happy grin and flashed one at Andy. When he had finished signing, the man beckoned his daughter, who stood waiting near the lodge for his signal. Stooping to scoop up the clothing she and her mother had been working on, she hurried forward. Approaching Andy with it, she gestured for him to dismount, where she presented the clothes to him and stepped back to her father's side, watching with anticipation. She beamed proudly while Andy admired his gift, but was quickly sent to fetch a similar pile for Badger. His clothes she thrust into his hands, quickly returning her attention to the white boy.

Both had been gifted a breechclout, leggings, three pairs of moccasins, and a handsome, pullover shirt, all made of soft leather. Andy's shirt, when he tried it on, fit perfectly. Heavier than the cotton shirts he had worn most of his life, it would be too warm for a day like today, and certainly too warm for the hot weather they had been experiencing over the last number of days. While they were trying on their new clothes, the girl's mother handed them each a vest-like garment, open down the front and sleeveless.

Excited about their gifts, Andy was even more excited when Badger told him the rest of the news. Pointing at the horse Andy had been riding, he announced, "You, horse!" and pointing to the one he had been riding, he said, "Me, horse." Then in Blackfoot, he said, *"Yours,"* pointing to Andy's horse and, *"mine,"* pointing to his own. *"He has given them to us!"*

Not sure he had understood, Andy turned to the girl. *"Yes!"* she exclaimed, in her language, nodding her head. *"From my parents! I helped my mother make the clothes! You saw me making them!"* The big man and his wife were both grinning and nodding, and from their gestures, Andy understood.

"Thank you! Thank you so much!" he blurted. On an impulse, he grabbed the woman and gave her a hug, which surprised her completely. He then grabbed the girl and hugged her, too. Taken off guard by it, she had difficulty concealing her delight.

"Come!" Badger urged. *"We need to try out these horses!"* Quickly donning his vest, and handing the rest of the clothing back to the girl to put somewhere, he gestured for Andy to do the same. Hopping onto his animal's back, he waited for his friend, who was not nearly so graceful at getting on. He then led him out of the valley—a precarious venture for Andy, who almost slid off

his horse. They spent the rest of the racing and riding their new mounts on the open prairie with Wolf Tail.

Returning to camp for something to eat, the afternoon was spent at target practice with others their age. Badger used a bow lent to him by Wolf Tail and won arrows off most of the others. In the end, he and Wolf Tail were at an even tie, so someone fastened a long piece of rope to the hanging target, so it could be whipped around continuously. The two finalists then stood at the same distance from their wildly swinging mark, each with just three arrows. Wolf Tail hit the target with his first two, and the third flew wide, but Badger hit all three! The *Atsíína* boy was gracious in presenting the winner with the bow he had been using, and keeping only a few of his own arrows, he gave the victor the rest along with the quiver. Together with the arrows he had won, Badger had a good start on a quiver full of arrows.

The sun was down by the time they returned to the camp. Toward the end of their target practice, they had heard the drumming start and returned to camp to find the men—young and old—dancing around a fire. Andy became so engrossed in watching them that he lost track of the others.

He had been watching the dancers for a while, when one more beautiful than the rest joined the dancing. The newcomer's outfit made him stand out from the others. His high-topped moccasins were decorated with colourful quills and trimmed around the top with winter ermine skins. From his waist, hung from a narrow belt, was a white leather breechclout, hanging to his knees. Over his shoulders hung a vest of the same white leather, adorned with coloured quills and winter ermine skins. The vest hung open at the front and contrasted against the dark skin of the dancer's chest and rippling belly. A necklace of elk teeth and feathers was around his neck. His braids were trimmed with winter ermine, and he wore on his head a cap of straight, upright fur. In each hand, he held an adornment of feathers, which he waved about in time with the drum. His face was entirely painted. Above his eyes was black and below, white. The two colours were separated by a bright, yellow line running horizontally through the eyes and across the bridge of his nose. Lines radiated from each eye, four white ones above the eye, and four black below the eye. The colours were so vivid that Andy could see them plainly, even in the twilight. He squirmed through the spectators to get a closer look.

The ornate dancer kept perfect time with the drum, which began to pick up the tempo as soon as he appeared. Before long, he was the only one dancing, the others having retired to watch him. His dark skin soon glistened with sweat. Faster and faster, the drum pounded, and faster and faster, the agile dancer moved. Andy found his heart racing as if he were also dancing until, almost imperceptibly, the rhythm began to slow. When the end seemed near, Andy wanted to shout his appreciation, but everyone else seemed too solemn for that, almost reverent. He dared not. But suddenly, the tempo picked up until the drums were beating frantically. Finally, with one resounding, final boom, the dance was finished with the dancer diving to his hands and knees, face to the ground, his sides heaving!

Andy looked around, ready to applaud, but nobody else made any such move. They were all still and solemn! For a long moment, the only movement from the dancer was his heaving sides, then slowly he lifted himself up and began to search the faces around him. Sitting back on his heels, he continued searching, not stopping until he found the white boy and fixed his eyes upon him.

It took a moment for Andy to notice that the figure's expressionless gaze was directly upon him. The painted face was haunting as the mysterious dancer now stood, slowly, to face him. Breathing heavily, the figure's smooth belly glistened with every breath while he continued to watch just Andy, his eyes fixed and unmoving.

Andy became nervous, not understanding why he had been singled out. He looked around to see where his friends were, but glancing back found the dancer's eyes still glued upon him. Feeling even more uncomfortable, he turned his back and started to walk to where he had last seen Badger. The crowd was drifting away, and when he looked again, to his relief, the eerie figure had disappeared.

The twins were in Badger's company, jabbering excitedly, eventually suggesting that they find something to eat, leading in the direction of their lodge. Following them inside, both Badger and Andy were shocked to discover the mysterious dancer, standing on the other side of the bright fire.

"You?" Andy exclaimed, recognizing Wolf Tail, who greeted him with a broad grin. His mother was helping him out of his attire. Carefully, she lifted the vest off him, taking great care not to get the face paint on the white leather, before he removed his breechclout and handed it to her to put away. The boy's body still glistened with sweat. Giving a nod to his friends, he queried, "River?" using Andy's language.

The cool, evening air made the river seem warm, and they lingered in the water after Wolf Tail had scrubbed the paint off him. Knees bent, so just their heads were out, they held themselves against the gentle current and looked at the reflection of the fires glittering across the water. In the sky, Badger pointed out *the seven persons*. "That's the dipper!" Andy exclaimed. They all attempted to point out other shapes they recognized among the stars, but none of them knew enough of the others' language to be able to make them see what it was they were pointing out.

When they returned to the camp, the men were again lingering around the outside fire. Remembering how bored he had been the night before, not understanding anything that was being said, Andy convinced the others to go inside. There, without a fire, they sat in the dark, atop their robes, trying to converse. Their attempts at conversation were punctuated with jostling and poking, witnessed by the women and the girl, who watched idly, speaking quietly. When a couple of them slipped outside to relieve themselves, the light from the outside fire illuminated the inside, and in the dim light, Andy caught the girl's eye. Once more, when the door flap was pulled aside for the women to re-enter, they both locked eyes in the brief light.

Eventually, the boys settled down and became quiet. Badger, this time, was lying awake. He was thinking about the *Káínaa*. He had asked to accompany them in the hopes of returning to his homeland, but inside he knew it was a bad idea. Before returning to their homeland, the men were intent on making a raid on the *Liars*. It would be utter foolishness to accompany them. He feared they would be killed! Better, he thought, they should stay with the *Atsíína*, and maybe travel with them. Sometimes the *Atsíína* joined his people at their Sun dance—he would find his family there.

When the men finally came in, they were noisy and did not seem concerned that others might be sleeping.

In the night, it rained. Alone with his thoughts, it was the steady drumming of the rain on the hide shelter that finally lulled Badger to sleep.

The dawn was cool and overcast, drizzling off and on. The smell of the wet earth, after the long hot spell, was refreshing when everyone went for their morning bath.

On their return, the boys prepared to ride out to the horse herd again, and Badger hurried the others along, hoping the *Káínaa* might be gone by the time they returned. They hadn't seemed all that interested in having the boys along anyway.

Both he and Andy donned their new clothes, including their leggings, anticipating that they would be riding through the wet brush at the river. Badger wore his new bow and quiver across his back, delighted to have it.

Bringing their horses to the front of the tipi, Wolf Tail put a kind of saddle on Andy's mount. It formed a soft padding, strapped around the animal's body. A leather handle stitched to it let Andy swing himself up and hold on. Once he had practised mounting a few times and was seated on his horse, Wolf Tail tied two large, leather bags over the saddle in front of him. Into these, his mother stuffed some things for them to take. She was sure it would rain again, and just in case they might have to sit out a rainstorm, she showed up with a large, tanned hide, rolled up, which was tied on behind.

Andy was unhappy that his was going to be the packhorse. He would have liked to complain and suggest that the others take their share of the load, but he lacked the words to do so. When he pointed to his load and then at the others, they both shrugged indifferently and turned their horses toward the river.

Badger saw that the *Káínaa* seemed to be getting ready to leave, too. Good, he thought! They would be gone by the time they got back! He was relieved, certain that it would have been a mistake to accompany them.

The twins were coming again today, riding double on the same old horse they had ridden the day before. Badger and Andy each had their own horses, while Wolf Tail rode a different horse. It was a buffalo runner, a gift from his father, given to him upon the occasion of killing his first buffalo. He was excited to show it off to the others.

As his mother had predicted, it started raining even before they found the herd—not heavily, but it spoke of more to come.

Finding the horses nearer the river this morning, they pushed them down the same trail as before. While the herd went to water, the boys tied their mounts in the trees, taking shelter from the drizzle under a large cottonwood.

The horses began to move back into the shelter of the trees when they finished drinking from the river, and Wolf Tail was thinking about watering their mounts when they heard horses approaching rapidly, from the direction of the camp. Instinctively, ducking for cover, Badger and Wolf Tail lifted their heads to see who was arriving in such a hurry. When he saw it was the *Káínaa*, Badger's heart fell, but he stepped out into the open, letting himself be seen. Pulling their horses to a halt nearby, the men quickly tethered them.

Their arrival puzzled the boys until the huge man hollered to Badger, *"We have word from their father!"* Alarmed as to what it could be, Badger signed to Wolf Tail what had been said. Before the boys could react, the men rushed quickly toward them, and without any warning, the giant Indian slipped his knife from its sheath and plunged it deep into Wolf Tail's chest. The weapon was driven with such force that the tip of the blade came out the boy's back, protruding briefly through his leather shirt before he was flung to the ground. Badger and Andy were both frozen with shock and horror as they watched the big man and his comrades quickly and efficiently slaughter their friends before their eyes. With practiced moves, the killers stooped over their hapless victims and sliced a braid from each of them.

The attack had been executed so swiftly and so efficiently that neither Badger nor Andy had been able to do a thing! Horrified, Andy raced to his fallen friend and fell to his knees beside him as soon as the giant *Káínaa* abandoned him to his death. The boy gasped desperately, a horrible sucking sound coming from his wounds, his terrified eyes locked upon Andy's. Bright red blood oozed from the ugly, raw patch of skull, where his scalp had been taken. His mouth opened and closed repeatedly, his lips pursing as he struggled for breath. His eyes pleading for help, with two short, pained groans, the young dancer's body went limp. By the boy's eye was a bit of yellow paint that he had missed the night before.

Paralyzed by shock and fear, Andy just sat there, unable to move or think. He was oblivious to what was happening around him—just him and his friend's lifeless body. His mind reeling, he stared into the boy's lifeless face. Images of Matthew's body raced through his mind when suddenly, the giant was beside him once more, muttering something unintelligible. Before Andy could react in defence of his friend's body, the man shoved him out of the way with his knee. Roughly he rolled the dead boy over and ripped the bow and quiver of arrows from his back, tossing them in the direction of his horse. Grabbing the boy's shirt by the sleeves, the man lifted him and shook him until it slipped off, and the body slumped to the ground. With a quick movement of his blade, he slit the belt around the boy's waist and removed the breechclout and leggings in a similarly brusque manner. Lastly, he pulled off the moccasins, leaving the pitiful body naked. Remembering the mutilation visited upon the Cree, Andy was roused from his stupor. He steeled himself to leap forward to prevent the indignity, but the big man was gone.

Equally horrified by what had happened, Badger watched helplessly while the other *Káínaa* stripped the twins' bodies. Dreading the thought of their young bodies being cut and mutilated, he was relieved when the attackers stopped short of it. Stunned by the swiftness and the brutality of the attack, he stood glued to the ground and gaped in horror.

At first, the voice seemed to emanate from somewhere outside Badger's consciousness, but he turned slowly to face the source of it. *"Quickly! We must ride!"* the giant *Káínaa* ordered, stuffing Wolf Tail's braid and his clothing into a sack, hanging from his horse. *"We will capture these horses and take you home!"* Badger could only stare blankly at the man who now approached him, wearing a sinister grin. *"Come, little brother! Bring your friend! We must hurry! You must come with us!"*

"We are not going!" Badger uttered, emotionless.

"Are you a fool?" the giant roared at him, *"They will kill you like flies! We have killed his sons! He will cut your bodies into small pieces and feed it to the dogs! Come! You must leave with us!"*

Badger did not know what to do. Imagining the grief the boys' father would feel, he knew the *Káínaa* was right. Revenge would be swift and certain. Besides the loss of his sons, having his horses stolen too would only fuel the man's fury. There could be no mercy for those who had perpetrated such a deed!

They would have to flee! Recognizing no other option in the horror and confusion of the moment, he raced for their horses, shouting, "Andy! *Come quickly, or we will end up like these ones! Come quickly! We are going with them!*" Already the *Káínaa* were on their mounts and beginning to usher the herd across the river.

Andy had not moved from where he was kneeling beside Wolf Tail's body with a look of horror on his face. Badger got his horse and took it to him, shaking him by the shoulder. "*Come! Get on your horse! We must ride fast! You must get up, my friend. Come on!*"

Trance-like, Andy could not grasp what his friend was saying as he tugged desperately on his arm. Slowly, he got to his feet and turned to face him, the fear and torment in Badger's face adding to his confusion. "*Please! Come now, my friend! I do not want you to die, too! We must flee!*" Badger begged him, wide-eyed with fear, dragging him to his horse, where the bewildered white boy just stood in shock, making no move to get on. "*Get on! Please!*"—the desperate Indian pleaded, frantically— "*Now!*" —trying to get Andy to mount his horse.

"*You will be food for the coyotes, you fools!*" cried one of the *Káínaa* from the edge of the river, not waiting.

"We have to help them!" Andy blurted, his eyes moving from one body to the next.

"*Get on your horse!*" Badger ordered, trying futilely to lift his friend onto his mount. The white boy just stared in disbelief at one of the twins, lying nearby, his neck gaping, his face smeared with blood where his shirt had been pulled over his head.

"We have to help them!" he sobbed desperately.

Badger now squatted behind him and wrapped his arms around his hips. With all his strength, he lifted Andy up, hoping he would put his leg over the horse's back. It did not work, and now he could only hold him against the horse's side as it fussed and tried to move away from him. *"Get on! Get on!"* Badger screamed frantically, his voice high-pitched, trying to get his disoriented friend onto the horse. Managing to get his shoulder under him, he could lift him enough that Andy finally swung his leg over the animal's back and pulled himself on. *"Hold on!"* Badger tried to make Andy grip the handle on the saddle he had been given that morning, relieved when he closed both his hands tightly around it. He then led the animal over to where his own horse was tied. But before mounting, he paused, looking thoughtfully at the *Atsiína* boys' horses, still tied in the bush. The killers had somehow missed them. He went and untied them. Grasping all the reins together in one hand, along with Andy's, he swung up onto his mount. *"Hold on!"* he barked at Andy, his voice breaking. He urged his mount toward the river, struggling to hang onto all the other reins in one hand, with the rest of the horses trying to crowd past to follow the herd.

The *Káínaa* had the last of their plunder over the top of the valley by the time the boys reached the water. Without letting their animals stop to drink, Badger frantically kicked his mount onward, watching Andy anxiously and checking nervously for anyone to show up behind them. Crossing the river, he led his friend up the ridge—homeward—out of the valley of death.

The tracks from the herd, plainly evident in the wet earth, could not go unnoticed. *"They will not miss those!"* Badger muttered as they came up onto the parkland above the river valley. The *Káínaa* were chasing the horses at a furious pace ahead of them, with one of their number riding out front, leading them.

Andy was in shock. At a time when he thought they should be racing to the boys' father for help, they were fleeing with their killers. Completely confused, his mind was filled with the gory images of the slaughter. And, remembering Badger trying to tell him something about going with the *Káínaa,* he was suddenly haunted by the worry that maybe his friend had been a part of it. It was all he could do to cling to the saddle using every bit of strength his body and spirit could muster.

Even after it started pouring rain—it was coming down in sheets—they rode as hard as they could. Badger kept them a short distance behind the *Káínaa*, who would occasionally turn to see if they were being followed. The *Atsíína* had been at peace with his people for a long time, but peace could be broken by any ambitious warrior looking for honour, which came through such endeavours as they had just witnessed. These hotheads, if they escaped successfully, would have double honour: they would boast of their killing and brag of capturing the horses. He doubted that they would tell anyone how they had betrayed a host's trust to accomplish it.

He, too, could not get the images of the slaughter out of his mind. The memory of Wolf Tail's dying body, impaled and suspended helplessly on the big *Káínaa's* knife, plagued his mind deeply. He kept imagining what it must have felt like to die—what Wolf Tail thought about in his final moments, impaled, with his life leaving him. Had he been afraid? Was he angry? Did he think his friends had betrayed him? Had he wondered why they did not help him? *"You nothing one!"* he cursed himself. *"You should never have asked them to take us along!"* He tried to pray to his gods, but it felt like his prayers were falling into the prairie mud, chewed up by the horses' hooves.

The harder it rained, the more triumphant the *Káínaa* became. *"See how the rain takes away our trail!"* they revelled. *"Sun has shown favour to us. He has given us victory!"*

All the rest of the day, the haughty thieves raced across the rolling parkland. Pausing only once, just long enough to catch fresh mounts from the herd, they pressed on without stopping to rest. Badger took that opportunity to switch horses, too, switching for those of their friends, leading their own by the reins when they raced on.

Soaked to the skin, Andy was getting cold. But for the warmth from his horse, he would have been shivering. The saddle and bags had been left on the first horse, and as he became aware of the heat from the horse's body, he was thankful as they raced on.

He had lost track of time when he realized that they were slowing. The trail ahead dropped steeply before them, and he became conscious of the fact that they were descending into a ravine. Looking around him, he could see neither the *Káínaa* nor the herd. At once, he became more alert.

"*Míísinsski!*" he called hoarsely to his friend. Badger heard him and pulled his horse up. Turning to look at the white boy, he was relieved to see him alert. It was the first thing he had uttered all day. Slipping off his mount, he tied all the horses and stepped back to where Andy remained seated on his horse. "What's going on? Where are they?" Andy asked, without considering that his companion would not understand him. Seeing his blank expression, he gestured behind him, "*They, horses—where?*"

"*We left them—a long way back. Maybe we are followed, can you keep riding?*" Frustrated that Andy could not understand him, and anxious that they not stop for long, Badger tried to explain. "They...they, no!" he stammered, shaking his head, and the few words he might have known escaped him. He could not figure out how to tell his friend that he had pulled away from the *Káínaa* a long way back. Seeing an opportunity, he had led his companion off the others' track, finally turning at a right angle from their trail in a heavy downpour. Riding hard, they had eventually come upon the river valley, which he had known would be there. He wanted to keep travelling so long as the rain obliterated their trail.

"Gotta pee," was Andy's response, and he slid from his horse. He was more alert and ready to squirm back onto his mount when he heard Badger call to him softly. When he turned around, the Indian boy's eyes were sad and rimmed with tears—pain was written on his young face. That was all it took to break the thin shell holding in Andy's grief and sadness. Both sobbing, they stumbled toward each other and fell on each other's shoulders. And Andy knew his friend had had nothing to do with the murders.

It was Andy who stopped sobbing first and stood holding onto his friend, who could not stop. When he finally managed and was silent, the white boy waited a moment before stepping back. At first, Badger could not look into his eyes and instead stared at his feet. "Hey," Andy said gently, causing him to lift his head. Looking deeply into each other's eyes, they knew without speaking a single word that their heartache was the same, and it bound them together.

It rained all day, a steady, obliterating rain. The grey clouds scudded low across the sodden prairie. After their brief stop, they pressed onward, crossing the river and finding the valley to be much like the one they had left that morning. On the other side, they climbed out of the valley and turned upstream to follow its northern edge, before Badger realized there was little time left for them to find a place to spend the night.

Returning to the river valley, hurriedly, he searched until he found a small clearing in the bush that would shield them from the keenest eyes. While he tethered the horses securely, he had Andy dig out the hide Wolf Tail's mother had sent with them, and together they created something of a shelter for them to crawl under.

Out of the rain, they rifled through the bags that had been tied onto Andy's saddle, pulling out the leather shirts, some dried meat, the bear claw which Wolf Tail had usually worn around his neck, and his knife. Seeing what they had, Andy looked up and murmured, "Thank you, God!" Shedding their wet clothes, they donned dry shirts and ate some of the dried meat. Afterward, they huddled together for warmth and tried to sleep.

8

The gloomy morning was accompanied by low clouds, hinting at more rain and reflecting the sadness both boys felt inside. Neither of them had slept very well. Haunting images of their friends' brutal slaughter had prevented them from getting much rest. For Andy, it was almost more than he could bear, bringing back the trauma of his brother's death. Badger, too, had been tormented most of the night and awoke deeply troubled.

When Badger stirred at first light and started to get up, Andy asked, *"Where you go?"* he asked.

"I am just going to check on the horses. We should get going!"

When he returned a short while later, he found Andy clutching Wolf Tail's claw, gazing at it sadly. *"Let me see it,"* the Indian said softly, reaching out an open hand.

Not really wanting to give it up, Andy passed it to his friend, who looked at it longingly before handing it back.

Andy had discovered something else, too. *"Knife!"* he murmured, digging into the bag for it. He passed their fallen friend's knife to Badger and watched as he pulled it from its sheath to study it and run his finger over the blade. When he had finished looking it over, he slid it back into its sheath and passed it back to Andy, who refused it. "No, you take it—*you!*" he said. "He'd want you to have it."

Not really understanding what he had heard, the Indian paused before suggesting, *"You keep the claw, and I will keep this!"* He demonstrated his wish by pressing the claw against Andy's chest and holding the knife to his own. Andy nodded his agreement, and the arrangement was complete. He slipped the claw around his neck while Badger stood and put the knife on his belt. *"I wonder why he never wore it like this,"* he muttered to himself.

Not looking forward to the rain which had begun to fall again, they huddled in their shelter, snacking on the dried meat. When the rain came more heavily, Badger thought they had better get going, still worried about trailing vengeance seekers. "We go," he said solemnly, looking at Andy. Sensing reluctance, he pressed his foot into the soft ground and stepped back to reveal his footprint, "Rain. *We will leave no tracks,"* he explained, and Andy nodded his understanding. *"We need to get into our wet things—we have to keep these ones dry,"* Badger said, pulling off his shirt. He donned the clothes that were cold and wet from the previous day without flinching. Andy watched, and with a sigh of resignation, did the same, keeping his discomfort himself. The dry clothes were then stuffed snugly into one of the sacks before they stepped out into the rain. Badger put Andy's saddle onto the twins' horse and helped him tie their things onto it. Next, he used the hide, which had been their shelter to cover the load, hoping to ensure that their dry clothes remained so.

Once again leading their friends' horses, they headed southwest. Staying far enough away from the valley to avoid its meandering ravines, they pressed on in heavy rain. Rainwater coursed across the plain, like fingers reaching down to the river below, and most of their morning ride was cold and grey.

The skies began to clear around midday, but Badger was worried that they might still be in hostile territory. Uncomfortable with travelling in the daylight, as the weather cleared, he wanted to wait for nightfall before continuing.

They stopped along a swift prairie stream, which, two days earlier, would have been bone dry. Frothing with foam and debris, it now flushed the heavy rain from the land. After the horses had drunk from it, Badger tethered them in nearby bush, spreading out the hide so they would not have to sit in the prairie mud.

Realizing that their food was limited, they carefully rationed what was left of the dried meat. Only sent along as a snack, there had never been much to begin with.

Glad for the sun to return, they munched on the dried meat and tried to talk. Finally, with a little daylight left, they slept. Weary from a lack of sleep the night before, and their hard ride, neither awoke until after dark. Sometime time during the night, Badger stirred and poked Andy before fetching the horses.

Preparing to mount, Andy wondered what his friend was doing when he saw him pull his breechclout out from under his belt and remove it, tucking it in with their gear on one of the other horses. *"What? Why do that?"* he wondered aloud.

"It is more comfortable this way! That thing bunches up and squishes my stones! You should try it!" It took a little more explanation, but when he understood, Andy decided to try it. He had already experienced the leather garment's discomfort and slipped off his horse to remove it.

After following Badger for a while, Andy kicked his horse to ride abreast of him, so they could talk, something which was much more difficult in the dark—so much of it involving gesture. They rode that way until the eastern sky began to lighten. *"We slept too long—the night was too short!"* Badger observed. *"We will have to get out of sight, soon!"*

Riding until they found a suitable place to conceal themselves, they holed up for another day. After two more night rides without food, the Indian announced that they would now ride during the day. *"And, the first thing I am going to do is get us something to eat!"* he exclaimed optimistically.

On the move again, they were enjoying the warmth of the sun, when Badger spotted a buffalo herd that looked to be a good prospect. In approaching them, though, he was careless with the wind, and the animals took flight before he could get into a proper position. Frustrated and upset with himself, he returned to Andy and grumpily grabbed the rein for the horse he had been leading and headed off without a word.

Vowing to be much more careful the next time, he kept watching for another opportunity and stopped when he noticed a single calf disappear into a hollow, at some distance. When the animal did not reappear and seeing no others, he concluded that there was a good chance that the calf was with others, which were out of sight in the hollow. He would make another attempt. Having Andy hold onto the rest of the horses, optimistically, he instructed him to remain well behind until the chase was over.

Closer to the hollow, he discovered a band of bush growing out from it, which let him get to within the distance of an arrow's flight from the spot where he had seen the calf disappear. Riding Wolf Tail's horse, he broke from the cover at a full gallop and found that his suspicion had been correct. Almost at once, he was on top of a herd of about twenty buffalo, most bedded down. Scrambling to their feet, they took flight immediately, tails held upright over their rumps.

Wolf Tail's horse was a good one—a trained buffalo runner, intelligent and dependable. Such a horse could be expected to pick up on the animal its rider had selected and run close to its right side, waiting for the rider to shoot. When the hunter shot his arrow, it would pull away and close in again on the same animal, if it did not fall. The hopeful hunter picked out a young cow.

Never having taken on a full-grown buffalo before, he was nervous. Without a father or an uncle that cared for him, he had never had anyone that properly trained him in the hunt. All he really knew was from the stories of others. Only a couple of times in the past two summers had he been allowed to accompany the hunters on their summer hunts. On such occasions, the hunters would often let the younger boys ride after the calves, which trailed at the end of the stampeding herd. He had been a little older than the other calf hunters, but he had been eager to prove himself. Serious hunters always chose the cows and young bulls leading the herd. Behind these came the much bigger, older bulls, which were usually only hunted for their thick hide, while the frightened calves came at the rear, harassed by the young hopefuls. On those occasions, Badger's little horse had shown its mettle and had stayed right beside each calf he had selected. Having practised and practised with his bow, he had brought down every calf he pursued. This time, he did not want to fail.

Running the buffalo was a dangerous endeavour! A horse could stumble or lurch and throw its rider under the thundering hooves of the frantic herd, or step in a badger hole and take down its rider. A hunter, in that case, was usually trampled, but if he was lucky and was uninjured in the spill, he might be able to retrieve his mount using the long rein which he had coiled up and tucked into his belt. Right at the front of the herd, Badger knew any mistake would be perilous.

He had started the chase with two arrows in his mouth and another already in his bow, clenched in his hand. The horse followed its rider's urging and drew alongside a young cow. Holding onto the horse using just the strength of his legs, Badger let go of the rein and drew back the bow. Countless times he had practised the manoeuvre atop his treasured pony, wishing success in the hunt would help him distinguish himself and gain the respect of others. But now, this was not practise—it was as real as it gets! With determination, he took aim just behind the wild-eyed buffalo's pounding front leg as it raced along beside him.

The arrow had not far to fly after he released it. The animal lurched and let out a bawl but kept going. Sure he had scored a good hit, Badger snatched an arrow from his mouth. The horse had pulled away slightly, with the shot, but now came in close again. His second arrow also found its mark. Once again, the cow bawled, but this time it faltered. Its gait impaired, buffeted by others, it quickly fell behind. Horse and rider pulled away to the right as the rest of the herd thundered past the stricken animal. Out of danger now, the hunter checked behind him to see his companion coming hard.

The doomed beast was still afoot when the triumphant hunter returned his attention to it. Facing him defiantly, breathing heavily and blood spraying from its nostrils, it stood its ground as he approached it. The ecstatic boy's heart was pounding with excitement. Thrilled with his success, he let out a whoop and sang a victory song. Holding his bow aloft, he was still singing when an excited Andy came alongside him.

The dying buffalo's front legs gave way slowly, and it dropped to its knees, its tail twitching above its rump. Gradually, its hindquarters wobbled and slumped to the ground, and its eyelids began to droop. Badger dismounted and approached the creature boldly. It opened its eyes wide and shook its head and gave a bloody snort, but it could do little more than watch his approach. Eyes locked on the boy, it put its chin to the ground and gasped its last. Badger sang his song once more and began to dance.

Andy dismounted and hurried to inspect the dead animal. "Gosh! Look at this!" he exclaimed. *"Look!"* The arrows were almost buried in the beast's side, showing the force given them by his friend's bow.

Finished his celebration, Badger had Andy help him hobble a couple of their horses to keep the others from wandering before setting to work on the buffalo. Andy watched with interest what he was doing.

Using Wolf Tail's knife, the Indian slit the animal's hide from the back of its neck to the top of its tail. Cutting and peeling it down each side and down the back of each hind leg, he cut it away, exposing the flesh beneath. Searching for the right place to make his cut, he sliced into the brilliant, red meat, and hacked into it until he had his arm, past his elbow, inside the carcass. Andy watched in amazement as the muttering boy then got both hands inside, tugging. He pulled and worked until he extracted the animal's liver.

With a look of delight, he held it up to his friend and exclaimed, *"What a feast we will have!"* Slicing off a piece of the still-warm organ, he offered it to Andy and got a look of disgust in return. Grinning with relish, the Indian popped it into his own mouth. He showed such fondness for its taste and was so animated in his enjoyment of it that Andy finally took a piece and choked it down. One ate with pleasure, the other nibbled squeamishly. Only Badger ate his fill before giving his attention to the rest of the carcass, cutting large chunks of meat off the hindquarters and the back. With the first such piece he removed, he shouted to Andy, *"Nitapi waksin!"* And, Andy understood what he had said.

Piling the meat on the grass, Badger returned to the carcass and hacked out the animal's tongue, turning to lift it up to Sun. *"O, great Sun, you have shown pity on me and my friend. Now, I know that we will succeed in our journey. Protect us as we travel and protect us from our enemies. For the life I have taken, I offer this back to you."* With that, he laid the most cherished part of the animal on a small bush. Backing away from his offering, he turned to Andy and said, *"Too bad we do not have your fire-thing!"* It had been left in Wolf Tail's lodge. *"We will have to dry this meat in the sun,"* he sighed before turning to begin slicing the chunks of meat into thin strips. Having Andy lay it out on the grass to dry, when he was done, he returned to the buffalo carcass.

Throwing back the hide, he retrieved his two arrows, frowning when he found that one of the stone tips had come off and remained inside the beast. Wiping them on the animal's fur, he deposited them into his quiver, putting the pointless one tip-up, before stretching himself out in the sun. It was to be a day off.

By the time the sun went down, the thin slices of meat were not even close to dry, so Badger said they would leave it until morning. *"We might have to chase the coyotes away,"* he kidded to his friend, hoping to alarm him. But no animal came near them, and long before first light, he was up, stuffing their bounty into the meat bag. The bag went on with the rest of their things, and they were underway.

The meat did not last very long before it went utterly rotten. Badger concluded that it had not been dried enough before going into the bag. *"I guess I should have paid more attention to how they do that!"* he lamented when they had to abandon most of it. *"I wish you had that fire-thing! We need to find someone to give us fire!"* Although he was not averse to eating raw meat, he knew Andy had no taste for it and went hungry a lot.

One evening, when they had stopped early, Andy tried to get his friend to understand that he wanted to know where they were headed. *"We are going to my people,"* he was told.

"I wanna try and find my father! He's out here somewhere," Andy replied.

"I do not understand—I understand your father, but I do not know what else you said."

"*Father*, Edmonton House. *Go* Edmonton House. *Where is* Edmonton House?" Badger still did not understand what he was trying to say, until he tried something else. *"Napikawan. Father—where napikawan, um, camp."*

"Yes, your father is at the napikawan camp?" Badger asked.

"Yes, napikawan camp. Where? Where napikawan camp?"

"There," Badger replied, pointing to the north with his lips.

"There?" Andy queried, pointing a finger in the same direction.

"Yes. Many sleeps!"

"Many sleeps?" The inflection of Andy's voice indicated it as a question.

Badger thought for a moment, and as he held up ten fingers, he replied, *"Maybe ten. I do not know. I have never been there."*

"Can you take us there?" Badger did not understand, so Andy tried again, *"We go, uh, to napikawan camp. Father,"* trying with a gesture to give meaning to his words.

Badger nodded his understanding, but was silent, looking off to the southwest. After a lengthy period of thoughtfulness, he asked, hedging, *"I guess so. Will you leave me then—when you find your father?"*

"Leave you? I do not understand!"

"You know! You will want to go with your father, and I will have nobody. What will I do then?" Badger answered, sounding disappointed.

Andy thought he got the gist of what he had said and responded, "You are my friend! We will stay together!" The Indian's blank look made him try again. *"You, me, friends! We friends—stay—me, you!"*

"Me and you? We will stay together?"

"Yes, you, me, father—stay together!"

Somewhat encouraged by his companion's answer, Badger did not know for sure where to find the *napikawan* camp. He had not heard much good about it. It was a place his people occasionally went during the winter, to trade. And, it was within the *Liars'* territory, who had made an alliance with the *napikawan*. An encounter with the *Liars* could be fatal for him. But he did not want to become separated from his white friend, so, with a sigh of resignation, he said, *"I can take you there."*

Starting out in a new direction the next morning, they encountered occasional lakes and streams along the way, making water less of a problem. Buffalo and other game remained plentiful, but Badger always preferred *nitapi waksin*, preferring to go hungry rather than kill anything else to eat. His companion ate a lot of berries.

Late one afternoon, Badger pointed out a track and reported that there was someone ahead of them. *"There are too many to be a war party,"* he told his companion. *"They are probably Siksika—like the Káinaa, only different—friends,"* he assured Andy, who expressed his concern, preferring to be cautious and avoid them. But after discovering an abandoned campsite, Badger examined it and was able to convince him. *"We will let their scouts see us. You will see—I am right!"* And, he was. The camp's rear guard discovered them coming up from behind and came back to investigate.

As the riders approached, Badger called out to them. When they were able to converse, Andy breathed a sigh of relief. Badger confirmed it when he turned to Andy to say, *"They are not travelling there, but they say there is a camp of my people not far from here. One of them thinks they might be going to the napikawan camp."* When Andy understood, he suddenly changed his mind and wanted to find this other camp.

The next day, after travelling in a more westerly direction, they came across the track of the other camp. Seeing that it was headed in the direction of the *napikawan camp,* Badger decided that it must be the group the others had mentioned but urged usual caution as he turned to follow the track. Near the middle of the next day, they came upon a campsite where the camp had spent the night. Judging from the fact that the embers of the fires were still warm, it had been abandoned just that morning. *"See those things—they are drying racks,"* Badger pointed out. Andy nodded his understanding as the Indian continued. *"That means they are hunting and drying the meat as they move, which tells me they are going to trade it."*

"How you know?" Andy wondered.

His companion just shrugged. *"I know!"* he said.

Once again, he was right. Andy was the first to spot a rider, the next day, watching them from a distance. Pointing him out to his friend, he searched Badger's face for some clue whether the stranger was friend or foe. Badger did not seem alarmed, and before they reached the rider, another had joined him. *"Piikáni,"* Badger announced with confidence, making their way toward the pair. But just because he recognized them, did not mean that they would recognize him. By approaching directly, with no sign of aggression, he hoped to indicate that they meant no harm. *"It is good to see you, my friend!"* he said in a loud voice when he thought they would hear him, conscious of the fact that his voice was not yet that of a man.

"Hai, who are you, and why do you follow us?" came a man's reply.

Happy to hear his own tongue, the young Indian continued. *"We are Piikáni! Who are you?"*

One of them replied, *"You might be Piikáni, but that one is not,"* pointing with his lips in Andy's direction, giving a chuckle. *"Is he like the white buffalo?"* the man asked, grinning at his own sense of humour. The boys drew up beside the riders who, though wary, showed no hostility. Andy reckoned them to be well into their twenties. Each had a bow and quiver slung over his back.

"Hai, you are my brothers! Where are you from?" Badger inquired.

"We winter along Makhabn, high up. We have been hunting buffalo to trade with the napikawan. I see you ride with one!" The same rider was doing all the talking, as both examined Andy. Still feeling good about his sense of humour, he asked, *"What is he called? White Buffalo?"* And, the other scout gave a chuckle.

"*No, he is my brother! His father is at the napikawan camp. Are you going there?*"

Ignoring his question, one of the others urged his horse up alongside Andy. Reaching out, he touched his hair and exclaimed, "*What strange hair! Where did you get him?*"

Badger motioned for Andy to lift his shirt. "*Look at this,*" he said, leaning over and tugging at his friend's shirt. "*Take your shirt off,*" he ordered. Andy was still getting used to the Indians' fascination with the colour of his hair and skin, but obliged his friend, hoping it would ensure them goodwill. "*See. It is all over his body,*" Badger said, grabbing Andy's arm and pointing to its golden sheen.

"*Where did you get him?*" the other scout repeated.

"*I rescued him from the Liars. They had killed his brother when my friends and I came upon them. We killed the Liars.*"

"*Are you alone? Where are the others?*"

"*The others were afraid to go to the napikawan camp. But not me! I agreed to take this one to his father, and now he is a brother to me.*" Pausing briefly, he continued, "*We would like to go with you to the napikawan camp. Is that where you are going?*"

"*Yes, come ride with us until we join the others.*" Both turned their horses, and Badger fell in beside them. Andy kicked his horse to catch up, pulling his shirt back on.

Shortly, a third scout joined them and was informed by one of his comrades what they had learned. After giving the white boy a looking over, two of them split off, one to the right and the other to the left, until they were just able to see the centre one, who rode on the main track with the newcomers.

Badger spoke with the scout while they rode and did his best to keep Andy informed of what they were saying. Excited with the prospect of finding his father, all Andy wanted to know was how long the journey would take. When the scout indicated that they were maybe four or five nights away, it was hard for him to contain his delight.

Late that afternoon, they caught up to the camp, which had stopped only a short while before. The lodges had not yet been set up, but some of the women were busy setting up the poles. Others were unpacking horses and travois, while boys tended the animals as soon as the women were finished with them. They all eyed the strange-looking newcomer as soon as they spotted him.

Badger did the talking as the scouts introduced them to the men, who were sitting in the shade together talking. One rose to his feet and reached out to shake Badger's hand. When he had finished speaking, Badger, turned to his companion, "You, me—sleep here. Man, all friend. All is. It is good!" It was more of an attempt at speaking English than Andy had heard before. Badger usually preferred to speak in his own tongue, and had shown little interest in learning Andy's language. Was he trying to impress their hosts with it? "You understand?" he finished.

Amused by his friend's behaviour, Andy replied, "Yes. *Yes! I understand.*"

Following introductions and some further conversation, the boys were directed to tether their horses with those of the camp, and Badger gestured for Andy to accompany him.

The boys who had been busy looking after the women's horses all stopped what they were doing and stood watching Andy as he approached. Badger spoke to them, "*We are friends! We come from Napi-tahta to join you on your journey to the napikawan camp. Come see my friend!*" He was speaking a little faster than he usually did around Andy, who struggled to understand what was being said. "*You should look at him! Maybe I will let you touch him,*" Badger said to the curious boys, most of them younger, who hurried to finish what they had been doing and came to examine the white stranger.

As soon as the first two approached him, Badger continued, *"But first, you must tether our horses. The one who does so may feel his hair—see here?"* He reached out to rub the hair on Andy's head. On hearing his offer, another boy pushed forward and grabbed Andy's reins, giving him a grin and keeping an eye on him as he led the animals away, not wanting to miss anything. Badger held out his reins to one of the others, who tried to pass them off to another. When that one would not take them, the first one had to do it and hurried to his task. Badger kept the rest at bay until the one who had taken up his offer returned. *"We are happy to have you as friends. What is he called?"* Badger asked, gesturing toward the boy.

"He is called Brings Laughter," one of the other boys answered.

"Brings Laughter, you may touch him. Feel his hair. Shirt! Shirt—off!" he ordered Andy, gesturing for him to remove his shirt. Dutifully, Andy pulled it off. *"See here,"*—Badger said to the boys— *"he has this hair that shines, all over his body,"* pointing to the fine, golden hair on his friend's arms. *"See here,"* he continued, pointing out what grew on his calves. *"And you should see what he has here!"* he added with a smirk, tapping Andy in the crotch. His friend gave him a look of warning, which Badger ignored, continuing, *"See here!"* he said, lifting Andy's arm to show them the hair under there. *"But you should see down here!"* he gloated, tapping him once again in the crotch.

Andy warned, "Unh-uh!"

Badger heard his protest and brushed it off saying, *"We will have to see about that, but if he shows you, you must give us something!"* Andy shook his head, but the boys were now more interested than ever.

"What do you want?" one of the youngsters replied, curious.

Badger thought for another moment. *"We need a saddle—"*

"That is too much!" he was interrupted. *"What could be so special about him?"*

"You give us a saddle or some arrows, and you may see. He is different! How about a knife?"

"What do you mean, different?" another asked.

"You are greedy!" protested the first. *"We do not need to see!"*

A few of the others showed some interest, one of them volunteering, *"Maybe, I have some arrows,"* while another offered something similar.

"Where will we do it? Let us go over there!" one of them suggested with anticipation, pointing to the nearby bushes.

"Unh-uh!" the white boy protested, getting a sense of what was going on. "I'm not gonna!"

"Ten arrows!" Badger came back, flashing five fingers twice.

"No!" from Andy.

"Five arrows!" was offered.

"No!" the white boy again refused.

"No!" Badger replied to the offer. "Come," he said, turning his back on the boys and grabbing Andy by the arm, ready to walk away.

"Seven arrows!" The bid was raised. Badger started walking, with Andy slipping his shirt back over his head.

"All right! Ten arrows!"

Badger stopped and turned to face them. *"All right, where do you want to do it?"*

Andy was not prepared to be exhibited—not even for ten arrows. "No!" he said emphatically. *"No! Not here!* Not with everyone around!"

"Why not? I need some arrows!" Badger argued. *"We might even get a saddle if you would do what they want!"*

"What is wrong?" one of the older boys inquired suspiciously, while the others crowded to hear what was going on.

"I'm not gonna do it! Not here! There's people here!" Andy protested.

"I cannot understand you! Speak so I can understand!" Badger insisted impatiently, speaking through clenched teeth. He was getting frustrated.

Equally frustrated, Andy said firmly, *"No! People—see!"* refusing to give in. Seeing his intransigence, his friend tried to make an excuse and promised the boys that he would let them see later, but they accused him of reneging on the deal.

"I will show you, I will show you!" he responded, irritated with his friend. *"He does not want to do it right now! He is—I do not know! He does not wish to, or something."*

With the disappointed boys insisting he was reneging, Badger led Andy away. *"Why not?"* he hissed at his friend once they were out of earshot. *"I could have got ten arrows, and probably a saddle!"*

"I do not—people see," Andy responded.

"We were not going to do it there! We would go somewhere else! You still better do it—I will be shamed if you do not! They will think I am a nothing one!" Andy had never seen him so agitated.

"What? What is wrong? Why are you so mad?"

"I cannot understand you! They will think I am a nothing one!"

A nothing one! Suddenly, Andy put it all together and realized that his friend did not wish to lose face. He had learned that no Indian ever wanted to be humiliated and be thought a "nothing one." *"All right,"* he sighed, realizing how important it was to Badger. "I'll do it," he agreed, not sure what he was going to be expected to do to gain the reward.

Badger stopped at once, and his face lit up. *"You will do it?"*

"I guess so," Andy sighed and turned around.

"Hai!" Badger cried to the boys who were still milling around.

It was sometime later that they returned from outside the camp, with Badger examining his new arrows.

Before long, one of the men spotted them and beckoned. After speaking with the man, Badger told Andy, "We sleep—there," pointing in the direction of one of the lodges that had just been set up. Turning back to the man, he continued in Blackfoot, *"Here is my friend, he is called* Andy."

The man was introduced as Crane with Many Horses, and he reached out his hand to Andy. *"My friend! Welcome,"* he said. Andy clasped his hand firmly but did not shake it. He had discovered that Indians did not seem to shake hands in the manner of his own people. *"You will be my guests tonight,"* the man said. Looking at Badger, he continued, *"The boys are out with the hunters. They will return soon. You watch for them to arrive. My son is among them."* Andy could understand little of what was being said, for they spoke much too quickly for him to be able to follow. He needed Badger to help him, but his friend was paying little attention to him as he spoke with the man.

Afterward, however, he took the time to explain what had been said. *"We will stay in the lodge of that man,"* he explained carefully. *"He has a son—a boy our age, who is hunting. They will return soon. He will be our friend."* While they waited for the hunters' return, they walked around and watched the women finish setting up the camp.

"Wait!" Andy exclaimed when he saw that some of the women were beginning to set up their lodge. *"Stop! I see!"* he added, wishing to watch them. The others had all been set up while they were off entertaining the boys.

Working together, the women first lashed four poles together, standing them upright before spreading them apart at the bottom. Next, they stood the remaining poles on end and leaned them against the first four, spacing them out, creating a cone-shaped frame. Unfolding the heavy covering, made of several buffalo hides stitched together, one of them used a pole to lift one edge of it up to the top of the cone. The other women draped and adjusted it over the poles before bringing the two sides together at the front. There, wooden pegs were inserted into holes where the edges of the hide overlapped in the front, fastening them together.

Spreading all the poles from the inside, then, to make the sides taut, two more poles were set up, outside, to hold open two flaps at the top, creating a smoke hole at the top. *"They call those the ears,"* his friend told him. *"They can adjust them for the wind."*

Seeing how closely Andy was watching them, the women gave him a smile as they placed a few rocks around the edges at the bottom, and the lodge was ready for occupancy.

"Do you want to help us?" one of the women asked.

"What? I don't...*I do not understand."*

"They want you to help them," his friend told him, so he could understand.

"Should I? *I do?"*

"Do—you do. I sit. Sit here, see you," his friend responded. Andy recognized that Badger was showing off again by speaking English. He sat and watched as the white boy pitched in to help the women move their man's belongings inside, carrying in several bundles and rawhide pouches, which had been unloaded from the horses.

In short order, everything was stowed, and one of the women got a fire going outside. This was the signal for the women's husband to move to the fire. When she saw him approaching, the other woman went inside and returned with a willow backrest, which she set beside the fire for him. The man then took his seat on the ground, reclining against the backrest, and presently, other women brought backrests for other men as they joined him at his fire.

Badger had just begun to tell the men about their journey when the hunters returned with whoops of success, interrupting everything as everyone hurried to meet them. Giving an animated description of their accomplishments, the hunters showed off their spoils and bragged of the chase. Girls and young boys helped the women remove the meat that hung from the horses. At once, the women and the girls began to work on it. Some had already started to build drying racks out of sticks and branches, while others set about cutting up the meat and laying it on the racks to dry.

The hunters, meanwhile, were finished their work. Younger boys took their horses to tend them, while the hunters joined the men at the fire, waiting to hear the stories of the hunt. But first, the man they were to stay with, beckoned his son and introduced them.

Sits in the Middle had seen 15 winters and was eager to talk about the hunt as well as brag about his accomplishments in war. He had been on two raids already. But for every story he told, Badger had another, and after they had been joined by a few others their age, Andy soon realized that this was the way Indian boys gained stature among their peers. Each one spoke about his endeavours, while the others listened respectfully, and although Andy had difficulty following all that was being said, he got the idea that a boy or young man without a story to tell was not very well-regarded.

It was very late when some of the others finally went off to find their sleeping places. *"I have to sleep out here by the fire!"* Sits in the Middle informed his guests when everyone else had left. *"My mother wants some of us to sleep out by the meat and keep the fires going. I will get some robes."* Without waiting for a response from his guests, he headed for his lodge and returned a short time later lugging a couple of robes.

9

Morning came. The black and white *long tails* announced their arrival at first light with their raucous voices, a little ahead of the women and girls, who soon appeared to see how well the meat had dried overnight. Their activity brought forth the dogs, and the girls created a ruckus trying to keep them away. Badger was trying to cover his head with the robe when Sits in the Middle suggested they retire to his lodge. The others agreed, hurriedly gathering the robes and following him to his mother's lodge.

Inside, it looked much like Wolf Tail's lodge. There were willow backrests at the back and a number robes, some of which still had someone sleeping under them and some of which had already been abandoned by the women. Sits in the Middle laid out his robe in an open space, and they lay on top of it to try to go back to sleep. The two Indians made it, but Andy was wide-awake, and after a while, decided that it might be an appropriate time to wash up.

Leaving the lodge quietly, he looked around at the activity of the women before heading to where he had seen some of the girls hauling water, the night before. A short walk through the bushes led him to a pleasant little stream. Finding a secluded place to bathe, when he was finished, he decided to have a look around.

In a meadow nearby, he discovered the camp's horses. A number were hobbled, and some were tethered, while the rest seemed content to remain close by, without any restraint. They had spotted him and were watching him with ears forward, when three Indian boys came silently out of the bush, not far from him. They spied him immediately and stopped short. Recognizing him as the golden-haired stranger, they eyed him warily before continuing toward the horses.

"Oki! Tsa niitapi?" Andy hollered to greet them, and they responded warmly, switching their course toward him. All were about his age. He had never met them, though he recognized two of them from the previous evening.

"Where do you come from, napikawan?" one of them asked.

Feeling good about understanding him, the white boy gave a gesture toward *the place where Sun rises* and said, *"Many sleeps, there,"* he replied.

"The napikawan we know live that way," the boy said, giving a nod to the north.

Taking a moment to figure out what he had been said, Andy responded, *"When, uh, how, uh...how far?"*

"One more night—maybe two or three," the boy replied. It was clear he did not know.

But Andy was excited to learn that they might be that close, and suddenly the prospect of seeing his father loomed larger than anything else. He wondered about starting out right away, not waiting for these people. Wishing to get back to tell Badger the news, he was interrupted when one of the boys asked him, *"Will you help us gather horses?"* He understood the boy's question and decided to give them a hand.

"Sure!" Getting a puzzled look, he said, *"Yes!"*

Two of them immediately trotted toward the horses, while the other one said, *"We will wait here! Wait for them!"* The pair worked their way among the animals and began to separate certain of them out. Andy watched what they were doing, and soon his companion motioned for him to help keep those selected from rejoining the others. After a number had been chosen, they drove them back toward the camp to join those that had been tethered there, allowing the boys to walk up and put ropes around their necks.

As soon as they had finished, Andy sought out Badger and found him with Sits in the Middle, going to bathe. *"Hai!"* he called and trotted toward them. "These guys with the horses said that my father's place is just—" The look on Badger's face told him immediately that he would have to use Blackfoot. *"Napikawan camp— one night, uh, er, two. We go?"* he asked, approaching his friend.

"What are you saying?" Badger did not understand what he was talking about.

"One sleep, two, napikawan camp. There!" he said, pointing in the direction that had been indicated to him. *"We go?"*

"No! We are going to help them hunt today. We will go with them when they are done."

"Aww! But I really wanna go now! *Please!"* Andy pleaded.

"You want to go now?"

Andy nodded his head emphatically. "Yeah! I mean, *Yes...uh...*I mean,"— he stammered— *"you and me, go there...now, see father."*

"Father?"

"Yes! Can we go there? Leave now?"

"Go?"

"Yes, go now!"

"We are supposed to join the hunt today, but I guess we could—if you want. We could leave right away and not hunt," Badger allowed. He spoke quickly, and Andy had to ask him to repeat himself.

"We leave now?" Andy confirmed.

"Yes! I will find out where to go."

It was hard for Andy to contain his excitement. "I'll get our stuff! And, get the horses," he blurted, hurrying off while Badger went to bathe before asking Sits in the Middle's father about it. When Andy saw him next, he looked solemn. "What?" he queried.

"He says we should not go. The Liars—uh, the enemy—keep watch on the napikawan camp," he replied, signing as he spoke. "We should not go alone!"

"Speak slowly. I do not understand! Enemies?"

"Yes, Liars! You know! Liars! He says it would not be good to go alone. Not safe!" Badger replied, speaking slowly.

Andy knew who the Liars were and was bitterly disappointed by his friend's news. "When will they be going?" he asked, having difficulty concealing his sudden disappointment.

"When will they go there?" Badger asked for clarification.

"Yes, when will they go there?"

"They hunt two more days, then in two more days after that, they go."

"Darn!" Andy exclaimed. "Are you sure we can't go by ourselves?" Badger's puzzled look told him that he had not understood. "I want...we go now!"

"It would be too dangerous! We need to wait and go with them."

Andy suddenly felt tears of disappointment welling up in his eyes. He turned away when he spotted Sits in the Middle approaching, turning his back to conceal his emotion from him.

But Sits in the Middle had already seen his distress. "What is the matter with him?" he inquired of Badger.

"His father is at the napikawan camp. He wants us to go there today."

"Are you leaving?"

"Your father tells me that we should not go alone."

"I will go with you! I will go speak to my father."

Andy perked up when he thought he had understood what the boy had said. As Sits in the Middle left, he asked Badger, *"Him go with we?"*

"Yes, he will go with us. He is going to speak to his father."

His hope renewed, Andy trotted after Sits in the Middle, hoping to hear what was going to be said. The boy spoke with his father, and the man seemed to be pointing here and there as he responded. When the young man turned to Andy, though, a grin preceded his answer. *"He says we should not travel with less than five. I will get my friends to come with us!"*

Not understanding him, Andy asked Badger, who had joined them, "Are we going?"

"It sounds like we are. He is getting some of his friends to go with us."

"We go?"

"Yes, we go."

Sits in the Middle brought three of his friends, having turned down others who had heard of the venture and wished to join them. All bore weapons. Each carried a bow and a quiver of arrows and a large knife. Sits in the Middle and two of the others each carried a stone club. One of them, a boy who seemed younger than the rest, also held what looked to Andy like a narrow staff, from which hung two clumps of black hair. He wondered if they might be scalps but couldn't believe that one so young would possess such a thing. The fourth boy carried something concealed in a long, leather scabbard slung over his back, beside his bow and quiver. With only brief introductions, they wasted no time getting onto their horses.

It seemed as though everyone, by then, had heard of their expedition and came to see them off and offer advice. People were still offering words of encouragement and advice as one of the boys led the others to where an old man stood outside a lodge, waiting. They stopped and dismounted to stand in front of him, while the man motioned for the two strangers to join them. Dismounting to stand beside the others, Badger whispered to Andy, *"This old man is probably going to pray for us. He is probably a man who has strong medicine."*

All of them stood solemnly before the old man who, after looking them over carefully, turned to face the morning sun, beginning to pray aloud. Andy looked around and saw that even the youngsters seemed to join the old man in his prayers. He prayed rapidly and very softly. Almost mumbling, it was difficult for Andy to be able to make out anything of what he was saying. The white boy was only able to catch a few words that seemed familiar, the man speaking far too quickly for him to be able to pick up the context. He went on and on, while none of the Indians moved. Andy had bowed his head and closed his eyes when, finally, the man ceased. Chancing a peep about, he saw that everyone was now watching the old man. "Amen," he whispered softly, waiting to see what would happen next.

The old man shuffled around behind his tipi, but nobody else moved. All were silent and solemn as they watched for him to return. In a moment, the man appeared, bringing with him a leather bundle, which he placed on the ground before him. Returning to prayer for a few moments, he finished and knelt to unwrap the bundle, inspecting one item at a time as he unravelled its contents. Uncovering a bunch of black feathers, he carefully selected one of them before gesturing to an old woman beside him, who promptly stepped forward and began putting the bundle back together, rolling it up as she finished. He watched her patiently, and once she had completed her task and stepped away with the bundle, he began to speak to the boys.

"I have strong medicine for you! Our brother, Raven, will protect you on your journey and give you success. I have prayed to him and to our great Sun, and I am certain you will not come to any harm. Raven is always vigilant—he sees everything—and will keep watch for you. He will fly ahead of you and warn you of any danger. When you see him, you should pay attention to what he tells you. He sees where you cannot see! He will warn you if an enemy lies in wait for you. Do as he instructs you!" He now motioned to one of the boys to step forward, handing him the feather. *"Our brother will recognize you because you carry this feather. He will recognize it because it belonged to one of his brothers who gave it to me."* The boy handled it reverently and returned to his horse to tuck it into a small leather pouch hanging from his saddle. After that, the boys were released, and thanking the medicine man, they swung up onto their horses, leaving the camp amid the shouts and admonitions of their families and friends.

Andy rode close to Badger, filled with questions. "Are those scalps?" he asked, pointing to the one carrying the staff.

Badger did not understand his question. He looked at him and chided, *"Speak so I can understand you!"*

Pointing again at the staff, Andy asked, *"Hair? Uh, enemy hair?"* grabbing his own and tugging it.

"Scalps! Yes! That is his honour stick!"

"What is it? He kill?"

"I guess so."

"What is that?"

"What?"

"That stick," Andy pressed to know what it was.

"Unh. Honour stick. It is used to strike an enemy and show off the scalps of those he has killed."

It gave Andy some comfort to know that someone among them had some experience—apparently. It made him feel slightly more secure. But he was surprised to find their protector so young. Awed by the thought of a boy, younger than him, having killed someone, he was at the same time intimidated by him. After a while, though, he gathered the courage to ride over beside the boy, who gave him a ready smile.

"*Hai,* Andy!" the boy greeted him, already aware of his name and speaking it perfectly. He seemed glad to have company. Smaller than the rest, he was wiry. His long hair was neat, in tight braids; his dark-brown eyes looked black, and his smile seemed genuine.

Surprised that the fellow already knew his name, Andy responded, out of habit, "Hi! How're ya doin'!" Realizing he would not be understood, he continued, "*Oki, tsa niitapi?*"

"*Iksokapi,*" came the reply. This fellow was not even a little shy. "*I see that Sun makes your hair shine. I will call you, Sun Shines on Him. Hai!*" he shouted to the others with a grin. "*We will call this one, Sun Shines on Him. He is Sun Shines on Him!*" he decreed. Turning back to grin at Andy, he looked very proud of himself for having come up with the name.

"*Hai, Sun Shines on Him!*" Badger raised his voice.

Not quite sure what they were saying, Andy asked, "*Hai, Míisinsski, what talk him?*"

Badger rode a little closer. Speaking slowly, he said, "*He says he calls you Sun Shines on Him.*" Grabbing his own hair, he said, "Hair. *Your hair makes it look like Sun shines on you. Sun Shines on Him. Do you understand?*" The white boy nodded thoughtfully.

Feeling honoured to have been recognized in that way, Andy took an immediate liking to the boy, but he could not get over the scalps. Wishing to ask about them, he chose not to be too direct. "*What are you called?*" he asked the boy, not yet having figured out that the Blackfoot did not like to speak their own names.

The boy hesitated and looked to someone else to respond. One of them answered, "*He is called White Quill.*"

"*White Quill! My heart feels warm toward you. How many winters?*" Andy asked awkwardly, having learned how Indians marked the years.

The boy flashed five fingers, twice, followed by four more, as he said, "*Ten and four. I was born in the season when the grass comes green.*" Like many other Indians Andy had seen, he signed as he spoke.

Andy was surprised to learn he was so young. Pointing to his staff, he asked, "*What is that?*"

"*It is my honour stick. I have two honours—I have killed two enemies,*" the young boy answered. Uncharacteristic for a young warrior, he seemed very unassuming about it—almost bashful.

Not one, but two! Andy was not quite sure how to ask what he wanted to know, so he said to Badger, "Ask him how he killed them."

It took a bit of questioning for Badger to understand what he wanted to know. When he finally understood it, he obliged. "*Our friend wants to know how you killed your enemies. What happened?*"

Trying to parrot what he had heard, Andy asked, "*How you killed your enemies?*"

"*We were keeping watch on the horses for my father when I saw two enemies lying in wait for my friend. They did not see me—but I saw them. They were waiting for my friend...to come close enough to kill him and steal our horses. I was able to kill them and save his life!*"

"*How you...um, kill, how you kill?*" Andy asked again, seeking more detail.

"*With my arrows—I shot them. The first one was not dead, so I had to shoot two arrows into him.*"

"*How?*" Andy asked.

It was Sits in the Middle, who explained. "*That fellow, he fell, then got up again. The second one, he was dead, but that fellow was*" *staggering around, trying to get an arrow in his bow. My friend ran up close and shot him again."*

Andy could not get over the killer's young age and how casually he spoke of the incident. "Ask him, who were they? *Who?*" he said to Badger, still watching the young Indian.

"Who were they? Crow?" his friend asked.

"Yes, Crow!" White Quill answered. *"Our worst enemies! They are always stealing our horses!"*

"Wow!" Andy exclaimed, awed by this fellow's accomplishment, trying to picture it.

"How did you come to understand his tongue?" the young Indian asked, turning to Badger. He did not seem to want to speak any further about his experience.

"I learned it after I rescued him from the Liars. They killed his brother." Badger looked at Andy to see if there was going to be any reaction to what he was saying.

Seeing the look he was getting, Andy whispered, "Oh?"

Badger continued, *"He has no more family except his father, who we go now to find. They would have killed him, but I saved him—like you!"*

"What did you do?" one of the others asked him.

Turning to another, Badger asked, "What is he called?" And, the young man was identified as Elk Hollers in the Trees. He was their apparent leader.

Badger explained, *"They were ready to kill him and his brother. My friends and I came along and killed them."*

"How many?" one of the others asked. Badger held up five fingers.

"How many?" repeated Sits in the Middle, who was behind them and could not see how many fingers he had held up.

"Five," White Quill answered for Badger, anxious for him to continue.

"How many did you kill? Where are your scalps?" Elk Hollers in the Trees asked, coming up alongside them.

"I do not have them. We were almost taken by the Underwater People—crossing a river—after—on our way home. Sun Shines on Him was riding behind me and fell off in the river. I jumped off to rescue him—into the water. We were both carried down the river— the current was strong from the rains—did you people get all that rain? My friends thought we had been taken, so they took our horses and left."

"I don't know if I understood all that. It didn't sound right to me," Andy ventured, just loud enough that Badger could hear him.

"I am angry at them for leaving us!" Badger continued. *"They took our horses! And, probably claimed my scalps! They probably told everyone that the Liars killed me,"* he added, thinking that it was likely the case.

Two of them seemed to be buying it, but Elk Hollers in the Trees still pressed him for an answer to his question, sounding suspicious. *"How many Liars did you kill—did you get honours?"* he asked.

"I shot one with an arrow. The Liar fell, but not dead. I stabbed him in the throat then put my friend on my horse to get him out of there. The others killed the rest."

Andy had understood enough to know that what his friend was saying was not true, and fearing he might be found out and embarrassed, he tried to get off the topic. He turned to Elk Hollers in the Trees. *"Friend! How many winters?"*

"Ten and six," he replied, holding up five fingers three times and one finger once.

"How many winters?" Andy asked the one who had the long leather sheath. The young man looked away and would not answer. *"What him called?"* Andy asked another.

"He is called Night Shoot." Elk Hollers in the Trees responded. *"He is my cousin."*

Andy did not recognize what he was saying. Nonetheless, he asked, *"What is?"* pointing to the thing that hung from the boy's shoulder.

Again, Elk Hollers in the Trees answered, *"He has a fire-stick."* Badger and Andy both wondered why he answered for his cousin, when he asked them, *"Where did you get these horses?"* He seemed to want to know more about their past.

Andy decided to answer before Badger got a chance. *"Gut People!"* he replied, not allowing his friend to respond. *"We come their camp,"* he said, speaking awkwardly, searching for the words. *"Friends. Chief like we."* He indicated himself and Badger with his hand. *"Give. Want, uh, want help we—uh—find father."* Andy used his hand to try and give meaning to his words. Elk Hollers in the Trees just gave a shrug and asked nothing more.

They had been keeping to a well-defined trail through the bush and occasional meadows. When they reached a place where the bush opened into a wide-open plain, Elk Hollers in the Trees signalled a stop. *"We must not ride together!"* he commanded. *"We must spread out. We will ride in twos with plenty of space between us."*

"I will ride with Sun Shines on Him!" White Quill volunteered quickly.

"We should take turns riding with him," Sits in the Middle responded, sounding disappointed. It was clear he wanted to be the one to ride with Andy.

"I have the first turn, then," the youngest insisted.

"Míisinsski, ride with me, out front!" Elk Hollers in the Trees spoke decisively. *"White Quill will follow with Sun Shines on Him and you two in the rear."* The others readily deferred to him—he was clearly the leader.

Elk Hollers in the Trees moved on ahead with Badger beside him, but as soon as they were out of earshot, Sits in the Middle turned to Andy. *"Is it true what your friend tells us about the Liars?"*

Getting him to repeat himself and speak more slowly so he could understand, Andy felt put on the spot and found it difficult to answer. He really didn't know what the truth was. *"Him help! Him help me!"* he responded, satisfied that there was at least some truth in his answer. With that, his companions seemed to accept all that Badger had told them.

"It is hot!" Sits in the Middle announced as they waited for the other two to put some distance between them. *"Let us remove our shirts,"* pulling his shirt off and watching to see if Andy would do the same. Andy noticed the others watching him closely, while they stripped off their shirts and knew they wanted to get a look at him.

"Here we go again!" he sighed. Amused by their curiosity, he pulled his shirt over his head. Letting them look him over, he got off to tie it onto the horse he had been leading. He was getting used to the Indians' fascination with his appearance and felt good about the attention it brought him. Badger had pointed out how he could win the favour and respect of the Indian boys by satisfying their curiosity. Walking over to White Quill, he put his arm alongside the Indian's smooth, hairless arm. *"See?"* he said, stroking the golden sheen on his forearm. The others crowded around him to give him a good looking-over, each of them holding out his arm and placing it beside his. Lifting a leg, he let them see the golden hair on his calves. None of the Indians bore much hair on their bodies—what grew on their calves was sparse compared to his. Finally, he lifted his arm to show what he had there. None of them had anything like it.

Andy grinned before noticing the two out front beckoning. *"We go. See?"* he observed, pointing in their direction. Elk Hollers in the Trees was turned around on his horse, waving for them to get moving.

"We need to get going!" Sits in the Middle responded, hopping onto his horse.

When Andy was mounted, White Quill directed his horse alongside him, and they kicked their mounts. Riding side by side, they talked continuously. White Quill knew no English whatsoever, but Andy had learned enough Blackfoot that with some blank looks and questions, accompanied by gestures and facial expression, they could understand each other reasonably well. White Quill communicated much more readily than Badger.

Andy learned that White Quill's people wintered near a river he called *Makhabn*. It was close to *Mistakis*. He recognized that word. Badger had explained its meaning to him by running his fingers over his spine, making him understand that it had something to do with a spine and hills. He had been anxious to see what that looked like because he had no sense of what it was, but when White Quill explained it was very high hills, Andy wondered if might it be the vast mountains his father had written about.

White Quill explained that his people were on their way to the *napikawan camp* to trade meat, buffalo robes, and a few furs they had accumulated. The women, he said, spoke of getting things with which to cook and make clothing, but he thought that the men were mostly interested in getting *napiohke*.

"What is that?" Andy asked.

"Napiohke! Hai, you should know! It is a kind of water that comes from the napikawan that burns when you drink it and makes you feel good! They say we will like it! That is why my friends wanted to come—they are hoping to get some."

Andy realized that he was speaking about the liquor which the traders gave to the Indians. In his letters, his father had described that too, and how it turned the Indians into madmen. Understanding the others' intent made Andy worry about what might happen to them. He and his brother had seen some of the men on the boats get drunk. Usually, they had behaved ridiculously and foolishly, but sometimes, some of them had become downright mean and violent. There had been terrible fights, alarming them both, making them recall that their Bible warned against drunkenness. Periodically, they had seen the piteous behaviour of Indians who had been fed the stuff at one of their stops. He knew why their father had been concerned about the practice of giving it to them.

"Me know, uh...what is it called?

"Napiohke?"

"Napiohke! Me know! Bad! Napiohke bad. You drink—no!" Andy said awkwardly, shaking his head and watching for White Quill's reaction.

The Indian looked at him quizzically. "What do you mean? It is supposed to be good. We are supposed to like it!"

"Me see! Bad! It hurt you!"

"We would not get hurt! How could it hurt you?"

"Napiohke bad! Not drink!" Andy responded firmly, trying to dissuade him from it. "You drink—napiohke?"

"No, not yet,"

"No! Bad!" Andy tried to look disappointed. It seemed to have an impact on his companion, who now looked troubled. "Me— not drink!" the white boy proclaimed. "White Quill not drink napiohke!" Feeling bolder, because the Indian now bore a look of uncertainty, he continued, "Sun Shines on Him not want you drink napiohke! You my friend!" White Quill looked puzzled but did not say anything.

They rode in silence for quite a while before either of them spoke again. Finally, it was the Indian who broke the silence. "I would like to be your friend! You should stay with me! You could stay in the lodge of my mother with me and my family."

Andy replied. "You? Family?"

"No! I am too young to have a family! I live with my mother—and my father." Andy thought he could detect a note of disdain in his friend's voice when he mentioned his father but let him continue.

"*I have a sister, older than me, and I have two brothers—they are just little. You do not have a wife, do you?*"

"*No,*" Andy chuckled and shook his head. "*Mother dead. Brother dead. Father napikawan camp.*"

"*Yes, we are taking you to him!*"

"*Yes. You go napikawan camp—*" Andy did not know the word he was looking for, but the inflection of his voice gave meaning to his words, which White Quill understood.

"*Have I been there before? No. Sometimes my people travel there, but most of the time, they go when the buffalo calves are black.*" Seeing the white boy's confused look, he added, "*When Cold Maker brings the snow,*" wrapping his arms around his shoulders and shivering exaggeratedly.

Andy liked this fellow and learned his language easily from him. They talked a lot, and he was disappointed when they found Elk Hollers in the Trees and Badger waiting for them early in the afternoon. They had stopped at a point overlooking a river and were waiting for the others to catch up. When they were all together, they opened their bags and ate.

Afterward, Sits in the Middle joined Andy, and White Quill rode with Badger as rear guard. Sits in the Middle was not nearly as talkative as White Quill. It was harder for him to understand Andy's Blackfoot, and he was not as patient as White Quill in explaining himself. The older boy spent most of his time bragging. Anything he asked, it seemed, was aimed at finding out who was the better of them. Andy was afraid that he was not going to measure up very well, but the fellow was likeable enough, and he enjoyed his company.

Badger and White Quill talked a lot. White Quill asked lots of questions about the *Liars* and had Badger describe how he felt about killing one. Badger hedged, telling him that it had felt good and made him wish to go on another war party. The younger boy wrinkled his nose and admitted, "*I do not feel that good about it. I killed two, and I am supposed to be great, but—"* and he would not elaborate further. When pressed, he said he would rather not have killed the two intruders, acknowledging he had to do it.

"What about that girl I saw last night—the one with the elk teeth around her neck—she talked to your mother," Badger changed the subject.

"That is my cousin—why?"

"She looked pretty! You should introduce us—have you ever been with a girl? I mean—you know—done sex?" The younger boy hesitated and looked straight ahead, admitting he had not. Badger then began to speak about others' experiences with girls as if they were his own, and finding that this piqued the younger one's curiosity, he began to embellish them. Feeling like he now had the upper hand on the young warrior, Badger asked him if he thought his cousin might do sex with him.

After a lengthy silence, the younger boy looked him in the eye and warned, *"You had better not do that! We are supposed to remain pure until we take a wife! That is what I am going to do, anyway. And she is my cousin! I do not think I would like it if you did that!"* Badger was taken aback by the younger one's rebuke. He did not say anything else about the matter, and they moved on to find common ground in talking about horses.

The land had become undulating, back to more trees and bush, and the grassy meadows were becoming less frequent. In the evening, Elk Hollers in the Trees ordered a halt on the shore of a large lake. It was one of the most significant bodies of water Andy had seen since leaving the big lake, north of the Red River settlement.

Finding a suitable site along the lakeshore, they removed their gear from the horses and tethered them deep in the bush, before sitting in the grass beside the water, swatting at the mosquitoes and the black flies.

"We swim?" Andy suggested. He wanted to get into the water, so he had less skin exposed to the vicious insects.

"I will go with you!" exclaimed White Quill, and the rest seemed just as eager.

Elk Hollers in the Trees, though, would not take part in their rough-housing. Taking his role as leader very seriously, he separated himself from the others. Keeping only his head above the water, avoiding the insects, he would have none of their shenanigans. After they had finished, he declared that they would have no fire, so they spent the evening sitting together, telling of their accomplishments, and swatting at the hordes of mosquitoes that came at dusk. Andy was content to listen and was happy to discover that he was beginning to understand more and more of what they were saying.

The next day was slower-going, through the bush. Though there was a reasonably well-defined trail, Elk Hollers in the Trees urged a great deal of caution, believing they could be approaching the *napikawan* camp, where Sits in the Middle's father had warned them that they might encounter the *Liars*. Andy spent most of the day riding with White Quill, enjoying his company—he was always joking and pulling pranks.

Their second night was spent on the edge of a vast, open prairie. Again, their leader allowed no fire, and Andy continued to be captivated by the boys' stories. They were all keen to tell of their own exploits but also spoke of the deeds of noted warriors and hunters from their camp. Each one listened quietly and patiently, while the others spoke, contrasting sharply with the banter Andy had experienced at home, where his own friends were always interrupting one another and interjecting loudly, even when someone else was speaking. Badger talked more than Andy had ever seen before; it seemed like the other boys' stories stimulated him. He learned a lot about his friend from his stories.

When he got a chance to speak, Andy tried to describe the sailing ship upon which he had crossed the ocean before coming to the settlement. He had much difficulty finding words to describe something about which his listeners had no concept, and in the end, he wondered what they had understood. Even if he had known their language well, he wondered if he would have been able to make them understand. They were in disbelief when he spoke of the rows of square lodges where he had lived in England. Still lacking the words to describe the brick and mortar houses, with doors and glass windows, the best he could do was describe them as rock and mud, but none of them seemed to understand what he meant. Most of the things that were common in his world were utterly unknown to these boys.

Their lives seemed to have been filled with things about which Andy knew nothing—training and preparation for hunting and for war. Their talk was filled with stories of achievement and bravery in both those areas and little else. Each boy's aspiration seemed, simply, to be a respected hunter and a brave warrior, and to have good wives who worked hard.

Only one thing seemed to occupy their minds more than hunting and war, and they often spoke of their interest in sex. Andy was surprised how much they sounded like his friends back at the settlement, describing the physical attributes they desired in a girl and speculating what it was like to do sex. He decided that none of them had ever had the experience. When he admitted his own inexperience, White Quill and Sits in the Middle both admitted theirs, but Badger and Elk Hollers in the Trees remained silent. Night Shoot never said anything. They had learned that, for some reason, he had never been able to speak, and he only sat and grinned during such discussions.

The next morning, they were underway before sun-up. At mid-morning, the small party came upon another lake where they stopped to eat, and it was evening when they made their camp along another river. They had seen evidence that they were paralleling the river valley for a while before Elk Hollers in the Trees steered them down through dense brush to camp near the river's edge.

After they had tethered the horses, Andy announced that he was going for a swim, and the rest scrambled to join him. The river reminded him of the great river which had brought him to the west, and the more he thought about it, the more he began to wonder if they had come upon it once again. Knowing that Edmonton House stood upon its banks, he became very excited.

After swimming, they ate and talked, and it was the same as the night before. Fighting the mosquitoes and black flies, which maintained a constant assault upon any skin left uncovered, they frequently resorted to the river to get away from them. Eventually, they made themselves ready for sleep.

Badger was apprehensive and could not sleep. He had never been to a *napikawan* camp before and was nervous. More than that, he had been concerned about what would happen once Andy found his father. Having grown very fond of him, he was worried that the reunion might spell the end of their friendship.

Andy, as well, had too much on his mind to sleep. The anticipation of seeing his father was overshadowed by the prospect of telling him about Matthew's death. Thoughts of his brother brought him tears. It had been a while since he had felt that way. There had been so much going on since the tragedy that had kept him from thinking about it. And, he could not know for sure whether his father would have heard about his mother's death, uncertain if he had got any of their letters. It could be a double blow for him. In any event, he would be excited to tell of all the things he had experienced during his time with Badger and his close friendship with the Indian.

"Do you sleep?" Andy was startled by the sound of his friend's voice.

"No. Too excited, I guess."

"I cannot understand you!" his friend growled.

Andy was a little exasperated. Before joining up with the others, Badger had been learning and trying to use some of his language. Now, he seldom attempted it—only to show off. *"My father,"* he whispered, turning on his side to face his friend, who turned to face him.

"I hope we can stay together—I hope I can stay with you," the Indian boy said quietly. *"And your father,"* he added softly.

"I would like you, um, to stay with us," Andy answered slowly, having to think about what he was saying. *"My father, uh, feels very warm toward you."*

"I hope so! We are brothers, you and me! Maybe—do you think maybe he would take me as his son? Like you?"

"Yes! I know he would! That would be really good!"

"What?"

"Yes, I wish that!" After a few moments of silence, Andy said, "I would really like it if you were my brother!"

"I guess I should learn your tongue—what did you say?"

"Yes. I want you...be my brother."

"Me too," Badger whispered. *"I hope we can be!"*

White Quill had been listening to their conversation, but he remained silent and let them think he was sleeping. He too longed for a friend like Andy, who seemed so unlike the other Indian boys his age.

10

The sound of gunfire wakened them during the night. In the stillness, it seemed close, but they decided that there was nothing to worry about—they were well-hidden, and nobody would see their trail in the dark. Elk Hollers in the Trees said that it was probably coming from the *napikawan camp*.

He was up before first light, rousing the others, telling them that they needed to break camp and get on the trail early. He did not want anyone to surprise them while they were unprepared, which worried Andy. He had thought that the *napikawan camp* ought to be a safer place than Elk Hollers in the Trees seemed to think.

They broke camp without eating and were on the trail by the time the sun came up. Riding out of the sanctuary of the river valley, they rejoined the trail they had been following the day before. At a fork, Elk Hollers in the Trees stopped to ponder their course, with one trail staying on top of the river valley and the other descending into the bush in the direction of the river. He was still thinking when they heard the familiar croak of a raven. Whirling to see where the voice had come from, they spied the big, black bird on top of an evergreen tree standing over the lower trail.

"Hai-ya!" Elk Hollers in the Trees exclaimed. *"Did our grandfather not tell us to listen to our brother, Raven? He is telling us which trail we should follow. Thank you, brother!"* he hollered toward the bird. It croaked again as if to answer him and quit its perch to fall on silent wings toward the river valley. Confidently, Elk Hollers in the Trees led the others down the trail Raven had indicated. It took them right down to the water's edge, where Badger pointed out a haze of smoke hanging over the placid water. When their leader observed that it must be from the *napikawan camp,* Andy could hardly wait and grew anxious to get going a little faster. Eventually, rounding a bend in the river, they got their first view of the fort on the opposite side.

"How we go?" Andy asked impatiently, crowding past the others to join Elk Hollers in the Trees, in the lead.

"We must find a place where we can cross," he replied. *"There is a ford somewhere."*

"What is that?" Andy asked impatiently.

"A place we can cross."

"How far?" Nobody knew.

Following the trail they were on, they began to see the structure more clearly. It stood at a higher elevation, above the river; its impressive bastions stood at opposite corners of imposing walls. People afoot and on horseback could be seen in the vicinity, and several tipis stood nearby. At the river's edge below it were overturned boats.

Andy was ready to plough into the water and get there as soon as he could. Still, Elk Hollers in the Trees insisted there would be a place to cross, and shortly, the ford became obvious. But he urged the others to be vigilant while crossing, where they would be vulnerable to attack. He told Andy to lead them. *"And, take your shirt off so they can see who you are!"* he commanded.

Doing as he had been told, Andy nervously slipped his shirt off. Tossing it to Badger, he asked him anxiously, *"What me do?"*

"Ride ahead of me," his friend responded, tucking his friend's shirt under his arm. *"If your horse starts to swim, hold on to its mane. If it starts to flounder, slide off its rump and hold on to its tail. Be careful not to get hit by its legs! They really hurt! Give me the rein of your other horse,"* Badger instructed, reaching out to take it from him, his hands now full. *"And, never let go of the rein!"* Andy had not understood most of what he had said but began to urge his horse into the water, taking the lead. The others followed one at a time, leaving plenty of space between them.

Even before reaching the middle, the water was well up on the horses' sides, where Andy's mount hesitated in the deeper water. It was difficult for him to kick it in the ribs—his feet were now in the water, impeding his effort. *"Whip it with your rein!"* Badger urged from behind. Slapping the horse on the rump with the long end of the rein, Andy was nervous. He had never been in this type of water on horseback, where the current was so swift. The water kept rising on the horse's side, and soon it would be at its back—it would have to swim. Glancing nervously behind him, Andy was reassured by the look of confidence on his friend's face, but he had moved a bit more upstream.

Suddenly, Andy's horse plunged into deeper water, which was around its young rider's waist, making it difficult for him to stay on. The animal's feet still had purchase, and with its head high, it lunged ahead, nostrils flared, and ears laid back. Too frightened to look back, Andy heard Badger yell, when suddenly, the animal seemed to rise out of the water—it had come upon a bar and seemed to settle. Turning to look for Badger, he found him even more distant—upstream. He, too, appeared to be on a bar.

The white boy's mount now became determined to get out of the water. Advancing at a lunging trot, it was making little headway into the current. Realizing that it was angling upstream, where the opposite shore was nearest, Andy steered the animal slightly downstream. They were making better headway when, suddenly, the horse disappeared from under him, in deep water, and Andy was off its back. As quick as it had gone under, the animal's head broke the surface, and Andy grabbed for its mane. He knew it was swimming, and he wished he had understood Badger's instructions more clearly. Gripping the animal's mane tightly and kicking with his legs, he tried to keep himself over its back until once again it seemed to gain its footing on another bar and rise out of the water. There, Andy lost his grip entirely and slid into the water, struggling to gain his footing with the water chest-deep. Still grasping the long rein in one hand, he could not stand against the strong current. Unencumbered, the horse lunged ahead, pulling the rein from his hand.

"H-help me!" the boy cried, announcing his plight to his friend. Badger and White Quill had both seen his difficulty, and White Quill got to him first, hoisting him on behind.

"Hold on to me!" he shouted, as his horse struggled under the weight of the extra rider. Overcoming the animal's impulse to go toward the nearest shore, he directed it toward the bar he knew to be just up from them. Lunging against the rushing water, in a moment, the animal reached the shallower water and began to settle down. Its ears back, it shook its head as the water got shallower toward the shore.

Andy watched his own mount scramble from the water. Taking a few steps, it stopped to shake itself vigorously, before starting to nose the vegetation near the water's edge, dragging the long rein.

White Quill and Badger both had their eyes fixed on something else. Trying to see where they were looking, Andy spotted three figures standing on the slope not far above them, each holding a firearm. Turning around, he saw that Elk Hollers in the Trees was watching them, too. Their other companions, though, seemed to be paying no attention at all, both concentrating on getting across the river.

Coming out of the water, White Quill guided his mount over to Andy's horse and scooped up the long, trailing rein. *"Are you all right?"* he asked his passenger.

"Yes," Andy replied, slipping off to take his horse. "Thank you!" he said, hurrying to climb back on, in a hurry to keep going.

Running his fingers through his wet hair, trying to show the figures above them that he was white, Andy headed for the trail that led up from the ford. "Hello!" he shouted as he closed the distance between.

"Hallo!" came the reply. Andy was thrilled to hear someone speak his language. Finding a network of trails, he chose one that looked like it would take him closest to the three men. When he came in sight of them, he greeted them again, eventually pulling his horse up in front of them. All three were white.

"Who ye got wi' ye laddie?" one of the men asked, with a deep Scottish brogue. Badger had stopped just behind Andy and watched, joined almost immediately by the others.

"These are my friends! They brought me here," Andy replied, hoping the men would give them a better reception than had the boatmen.

"They Bla'foot, then?" the same man asked, watching the other Indians gather behind Badger.

"Whadda ya mean?" Andy responded.

"'Re they Blackfoot injuns?" the man asked, taking more care to make himself understood.

"No, they're, uh, I think they're *Piikáni,*" was Andy's answer.

"Aye, tha's wha' ah figgered. They're na' dressed fer war. They cumin' to trade wi' us?"

"No, I mean, yes, er...no, they just brought me. There's others coming to trade. I'm looking for my father, Will Preston—Reverend William Preston. Do you know him?"

"Nah, never heard o' 'im," the same man answered, turning to the others. "Ye heard o' 'im?" he asked them.

"Never!" came the reply, and Andy's heart sank.

"A man o' the cloth, yuh say?"

"Yessir, he's a minister. Do you live here?"

"Aye, most o' th' tyme."

"Maybe someone else has heard of him. How many people live here?"

"Reckon there be nigh on a hun'erd 'bout now. Ye c'n ask a' the fort. Ol' One Poun' One may know 'im. Ain't no preachers 'ere, though, laddie."

"Who's that?" Andy queried

"Who's One Pound One?" the second man asked derisively, turning to his companions with a disdainful grin. Looking at Andy, he continued, "He's just the worst streak o' misery you'll ever come across in these parts—mean as the Blackfoot! The sonofabitch that runs this place! Reckon his momma called him, John—we calls 'im One Pound One, to be p'lite." He chuckled and looked to the others who grinned at his description of the factor at Edmonton House, nodding their heads in agreement.

"Where is he? Can I talk to him?" Andy queried, not realizing the intimidating nature of the man they were describing to him.

"Aye. Reckon 'e's up there a' the fort," the Scot replied.

"How do we get there?"

"Jus' be followin' tha' wee trail yer on, lad."

"Thank you, sir!" Andy responded, turning his horse and directing it up the trail.

"Make sure you keep them injuns outta trouble," one of the men hollered behind him.

Turning to check on his friends, he saw them eyeing the three white men suspiciously, riding past them. Elk Hollers in the Trees nudged his way past Badger and came up beside Andy.

"*What did they say?*" he demanded to know.

"*We go to camp,*" said Andy urging his horse along a little faster, anxious to get to the fort.

"*Slow down! Slow down!*" Elk Hollers in the Trees commanded, "*They will think we come to make war!*"

"What?" Andy asked impatiently, reining back his horse. Realizing Elk Hollers in the Trees could not understand what he had said, he asked, "*What?*"

"*We must ride slowly, and we must keep spread out!*" Elk Hollers in the Trees scolded. "*When we come out of the trees, you must let us spread out!*" But when they reached the open, grassy flat beside the fort, Andy did not stop. "*Stop!*" Elk Hollers in the Trees commanded.

Hearing what was going on ahead of him, Badger hollered, "Andy! Stop!" Andy finally reined his horse in, impatient.

Men were visible along the walls of the fort, watching them. Someone with a firearm stood in the open gate. Behind the fort to the north was a cultivated field, the first Andy had seen since leaving Red River.

"*Go! Slow!*" Elk Hollers in the Trees now told Andy, waiting to direct the others.

At the fort, they had become the centre of everyone's attention.

"*Arrêtez!*" someone yelled from the top of the barricade as the riders approached. "Hold up, right there!" another voice commanded. "Hold up!" still another, all at the same time. Andy pulled up his horse, signalling for the others to stop, but Badger rode right up and stopped beside him. All the Indians were tense.

"Whadda ya want?" a man standing in the gate called out.

"We are friendly," Andy assured the man, "I am looking for someone—my—"

"Who's yer friends," the man interrupted, jabbing his weapon in the direction of the Indians.

"They're friendly," Andy answered. "They brought me here. They're *Piikáni.*"

"I know that! Tell 'em to wait where they are—you kin come inside," the man said gruffly.

"Stay here," Andy told Badger, who turned and told the others to wait.

Without waiting for a response from those accompanying him, the white boy eagerly slipped off his horse, tossing the rein to Badger. Retrieving his shirt from him, he hurried toward the gate, pulling the wet garment on over his head. As soon as he was through the gate, the man stepped aside and ordered others to close it.

Andy strode up to the man as the big gate closed behind him. Reaching out his hand, he introduced himself, "My name is Andrew Preston, and I'm looking for my father. Do you know Will Preston—Reverend William Preston?"

"Samuel," the man announced his name gruffly, shaking the boy's hand only briefly. "Samuel Hathaway. He a preacher?"

"Hi, Mr. Hathaway. Yes, sir, but he doesn't dress like a preacher. He doesn't wear a robe and tie."

"Nope, don't know any preachers. But thur's bin a couple 'round here. Where yuh from, kid?"

"Red River settlement."

"How'd you do that? Where'd yuh pick up them injuns?"

"I came with Mr. McConnell. Do you know him?"

"Yeah, him, we know. Reckon maybe we heard 'boutcha, then. How'd yuh get here?"

Hearing that the man apparently knew of McConnell, he told him, "I came up the river with Mr. McConnell...part of the way. Then some Indians killed my brother—and some hunters—Cree. The boats wouldn't pick us up. They just left us there, on the river."

"Where 'bouts?"

"I don't know. Somewhere past some fort—"

"Carlton? Pitt?" the man interrupted.

"Yeah, Fort Carlton, I think. 'Bout a month ago, maybe. Downriver somewhere. Is this Edmonton House?"

"Sure is."

"Are you the guy in charge?" Andy asked.

"Nope. That's Mister Rowand—he's over there," the man said, giving a nod in the direction of a tall, three-storey log building.

"Can I talk to him?"

"Shore can! I'll hafta take yuh."

The man led the way, and Andy followed. Walking across the yard at the man's side, he examined his surroundings. There were a number of log structures, inside the stout log walls. Along the top of the walls was a platform upon which a few men, armed with firearms, stood watch on his companions outside the fort. The walls supported solid-looking bastions, which showed the presence of brass cannon.

Approaching one of the buildings, the man rapped firmly on the wooden door and said, "Got someone to see yuh, sir." Andy heard a muffled response from within, while the man proceeded to open the door.

"Got a kid who showed up with a bunch of pecunnies. They don't look like they're up t' nothin'—not yet, anyhow. Says he's lookin' fer his old man—some preacher or somethin'."

"I'm the trader here," the man said gruffly, getting up from his table and stepping toward them. He was a stout man, not tall—but imposing—with a round face framed with mutton chops and a scruffy beard. "What the hell you doin' in my fort, kid?"

"Pleased to meet you, sir. My name is Andrew Preston," Andy stepped forward and held out his hand. The man ignored it, bringing him to withdraw it awkwardly. But he continued, "My father is Reverend William Preston. Do you know him?"

Studying the boy for a moment, the man replied, "Sure do! Came through here a while back—on his way downriver—lookin' fer someone. That you?"

"He's already been here?" Andy stammered, shocked. "When was that? How?" he asked urgently.

"Hell! He come through here a few weeks back. Come through from the upper house. Got a letter that 'is wife had died. Where the hell you been, kid? Were you out here with 'im?"

"No, sir. My mum died, and my brother and I came out to find him. We wrote him, and he never wrote back, so we decided we'd come find him."

"Your brother? Where's he?"

"Oh, no! He's dead. We went hunting with some Indians, and some other Indians killed 'em. Another one helped me, though, and he's the one that brought me here, but my brother's dead. We buried him back there somewhere—I'm not even sure where."

"Un-huh. Dam', we heard 'bout that. You was with McConnell!"

"Yes! Mr. McConnell! Do you know him? Is he here? We came with him."

"Hell no! Dropped off at Pitt, down from here, where he belongs. Wouldn't have that sonofabitch around here! Word travels pretty dam' good out here though—I heard 'boutcha. Wouldn't leave the injun behind, huh?"

Andy was amazed to discover that the man seemed to know all about him. "Yeah, that's right! They wouldn't even stop for us! I'm pretty annoyed about that—are you his boss?" Andy was temporarily distracted from his quest.

Rowand laughed. "Boss? Hell, I reckon you could say that. I pretty much run everything west of Cumberland House, right through to the salt chuck. That sonofabitch pretty much works for me, hell yeah! Everyone out here that ain't injun works for me!"

"Well, he left me behind and without help from my friend, I probably never would have made it!"

Rowand's response was curt. "Without yer injun friend, McConnell woulda picked you up. Matter o' fact you'da probably met up with yer daddy!"

For the second time in a very few minutes, Andy was stunned by what the man had to tell him. The issue of McConnell's failings vanished from his mind. "What do you mean?" he asked, much subdued.

"Hell! Yer daddy came through here an' went on to Fort Pitt—gettin' out of here in a great big rush, he was. Got to Pitt just after McConnell."

"What do you mean? My pa? He met McConnell?"

"Dam' right 'e did! McConnell had just got in, an' by 'n' by yer daddy shows up. That's where McConnell is, Fort Pitt. They run into each other there, I reckon—that's what we heard."

"Why didn't he come looking for us, then?" Andy asked desperately.

"Who knows? Maybe he'd heard the whole dam' lot of yuh was killed! I dunno!"

"That's not true! Is that what he said?"

"I dunno. Hell, I wasn't there! It's just something we hear, but it's probably pretty close to right—guess maybe not, if you're here!" Andy was shocked and bitterly disappointed to hear that he had so narrowly missed his father.

Rowand could see his state of mind and sized him up while he waited for him to say something. Finally, the man spoke again. "How'd you get hooked up with the injun? Why'd you wanna stay with him rather than get back in the boat?"

"He helped me, sir," Andy replied, much subdued. He tried to explain more fully how he had ended up with Badger.

When he had told his story, Rowand quizzed him. "Tied him up? What is he? Why didn't they kill him?" Clearly, he was puzzled by what he had been told.

"I don't know—he's—he's not a Blackfoot or whatever, he's *Piikáni*. That's what the others are—the ones that brought me, they're all *Piikáni*."

"Blackfoot!"

"No. I think they're *Piikáni*," Andy corrected him.

"That's Blackfoot, boy. *Piikáni, Káínaa, Siksika,* they're all Blackfoot. Dam' buggers give us more trouble than all the rest put together!"

"Blackfoot, then—"

"They's outside," the other man interrupted Andy. He had been standing behind, listening to the conversation. "They the buggers that did yer brother in—an' the Cree?" He, too, seemed puzzled by Andy's version of the events they had only heard about.

Andy turned and tried to explain to both of them. Frustrated, he stammered, "I don't know! This guy—my friend—the one outside. He helped me. You see—I don't know!" he stammered. He ended by telling them, "This guy helped me!" He was feeling exasperated.

"This the one they tied to yer brother?" Rowand asked in disbelief. "What the hell are you saying, boy? I'm not getting' it!"

"I don't know! I haven't really been able to find that out. His name is *Míísinsski*. He didn't kill anyone. Whoever killed them— the Cree— I don't know!" Andy blurted in response. He did not like talking about this and wanted to learn more about his father. "Can we talk about my father first? Where is he? Do you know where he is?"

Rowand, equally frustrated and not understanding what Andy was trying to say, said firmly, "Kid, yer daddy was goin' back to find you!" He continued to explain, "You two, I reckon. There was a letter come here, way last spring. He'd been here for a while, but last winter he spent somewhere out 'round the upper house, one of our forts, west o' here—Rocky Mountain House. That letter sat here for a long time. Hell! Months! Then when he didn't show up here this spring, I sent it on to the other house, for 'im. He got it not long ago 'cause he come right here, soon as he got it. Come through a couple of weeks ago. Left with a bunch that was goin' 'cross by horseback. Said he was gonna bring you boys back next spring."

The man's revelation left Andy's head spinning. He had never even imagined such a thing!

Reading the shock on the boy's face, Rowand said, "Sorry t' hafta break that to you, boy. How old are yuh?"

"Fifteen, sir."

"Hell, maybe you want to stay here 'til your daddy comes back! He's a dam' good man. If you're half the kid yer daddy is, I'd dam' well put you to work right here—for the winter. You could wait for him to come back in spring." Rowand was beginning to see a way he could capitalize on the boy's plight.

"What if he doesn't come back? What if he goes back to England—if we're supposed to be, uh, dead?" Andy asked dismally.

"Hell, didn't sound like that t' me. Yer daddy's had a real fire in 'is belly—had quite a influence out here. He's 'way different from the other dam' preachers who just come and go. He talked with lotsa spunk—'bout them Blackfoot. Tamed some of 'em right down." Letting that sink in for a moment, he continued, "No, kid, yur daddy'll be back! You better dam' well stay right here an' wait fer 'im. Do yuh hunt? We always need hunters. We need lotsa meat to get this crew through the winter."

Wholly disheartened, the boy replied, "No. I mean, yes, I do. Maybe not very well." He hung his head. "My brother was the hunter. I've shot deer an' I shot a moose once, and things. What about my friend? Could he? Where would we stay?"

"You'd stay here. We'd find a place for you. Who's yer friend? The injun?"

"Yes. The one that brought me here."

"Well, he sure as hell ain't stayin' here! We'd have hell t' pay, havin' a injun stay inside these walls!"

"Why? He's not—there's nothing wrong with him!" Andy retorted, resenting the man's attitude toward his friends.

"He's a Blackfoot injun!" Rowand roared. "No dam' injun like that's gonna put 'is head down inside these walls!"

"He's not an Indian!" Andy blurted in response. "I mean"—he corrected himself, realizing how foolish he was sounding— "he's an Indian, but he's not bad! He won't do anything!"

"Listen, t' me, boy!" Hathaway interrupted again. Trying to make Andy understand that Badger would not be allowed inside the fort, he explained, "If he's one o' them outside the gate, he's a Blackfoot, an' if he's a Blackfoot, he's trouble. Yuh dare to put yer head down to sleep with one o' them inside these walls, an' yuh got all hell to pay! Hell to pay!"

"That's not true!" Andy replied angrily. If he was not going to be able to join his father, he was certainly not prepared to abandon his only friend in favour of these kinds of men. Having turned to face Hathaway, he continued, "Listen! I'd put my life in his hands. He's my friend!" Turning to Rowand, he continued, his voice raised. "I don't know! I'm not stayin' around here if he can't stay! Maybe we can catch up to my father. Do you know which way they went?"

"Don't be a dam' fool, boy!" Rowand replied unsympathetically. "Yer old man's a good three weeks ahead of yuh. He'll be more 'n halfway there by now. Where the hell's he goin'? Where'd yuh live?"

"Just down the river from where Fort Garry was, sir, 'bout halfway to the lake."

"Well I'm just as sure as I'm sittin' here that he's comin' back! He was bent on that! But hell, it's nigh the middle of September. Won't be any boats comin' up from there anymore this year. I doubt if he'd turn 'round and come back overland. September might be all right, but any time after September, we dam' well expect snow anytime. My money's on 'im showin' up here first thing in spring— with the first boats."

"When is it, anyway? You said it's September?"

"It's the middle of September— 'round the fifteenth."

"What if he doesn't come back?"

"You'll hafta figger that one out—he's yer daddy. But like I sez, my money's on 'im comin' back!"

"How come he said we were both killed? McConnell, I mean."

"Give it up, kid! Sometimes the moccasin telegraph ain't quite that reliable."

"I don't know. I'll have to think about it," Andy said. "Can I talk to my friend?"

"Suit yerself. Hathaway here'll find yuh a place to bunk in."

"No thank you, sir! Not unless my friend can stay here, too."

"There'll be no chance of that! Do whatcha like. Lemme know what yur gonna do. I'm prepared for you to start right away. Maybe you and yur injun friend can both hunt for me. You should take me up on my offer an' you'll be right here when yer daddy comes back next spring."

"Well, he could hunt, that's for sure."

"Yeah, them buggers can hunt—if yuh can get 'em to do it! Lemme know what yer gonna do, then!"

"Yes, thank you, sir. I will"

"Git to hell outta here, then! I gots work to do!" Mr. Rowand turned his back and went to his table, and Andy turned to go.

Reaching the door, he turned around to ask, "How long does it take to get back to Fort Garry from here?"

Looking up at him with a scowl, Rowand replied, "Hell! You gotta count on five to eight weeks, at least! Yuh better not try that one!" He did not want the boy to leave; he was hoping he could convince the boy to stay and work for the winter.

Disappointed, Andy turned and stepped out the door, not sure what to do.

Things inside the fort seemed to have settled down from the commotion of his arrival. There were only a couple of men along the top of the wall who seemed to be watching his companions. The gate was still closed, and as Hathaway led him toward it, Andy took notice of the people he saw inside the fort. Mostly men, the only women appeared to be Indian women, dressed in the garb of the whites.

"You watch those Blackfoot, boy!" Hathaway warned when he reached the gate. "If they're gonna get into the liquor here, they'll be actin' up, plumb wild. You be careful! The Cree and the others, we can trust better, but not Bug's Boys."

"What's Bug's Boys?" Andy asked him, recalling the American using the same expression.

"Bug's Boys! Blackfoot—means the devil's own!"

"What do you mean?" Andy asked him.

"They're the devil's own—they belong to the devil!" He left Andy to ponder what he had said and hollered for the gate to be opened. As it swung open, Andy saw his companions waiting for him.

"Did you find him?" Badger asked as his friend approached.

"Him not here. Go river...home...far," he reported, deep disappointment etched on his face.

"Why did he leave?" White Quill asked. *"Why did he not wait for you?"*

Andy was too glum to try very hard to communicate with them. He was feeling overwhelmed. *"He not—"* Stammering dismally, he waved his hand uncertainly, not coming up with the right words.

"What are you going to do?" Badger wondered, still worried about being parted.

"I don't know," Andy replied. He stepped behind Badger's horse, so the others would not see the tears he felt welling up.

His friend saw what was happening and snapped at the others. *"Leave us! Leave us! Wait over there!"* he insisted, pointing to the edge of the clearing. Not understanding what was going on, all but White Quill obliged. Seeing his concern, Badger said nothing to him and slipped to the ground as the rest wheeled their horses, looking back suspiciously. He put his hand on his friend's shoulder while White Quill dismounted and stood close. Caring for the white boy, he did not feel confident enough to get any closer.

"O Jesus, what am I gonna do? I haven't even been praying! Please help me! I want my pa!" Andy whimpered softly. Not understanding him, Badger had nothing to say.

In a moment, Andy turned and wiped his tears on his sleeve, still soaked from the river crossing. He tried to explain to his friend what had happened. *"My father...know"*—he emphasized his point by tapping his head— *"my mother dead."* He spoke slowly and deliberately, searching for the right words. *"Travel to my, uh, lodge. He goes there...far,"*—sweeping his hand toward the east— *"many nights—two moons. Napikawan say not go."* Andy shook his head and continued, making the motion of pulling a bow. *"He say we hunt...bring meat, you and me."*

"Will your father return?"

"Him say yes. Me?" Andy shrugged his shoulders to signify that he did know the answer.

"What are you going to do?"

Andy just shook his head. *"Him say camp here, hunt. Me want father. Him say—he say, not travel. Go there, no. You, me stay... hunt. Father come here, long time—when grass green."*

"Your father is not here?" Badger tried to confirm what he understood his friend to be telling him.

"No."

"You are going to find him?" the Indian asked, feeling optimistic. If his friend's father was not at the fort, perhaps they would remain together.

"No, stay here, you, me."

Feeling immense relief, Badger asked more questions. *"You and me? We will stay here and hunt for the napikawan?"*

"Yes."

"Good! I will teach you to hunt buffalo!" Understanding they would remain together, the suggestion of hunting together was even more exciting.

Andy did not wish to tell him that he would not be welcome in the fort. He had not figured that out yet. He could not understand why the Indians were held in such contempt. Not wanting to hurt Badger's feelings, he just said they had no room for them to stay at the fort.

"We can make camp nearby, hunt buffalo for them and trade for fire-sticks and napiohke," his friend responded.

"No!" Andy snapped. That was the last thing he wanted to have to worry about just then. *"Not drink—napiohke! Bad!* Please don't!"

Surprised by his friend's sudden angry response, the Indian countered, *"The others came here to get it! They want us to try it."*

"No, please, no!" Andy begged his friend. "I can't take this!" he exclaimed, pulling his hand through his hair, trying to figure things out.

Badger could not understand why his friend seemed so upset by the *napiohke.* The others could hardly wait to try it, but seeing his friend's reaction, he decided to keep quiet about it.

Thinking he had relented, Andy sighed, "Thank you. I don't need that right now!"

"What do you mean? I do not understand what you say."

"Thank you. Just thank you—*you are my friend!"*

"What are we going to do now?" Badger asked.

"I do not know. I want my father!"

"I will go with you. Are we going to find him?"

"I will go...talk napikawan. Sleep first."

"We should join our friends, then," Badger suggested and led the way to where the others were waiting at the edge of the clearing.

There, Badger responded when they asked Andy about his father. He explained, *"His father travels to the land of the napi-kawan by the great water. He travels two moons to his lodge."*

"*What will he do now?*"

"*He wants me to stay with him and hunt buffalo for these napi-kawan.*" As Badger explained their friend's circumstances to the others, White Quill felt left out, wishing he, too, could stay connected to their white friend. But he kept it to himself.

Andy had been listening to Badger and interjected, "*Yes, stay here...hunt...until grass becomes green.*"

"*He should ask my father what he should do,*" Sits in the Middle offered. "*We have a few more nights before they arrive.*

"*Now, how can we get napiohke?*" he wondered, changing the subject.

"*Yes! How do we get napiohke? That is what we came for!*" Elk Hollers in the Trees agreed, and Night Shoot nodded his head, showing his enthusiasm for the idea.

"*No!*" Andy interjected. The others looked at him strangely, not understanding his objection; they thought he must be joking.

Sits in the Middle laughed it off, asking, "*Why not? We came all this way to get it!*"

Andy did not have the words to explain himself. "*Napiohke bad! Hurt you!*"

"*No! My friend says that it makes you feel good!*" Sits in the Middle responded, grinning with anticipation.

"*No, napiohke...make you, uh, feel bad—you hurt,*" Andy tried to dissuade them, lacking the proper words.

"*Have you had it?*" Elk Hollers in the Trees asked aggressively.

"*No. Me see man...drink napiohke! Not good. Not drink!* Please!"

"*You do not know! It is supposed to make you feel good!*" Sits in the Middle insisted. Turning to his friends, he said, "*How can we get some? We have nothing to trade!*"

"*Maybe we should do as we talked about—find some Liars who have it and take it,*" Elk Hollers in the Trees reminded the others of something they had apparently discussed previously. "*See? They* are all over the place! *They have been watching us ever since we got here!*"

"*We should wait for the others!*" White Quill cautioned them. "*This is their camp—there are too many! We are few! The napi-kawan favours the Liars. They will help them if you try anything,*"

"*No! Not here, you nothing one!*" Sits in the Middle countered. "*We will find a place to wait in ambush—along a trail somewhere.*"

"*Yes,*" Elk Hollers in the Trees agreed. "*But we will stay on this side of the river. The Liars are afraid of our people over there,*" he said, pointing with his lips to the south side of the river—the Blackfoot side. "*We need to stay on this side. We need to find a place for an ambush.*"

"*Miisinsski,*" Andy said desperately, "say no! Don't go with them!"

"I...you," Badger stammered, before speaking out. "*Sun Shines on Him and I are not going with you! He wants me to go back with him and speak with the napikawan. We will see which way you go, then come after,*" he told the others, though he had no intention of following through with it.

"*Why does he have to speak again to the napikawan?*" Elk Hollers in the Trees asked suspiciously. "*He has already spoken with him.*"

Without hesitating, Badger replied, "*We have more to say to him, Sun Shines on Him and me. He wants both of us to hunt for him.*" Which left White Quill feeling even more disappointed.

"*Maybe he gives you napiohke,*" Sits in the Middle said with a sarcastic grin on his face.

"*No! Maybe he gives us fire-sticks—that is what I want!*" Badger retorted.

"*You stay, then,*" Sits in the Middle said. "*We will find a place to keep watch on the Liars,*" he urged the older ones. "*You can find us later,*" he said to Badger.

"*Yes!*" Elk Hollers in the Trees agreed. "*We will look around and find a trail—there has to be one somewhere,*" he said, kicking his horse. *"But come with us until we find a trail"*—he told Badger—*"so you will know where to find us!"* So he and Andy followed, with White Quill.

Conscious of the Cree watching them closely, they rode past a cultivated field beside the fort, almost at once discovering a trail leaving the area, heading northeast. Pausing, Elk Hollers in the Trees said to Badger and his white friend, *"We will be down this trail. We will find a place to wait in ambush. We will watch for you! Hurry back! Get napiohke if you can!"*

Reluctant to go along with the older ones, White Quill was happy to hear Andy say to him, *"White Quill! Come!"*

Agreeing with him, Badger said, *"Maybe you will hunt with us. Come! We will see if the napikawan will give us fire-sticks!"*

But Elk Hollers in the Trees had other plans for the youngster. *"No! We need him! He comes with us!"* White Quill's countenance fell when he heard it, and he hesitated. Until the leader barked at him, *"Come! We must hurry—in case they follow us!"*

"Us, um...we bring White Quill!" Andy tried to say.

"No!" Elk Hollers in the Trees disagreed firmly, *"We need him against the Liars."*

White Quill felt he had no choice in the matter and turned his horse to follow the troublemakers. Seeing that, Andy was afraid for him and asked Badger, *"What we do?"*

"Nothing," Badger responded. *"We cannot go against that other one!"* he said so only Andy would hear. And, the two of them watched their young friend fall in behind the others.

"He does not want to go!" Badger observed.

"What do we do?" Andy asked again, not happy that White Quill had to go against his will.

"There is nothing to be done!" the Indian responded. *"That fellow wants him, and he must go!"*

Watching until the others were out of sight, Badger wheeled his horse and headed for the fort. Neither of them said much, worried about their friend.

By the time they reached the fort, again, Andy had decided to go and have another talk with Rowand.

Back at the fort, he dropped to the ground and told Badger to wait for him and hold the horses, handing him his rein.

Once again, Andy was given admittance to the fort. Hathaway met him, and they spoke in the open gateway. "Can I see that guy again, the trader. What's his name? Mr. Pound?" Andy asked.

"One Pound One! That's right! You call him that!"—Hathaway chuckled— "an' he'll have your sack for a tobacco pouch! It's Mr. Rowand. An' he don't like to be bothered. Whadda yuh need?"

"These other guys want liquor, but I don't want them to have it. Can you give them something else and not give them liquor?"

"Not on your life, boy! That's our best card! If they ain't satisfied, they goes t' the Yanks, an' don't come back. B'sides! We don't trade it like the Yanks do—just give 'em a little enticement—a gift!"

"But they're just boys, like me!"

"Boys hell! Boys who'd just as soon kill yuh, un-huh! They're troublemakers, all of 'em and they like their firewater! Lotsa them don't even live long enough t' have a woman! Most of 'em been out raisin' hell before they's yer age. Bet some of 'em counted coup already!"

"What's that? Counting what?"

"Counting coup? Takin' scalps. They'll skin that pretty hair o' yers off in no time. Bet some of 'em done it already." Andy thought about White Quill.

He was not sure what he should do. If he did not leave the fort with something, the others might be suspicious of his reason for being there. "Mister—what's his name? Rowand? He wanted us to hunt buffalo for him. Do you think he'd give us a couple of guns?"

"You'd have to—" Suddenly, Hathaway was interrupted by a commotion behind Andy. "Look out!" he shouted. Hearing the sudden pounding of horses' hooves behind him, Andy whirled around to see what was happening.

"Watch out!" he screamed, seeing three Cree on horseback racing toward Badger, two with bows drawn, the third brandishing a war club. His friend had seen the attack coming and was whipping his horse for the gate, but Hathaway was shouting for it to be closed. Even as he spoke, those manning the gate had it almost closed.

"No! Let him in!" Andy screamed frantically when he saw what was happening. "Wait! Keep it open!" The men on the gate paid no heed to him, so he turned and threw his weight against it, to prevent them from closing it. One of the men stepped forward and threw him to the ground, but not before Badger barged through the gate, his horse hitting it and bowling over those who had been trying to get it closed. Andy scrambled to get inside just as they managed to push the big gate shut.

"The injun got in!" someone shouted from the walkway along the walls above him. Scrambling to his feet, Andy heard a man yell, *"Stop! Stop!"* in Blackfoot. The startled boy raced to assist his friend, who was being dragged from his horse, where a handful of agitated men quickly surrounded him. Others were hurrying to join them, and almost everyone inside the walls had a gun trained on the intruder.

"Míísinsski! Don't move! Stay there!" Andy yelled, trying to claw his way to him.

"Toss 'im out!" someone yelled.

The white boy was alarmed by the murderous threats being directed toward his friend, positioning himself between him and the angry men. "He's all right! He's my friend! He won't hurt anyone!" he shouted, shocked by their hostility.

"Git 'im out!" someone shouted.

"Hold it!" Andy protested, being pushed around. "They were after him!" The men tried to push him out of the way to get at Badger, but he shoved right back.

"—scalp 'im!"

"No! Wait!" the white boy cried, being overwhelmed by the growing mob.

"Get 'im outta here!" one of the men hollered, using the barrel of his gun to try to push Andy aside. "Yer in the way, boy," the man said, giving him a fierce thrust with the weapon.

"No! Stop!" Andy yelled, shoving the gun away and standing his ground. "He won't hurt you! He's all right!"

"What the hell's goin' on here!" came a booming voice from behind. Everyone turned to see Rowand, his hands on his hips, looking furious. There was a general commotion while everyone shouted an answer. "Hathaway! What the hell yuh got goin' on?" Rowand shouted, red-faced. "What's that injun doin' in my fort!" Some of the men turned and looked at Hathaway.

"A bunch of Cree, sir. They came after this one. He's pecunnie, all alone—was waitin' for the kid here," Hathaway responded, pointing to the white boy. "Come right through the gate 'fore we could get it closed, sir."

"Boy!" Rowand roared at Andy, striding toward him, the men parting like a wave before him. "He the one that's with you?"

"Yes, sir," Andy blurted fearfully. "This is *Míísinsski*. He's the one I told you about. He's my friend—he won't hurt anyone, I promise. The other Indians were—"

"Shut up! I don't wanna hear it!" the man shouted angrily. Some of the men held their weapons a little lower, as Rowand advanced, standing over the two boys. He looked Badger over then turned to the white boy. "Your friend, is he?" he sneered. "Git 'is weapons!" he ordered Hathaway. The young Indian tried to resist, but Andy gestured that he should let them take them.

"Yes, sir. He's my friend! I'd trust him with my life!" he said, turning back to Rowand.

"He may just have to trust you with his! If I turn him out now, with them Cree outside, they'll have 'is scalp before you can say cuttlefish." And, several of those standing around them urged him to do just that.

"You can't do that! An' they got our horses—he had our horses—they probably got 'em!"

"I can do as I dam' well please!"

"Please don't give him to them! He's all I got!" Andy pleaded. "He's like my brother! Please help us! And you gotta help us get those horses!"

"We'll have to lock 'im up! Maybe put 'im the hell out after it gets dark!" he said, directing his comment more to Hathaway than Andy.

"Why do you have to put him out?" Andy asked. "Couldn't we just stay here for a little while? I need to talk to you!"

"Listen, kid, those Blackfoot are the worst kinda injun we got! If we're gonna have trouble, it'll come from them! Some injuns come in here just fine, do their business an' leave. These guys raise bloody hell, all the time! Always stealin' our horses an' shootin' the dam' place up! We only let 'em in here maybe two or three at a time, that's how careful we watch 'em. To trade! We don't let 'em in 'cept to trade! Just a couple at a time. If I'm to bloody let 'im stay, he'll hafta be locked up."

"Where will you lock him up?" Andy demanded to know.

"We got a cellar under one o' the storerooms. We'll put 'im in there."

"Where will I be?"

"You c'n bunk with the others in the bunkhouse."

"Why does he have to be locked up? Can't he just stay with me?"

"You heard me, boy! In the hole or the hell out the gate!" the man snarled.

"I hear you, sir. Can I stay with him?"

"In the bloody hole? Are you crazy, boy?"

"Sir, he's my friend! Where he goes, I go!" Andy declared stubbornly, putting his hand on Badger's shoulder, hearing the men mock him.

"Damn, you think a lot of them savages! You talk just like yer old man!" Rowand growled. "Come with me! Bring the injun! Hathaway—look after the injun's dam' horse. Put it over there with mine!" he said, pointing to a fenced area between two of the structures. "An' get their others—go tear their red asses off! Tell 'em I'll be payin' 'em a visit if we don't have 'em in here by the time Sun goes down!" He was clearly outraged by the disturbance. "C'mon then!" he ordered the boys.

"Come, my friend," Andy said to Badger. *"Sleep here."*

Someone standing nearby said to Rowand, as he left, "M'sieur, you let da sauvage stay 'ere? Ees not good!"

"Never mind what the hell you think, Mitterand!" Rowand was still angry. "I'll handle this! You stay the hell out of it! Just get those damn horses back!" he snarled. "C'mon kid, I said! Bring yer injun!"

Andy took Badger by the arm and followed the trader. Most of the men grudgingly made way for them, but one big man who spoke French to the fellow beside him would not move, forcing them to walk around him and hurry to catch up.

Rowand led them to the place Andy had met him before. Opening the door, he let the boys enter ahead of him. Inside, Andy led Badger over to the big table while Rowand closed the door and walked to a hutch at the side of the room. "Pull this chair up for the injun," he told Andy, pointing to one beside the hutch, his manner now much subdued. Badger followed his friend nervously while he retrieved the chair and moved it beside one that was in front of Rowand's table. Badger had never seen a chair before and looked them over carefully while Rowand poured something from a cut-glass bottle into a squat, stemmed glass. The Indian gaped wide-eyed at the beautiful vessels.

Finished pouring himself a drink, Rowand returned to his table and invited the boys to sit. Not used to sitting in this fashion, Badger watched Andy take a seat and carefully lowered himself onto the other chair wriggling his backside in it suspiciously to make sure it would hold him.

"Brandy! Damn good brandy!" Rowand exclaimed, holding the glass up before taking it to his lips. "Ahhh!" he exclaimed after a sip. "Not the rot-gut shit we feed your friends.

"I don't need to ask you if you want a glass. You strike me as bein' pretty much like yer daddy. He never would accept my offer of a glass, an' I'll not offer a glass to the injun'!" He took another sip and leaned back in his chair.

"Kid, I admire yer daddy! He had a helluva time out at the upper house—workin' with the injuns. I tell you what! When he comes back, he'll have 'em eatin' outta his bloody hand again. And I like that! I ain't seen none of them black robes get the kinda respect these boys give him. He has a real way with 'em—he charms 'em! An' I want 'im back here! They're a lot easier to deal with when he's around."

"Wow! Thank you, sir!" Andy breathed, somewhat surprised.

"You gonna be doin' the same as him?" the big man asked.

"That's what my brother was going to do, sir. I suppose I might have. Now, I don't know what I'll do—maybe I'll help him—I don't know."

"I made 'im promise he'd come back. I even offered him a wage with the dam' company, but he was pretty adamant that his lord wouldn't fancy that much. Promised he'd come back, though! He spoke pretty high of you and your brother and wanted the two of yuh out here with 'im. How the hell old was your brother?"

"Seventeen."

"And how old didja say you were?"

"Fifteen, sir."

"And do you know how old the injun is?"

"Same as me—fifteen or so."

"They start makin' war at that age—has he counted coup? Do you know what the hell that is?"

"I think so, sir."

"Killin'! Has 'e killed anyone yet!"

"No! An' I don't think he will, either. He doesn't like killing."

Rowand sneered. "A Blackfoot that doesn't like killin'? Let me tell you, boy, it's in their blood!"

"I don't think so, sir. I know him pretty well!" Andy answered with adolescent confidence.

"How the hell long did you say you been runnin' with 'im? A month?"

"I reckon it's been about that, sir."

"A month! An' where'd yuh run into 'im?"

"I'm not really sure—somewhere down the river."

"So, that makes you the expert, huh?" Andy could only give a frown in response. "I been with 'em since Christ was a ship's boy!"

Rowand's demeanour shifted, and a pensive expression crossed his face. In a moment, pulling on his bushy sideburns, the man spoke slowly, as if working something out in his mind as he spoke. "Here's what we'll do. We'll send word to yer daddy that you're here, well an' safe. We'll tell 'im that you're gonna spend the winter workin' for me—makin' a wage—an' that you're lookin' forward to 'is comin' back just as soon as he c'n make it back out here, next spring. Meantime, I'll hire yuh! I'll even hire the injun! I'll give yuh everythin' yuh need. Horses? Yuh got horses, doncha? If we get 'em back for yuh!"

"Yes, sir—well, we did! Do you think you can get them back for us?"

"I'll see what I can do. That's all right. I'll give yuh an extra, maybe a couple. You'll need 'em—pack horses. You and the injun.

I'll give yuh each a gun, powder, ball, bit o' grub, duds, if yuh like—everythin' yuh need. An' then I'll give yuh fifteen pounds to go with your injun friend—to 'is people. The money's just for you—he don't know how to use it! Hunt with 'em—spend the winter with 'em. I'll give yuh some things to take as gifts from me. All yuh need to do is get 'em to come back here in the spring with furs—lotsa furs! I'll send you with traps, too. We'll treat 'em right! Then, next spring, yer back here to meet yer daddy. How's that sound to yuh?"

Andy could not believe it! It was far more than he had hoped for! "You mean you'll pay me to do that?"

"That's right, boy! Fifteen pounds! I do you a favour, an' you do me one. 'Cept, you get paid for yours. I'm sure yer daddy'll be proud of yuh for earnin' that kinda money! It's probably more 'n he'll make in a year! Maybe you can help 'im out some next year. Whatcha figger?"

"Can I talk to my friend?" Andy asked. He was suspicious—the offer seemed a little too good to be true.

"Sure, go right ahead," Rowand said, shuffling some papers on the big table.

"*My friend,*"—Andy said, turning toward Badger— "*napikawan, um...want me and you...go your people. He give we horses, uh... fire-sticks. He give—*" Realizing that he knew no word in Badger's language to describe pay or money, he had to think for a moment before continuing. "*He give...uh...things, me and you...help him.*" His friend looked puzzled. "*Do you understand?*" Andy asked.

"*He wants us to help him, and he will give us things for it? What kinds of things? What is in his head? How do we help him?*" Badger asked.

"*Yes, napikawan wants...your uh, your brothers and them...go here, um, give, um—*" waving his hand, he tried to think of a word.

Suddenly, Rowand interrupted him. "*You have your people come here, to this place, when the jackrabbit whistles at night,*" he said,

Blackfoot flowing from his tongue as if he was born with it. *"They come here to trade, and I will give them good gifts. They can trade furs and meat for many good things. I will give you some gifts to take with you."* He spoke Blackfoot so fluently that Andy could not understand what he was saying. *"Tobacco—you like tobacco?"* The Indian looked up and nodded slightly, before dropping his eyes again to the floor. *"I give you tobacco and things for the women."* The man continued, *"Things to cook with, blankets and beads. They will like it! It will bring you honour. I will honour you in front of the other men!"*

Badger was listening carefully, but he did not say anything, his eyes still fixed on the floor.

Surprised by what had just happened, Andy asked the man, "You speak his language?"

"A little," Rowand responded, without paying any attention to him. Still looking at the Indian, he continued. *"Do you hear what I say? You go? Do as I ask? I give you good gifts, smoke, maybe a fire-stick!"* His voice was loud and his manner gruff, and Badger shrank back in his seat. Giving the young Indian a moment to think about it, Rowand spoke again. *"You do as I ask? I will give you gifts!"*

Looking up at the man only briefly, Badger grunted, *"Yes,"* and again looked down.

Andy had never seen him so withdrawn and wondered what was wrong. *"We do?"* he asked his friend.

Making eye contact with Andy, the Indian just shrugged his shoulders and grunted, *"Yes."*

"That's great," Rowand said, standing up and reaching out his hand toward the white boy. "Welcome to the Company."

Andy was puzzled. "You understand his language!" he exclaimed.

"Just a bit. Enough to know he's with us," Rowand said, still holding his hand out to Andy.

"All right," Andy said uncertainly. Standing and taking the man's hand, he shook it firmly. "There's already some of them coming to the fort. They should be here in a couple of days," he announced confidently, as Badger stood up and moved over beside him. "Do they count?"

"How's that?" Rowand asked.

"We came on ahead, him and me, an' the others. The rest of them are comin' along behind, to trade."

The man nodded his head knowingly, "Very good then! We'll see how well you do.

"Meantime, you need some clothes," Rowand exclaimed. "You both need 'em, an' get the hell out of those injun things." Walking to the door, he opened it and hollered for Hathaway. When he arrived, a moment later, the factor told him, "The boys'll be with us for a bit. Get 'em each a set o' duds, but first, take 'em out to the trough and get 'em clean."

"Yes, sir. What do I tell the men?"

"Tell 'em nothin'! I'll tell 'em what they need to know at evening meal. Leave 'em t' me." Turning back to the boys, Rowand said to Andy, "Samuel here'll fix yuh up with some proper duds. You wait out here," he said, leading them to a door at the back of the room. Opening it, he ushered the boys into a small room, stacked to the ceiling with bales of furs. "Go through here an' out that door an' wait 'til he comes with your duds," he ordered them.

The boys walked through the room, and Andy pushed on the other door. It opened into a yard between two buildings. Bounded on the back by the stockade and on the front by a rail fence, it held Badger's horse, as well as three other fine-looking mounts. Complaining about the loss of their other horses to the Cree, they waited for several minutes before Hathaway returned with the clothes.

"Skin off and get into the water, then," he said gruffly. "There's the trough." Andy walked over and inspected it. The water was clear, but sediment covered the bottom. Pulling his shirt off, he hesitated at his breechclout. "Do you hafta watch us?" he asked, seeing that the man was staring.

"Someone's gotta watch the injun. You guys ain't got nuttin' I ain't already seen before. Get along now!"

"What does he say?" Badger asked his friend.

"We bathe," Andy informed his friend, making the gesture of scrubbing himself, pointing to the trough.

Both boys stripped off and took turns in the trough, nervous because of Hathaway staring at their nakedness. Wiping the water off his skin when he was done, Badger picked up the company clothes and inspected them suspiciously before awkwardly getting into them. He observed that they were the most uncomfortable things he had ever worn, and Andy had to agree. The pants were wool and immediately began to irritate their skin. Andy made sure he retrieved their soft leather garments and kept them with him.

"Yuh done?" Hathaway asked.

"I reckon so," Andy replied.

"Aw right then. At least the injun don't stink so bad! You wait in here." Hathaway growled and stepped away from the door for them to enter the storeroom.

"He doesn't stink as bad as you!" Andy muttered as they stepped inside, wondering what was going to happen next.

The door slammed shut behind them, and he was surprised when he recognized the sound of a bar being placed over it. Stepping through the small room, they entered the spacious room where they had spoken with Rowand, who was no longer present. In a moment, Hathaway walked through the front door, having come around the building. Crossing the room, he picked up a couple of blankets that had been sitting on the chair Andy had sat upon.

"Here! Put these in there," he ordered, tossing them to Andy and nodding his head to indicate he should put them into the small room. Following them to the door, he ushered them inside. "Holler if you need anything!" he uttered. Stepping back quickly, he closed the door on them, and they heard a bar being placed across it. Trying it at once, Andy found that it too had been barred.

"Hey! Open the door!" he cried, pounding on the door. "What're you doing?" There was no reply. When they heard the outer door close, they knew the man had left. Groping his way through the sudden darkness, Andy tried the outside door and found, as he had suspected, that it was barred from the outside. He was angry to discover that they had been locked in.

"*Dog!*" he cursed. Pounding on the door with his fists, he yelled, "Hey! Let us outta here! Open up!" There was no indication that anyone had heard.

"*What is happening? What are they doing to us?*" the Indian asked nervously. "*Are we in danger? I do not even have my weapons!*"

"*No, I...I do not know.*" Andy was upset over being treated in such a manner.

Badger was nervous. "*What are they going to do to us? I do not like this! I cannot get out!*" he exclaimed, testing the doors and walls and beginning to pace. Each one sensed the other's tension and became more and more agitated. The only light came from the cracks around the outside door, but it was enough that they could eventually make out their surroundings. Indignant, they continued to gripe. While his companion prowled nervously, Andy pounded on both doors and yelled for Rowand, but got no response.

Tired of yelling, all they could do was sit on the blankets and talk and eventually lie down to sleep. Sometime in the night, someone opening the door awakened them. Neither one could see who held the lantern as a bucket was kicked inside, and a couple of pieces of dried meat were tossed at them. The door closed as quickly as it had been opened, before they could react. "Let us out! We gotta pee!" Andy scrambled to his feet and rushed the door, pounding it with his fists.

"Shut up! You'll wake the dead," a strange voice replied through the door. "That's what the bucket's for."

"I need to talk to Mr. Rowand!" Andy shouted.

"He ain't here!" came the reply.

"Go and get 'im! I need to speak to 'im!" Andy demanded angrily. They heard the outer door close, and further shouting brought no response. Feeling around on the floor, they found the scraps of meat and ate, grumbling, before returning to a fitful sleep.

11

The captive pair were awake to see the light beginning to show through the cracks around the outside door. When Badger heard the crowing of roosters, he shrieked, *"What is that!"* He had been up and pacing, feeling very nervous, and the strange sound jolted him.

With a chuckle, Andy explained, "They are birds! *Birds,"* he said again, in the language of his friend. *"Birds—we see yesterday."*

"Ah," Badger replied, although he did not remember seeing anything he thought might sound like that. He was very nervous—he had never been confined before. Behind solid walls and doors, it reminded him of being a cave. The more he paced, the more upset he got, testing the doors continually and searching for a way out.

Andy had resigned himself to their captivity, believing that they would soon be released, and he was right. As soon as he heard someone enter the outer room, he got ready for the bar to be lifted. When the door began to open, he hit it—with Badger right behind him—both spilling out into the room, almost bowling Hathaway over. "Whoa!" exclaimed the man. "What're yuh doin'?"

"Why did you lock us in there?" Andy blurted angrily. "Where's Mr. Roland? We're gettin' outta here!"

"He said the injun had to be locked up!" Hathaway said, flustered. "An' you said you was gonna stay with him! Whadda yuh expect?"

"What do you think? We're robbers? Where's Mr. Roland! I wanna speak to him!"

"Hold yer horses, boy! I's comin' to git yuh t' have some grub with 'im. Come on with me—an' it's Rowand, not Roland! You better get that right! And, sir 'im lots."

Fuming, Andy turned to Badger and said, *"Come, we eat... see, uh, see chief."* He let Hathaway lead them across the yard to another building. There were just a few men on the walls, and the main gate was standing wide open. Upon entering the other building, the boys understood why there had been nobody in the yard; all were inside, eating. As soon as the door opened, the din of conversation ceased, and every eye was upon them. Andy would have preferred the curiosity of the Indians to the suspicious contempt in the eyes of these men. They all glowered at Badger as the pair moved to where the factor was sitting, alone.

A murmur of discontent was silenced by Rowand, who stood up and roared, "These boys dam' well work for me! You get it? Both of 'em! You leave 'em t' hell be! I'm gonna have the injun watched as long as he's inside these walls, which won't be bloody long! See to it that none of you touches 'em, or you'll be answering to me!" Turning to the boys, he softened his tone and pointed to a big pot on the stove, saying, "There's your grub. Get to it!"

Badger followed his friend to the pot. Not realizing what the stove was, he touched it and burned his hand, bringing mockery from those who saw it. At once, the room returned to its previous din as Andy picked up a filthy piece of cloth to remove the lid.

Inside, they found a thick layer of grease atop what turned out to be a stew. Using a big ladle that stood in it, the white boy took a banged-up metal bowl and filled it for Badger, filling another for himself. He picked up two spoons and plopped one into each bowl before returning to Rowand's table, sitting across from him on a wooden bench.

Watching Andy apply the spoon to his meal, Badger attempted to do the same. He had never used a metal spoon, being more familiar with one made from a buffalo horn or one carved of bone. Usually, he ate with his fingers and quickly resorted to doing so, picking whatever he could out of the broth, which he then sipped from the bowl. Those who saw him snickered.

Before eating, Andy scolded the factor. "I didn't appreciate being locked in that room last night! Is that how you treat people who work for you?" he said boldly.

"Now, boy, what the hell was I to do?" the man replied, his tone condescending. "Didn't you tell me you preferred to stay with the injun? I offered you a dam' bunk, but hell no, you said you'd spend the night in the cellar with the injun. At least I didn't putcha in the cellar!" His voice now became more sinister. "You can fend for yourself on the outside if you like, but as long as the injun's inside these walls, he's under guard an' locked up. Yuh got that?"

The man's forcefulness cooled Andy's temper a little. "Yes, sir," he said, "I reckon we'll be leavin' today, then."

"Suit yourself. You work for me now. Remember that!"

"Yeah, I reckon I'll just do my job like you asked me to. I think I'll live with him," Andy said, nodding in Badger's direction. "That'll suit me better."

"Have it yer way, kid. You just get 'em comin' here to trade. Didn't you say you had some of 'em on their way here now?"

"Yeah, maybe we'll ride out to meet 'em."

"That'll be fine by me. We'll getcha set up with some tobacco and other gifts and some things for their women."

"An' we're not wearin' these things, either!" Andy grumbled, tugging at the clothes he had been given. "My legs feel like they're gonna fall off!" Rowand just shrugged and kept eating.

They continued in silence until Rowand, gnawing at a bone, motioned toward Badger and asked Andy, "Whadda yuh know 'bout his people?"

"Not much, I reckon. I just know they've treated me a sight better than these guys," he responded, nodding at those seated around them. "I kinda like 'em. They've treated me pretty good."

"Maybe they treat you pretty good, kid, but they don't take too kindly to any of the other injuns 'round here."

Andy thought instantly of the attack upon the Cree and his brother, and what the *Káínaa* had done to Wolf Tail and his brothers, but he responded defensively. "I wouldn't know about that."

"Well, let me tell you, boy! Those dam' Blackfoot 're at war with every bloody tribe around 'em. None o' their dam' neighbours can live at peace with 'em 'cause they're always raidin' an' stealin' an' killin' an' scalpin'. Your bloody pecunnies 're more interested in war and stealin' horses than givin' their women any o' the good things we got for 'em. We've tried to get 'em to trap for us and bring us decent pelts, and they can't be the least bloody bit bothered. Only thing we can interest 'em in is guns an' tobacco...an' the liquor yer old man hates so much."

"And I hate it, too!" Andy snapped at him.

"Now, why the hell would you say that? Even Jesus made a little wine fer 'is friends! An' it was probably pretty good stuff, too! Anyway, they come in here wantin' a little something to lighten their spirits an' we give it to 'em. They don't have much in the way of a life, yuh know—they're a dour bloody lot! Don't get to enjoy life atall, less it's killin' an' raisin' hell! Can't seem t' ever have any fun, like we do, so we indulge 'em with a little libation to make their life a little better."

Andy wondered what this man could be talking about, recalling the wonderful times he had seen his Indian hosts enjoying, remembering Wolf Tail and the splendour of his dance and his father's generosity, recalling their humour—always looking for ways to play jokes on others. They seemed to enjoy a much better disposition than the men with whom he was eating, and he wondered how much Rowand really knew about them.

"Have you ever lived with 'em?" Andy asked.

"Have I ever lived with 'em?" Rowand exclaimed sarcastically. "Hell! I've lived with 'em most o' my life! An' I live with 'em all around me, boy! Every day! Spent years out here, and the other houses—travelled all over. Bin to the salt chuck an' I've seen 'em all; a helluva lot more than you, kid. Damn, I've seen 'em steal us blind! I've seen 'em kill each other over nuthin' at all. An' kill anyone that comes in their way. They're downright bloody nasty to us when we try to trade with some of the tribes across the mountains—want to keep it all fer themselves. Want to keep any other injuns from gettin' guns so's they'll always be able to whip 'em." Rowand paused for a moment to chew something before continuing, "That's why I like yer old man out there so much! His preachin' or whatever he says to 'em has a real good effect. Calms 'em right down!"

Rowand's unexpected compliment toward Andy's father took the edge off the boy's feistiness. "Yeah, well, I've sure never seen 'em like you say. They sure haven't locked me up, anyway," he responded.

"Yeah, well, maybe that's just 'cause a scrawny little, white-ass kid don't pose much of a threat to 'em. You just be careful, kid! They'll stick an arrow through you an' that fair hair o' yers'll be hangin' off some buck's coup stick!" Rowand warned, pushing himself away from the table. "I gots work to do," he muttered, by way of excusing himself, and walked over to one of the men at another table. After speaking quietly to him, the two returned together. "This is Mitterand. He doesn't speak much English. Just French an' Cree—an' a little Blackfoot. You don't leave his dam' sight as long as you have that injun inside these walls. You got it?"

"Yeah, I got it," Andy said curtly, standing up. "We're leaving right now, anyway. Do you know if they got our horses? An' you said you were gonna give us some stuff?"

"Suits me," Rowand replied. Turning to Mitterand, he told him to show them where their horses were. Next, he spoke to Hathaway, who by then was putting back his meal at another table. Hathaway was instructed to put together some items for Andy to take to the Indians he had said he was expecting. Returning his attention to the boy, he said, "Tell your injun friends that these are gifts from me. Be sure to tell 'em that I'm ycr friend an' I got more gifts for 'em when—"

"Gifts! Right!" Andy muttered sarcastically.

"Damn you, boy!" the big man roared angrily. "This is my dam' ship, and you'll dam' well do as I tell you! You dam' well lose that attitude, or I'll give yuh both to the Cree! You got that?" he yelled, red in the face and the veins sticking out on his neck. The room had fallen silent at the outburst, and the men once again stared. Badger looked around nervously and edged closer to his friend.

"I guess so," Andy responded sullenly, not sure he was doing the right thing by going to work for a fellow like this. But it seemed like the only way to get to his father. He saw no other option.

"All right then," the man settled down and continued where he had left off. "When they get here, give the tobacco to the head man. Tell 'im you expect he'll know best how to share it with the others. Find out who his wives are and give 'em some of the beads an' yard goods. Tell 'em we got metal pots, blades an' points, an' lotsa things they c'n use. I'm countin' on yuh, boy. This is your chance!"

"Wives?" Andy asked.

"Yeah! Bloody wives!" the man snapped. "If he's a chief, he'll have a bunch of wives! I thought you lived with 'em!" Without waiting for a response, Rowand put an end to the conversation by heading for the door. The boys followed with Mitterand and Hathaway, who grumbled about having to leave his meal.

After letting the boys pick up their horses, which they were happy to discover had appeared overnight, Mitterand led the pair to a long, low building with chimneys on each end, high windows, and holes bored through the log walls. Puzzled by the holes, Andy asked what they were. "They're fer shootin' injuns when we gotta. Wait here!" Hathaway responded, before disappearing inside the building, calling Mitterand to help him.

Left alone, the boys observed those on the walls watching them closely, guns in hand. Some of the men from the eating hall were starting to file out into the yard, glaring at Badger while they went about their business.

Waiting a long time for Hathaway, the boys wondered what was keeping him when he suddenly appeared with his hands full. He carried a couple of bulky leather sacks, joined in the middle, and Mitterand followed with another bulging sack. Setting the leather bags on the ground, the factor's deputy listed their contents, "Tobacco, ball, powder, some cloth, a couple o' pots, an' some other things fer their women—knives an' things." Mitterand carefully handed Hathaway the sack he had been carrying. "Sugar!" he announced, holding it out for Andy to heft before taking it and stuffing it into the top of one of the big leather bags. "Be sure to give the 'baccy to the chief. Give 'im it an' the sugar. Tell 'im to give it out right away. Be sure to tell 'im it's from the trader and have 'im give it out first. Once he's giv' out the sugar, you give 'im the rest o' the stuff and tell 'im to give it to his people. Let him decide, yuh got that?"

"Yeah, tobacco, and then the sugar to the chief to give out, then the rest of the stuff. It's all from him," Andy confirmed, anxious to be gone.

"An' tell 'im we got lots more stuff for 'im when 'e gets in here."

"That's it? No liquor?"

"Kid, do you think we'd give you any of that stuff? The old man says you're just like a preacher! You just watch your scalp! Bring your horses to the gate, and we'll letcha out."

"He said we'd get muskets. What about the muskets?"

"Not this trip, kid! See how yuh do with this stuff."

"We need our other clothes," Andy demanded.

"Couldn't have yuh lookin' like you was human, could we?" Hathaway muttered.

"And, my friend's bow and arrows!" Andy demanded. "And his knife!"

"Yeah, yeah!" the man continued. They followed him to retrieve their things while Mitterand waited with the horses. Finding their buckskin clothes in the room where they had been confined, they changed quickly, while the man retrieved Badger's weapons. Andy brought the company clothes with him when they left and tied them onto his saddle. He figured he might give them away—a gift of his own.

As they were about to leave, he remembered Badger's narrow escape the day before. "Will we be all right out there?" he asked Hathaway. "What about those Indians who went after him?"

"Better not have to worry 'bout 'em! One Poun' One had 'em bawled out yesterday—when they fetched your horses. Told 'em this one's his messenger and they'd better leave 'im be. They're all ascared of 'im now, an' buggered off." Approaching the gate, he looked up to a man on the wall. "All clear?"

"Mostly gone!" came the reply. "Open 'er up!"

"Open up!" Hathaway repeated the order to the man on the gate, who lifted the heavy bar. The gate swung open, and once it was wide enough, Andy stepped toward the opening, but Badger grabbed him by the arm.

"*What about the Liars?*" he asked, reaching for his bow.

"They are gone!" his friend assured him and paid so little attention to his concern that the Indian wondered if he had heard him.

"The almighty watch over yuh boy," Hathaway said, watching the boys hop onto their mounts. Andy was surprised that he would say such a thing.

"They are gone!" Badger observed, as soon as the gate swung shut behind them. He had already taken his bow off his shoulder, anticipating trouble, and now put it back.

"Yes. *Chief say*...I don't know. Yeah, they're gone."

"Where are we going?"

"Find friends, take gifts to chief."

"We should go this way, then," said Badger, asserting his leadership and heading his horse to where they had left the others.

"Yeah, let's hope they're still around! I hope they're all right!"

Glad to be leaving the fort, the boys kicked their horses and headed off to find their comrades. Finding the trail where they had parted company, Badger pointed out how their tracks from the day before had been obliterated by many others. *"It is probably the Liars, leaving,"* he suggested. He, too, was hoping the others were all right.

After following the trail for some time, Andy began to worry that their friends may have encountered the Cree. Fearing the worst, he suggested they turn back. Badger wanted to keep going, but when he took his bow off his shoulder and placed an arrow in it, Andy became even more nervous. *"They have not turned off the trail yet,"* Badger assured him; he had his eyes glued to the trail.

Andy was getting ready to insist that they turn around, when suddenly, from the dense brush beside them, someone yelled, *"Hai!"* His heart stopped. Badger whirled around, drawing his bow, when they both saw a solitary figure arise from the cover.

Pulling up his startled horse, Badger cried, *"Hai, it is him!"* as White Quill, stepped out onto the trail. Looking around expectantly and finding no sign of the others, Badger asked, *"Where are the others?"*

White Quill answered, *"They are in there somewhere."* Turning, he pointed with his lips behind him. *"They got a girl!"* he said, approaching his curious friends. At once, they could see that he was wearing only one legging, and he had an angry wound on his thigh.

"What is that?" Andy asked, alarmed. Badger wondered the same thing.

"All those Liars came this way—they must have all left or something. That fellow, he said that Raven had showed him in a dream a good spot to lie in wait—so he looked for it, and we did. He told us, 'Wait here,' so we hid in the bushes to see what would happen. We waited, and they all came. There were a lot of them—too many. We could not do anything! There were too many of them!

"After they had all gone by, he said, 'Wait! There are still more.' And sure enough, we heard someone coming. They were coming fast—probably they were hurrying to catch up, and they were not keeping a good lookout. And, when he said, 'Now!' we all jumped up and just started attacking them—letting our arrows go. He says it was a family, maybe. I think I hit one of them, but then someone got me here—it went right through." He stuck his leg out for his friends to see. Andy dismounted to have a better look.

"Doesn't it hurt—*it hurt?"*

"No!" the boy replied, but when Andy exclaimed that it looked like it hurt, he conceded, *"Maybe a little!"* But the Indian was not going to be distracted from his story. *"It really did not hurt that much. At first, I did not even realize what it was. It just felt like being hit when someone throws a stone at you, really hard. Anyway, when I looked down, I did not see anything, because I had my legging on, and I wondered, 'Ki-yah! What was that?' And, so I just pulled out another arrow and kept going.*

"It was just about over. There was a man and his wife, and they had a couple of sons and this girl. She is probably about my age—no, your age—so of course, they made sure they did not hurt her.

"Those Liars did not know what was happening! We just let our arrows go and go, and then Night Shoot came out, swinging that fire-stick thing. It did not work like it was supposed to, and he just used it as a club, and he hit those boys with it. But that Sits in the Middle—he went straight for the girl and grabbed her, and he just held her down and did not let her get away.

"You know why they did that, do you?" Badger asked, flashing a knowing grin, but they could both tell from the puzzled look on Andy's face that he did not understand.

The wounded boy explained, "They are in there right now, doing sex with her! They said we should all do sex from her, but I said I was not going to do that because I made a vow to my mother and my sister not to do that. They laughed at me and tried to get me to, but that is something I take very seriously—my vow! You might think I am a nothing one, but that is important to me!"

Badger commented, "But that is what warriors do, I thought!" Looking at White Quill, he asked, "Is that not what everybody says? You capture an enemy girl, and she is yours to do what you want with!"

"Yes, but not me!" the young warrior vowed resolutely. "You can if you like."

"Not me!" Andy joined him in his resolve. The white boy had his own reasons for steering clear of that sort of thing. His father had pointed out strange words in his Bible, warning against it. Although it had always been a favourite subject among his friends, back home, none had ever had the opportunity. Free in this wild land from the influences which had always constrained him, though, the allure was a temptation. But he sided with White Quill and chose to heed his father's advice. He just shook his head. "I shouldn't."

"You do not want to?" the injured boy asked him.

"No!"

"What are we going to do now, then?" Badger wondered, sounding disappointed. *"Do we wait for them? What are we supposed to do?"*

"I have been waiting for you!" said White Quill. *"I am not waiting around here any longer! Who knows how long they will be? And, I do not want to be with them when they bring that girl into camp—my mother and my sister will think I have been doing sex with her, and I do not want that! I want to head back across the river and find our people."*

"We do?" Andy looked at Badger, who just shrugged his shoulders, disappointment on his face.

Returning to the river below the fort, they found the bar and crossed without incident. They spent the night on the trail and encountered the rest of the camp the next evening.

"What have you been doing, my son?" cried White Quill's mother, when she saw his injury. There was dismay in her voice.

"They—not these ones,"—he began, nodding toward his two companions— *"those other ones found some Liars and attacked them. I guess I got hit."*

"My son, I wish you would not do that! You are too young to make war!" his mother scolded. *"Let me have a look at your leg! I wish you would stay away from those boys! That one, the son of Crane with Many Horses—he is a troublemaker!"*

"Well, you should be proud of me, mother!" her son responded flatly. *"They captured a Liar girl, but I did not do anything with her. They all did, but I just left—we all left. None of us did anything with her."*

"Ah! That is good! You are such a good boy!" his mother crowed. *"Get off your horse then, and let me give you a hug!"* she ordered. Her son was happy to oblige, letting her make a fuss over him for a moment before she turned her attention to his leg. *"I want you*

to see the old woman and get her to do something with this before it goes bad! You know her! If you do not get it fixed up, it will go bad. She will put something on it, and it will heal."

"Hey!" Andy exclaimed. *"Go—I take gifts—to man.*

"No," the injured boy did not like that suggestion. *"I want to see too! I will do this after. Let us go find his father!"* Andy had not let his friends open anything up, thinking it was his responsibility to deliver everything intact.

Crane With Many Horses saw them approaching and stood to greet them. Alarmed that his son was not with them, his face showed concern. Badger saw it and assured him, *"Your son is all right! They did not come back with us. I think he is going to be at the napikawan camp when you get there."* He did not wish to give any more detail than that. The man nodded and appeared relieved, and it was Andy's turn to speak.

Haltingly, he announced, *"Me at napikawan camp—Chief give, uh...these uh, things...oh, yeah, gifts...gifts—you and...woman."* Lifting the bags off his horse and setting them on the ground in front of him, he opened the flap and said, *"Napikawan chief give, uh,* I don't remember, oh—tobacco"—handing the tobacco to the man— "sugar,"—he handed the sack to him— *"and—"*

"Kyai-yo! What is this?" the man exclaimed, interrupting him. *"I think I know what this is!"* he continued with delight, feeling something inside the sack of sugar. Those who had gathered watched while he handed the tobacco off to another and worked at opening the sugar. Plunging his hand into the bag and feeling around, he pulled out a small jug, carelessly spilling much of the sugar onto the ground at his feet. *"I am right—it is the napiohke!"* he exclaimed, holding the jug up for those around him to see. *"A very good gift! Thank you, my son!"*

Rowand had surely known that Andy would never deliver liquor and must have instructed Hathaway to conceal it in the sugar. Andy felt stupid! *"Tell your chief that we have much dried meat to trade for more of this!"* Crane with Many Horses said enthusiastically, clasping him by his shoulder. Removing the plug from the jug with his teeth, he spat it away and held the jug aloft, crying, *"My friends! This is just a little taste, for now! Come! Have some!"* Tipping the bottle to his lips, he took considerably more than just a little taste. *"Augh!"* he gasped, wiping his mouth on his sleeve and making a face, before passing the jug to the nearest out-stretched hand. In no time, it was empty, and he addressed those around him. *"Soon, friends, our hearts will be light! Our women will need to be lively! Let us make ourselves ready to trade!"* Turning again to Andy, he said, *"What more have you got for us? Do you have any more of that?"*

Disheartened, the white boy just dumped the remaining items from the bags. "Just some other stuff for your stupid wives," he muttered angrily, spitting the words out and turning away disappointed.

Seeing that he was downcast, White Quill urged, *"Come! My leg hurts. I must get it fixed."* He led the others to the healer—an old medicine woman. When he recognized her lodge, he pounded on the leather cover and hollered, *"Old woman! Are you there? I need you!"*

"What do you want of me?" came an ancient voice from inside.

"I have been wounded! Do you have something for my wound?" White Quill replied. Shortly, the woman stuck her head out, revealing her gray hair and wrinkled face.

"White Quill! Not you! What have you done to yourself?" she exclaimed, looking him up and down, her eyes finally resting on his injured leg. Without lifting her eyes, she approached him and asked, *"Who are your friends?"*

"This one is Míísinsski. He is from Napi-tahta," he replied. Nodding his head toward Andy, he continued, *"This one is Sun Shines on Him. I have taken him as my brother."* Which was the first Andy had heard of it.

When she looked up to examine his friends, White Quill gave her a brief account of what had happened. *"You boys are too young to make war!"* she scolded, pounding him on the chest with the end of her small fist. *"Why do you want to die so young? Who is going to look after us old ones if you young ones keep going off and getting killed? Who is going to bring buffalo for us to eat? You should stay at home and look after us!"*

"I know, I know," White Quill tried to mollify the old woman, rolling his eyes for his friends. *"I will bring you all the buffalo you want! Do you have anything to fix my leg?"* he persisted.

"What about the others? Are you hurt?" she asked Badger, who just shook his head. Turning to Andy, she asked, *"And what about you, Sun Boy?"* He, too, shook his head, standing stiffly as she stepped toward him. Looking him over carefully, she turned abruptly and headed toward her lodge. *"Come in here!"* she commanded.

Inside, rummaging around in sacks piled at the back of her lodge, the old woman began to sing and continued softly while she brought a couple of pouches to where her young patient waited. Closing her eyes now, she broke into prayer. *"Sun, have pity on your poor servant and let her help this boy! She knows him, and he is a good boy. And he is so young! They are all so young!*

"Great Sun, you have given us life! You have given us the buffalo, who give us our every need, and we thank you for being so good to us! You have given your servant long life and she thanks you for that. Every day she thanks you for it. Great Sun, now let her have your power for this boy, that he might be healed. Sun, have pity on us, your people. Make these boys strong and keep them safe from harm. Make them want to care for us old people. Sun, I ask your healing power." With her head bowed, the old woman remained motionless and continued to mutter something which none of the others could make out.

Finished, she kept her head bowed for a moment before looking up to speak. *"I must make a potion that you must keep on the wound. Do not get it wet! If it comes off, you must come and see me!"* Turning away, she knelt and began mixing together a few items from different pouches, spitting, from time to time, into the mixture. *"Where did you find Sun Boy?"* she asked as she worked, lifting her head periodically to look at him. White Quill let Badger tell his story, and she stopped what she had been doing to sit back on her heels and listen. *"He is a pretty one!"* she observed when he was done. Turning back to the injured boy, she applied the moist, green poultice to his wound, binding it with a soft piece of leather.

"There!" she said as she finished, *"Do not get it wet—and come and see me tomorrow. I will put more of this on it. Now you may go."* The potion started to burn as they took their leave.

"It is burning!" White Quill exclaimed.

"Hai-ya! What are you—a child?" the woman scolded.

"I will bring you one of the horses we captured," White Quill offered, stepping toward the door.

"No! You do not need to do that! You are only boys! Keep your horses! I do not want you to have to go around capturing horses just so you can give them to me when you get hurt! Just bring me nitapi waksin."

"I will! Thank you, old woman!" the young Indian said to her.

"Look after that pretty boy!" cried the old woman as they left her.

"Pretty Boy!" Badger exclaimed. *"We should have called him Pretty Boy!"*

12

The camp reached the North Saskatchewan River two days later, but not many crossed over to camp near the fort. Most remained on a flat not far from the river, before crossing the next morning. It was midday before the people began setting up outside the fort.

Andy and his friends found a place to sit and watch the activity. As soon as the women had finished setting up the lodges, they began putting together what the men would be trading at the fort. Andy walked around to see what they were packing—mostly hides and dried meat. Wishing to impress Rowand, when it looked like they were almost ready for trade, he headed for the fort to let him know.

As he neared the gate on foot, he noted figures with guns watching him from the walls. "It's the white kid!" one of them hollered to someone inside. "It's clear!" He heard the heavy bar being removed from inside the gate, and it slowly swung open, just enough for Hathaway to slip out.

"They ready to trade, boy?" he asked.

"Yes, sir. Go easy on the liquor, will you?"

"Shore will, boy—just as you say. You give 'em the stuff?"

"Yup, except we lost the sugar somewhere."

"What!" Hathaway exclaimed until he saw Andy's smirk. "Oh! Right—go fetch 'em in here then!"

"Dog!" Andy muttered to himself and turned back toward the camp. He heard the gate shut and the bar fall into place behind him.

A group of Indians had already set out from their camp, afoot, leading pack animals. Four mounted warriors led the procession, their faces painted; each of them carried a firearm at the ready. Andy had not expected anything like this—he had thought he would be the one to introduce Crane with Many Horses to Rowand. It turned out the Indians had something else in mind. Sits in the Middle was beside his father. Andy and his friends had not seen him arrive at the camp. His face painted, he was leading his father's pack animals. Four more young men, their weapons also at the ready, flanked them. Still farther back, others followed, leading packhorses. Seeing the procession, Andy waited near the gate, wondering how it was all going to turn out.

Crane with Many Horses stopped a short distance from him and surveyed the imposing structure, a look of anticipation upon his face. Catching the eye of those warriors standing out in front of him, he grinned and gave a nod. On his signal, the warriors raised their guns and fired into the air, startling Andy just as he was about to speak. Ducking, he whirled around to see what had gone wrong. At once, the rest of the warriors discharged their firearms and began singing. In response, the two brass cannon were discharged, their resounding report returning from the river valley and their smoke painting a ribbon on the slight breeze. There was a whoop from both sides of the wall, and the big gate creaked open.

Crane with Many Horses strode for it eagerly, leaving Andy to fall in beside him. Quickly falling in step with Sits in the Middle, Andy asked him, *"Why shoot fire-stick?"*

"They are now empty! It tells them that we come in peace, and the big mouth fire-sticks tell us we will be safe," the Indian replied, gesturing toward the cannon. *"There will be no fighting!"* He was watching anxiously to see what was going to happen as they followed his father cautiously through the gate. Andy walked slightly behind him.

Inside, in the main yard, Rowand was waiting for them. He wore a top hat, a white shirt and tie, and a dark suit with brightly polished brass buttons. Walking forward to Crane with Many Horses, he held out his hand to the Indian and said, *"Oki!"* He then turned to Hathaway, who stood beside him, similarly dressed.

"He is called Rowand," Hathaway announced. *"Your people call him Big Mountain."*

Andy was surprised to find that Hathaway's Blackfoot was just as good as Rowand's. He wondered how many others spoke it.

Crane with Many Horses turned to his son, who cleared his throat and spoke up nervously, *"He is called Crane with Many Horses."* He was behaving in a much more subdued manner than Andy had ever seen him—he looked downright timid. With that, his father faced the factor, and the two men shook hands.

Rowand then spoke with a loud voice, using perfect Blackfoot, *"We are much honoured that you have come to visit us! I welcome you!*

"My men and I are here to serve you and your people and to treat you well! Many gifts we have, which we would like to give you in gratitude for coming such a very great distance—to trade with us. I trust my young friend here has already given you some of my gifts."

Crane with Many Horses responded, saying, *"Yes! Indeed, we have travelled far to visit you! It was a long and difficult journey! I wish we did not have to travel so far—the journey is long and hard for our horses and women. You should make your camp closer to ours—to make it easier for us!"* Rowand nodded politely, and the Indian continued. *"We are honoured, however, that you have sent your gifts with this boy, who is a friend to my son here. We are happy that you treat us so well! It is good for us to meet together like this to show our people that we honour one another."*

Rowand responded, *"We have been busy getting ready for you to arrive. And we have many fine things for you and your women!*

"Come now! First, let us smoke together! And then, I will show you some of the things we have for you," the factor said, before turning to lead the entourage toward the long, low building with the chimney at each end.

Andy now noticed that the gate had been shut silently behind them, leaving most of the Indians outside the wall—only a few of the leading men having been admitted. The guards atop the walls kept a watch on both sides, while Rowand led the party toward the trading house.

Standing just outside, one of the factor's men had been waiting for them. He was holding a large pipe, which he handed to Rowand. Gesturing for the Indians to sit on the ground, he sat down with them, showing great flair in the way he handled the pipe. In silence, it was lit and passed back and forth, each Indian nodding toward the factor as he finished his smoke, before handing the pipe to the next. Four times, they passed the pipe, following which it was returned to Rowand. He then handed it ceremoniously to his assistant and got to his feet. Taking Crane with Many Horses by the arm to help him up, he led him toward the door. *"Come. Let me show you what we have for you."*

Inside, he introduced his guests to a man behind the chest-high counter before moving over to speak to Andy. "I want you the hell outside!" he ordered. "Go out there and tell them other injuns that their chief is getting treated very well in here, and he is getting gifts from me. Here, give this to the buggers," he added, turning to snatch another rope of tobacco from the counter, handing it to Andy.

"They don't want liquor, you know," Andy tried to tell Rowand, who escorted him toward the door.

"Like hell they don't! You can just be dam' thankful we water the stuff down, so it don't affect them that much, boy. Fact is—they love it! Can't get enough of it! That's what they're here for this time o' year. They got nuthin' we really want—just the meat—those buffalo hides are bloody useless to us. You just watch out for that little white ass o' yurs, and we'll be all right." From the doorway, Rowand summoned someone to let him out the gate.

Outside, Andy delivered the message and the gift to those waiting and lingered to see if his friends would show up. Shortly, however, they heard the bar being removed from the gate, and it swung open. Sits in the Middle hurried out to fetch a couple of the other head men, who scrambled to their feet and returned with him.

There was a long wait before the big gate creaked open again, preceded by a clamour and loud voices, and the entire party of Indians now exited the fort. Inordinately lively and jovial, they lurched toward the others, and it was apparent that they were under the influence of alcohol. Most brandished small jugs or cups of the stuff, as they made their way through those waiting and headed back to their lodges. Even Sits in the Middle hugged a small jug, looking very pleased with himself.

For much of the rest of the day, the *Piikáni* marched up to the gate and waited to do their trading. Every man who returned from the fort seemed much pleased with how well he had been treated. Many went directly to their lodges with their merchandise. A few went to their friends, who mingled in groups throughout the camp. Not all had gotten liquor, but those who had, carried it about with them, either guarding it very carefully or handing it out liberally. Andy had learned that the Indians could not trade for the liquor—it was given out only as a gift, and he wondered why some had it, and others did not.

Sits in the Middle was met by his friends, and he set about trying to recruit Badger and White Quill to help him consume the treasured drink he had been given. When Andy saw what was happening, he intervened. *"No! No napiohke. Not drink!"* he cautioned them.

White Quill was supportive. *"His words are good!"* he agreed and tried to convince the others. *"You know what happens when people bring that stuff into our camp. Two of my brothers now travel the Sand Hills because of it—you know what happened to them!"* Badger remained silent and appeared indecisive.

"Míisinsski—come with us!" Sits in the Middle tried to persuade him, trying to separate him from the other two. *"We have that girl, and you should come with us! We are not boys like these ones! Come!"*

Badger looked at Andy, then at White Quill. *"No,"* he began, *"We have made a vow!"*

"A vow!" Sits in the Middle sneered. *"You are cowards!"* he ridiculed, looking the trio over disdainfully. *"No wonder you left!"* he taunted White Quill. *"You are afraid to sex a worthless Liar girl! We will see you little boys later!"* he mocked, turning away. His other friends scowled at them and followed their leader.

Andy gave a sigh of relief that it was over. Standing with his friends, they watched the others swagger off together.

"You will never catch me drinking that stuff! Let us get out of here!" White Quill urged and set out in the direction of the river, leading the other two.

He told them he had learned the *Liar* girl had been brought back to camp on the end of a rope. As they made their way down toward the river, he told the others what he had heard. *"They took her to someone called One-Eared Wolf,"* he informed them. *"That fellow is in the Braves Society. They told him they wanted to join that society. They said they would let the Braves have that girl if they would be allowed to join their society. They are too young for that society, so they would not let them! They now are going to keep her for when they drink their napiohke."* His companions just shook their heads.

At the river, they looked over the boats that lay along the beach, most overturned and resting on logs above the high-water mark. The Indian boys were disinterested, but as they were about to leave, Andy noticed something about one of the boats. *"Look!"* he cried. *"Look—this!"* He pointed out the very faded image of a woman someone had long ago etched onto the bow of one of the boats. "This is my boat!" he exclaimed. "This is the boat I came up the river in!" Excited, he wanted to examine it and show it to the others. *"Help me!"* he urged them. The vessel was extremely heavy, and even with a mighty effort, they could not manage to flip it onto its keel.

Intrigued to find it there, he got down on his hands and knees to peer underneath it. Crawling beside the gunwale to his usual position in the boat, he spotted something and cried, "Hey, look!" He had found the brass ring, fastened to the gunwale, to which he had once twisted a piece of wire. "That's my wire! That's where I hung my tin cup!" he exclaimed. While he marvelled over the fact that the boat was now at Edmonton House, his friends watched, bewildered, not understanding anything he was saying. "I'm gonna take it!" he said to himself, twisting the piece of wire loose and winding it onto his belt. Feeling some attachment to the vessel, he stood for a long moment looking it over before his friends tried to get him to move on.

"No! Hear me! This mine!" he tried to explain to them. *"This, this uh"*—realizing he knew no Blackfoot word to describe such a vessel, he continued— *"this thing."* Gesturing to indicate he was speaking of the boat, he told them, *"This me—uh, come here."* It

took some more explaining, but White Quill figured it out and explained it to Badger.

Next, Andy took one of the long and heavy oars nearby and hauled it over to an upright boat, putting the oar in place to show them how he had rowed. Still, his comrades showed little interest in what he was trying to show them and wanted him to come with them as they moved along. Looking over his shoulder at his boat, as they moved on down the shore, he murmured, "That's amazing it's here!"

They poked along the river's edge until they found a place to sit together, beside the water. There, White Quill surprised them by saying, *"I do not want to grow up! I do not want to be a warrior— not yet!"*

Badger said that he was going to be a warrior. Knowing him well enough by now, Andy said, *"Your words are dung!"* His friend became silent, and there was an awkward moment.

"Yes, what a fool I am!" Badger admitted, looking up and giving Andy a half-smile. Turning to White Quill, he confessed, *"My friend is right! He knows what a coward I am! I did not kill any Liars—when I found him. My words were no good! I have never killed anyone! I have seen it—my friends—right in front of me... That is why I do not want any part of it! I do not think I could ever do it! We are both alike, him and me."* He looked expectantly at Andy. *"I guess we will have no friends but each other!"*

Andy was surprised by his sudden candour. *"I like to hear— happy, I be your friend!"*

"Your words are good to my ears," White Quill exclaimed. *"I thought I was the only one!"*

"What do you mean? You have two scalps!" Badger was surprised.

"No! I told our friend the other day, I do not like it!" White Quill admitted to him. *"I wish I had never been there! I do not want to be a warrior—I wish I could still play—and be a boy, instead of having*

to swagger around and boast all the time and always be trying to make a name for myself!"

Badger was astonished! This was the fellow who was the envy of most of his peers. *"Are your words good?"* he exclaimed. *"I thought you were the big warrior!"*

"No! I told our friend! I do not want it!" He continued, *"But I do not dare to tell anyone! I will be made a fool if you tell anyone! A real nothing one! You cannot tell anyone!"*

"No!" Andy interjected. *"We not tell anyone!"* he said, turning to look sternly at Badger.

"I cannot believe it! You mean, you are not what everyone thinks you are?" Badger asked.

"Hai!" White Quill blurted in reply. *"I am food for the dogs if you would tell!"*

"I vow!" Badger assured him. *"I will not tell if you will not tell—you vow?"*

"I vow!" White Quill agreed readily. *"You vow?"* he said, turning to Andy.

"What? I do not understand."

"I vow! You know! A vow—a promise—do as you say!" Badger reminded him.

"Oh yeah—*Yes, vow. Yes! I vow."*

"We are brothers!" Badger exclaimed, holding up his hand.

"Brothers!" White Quill agreed, giving it a slap.

"Brothers!" Andy confirmed, lifting his hand.

The other two gave it a slap, and all together, they cried, *"Brothers!"*

Suddenly, though, White Quill gave a look of alarm, looking closely at Andy's bare chest. *"What is that?"* he interrupted them, suddenly very serious.

Startled by his sudden alarm, Andy missed what he was up to and looked to see what he was talking about. Catching him off guard, the Indian grabbed him by the nipples and squeezed until he howled, "Oww! Let go! Let go! —*have pity! I surrender!*" Badger watched with a look envy on his face.

"Help me!" Andy squealed. Instantly, the Indian pounced on White Quill, and there was a free-for-all. Laughing and giggling, they tumbled to the ground, wrestling.

Until, suddenly, Andy screeched in pain. "Ow—ow!" he moaned, getting to his feet and holding his hand. *"My hand!"* he groaned, bending over and cradling it gently between his knees, grimacing and moaning. Both Indians stopped their rough-housing and stood to figure out what had happened. "Ouuuchhh," the white boy wept, angrily turning his back toward them. Suddenly, he swatted them both in the crotch. "Gotcha!" he squealed with delight, taking off as fast as he could. The others gave chase, bent on sweet revenge.

Spotting a fallen tree trunk, sticking out into the water, Andy ran for it, snatching up a stick along the way. Quickly scampering out onto the log, he turned and used the stick to keep his pursuers at bay. *"You are a female dog! I will have your sack!"* White Quill threatened, picking up his own stick to poke back at Andy. Badger resorted to throwing rocks into the water, splashing them both. Seeing him do that, White Quill cast his stick away and joined him. Finding a rock so huge that he struggled under its weight, he heaved it toward his adversary, drenching him totally. Surrender was immediate.

"All right, all right, I give up!" Andy said, dripping wet. *"I come! I come! Have pity! I come! Have pity!"* he begged as he shuffled submissively along the wet log toward them. Reaching a dry spot, just out of reach of his two vengeful comrades, he stopped. *"My hand!"* he reminded them. The others responded with another barrage of rocks. *"Wait! Wait!"* the pale one pleaded. Having an idea, he stopped and bent over to slip off his moccasins. Tossing them to the shore, he quickly slipped off his breechclout and tossed it after his footwear. Turning to wag his bare backside at his audience, he headed down the log and leapt into the waist-deep water. *"Come!"* he shouted, wading into deeper water without looking back to see if they would follow.

The others were quiet for a moment before Andy heard them giggling and scampering out onto the log, and with a great splash, they were both upon him. Wrestling in and out of the water for a long time, they finally took time to wash the mud off before clambering out onto the muddy shore, where they continued to jostle while they dried off.

A sudden gunshot from the camp startled them, and in the quiet of the river valley, they became aware of a commotion going on near the fort. While they listened, a second gunshot, and then another alarmed them, and they wondered what they would find when they got back up there.

"We wait—and not go up there!" Andy cautioned.

"Why not sleep down here by the river?" White Quill suggested.

"Yes, let us get our things and come back down here," Badger agreed.

Warily, the trio returned to the camp. Nothing Andy saw when they got there reminded him of what he had seen previously in Indian camps. He was used to seeing people around the fires, cheerfully telling stories or drumming and dancing. Tonight, there was none of that.

Following White Quill in the direction of his mother's lodge, Andy saw people who were loud and arguing; there was a shoving match and yelling and pushing among those who watched. *"What is going on?"* White Quill murmured in a hushed tone.

"It is the napiohke!" their white friend asserted.

Not wishing to be seen, they ducked into the bush a couple of times to avoid rowdy groups of men and young men who crashed about the camp. They spotted an older man who had a young boy by the arm and was yelling and hitting him. Andy had never seen such a thing in the short time he had spent among the Indians and was taken aback. Shouting and shrieking and raised voices could be heard throughout the camp. A group of men hounded a girl, who was quite obviously trying to get away from them. No children or women were anywhere in sight.

Nearing White Quill's lodge, they encountered a man leaving it with two others. When White Quill stepped up to speak to him, the man became belligerent and abusive. Andy was not able to make out anything of what was being said, though the man was very loud.

White Quill was troubled when he returned to his friends. *"That is my father! He has put a curse on me! While we were down at the river, Elk Hollers in the Trees and Night Shoot came around, looking for my sister. My father is full of that drink, and he wants me to find her and bring her to him. I do not like it! I must speak to my mother—come!"* Turning, he hurried toward his mother's lodge.

At the door, he slapped the side of the lodge and announced his arrival, and that he had friends with him. *"Stay out!"* a woman's voice sobbed.

Recognizing his mother's voice, the boy pulled the flap aside and stepped inside. His companions thought it best to wait outside—until they heard him cry, *"What has happened? Who did this to you?"* Scrambling in behind their friend, they saw an older woman on her knees, weeping, being attended by a younger woman kneeling beside her. The older woman's face was battered, and her upper lip and chin were bloodied. No one seemed to mind that her dress had been ripped down to her waist, exposing pendulous breasts. Two small children cowered in the back of the lodge. *"Mother! What happened?"* White Quill persisted.

The younger woman answered for her. *"White Quill, you and your friends should not see this! You must leave until things settle down! Take your little brothers and find Pretty Bird! I will look after our mother."*

"No! Tell me who did this? Was it him?" White Quill demanded to know.

"Please!" his mother groaned. *"Leave him alone! He will get over it when he returns to his head."*

"It was him!" White Quill asserted, his voice low. *"He did this to you!"* he growled.

"He is in a very bad mood! Just leave him alone! Take your brothers and go find Pretty Bird!" the younger woman begged him. *"Your friends are after her!"*

"Please, my son, take your brothers"—his mother pleaded—*"and you must find your sister. They are after her!"*

"What are you telling me, mother?" White Quill fell to his knees in front of her, taking her hand. *"Who is after her?"*

"It is your wicked friends!" The younger woman spoke bitterly. *"They came in here earlier, with your father, wanting to take her away. They have somehow lost that Liar girl they brought back here, and now they want your sister. They had given your father napiohke, and he was ready to let them take her! Your mother tried to stop them, and this is what she gets!"*

"Those dogs! Why do they have to go after my sister? Where is she? Tell me where she is!" White Quill screamed.

"She ran! You must find her! I am certain they are after her!" his older sister whimpered. Their mother had got to her knees, sobbing and tugging at her dress to cover herself. As the boys turned to leave, a woman's scream pierced the darkness, outside, alarming them all.

"I will kill them! We must find her!" White Quill was seething and hurried from the lodge. Running from lodge to lodge, looking inside each one, he called her name. *"Tell me if you see them!"* he demanded of his friends, who followed without a word. Neither one had yet met his sister, so they had no idea who they were looking for, but watched anxiously for any sign of the others.

A sudden movement in the shadows startled them. A man, naked from the waist down, barely able to stay on his feet, was being assisted by a woman. It was all she could do to keep him from falling while he groped her and tried to kiss her. *"Can you help me?"* she begged, obviously not interested in the affection the man was trying to inflict upon her. Andy wanted to help but felt he had to follow his friend, who ignored her.

Near the edge of the camp, a figure suddenly lunged out of the bushes and grabbed hold of White Quill. *"My brother! You must help me!"* a girl uttered, clinging to his arm.

Embracing her, White Quill blurted, *"Where are they? Are you all right?"*

"Yes—I do not know! I have been hiding in the bush! I am afraid!"

"Quickly, into the bush before we are seen!" he told her, shepherding the girl back into the cover of the bush. Crouching, he turned to the others. *"This is my sister!"* he blurted. Turning to face her, he asked, *"What is happening?"*

"Our father is out of his mind! He is full of napiohke! Those dogs you call friends gave him some—so he would let them have me! I ran away! They are horny dogs! I hate him!"

"I will kill them!" White Quill snarled between clenched teeth. Seeing his sister eyeing his friends, he took a moment to introduce them. *"These are my friends,"* he told her. *"You can trust them! They will look after you. I must get our brothers. You stay here and keep her safe!"* he said to his friends. *"Do not let anyone touch her!"* he demanded urgently. *"I will be back!"* Turning immediately, with only a glance back at them, he ran for his lodge.

When the familiar image of his home loomed in front of him, he heard his father's angry voice and his mother pleading with him. Tearing aside the door flap, he saw his father standing bare-chested over his mother, hammering her with his fist. His older sister hung onto the man's arm, trying to stop him. Seizing the first thing he saw, the boy brought a willow backrest down on his father's head. *"Leave her alone!"* he screamed, pounding him with the flimsy weapon until there was nothing left of it. His efforts only enraged the man, who now directed his attack on his son.

"You dog! I will crush you like a fly!" the man roared, turning to charge the boy, grabbing drunkenly at him. He was so pathetically incapacitated by the alcohol that White Quill had no difficulty in sidestepping the attack. The man tried again, and this time his son stepped aside and tripped him, sending him headlong into the fire. Shrieking and flailing, the angry man scrambled to get out, but White Quill put his foot on him and pushed him into the hot coals. At once, his mother screamed at him and tried to intervene. Striking at her son, she aided her husband out of the embers. As soon as the man tried to get up and regain his feet, howling with pain, the boy's older sister cracked him on the head with a piece of firewood. Stunned, he fell to his hands and knees before she struck him again, sending him to the ground. The man's wife crawled to his side and began wailing loudly over him.

"He deserves it!" White Quill screamed. *"Leave him alone!"* he blurted angrily, pulling his mother's hand away while she tried to wipe her husband's blackened face. *"Get me some rope so I can bind him!"* he ordered his sister.

"You must not do this to him!" his mother protested. *"He is your father!"*

A silent figure suddenly slipped through the door, followed by two others. Startled, White Quill turned to face them and recognized his aunt, who hurried to his mother's side.

"You must get her out of here!" White Quill urged the women.

"We will! Have you found your sister?" the woman spoke sharply and urgently.

"I have her! She is safe!" he assured her. *"I must get back to her. Will you look after my mother?"*

"Yes, certainly! Go!" she replied.

White Quill spun around and hurried to his little brothers, who were both howling over what they had witnessed. Scooping them into his arms and struggling to his feet, he rushed for the door.

"Take care of her!" he implored his aunt and slipped out with his anxious brothers.

Racing as quickly as he could to where he had left the others, and checking to make sure that nobody had seen him, he slipped into the bush, relieved to hear his sister's voice greeting him. He made his way toward the sound of her voice. *"Come here, babies,"* she murmured when he got there, kneeling to embrace the children as he set them down.

"We must be careful!" Badger whispered to White Quill. *"We saw Elk Hollers in the Trees and Night Shoot, just before you came back!"*

"Yes—be careful," Andy urged the others, very much alarmed.

"Míísinsski, we need to be farther away!" White Quill directed his friend. *"Wait! We need some robes! Wait here again,"* he said. *"I will get them!"* Checking to see that nobody was around, he plunged into the dark camp circle. Nobody was at his lodge when he reached it, not even his father, and he wondered where he had gotten to as he grabbed an armload of robes.

Returning to the others, he let Badger lead them deep into the underbrush, while the others followed, lugging the robes and the little boys. At a bit of a clearing, Badger stopped. *"How is this?"* he asked, turning to the others. The sound of the uproar in the camp was still clear, but they could barely see the fires through the bush.

"This should be good!" White Quill replied. *"I will lay these out for the little fellows,"* he said, tossing a robe to Andy, while he laid another down on the ground. Putting the little boys under the robes with Pretty Bird, the three boys sat together, and feeling safer, away from the camp, they talked about what they had just witnessed.

From the crisp air and excitement, Andy could not keep from shivering. *"Make room under the robe for this one!"* White Quill ordered his sister. *"He is coming under."* Not wishing to be thought a sissy, the white boy tried to protest but got shoved. He was put next to the little boys, and the two Indians took the outsides— White Quill beside his sister.

Only the little boys could get to sleep. The rest listened to the sounds from the unruly camp and spoke of what they had witnessed, speculating on what they thought must be happening. None of them had seen anything like it. Once more, they were startled by the sound of gunfire, and the shouting and screams continued, unabated. It took some time before the camp seemed to settle down, and when there was no more noise, sleep came.

The first rays of sunlight were beginning to illuminate their verdant cover when something startled Badger awake. Throwing the robe aside, he leapt to his feet to discover that it was White Quill. Awake since before first light, he had crept away to go into the camp to check on his mother and bring another robe, for he had spent most of the night uncovered. *"Everything is quiet. Only some of the women and children are awake,"* he reported, laying the robe over him and his sister.

Hearing them, Andy started to stir. "What's going on?" the sleepy one asked. White Quill began to tell him what he had done when suddenly, the very loud wail of a woman arose from the camp. Listening carefully, they heard another woman's voice join the lament.

"Someone is dead!" White Quill concluded soberly, with Badger nodding his head in agreement. *"Let us go and find out what happened! Míisinsski, come with me,"* he whispered. When Andy started to get up to join them, White Quill stopped him. *"No, you stay here with my sister and my brothers. Come!"* he said to Badger, not sure how much help Andy would be if they got into trouble.

After his friends had left, Andy glanced in the girl's direction and thought he saw her close her eyes. Sure she was feigning sleep, he studied her face in the soft morning light. She was beautiful! He wanted to say something but did not wish to embarrass her by letting on that he had seen her looking at him. Instead, he rolled onto his side, facing her, tossed back the robe a bit, and laid the back of his arm over his eyes so she would not see him watching her.

In a moment, her eyelids flickered and opened. He saw her lift her head, ever so slightly and look him over. With a sleepy sounding sigh, he moved his arms above his head to stretch, and opening his eyes as if awakening he looked over at her, and their eyes met. Her eyes were not like those of her brother—her deep brown eyes had a mysterious amber hue to them. He gazed into them without saying anything until she became uncomfortable and looked away. Checking on the little ones, sleeping between them, she looked again into his eyes, before letting him see her study at his bare chest and his arms.

"I see why they call you Sun Shines on Him," she murmured softly, giving him a timid smile. *"My friends told me about you,"* she continued, *"but I did not believe them. It is true! Sun shines on you!"*

Feeling a little awkward, having little experience with girls, yet wanting to impress her, Andy lifted a leg from beneath the robe. He moved it into the sun and said, *"See?"* With a look of intrigue on her face, she reached out to run her fingers across the golden hair on his calves, giving a little giggle as she withdrew her hand.

"Piikáni boys do not have that! Some of the older ones only have a few ugly black hairs there," she said. *"I pull them out when White Quill gets them."*

Andy was tongue-tied and had no idea what to say while she continued to look him over. *"What are you called?"* he asked when he began to feel self-conscious about it.

Hesitant to speak her own name, she responded shyly, *"Pretty Bird."*

"Pretty Bird." He repeated the name a couple of times. The girl smiled and looked down.

"How many winters have you seen?" she asked. Andy held up his fingers to show her. *"That is the same as me! I was born when the grass comes green. What about you?"*

Andy had understood most of what she had been saying; this, however, he did not understand. Not fully understanding how the Indians described the seasons and the passage of time, he responded, *"I do not understand."*

"I was born in the season when the grass comes green. When were you born?"

"In the fall, uh—" He tried to remember how Badger had described the autumn. "Oh—*yellow!*" he blurted. *"Yellow leaves!"*

Nodding her understanding, the girl observed, *"I guess I am older than you!"* There was a bit of awkward silence, and she spoke again. *"I like to look at you—your skin and your hair are so different!"*

"All right," Andy said. "Here you go!" He had kept his breechclout on that night and boldly tossed back the robe to let her see more. He was amused by the Indians' fascination with his appearance.

Pretty Bird giggled and grabbed the robe, trying to cover him up again. *"No! You are cold! I see your nipples standing out,"* she said, tucking the warm robe up against him.

"No, I am not," he protested, throwing it back again, putting his chin to his chest to see if his nipples had betrayed him.

"Yes, you are!" she exclaimed, giggling a little as she touched his nipple with her fingertip. *"See?"* At once, she snatched her hand away and looked toward the bushes. *"Someone is coming!"* she uttered and snuggled beneath her robe.

Andy scrambled to his feet, his heart in his mouth. He was relieved to catch sight of his friends, making their way toward them. *"It is them,"* he announced, watching their approach. Looking again at the girl, Andy discovered her feigning sleep and wondered why. *"You not sleep!"* he snickered knowingly.

"Yes, I am!" she whispered without opening her eyes.

Andy turned to face the others, who were just then stepping into their hideout. Believing him to be the only one awake, they spoke in a whisper. *"The women wail over a young man who is dead. Nobody knows what happened."* White Quill announced. *"I think we can return. I will waken my sister and brothers."*

Before he could do so, Andy bent over and gently shook the girl's shoulder. With a sleepy look on her face, she peered around as if awakened from a deep sleep. *"You wake—morning!"* Andy said softly as her beautiful eyes met his. *"We leave."* It thrilled him when she held his gaze a little longer than she needed to.

In short order, the little boys were awake and shuffling around sleepily, while the older ones gathered up the robes and trudged back to the camp.

The camp was still and quiet, but for the women who were wailing over the young man. It was soon learned that another of the young men was missing—a friend of the deceased. People suspected that he had killed his friend for some reason and fled.

Very few of the men were up and about, though it was still very early. The sun was just beginning to paint the top of White Quill's lodge when they arrived to find it still empty. It did not look like anyone had spent the night there, so they moved on to his aunt's lodge where they found the women. The little boys joined some other children who were at play close by.

Leaving Pretty Bird with her mother, Andy and his friends set out to survey the camp. Women were gathered in small groups, talking with hushed voices, and even the children were subdued. Some of the men were lying beside dead fires, sound asleep, and the camp was littered with small wooden kegs and glass bottles, with a few metal cups. Andy had never seen the Indians sleep outside and assumed it to be the result of their drunkenness. None of them could understand why several were naked or naked from the waist down. *"They were all after sex, last night,"* one of the older women growled when White Quill inquired. *"They were after the girls, and when they could not get the girls, they got upset!"* she said disdainfully.

Sits in the Middle and some of his other friends came looking for them at White Quill's lodge early in the afternoon. Elk Hollers in the Trees and Night Shoot had made off with the liquor he had got at the fort. In hushed voices, the older boys told them that they had then traded the use of the *Liar* girl for a little liquor and gone into the bushes to consume it. Downing it, they had enjoyed themselves with lots of joking and laughter. Hearing the commotion in the camp, they had elected to stay where they were, sleeping until midday.

By the middle of the afternoon, some of the Indians were again turning up at the fort. They were disappointed to find that they could not get liquor. The trader was no longer supplying it as a gift.

"Why?" Andy queried the others when they headed to the trees behind the fort to find shade from the afternoon sun. *"Why do they want more napiohke?"*

Sits in the Middle became defensive. *"Why not? It is not that bad! We liked it! We had a good time! You just have to be able to handle it."* Having tasted the substance only once, he seemed to consider himself an authority on the subject.

"It is evil!" White Quill said derisively. *"I hate this place! Did you not see all that was going on last night? Those horny dogs, Elk Hollers in the Trees and Night Shoot, were after my sister! It was your fault! You traded their Liar girl, and so they came after my sister!"* Sits in the Middle and his friends denied that the one had anything to do with the other. *"They are dogs!"* White Quill

continued. *"Anyway—people were hurt, and Eagle Moccasin got killed because girl dog, nothing ones were out of their heads!"* He spoke with usual temerity.

"Yes, and his father beat up his mother," Badger added, pointing with his lips at White Quill. *"Others got hurt, too!"*

"Yes, but they do not know how to handle it! You just have to know how to handle it!" one of Sits in the Middle's friends interjected, the others nodding their agreement.

"No, not good! Try stop them!" Andy ventured.

"Why should we? We can take care of ourselves," another friend added arrogantly.

"Does it not bother you that people get hurt from this drink?" Badger persisted, feeling support from his two friends. *"What if it was your sister that Night Shoot was after?"*

"I would not let that happen!" the arrogant boy came back. *"You are just cowards!"* he concluded.

"We are not cowards!" White Quill asserted. *"We are smart enough to know how to stay away from trouble! You will not make a very good warrior, behaving so foolish!"*

"You little worm! Eat my dung," hissed the arrogant one. He had always been jealous of the fact that White Quill had received honour for the incident with the two Crow raiders, and he did not care for the younger boy.

"Lick my stones," White Quill fired back, thrusting his hips in the direction of the foul-tempered boy.

"Lick your stones! You do not even have any! Sits in the Middle told us about you and that Liar girl! You were afraid to sex her!"

"I just want to keep myself pure—like we are supposed to!"

"Come on! We leave!" Andy interjected, feeling uncomfortable with the argument. He grabbed White Quill by the arm as he got up, and Badger stood to join them.

"Nothing one!" the arrogant boy hissed as he scrambled to his feet and began to advance upon White Quill. *"What is the matter,*

nothing one! Are you afraid? Are you running away?" the arrogant one taunted him.

"You are a girl! You are jealous because you have never claimed any war honours!" White Quill replied, aware of the reason for this fellow's jealousy toward him. *"Girl dog!"* the young one kept it up. *"Your father sexed a dog for you to be born!"* he mouthed off defiantly.

"You are the little girl dog!" the angry one snarled back.

White Quill ought to have left it alone, but he went too far. *"What did you fellows do last night, sex each other?"* That was too much for the arrogant boy. Enraged, he charged White Quill and was able to grab him by his long hair before he could dart out of the way. Being much bigger, the arrogant one held him by his hair and pummeled him in the face, before putting his foot to his stomach, pushing him violently to the ground. The smaller boy scrambled to face his attacker. Wiping the dirt from his mouth, he would not back down. *"Dog!"* he blurted. The boy stepped up quickly and kicked his injured leg.

Wincing, White Quill continued stubbornly, *"Dog!"* getting ready for another kick, shifting himself around to be able to fend it off with his feet. *"Dog!"* he sneered, when the other hesitated.

"Come on!" Sits in the Middle urged. *"Leave the little girl alone! We go!"*

The arrogant one turned as if to leave and suddenly whirled around to catch White Quill off-guard, kicking him in the groin and then in the face. *"Eat dung!"* the arrogant boy railed as he turned to join his friends.

"Dog!" White Quill croaked, still defiant, blood streaming from his mouth. Relieved that the troublemaker was leaving, Andy reached out to help his friend up. *"Oah-h, that did not work!"* the boy groaned, trying to get up. *"I better not try that again!"* Slowly making it to his feet, he had difficulty straightening up. *"Ohhh, he really got me! That really, really hurt!"* he repeated, shuffling to take

a few small steps, sticking his hand down the front of his breech-clout, checking himself out.

"Are you all right?" Badger wondered.

"I think so," White Quill whimpered. *"He really got me!"*

"Why you do—make angry?" Andy asked him, puzzled by his young friend's behaviour.

"I do not know! He is a dog! It was not supposed to work that way!"

"If your mouth is not big, you not kicked," Andy persisted. *"He is more big."* White Quill just groaned, and tightening his belt, began to hobble toward the camp.

"Míísinsski, go with him! I go napikawan chief," Andy told the others, starting out for the fort without awaiting a response. He had made up his mind about something.

At the fort, he got what he had been promised. When he was eventually able to see Rowand, the trader agreed to supply him with two packhorses, loaded with trade goods—lots of traps and no liquor—on the condition that the goods would be given as gifts to prominent Indians. He was given specific instructions and told to go and live among his friends' people for the sole purpose of encouraging them to return in the spring with furs.

While the pack animals were being loaded, he sat down at the factor's table and penned a letter to his father. He tried to tell him all that had happened and said he would see him next summer. Rowand made no promise that the letter would get out before freeze-up, and even if it did, it might not reach the settlement before spring. But he did promise that he would send the letter separately, with special instructions to see that it got through, from fort to fort, by the fastest means possible. He would send it immediately to McConnell at Fort Pitt, the next fort downstream, letting him know what it was and to make sure that it got through. Addressing it to both his father and to the minister, Reverend Jameson, Andy was confident of Rowand's assurance that it would get to his father. He entrusted the letter to the burly trader, and all the others of his kind along the way, and went to find Badger and White Quill. Both agreed that they should leave at once and avoid whatever was going to happen that night.

Badger and Andy set about getting their things on their horses while White Quill went to his lodge to get what he needed. He told his mother that they would wait on the other side of the river, but she insisted that he visit the old woman first, to have another look at his wound. Hurrying to find the others, he led them to the old woman. She fussed over them and scolded him for not taking better care of his injury. But before sending them away, she provided him with some more of the burning substance to put on each day after he had bathed. *"And, you have to pray!"* she warned him. *"It is Sun who does the healing!"*

When they were finally ready to leave the camp, Andy went alone to the fort, emerging from the gate leading the two loaded packhorses, proudly carrying a gun and wearing a broad smile. Badger joined him on Wolf Tail's horse, and White Quill showed up with Pretty Bird and their two younger brothers. They were on their way.

* * *

After several days on the river, Andy's father was not having a very good time of it. Having travelled by horseback from Edmonton House to Fort Pitt, there, he had received terrible news about his boys. He had been waiting to catch a ride downstream with the next boats leaving for the east when he had heard a story about a white boy who had been killed by Indians. Never imagining that it might have been his own son, he had not thought much about it until he had overheard talk that there had been two white boys, who had been heading west to find their father. Fear gripping his heart, he had sought more information and was directed to the man named McConnell, who was said to know all about the incident.

Mr. McConnell was the trader at the fort, and he hesitated for a moment before asking the troubled man for his boys' names. "Yep, that was them, all right!" he replied. "Nice lads. Went out huntin' with a group o' Cree, and they all got themselves killed by the Blackfoot."

"Both of them?" The boys' father had gasped.

"Yep. Killed 'em both—but it was more likely the Cree they were after!"

"Oh, dear God!" Will had exclaimed in shock. "What happened?"

"Sorry, parson! Nuttin', we coulda done! Found 'em laid out there by the river. It wasn't a pretty sight! We buried 'em back from the river a ways." McConnell had kept on telling the distraught father whatever he figured he needed to hear, hoping to discourage him from ever returning and learning the truth.

The boats had been ready to leave the next morning before dawn and overcome with grief, the heartbroken man had slumped himself in the bottom of one of them for his long journey of despair.

13

Leaving Edmonton House, Badger and White Quill rode on ahead to find the proper place to cross. Finding it, nobody needed to do more than lift their feet to keep them out of the water. They kept the lead, riding a short distance ahead of the others just in case they encountered anyone with unfriendly intentions. Behind them, and behind the packhorses and the extra horses, Andy and Pretty Bird rode with the little boys, talking to each other.

Pretty Bird communicated with Andy just as easily as her brother. She was curious about him and wanted to know everything. He answered her questions as best he could, asking lots of his own, too. He learned she was very close to her brother. Not only were they close in age, but they also spent much more time together than most siblings their age. *"We had two more brothers,"* she informed him. *"They were killed. And I have a sister who was taken as a wife last berries ripe season—she is a little older."* She spoke slowly, conscious of the fact that Andy was struggling to understand her. *"I miss her,"* she said with a sigh. *"And, that was my sister—another one—who was with my mother."*

"Your father—what...why—?"

"My father? He does not really come around that much. I do not like the way he treats my mother. He is all right to me—usually—but he is really mean to White Quill!"

"Why?"

"I do not know! My mother says that he wants to go live in the camp of his brother—she thinks he has another wife there. She thinks he might even have other children—he will never let her visit them—he just goes by there by himself and is gone for a long time." Andy gathered that her father was a bit of a rogue.

After riding for most of the morning, they found the other two waiting for them at the edge of a vast, open prairie. Some distance to the east, arising out of the meadow, was a low, tree-covered hillock. *"We will make our camp over there, so we can keep watch on the trail,"* Badger announced, pointing his horse in that direction. Among the trees, they found good cover, and with a thunderstorm looming, the Indian boys set about making a war lodge.

Pretty Bird stuck with Andy, and they busied themselves tethering the animals and unloading them to see what Rowand had sent. Two muskets had been apparent, tied atop the pack. Without having to think about it, he took the guns to his friends and said, trying to be sarcastic, *"Gifts! You take. Come to napikawan camp—trade!"* They inspected the gifts with awe, hurrying to finish their work so they could try them out.

Andy and Pretty Bird continued sorting through the goods, trying to keep the curious little boys from getting into everything. Pretty Bird was so patient with them! Andy noticed how she never raised her voice or scolded them. She had been showing them some red cloth, which Andy knew to be a favourite among the Indians, when he passed her a package of coloured beads and said, *"For you—and the cloth!"* Handing her also a knife and a hatchet, he grinned and said, *"And these—come to napikawan camp! Trade."* Trying to be sarcastic, he couldn't keep from smirking.

Continuing to rummage through the goods, to Pretty Bird's delight, Andy gave her anything she admired.

Before everything was put back into the packs, the other two were finished their shelter. Built out of fallen trees and dead branches, it was barely large enough for them all to squeeze into, and as soon as they were finished, Badger and White Quill were anxious to try out their new weapons. With Andy coaching them, they let forth a barrage of gunfire shortly before dark, just as the thunderstorm struck. It gave a mighty display of thunder and lightning, but little rain.

In the morning, the Indian boys were up before the others and gone with their new weapons, intending to return with something to eat. Pretty Bird and Andy stayed under their robes and whispered, waiting for the little boys to waken. She was quite happy to let them sleep while delighting in Andy's company. Andy was just as excited to have been left alone with her, and it pleased him when she shooed the little boys outside after they woke up. *"Go outside and play until your brother comes back with something for us to eat,"* she told them. After they had scrambled out, she turned on her side and gazed into Andy's eyes. *"What are you thinking about?"* she asked, using sign and gesture to help him understand.

"Oh," Andy paused, not sure how to answer. *"Um, nothing—I like you."* His answer made her face brighten. *"And your smile—and your eyes."* Not used to speaking with girls, he felt a bit awkward, but he liked her and tried to make a good impression.

Flattered by what he had said, Pretty Bird turned away for a moment before returning her gaze to him. *"I like you too!"* she said in a whisper. *"I am glad I know you!"* Andy beamed as she said it. *"And, I like your smile, also, and your eyes, and your hair,"* she continued, reaching to tousle the unkempt mop on his head. It had not seen any attention for weeks. *"Listen!"* she interrupted herself.

"Do you hear the lark? They do not usually sing in this season! He must be singing to us!"

The beautiful sound was interrupted by the distant report of a firearm, followed closely by another. Andy exclaimed, *"They!"* and the girl nodded. A few moments later, they heard another shot and another. Another pair of shots followed those a moment later, telling Andy they were firing together as soon as they had reloaded.

"Shall we go and see what they got?" Pretty Bird suggested when they heard no more shooting.

"They sure did a lot of shooting!" Andy exclaimed to himself, thinking they must have brought down an awful lot of game with it.

They were just crawling out from under the robes when the little boys came scampering in to announce that they had heard shots. *"I know! So, did we!"* their sister responded. *"Do you think your brother might have something for us to eat? Shall we go and see?"* The little boys squealed with excitement and complained when she made them put their moccasins on for the trek.

The shots had come from the direction of the morning sun, so leading one of the horses and taking an extra rope, they headed in that direction. Travelling only a short distance, Pretty Bird stopped and exclaimed, *"Wait!"* And, turning to run back to the shelter, a moment later, she emerged, happily brandishing her new knife and hatchet.

The prairie grass, showing a golden hue of fall, extended some distance to the east, where the bush took over. They were about halfway there when the hunters stepped out of its cover. *"We have meat!"* Badger yelled when they got within earshot. *"Come and see!"* When they met, he led them through the bush to another clearing, competing with White Quill to tell the story of their hunt, many times, while they hurried along. Finally, they reached their kill—a cow buffalo.

"What are the arrows?" Pretty Bird asked, seeing that the beast

had at least two arrows sticking out of it.

"*We could not kill it with these silly fire-sticks!*" her brother admitted. "*We only wounded—*"

"*You could not kill it!*" Badger interrupted his friend. "*He missed, but I hit it!*" he bragged.

"*Yes, but you could not kill it!*" the other protested, and the two of them argued until it came out that neither had dispatched the animal with his firearm. Wounded by Badger's first shot, they had continued to reload and fire, without appearing to have any effect on the wounded creature as it fled, probably because it had managed to get itself out of range. Abandoning their new weapons, they had given chase and killed it with their familiar arrows.

"*Give me your new knife,*" White Quill ordered his sister.

"*I will do it!*" she rebuffed him, keeping the knife from him and pushing past him to do the job herself. "*Roll it on its belly!*" she demanded. "*We will just take the best parts.*" Following her wish, they worked at getting the animal onto its belly and watched her work with her new tools. She removed the hindquarters, the back fat, and the loins, and while her brother loaded it onto the horse, she removed the tongue. "*This is the best part!*" she murmured.

All the way back, the hunters recounted their story but expressed disappointment with their new weapons. "You need to practice," Andy told them, but neither one understood him. "*Like Wolf Tail!*" Giving the gesture of the swinging target and shooting the bow, he said, "*Like...shoot and shoot, many times—to make good.*"

"*Practice! We need to practice—just like with our bows!*" White Quill agreed when he understood him.

At their camp, Pretty Bird cooked the tongue and some of the meat over a small fire. Rowand had provided Andy with several flints, making fire easy. Eating their fill, they spent the rest of the day in the trees where Andy and Pretty Bird stayed close, drying some of the meat over the fire and hanging the rest over branches to dry in the warm autumn sun.

Late in the afternoon, when it became apparent that the camp would not be showing up, White Quill asked Andy to accompany him to water the horses. Andy had been enjoying Pretty Bird's company and tried to put it off onto Badger.

"No! You come! I wish to talk to you," the girl's brother insisted.

They rode for a long time in complete silence, which was unusual for White Quill. Andy was not used to seeing him so quiet and wondered if something was wrong. He was ordinarily full of conversation and humour, but now, he wore a serious look on his face and seemed pensive. Not taking up the small talk Andy offered, finally, the young Indian turned to his friend and spoke. *"I see you like my sister!"*

"Yes!" the white boy replied happily. *"I like her!"*

It was a while before White Quill spoke again. *"You must not do anything to her,"* he warned. *"Do not hurt her—we are very close, her and me. And, I like you, but she is my sister—and she is my best friend,"* he continued awkwardly.

"Hurt her? I do not hurt her!" Andy assured him, unsure what his friend was getting at.

Finally, his companion came out with it. *"I am glad you speak of not sexing a girl until you take a wife!"* As soon as he heard it, Andy realized what he had been getting at, but let him continue. *"I worry, though. Others have been after her. She has never taken up with any of them, though some have tried. And, my father is being a dog about it! I just do not want anything to happen to her."*

"I will not! No!"

"No, you say, but I cannot be sure! I have not known you very long. Maybe you would try! I have made a vow to my mother that I will look after her, so—"

Andy had directed his horse over beside White Quill's and interrupted him by hitting him on the shoulder with the end of his fist, assuring him, *"I vow! Not sex! I wait...wife!"*

"I know, but you are a boy, just like me! I know what it is like

when—you know!" White Quill blurted as if he had been keeping the thought pent up, a worried expression upon his face.

Andy chuckled. *"I know! I vow! Not sex!"*

"And you will not touch her?"

"I will not touch her!"

"And, do not ask her to touch you—or do anything—you know!"

"No! I vow!"

Much relieved with his assurance, White Quill kept looking straight ahead, because he wondered if he had been foolish to bring it up. *"Do I sound foolish?"* he asked.

Andy admired his friend's integrity. *"No! She is your sister...and my heart is warm toward you!"*

Still, a little embarrassed for being so forward, the Indian replied, *"I know! And, my heart is warm toward you! If anyone was going to sex her, I would want it to be you!"* he said, beginning to soften his stance. *"But my people say that a girl should not let us boys sex her. She should keep herself pure until she becomes a wife, like I said to you before—and, the same for us! We are supposed to keep ourselves pure!"* After thinking about what he had just said, he exclaimed, *"Hai! Maybe you will take her as your wife!"*

Until that moment, Andy had never even thought of such a thing, but the notion was enchanting, and giving the idea some thought he said, "Who knows, maybe—*maybe, long time."*

"You are ten and five?"

"Soon ten and six!"

"Ten and six—some take a wife then. My father was ten and seven, and my mother was only ten and three. My sister was ten and five when she was taken as a wife."

"Hunh!" Andy grunted, shrugging his shoulders. He really liked Pretty Bird; he had never felt so comfortable with a girl before. In fact, he had never even courted a girl back home.

"I wonder what your babies would look like," his friend continued. *"Would they look like you or look like her?"*

"*Like her,*" Andy responded, having seen the offspring of the Indians along the river, spawned by white oarsmen and trappers. "*I see—look like mother.*"

"*Hmmm, a brown baby with yellow hair? I would like to see that!*"

"*No. Brown baby, your hair.*"

"*Black hair?*"

"*Yes, black hair.*"

"*Not your colour?*"

"*No.*"

"*Too bad! I would like to see what I would look like with hair like you!*" the Indian commented, trying to imagine it. When he was done with that thought, he went back to what they had been talking about before. "*I like you! And I am glad that you like my sister! She has never liked any other boy as much as she seems to like you.*" Andy remained silent and wished his friend would continue that topic because he enjoyed talking about the girl. But he rode without saying anything more.

Finally, when it was apparent that his friend had nothing more to say about it, Andy said, "*Yes, I like her much.*"

The Indian responded, "*I know! Maybe you will take her as your wife—maybe—sometime—that would be good!*" He was returning to his usual nature, seeming to have needed to get the matter off his chest. He grinned at Andy. "*I feel foolish! But I have made this vow to protect her. I love her, yet my heart is warm toward you, like a brother. It does not seem right to speak that way.*"

Once more, Andy was surprised by his friend's candour. Badger had never spoken in such a manner, and none of the other Indian boys had ever been so open. "*You heart is good! Good you vow protect his sister.*"

"*My sister!*" White Quill corrected him. "*You said, 'his sister.' You need to say, 'your sister.'*"

"*Your sister. Good you vow protect your sister,*" Andy nodded. "*Your heart is good!*"

"Race you!" the Indian suggested.

Andy responded by putting his heels to his horse's ribs, taking the lead. White Quill, though, soon passed him, laying low over his horse's neck, using the end of the rein to whip its flank. The other horses raced along with them until they reached the edge of the clearing, where the winner reined in to let his friend catch up. They plunged through the brush until they came to the water he and Badger had discovered earlier.

On their return, the Indian's good humour had fully returned, and he joked all the way. When they reached their camp, Pretty Bird was happy to have Andy back. She took both his hands in hers and held them while he told her about his trip, skipping the conversation about her brother's concerns. *"Much, much, I like your brother!"* he concluded.

The Indians listened with disbelief, that evening when Andy did his best to describe his world—talking almost until it was time for sleep. He tried to explain books to them, but they had a tough time understanding. When he spoke about trains and their belching steam engines, they thought he must be joking. They had a hard time believing him. Laughing at his antics as he described the piano his mother had played at the church, his audience was kept spellbound by other stories about his life in the settlement and what he could remember of England. They loved his stories and did not want him to stop.

The next day, the camp arrived—first the advance guards, riding solemnly. Being the first to spot them, White Quill ran to get his horse and broke out of the trees slowly, so the guards would not suspect an attack. At once, one of them broke off and headed in his direction. White Quill shouted a greeting and identified himself. With his companions hurrying to get their things together and onto the horses, by the time they could join him, the main body of the camp had passed.

Pretty Bird, with Andy riding close beside her, immediately

sought out her mother. When they found her, they were shocked by the sight of her bruised and swollen face. The woman was sullen and had not much to say. Pretty Bird was horrified, and although she wanted to tell her mother about Andy, she held off for the time being. Instead, she sought out some of her friends, shooing him away before telling the excited girls all about him.

Andy joined his friends, riding on the flank of the main group. White Quill observed that the people were unusually quiet. Even the children seemed subdued; something was not right. And, others confirmed it. Asking around, they learned that two young men, out of their minds with drink, had been caught with another man's wife. The woman's husband, also under the influence of the *napiohke*, killed one of them and then bludgeoned his wife to death while the other fled. Later, that night, tormented by grief and anger, the man had slashed himself with his knife and bled to death in front of his small children. There had been other fights, and some of the men were not on good terms with their wives. Many of them, and even a few of the women, complained of sore heads. Very few people sat around the fires that night.

Such was the pattern for the next few days, as the camp journeyed southward. Nobody talked much, and the good-natured fun and carefree attitude of the people was absent. Even Andy noticed it and commented upon it.

When he was not with Pretty Bird, Andy rode with Badger and White Quill. Sits in the Middle took notice of this and came to make up with them, apologizing to White Quill over his behaviour at the fort. He was still pretty cocky, though, when he spoke of their plans for the *Liar* girl. They had retaken possession of her, and she was being led, still with a rope around her neck. Even though she was seated on a horse, the sight of it made Andy angry, but his friends warned him against attempting to do anything about it.

Eventually, even the one who had beaten up White Quill came to him, offering him a favourite knife in return for the hand of friendship. The younger boy accepted the gift and the apology, but in a manner all his own, still insisted on calling him a dog. This time though, they all laughed.

After a few days, things seemed to be getting back to normal, but White Quill still had not spoken to his father. Not willing to return to his mother's lodge on account of it, he joined Badger and Andy in sleeping outside. The old woman made a fuss over them every time she saw them, pleased that his injury was healing up and praising Sun for it.

Many were anxious to know what Andy had on his packhorses. When his friends saw him keeping a close guard on it, they assured him, *"Do not worry! Nobody will touch it!"* And, he soon found out that he could leave anything unattended and find it exactly as he had left it. *"But you could never trust a Liar that way!"* he was warned.

At night, a fire felt good, and the long, hot days seemed to be giving way to cooler weather. Pretty Bird and her mother made sure the boys all had warmer clothes and adequate robes at night, and one morning, a sharp frost spoke of even cooler days to come. One of the old men had predicted that *Cold Maker* was going to be harsh with them, making everyone even more anxious to keep moving southward, where they intended to join others of their tribe. Everyone spoke of the fall hunt and readying themselves for the winter.

When Andy caught his first sight of the distant blue mountains, he was spellbound. He had never seen anything like them and exclaimed to Pretty Bird. Badger said that one day when they got closer to his home territory, he would take him into them. But White Quill told him of his own favourite place, which was much closer and said they should go there.

Every day, hunters would ride out in search of buffalo, and fresh meat was in constant supply. Only the best parts were taken and eaten fresh, and the rest left to the scavengers because the camp was on the move.

One day, after seeing White Quill cutting out the tongue of a buffalo, Andy learned something from him. *"They use them for the Sun dance—lots of them,"* Pretty Bird informed him. *"My mother did that once. I should get her to tell you about it."* That evening, she obliged.

"Hai-ya! It was a special time!" the woman began, a distant look of fondness in her eyes. *"It is a great honour for a woman to be chosen to put on the Sun dance! I never thought it would be me— but I was chosen once—because of my son—and I wanted to, I was happy about it.*

"He had been on a war party to capture horses from the Snakes, who live far away—down there," she said, pointing with her chin toward the south. *"They were very successful! They captured many very good horses! But on their return, they came into a war party— Crow."* She shook her head as she recalled the events as she had learned them. *"There were a lot of them, and some of his friends fell to their attack...then the rest of them—and him—they were pinned down while the enemy surrounded them—they were in those bushes, hiding in there—they had taken cover there. It was very bad! It did not look like they were going to get out of it...but my son—he had made a vow to Sun—that he would ask me to put on the Sun dance if he made it out alive...That is what he prayed. And, Moon hid her face that night, and it got very dark. He and two others—they were very brave to do this—they crawled on their bellies—just crawling along so carefully—right past the enemy...and they made it away! They made it away! And, they came all the way home on foot—my son came back to me, and I was so glad—of course, I would put on the Sun dance!*

"I had to do a great many things to put it on. I was a faithful wife—my husband was different then—it was different." The woman sighed and bowed her head in deep thought for a long moment before continuing. "A woman who puts on the Sun dance has to be pure—a good wife—one who has never been unfaithful to her husband. I have never been unfaithful—never! I have always been faithful to your father," she said, looking in turn at each of her children.

"I had to learn what to do—I had to go with other women who had done it before and be instructed and learn everything I must do—the prayers, the songs, and the ceremonies. As the time came closer—the home days, when we all get together—all the camps meet at that place, over near that Place of the Sweet Pine. We go there lots.

"The men would cut the timber and branches—for the lodge— and there would be much fasting and praying. I had to fast and pray for four days...before that big day. And, I was very weak and had to be helped to the ceremony, I was so weak. Your father could not touch me.

"Many people had been shown mercy and kindness by Sun that year, and they all brought offerings. Two people brought those white buffalo robes—they are very sacred and special—which were given as an offering to Sun.

"And, I said my prayers—I fasted, and I prayed, and I called out to Sun and thanked him for having pity on my sweet son—I wish he was still with us! And, Sun showed great favour on us that winter. It was very successful!

"Near the end—at the close of the ceremony, a few young men hung themselves from that pole. Maybe your friend does not know about that, does he?" Everyone looked at Andy, and when Badger and White Quill both shook their heads, she explained. "Sometimes, a young man will make his own sacrifice—torture himself. They hang themselves by ropes—a helper will cut into their chest—right here"—she said, indicating where the slits would be made on both sides of a man's chest— *"then that man puts wooden pegs or strong bones through the slits, like this"*—she demonstrated how the pegs were inserted under the strips of flesh— *"and ropes tied to those things and up to the main pole of the lodge...and those young men would dance and pull back, dance and pull back—always singing and praying—dancing, pulling back to increase the pain. Some of them would throw themselves against the ropes and lean hard against them—dancing, and pulling, dancing and pulling— until their flesh tears away, and they fall free.*

"Your brother, my son, did this...but he could not complete it— it was too much for him to endure. Your father cut his flesh to let him fall free, but there is no shame in that! He was very brave—he endured so much pain! But Sun showed him pity, and after that, he was very successful—he got many war honours—even that yellow leaves season! He was so proud of those scars!" Her face reflected great pride, yet the deep sorrow of loss as she finished her story with a sigh, sitting with her head bowed and her hands resting on her thighs.

Andy sat quietly, thinking about what she had said. Finally, he spoke. *"Is the sun your, uh medicine?"* he asked, respectfully, having heard the Indians speak of it as if it was a god.

"Everything comes from Sun," the woman replied, looking up. *"He gives us everything we need to live! We always pray to him for mercy and good fortune. When he gives us good things, we offer them back to him—that is why we always place a little food on the ground before we eat. When bad things happen to our people, we call upon Sun for his pity and mercy until he sends good upon us. He protects us!"*

"You know God or Jesus?" Andy asked curiously.

The woman shook her head and said, *"We do not know these things. What are they?"* she answered solemnly.

"Like Sun. Me, God and Jesus and Holy Ghost," he said. He wished he could describe his god, but he had no words they would

understand. "God *all around*. Jesus, *here—in here*," he told them, tapping his bare chest with his finger and seeing the puzzled look on their faces.

"*What is in there?*" Pretty Bird asked.

"Jesus *in—in me—my medicine. Inside me*," Andy said slowly and awkwardly, realizing they were having difficulty grasping what he was saying. Trying a different approach, he told them, "God *make Sun*. God *make all we, and this*," he said, waving his arm toward the trees, "*trees, buffalo, grass*." He grinned with anticipation when the woman began nodding her understanding.

"*Oh, now I know! We know him!*" she said with a chuckle and a half-grin. "*We call him, that fellow, Napi. Napi created everything—the trees, the buffalo—he created everything! Yes, we know that old trickster! We have many stories about him!*" Andy could not imagine she was talking about the same person, but it made him wonder if some of their beliefs might be similar to his own. He wished he knew the language better.

Like her children, Pretty Bird's mother could speak easily with Andy, and with them, asked endless questions about his family and his people. Enquiring about his ability as a hunter, she was pleased when Badger bragged about his skill with their musket and how well he was learning what they had been teaching him about shooting a bow and arrow. Both of his friends spoke of his growing ability to hunt from horseback, which brought more nodding approval from the woman. Andy was flattered by all the good things they had to tell her. It occurred to him that his friends were trying to impress the woman, on his behalf.

She seemed to like him. Seeing him hold hands with her daughter one day, she came up to them and clasped their hands together, saying nothing but smiling her approval.

One day, when she asked the boys to get her some meat, Badger and White Quill were more eager than Andy. He was reluctant to leave Pretty Bird's side, but when it was suggested that it would impress the girl's mother, he became more willing.

The rolling grassland was filled with game, as it had been ever since Andy had first come up out of the river valley onto the prairies, those many weeks prior. Seldom had they ever been out of sight of buffalo—except around the fort. Deer, elk, and antelope were plentiful, and the coyotes and wolves were always around, shadowing the grass eaters. *Sticky mouth* was constantly on the prowl in his relentless search for food, sticking his nose into everything and exploring everywhere. The bigger bear—*the real bear*—fascinated Andy. The Indians held the huge tawny and silvery, brown bears in great awe. It was Badger's aspiration to kill one. *"Anyone who kills a real bear gets its power!"* he said enviously. *"And, I would hang its claws around my neck, and everyone would respect me!"*

They had not travelled far when they began to encounter buffalo. Riding slowly among the scattered herds, they searched for one where they could get close, and it was not long before they began their stalk.

Andy carried one of the firearms, but the two Indians chose their more familiar weapons, claiming to be able to dispatch more animals using their bows and arrows. Staying out of sight behind a thicket, they managed to surprise a herd, coming out practically among them, and the startled buffalo stampeded in a storm of dust. Following his friends' advice, Andy directed his horse alongside the first animal he could. Giving the horse its head, he let go of the rein to use both hands to try to steady his weapon—which was almost impossible! From as close as he dared, he fired but did not see any result as his horse shied away from the sound of the gunshot, almost unseating him. Somehow, he managed to hang on, but it gave him a terrible fright as he looked down at the thundering hooves of the buffalo all around him.

There was no way he could recognize which beast he had just shot at, so he decided to attempt another shot. First, though, he had to figure out how he was going to reload the weapon, while the horse raced on amid the panicked buffalo. He had his hands full! Trying to stuff the load down the barrel, as well as stay astride his horse, he had no idea where the others were, and he had completely lost track of where he was in the herd. Managing to place his next ball and wad in the end of the barrel, and ramming them down with the rod, as he withdrew it, the rod slipped from his hand and was gone. "Damn!" he muttered, looking back, hoping he might be able to mark the spot and find it afterward. He could see nothing but a surging brown mass—all calves and lumbering old bulls—so he figured he must be near the tail end of the herd. He urged his horse up beside a calf. Easily keeping pace with the animal, he aimed and pulled the trigger, but nothing happened— the shot was a dud—and the young beast raced on.

By now, the herd had begun to scatter, and his horse was soaked with sweat. Turning from the chase, he looked around to see what success the others had achieved, surprised to discover that they were some distance behind, watching him. Returning to where White Quill sat on his horse, over a dead buffalo, he saw two other fallen beasts.

"Did you kill one?" the Indian asked, excitement in his voice.

"No! How many did you kill?" Andy asked, just as excited.

"Just this one! Our friend must have killed two because we have three down." Very excited, they headed toward Badger, who was coming toward them.

"Are we good?" Badger exclaimed when they approached, his excitement obvious. *"The napikawan kills his first buffalo!"*

"What do you mean? He says he did not kill anything!" the other Indian exclaimed.

"Well, someone shot that one over there with a fire-stick," he said, pointing with his lips at one of the dark forms.

"Well, I'll be!" the white boy exclaimed when he understood what his friend had said. "I gotta go have a look!" he said, kicking his horse in the direction of the fallen creature. As he stood over it, his friends came to thump him on the back, and they all their exchanged stories, as each one described his endeavours.

Taking the tongues and the best parts of the animals, they searched without success for Andy's ramrod. *"Hai-yah! Do not worry about it! I will cut you a branch—like an arrow—that will do just as well!"* Badger assured him as they loaded the horses.

It was late afternoon before they caught up to the camp as it slowly trudged along. Going first to White Quill's mother, they loaded enough meat onto her packhorse to satisfy her. Pretty Bird stood close to Andy while they told their story. Next, they went to the old woman who had healed White Quill and gave her all the meat she could handle. What was left, they distributed among the old people, and the women who they knew had nobody to hunt for them.

That night, Andy was invited to tell his story of the hunt. At the fire where they were sitting, a man asked him to relate his experience, which he did, haltingly, with much trepidation. When he was done, a man stood up and beckoned him. Giving him an embrace, he declared, *"This fellow would make a good Piikáni—he is a hunter! I have heard their story! He is just like one of our own sons. And, who knows, maybe he will make a warrior for us! He is called Sun Shines on Him!"* A few of the other men also repeated his name. He did not recognize the significance of it until his friends told him, afterward, that the elders had been honouring him by repeating his name in that manner.

14

Ever since getting his first glimpse of the blue mountains on the western horizon, Andy was captivated by them. Their rugged peaks stood jagged against the bright blue sky. Dark forests, accentuated by the fall colours and fresh snow in the high country, kept him enthralled as they journeyed southwest, getting ever closer to them. He could hardly wait for his friends to take him on the trip they had promised.

He was gazing at them in wonder, one day, when they were surprised by a group of Indians. It turned out to be a hunting party out from the main camp. Their destination was near, and there was great excitement among his companions as they were directed to its location.

When they reached the camp, the people who had been riding together quickly dispersed among the many lodges that were scattered among the trees beside a grey river. Andy and his companions rode with White Quill's mother as she sought the right place to erect her lodge, near friends. When she finally pulled up her horse, her son announced that he would be looking for somewhere else to stay. *"My father will be along soon—I think I will stay with my friends,"* he informed his mother, who could not persuade him otherwise. Andy waved wistfully to Pretty Bird and tagged along with his friends. He did so with reluctance since he had noticed some of the boys from this new camp already trying to attract Pretty Bird's attention. He did not wish to be gone long.

"We need to find Sits in the Middle—we can stay with him," White Quill announced after they had left his mother and sister, but their friend seemed to have vanished among the many lodges in this new camp. When their search brought them a second time upon Pretty Bird and her mother, Andy had had enough.

"Hai," he hollered to his friends. *"I stay,"* he yelled, pulling up his horse beside Pretty Bird.

"Tether your horses here with ours," she told him when she heard him tell his friends what he was doing. *"Then, come and sit while we put up our lodge!"* Andy tied his horse, but rather than sit and watch, he pitched in to help.

His actions soon drew the attention of others, and before long, several people were watching him. Aware no Indian boy his age would ever do this type of work, he wondered if it was that, or whether it was because of his appearance. Not really caring, he knew how he could get a reaction out of them. He took his shirt off, laying it aside while he toiled, smiling to himself as some of the onlookers exclaimed and called others to come and see. Before long, he was surrounded by curious children who took a step back in surprise when he greeted them. He was just starting to gain their confidence when Badger showed up.

"We found him!" he announced. *"We will stay with him tonight. Come!"* he insisted, waiting for Andy to say goodbye and get his horses.

It took just one night in the crowded lodge of Crane with Many Horses for Andy to wonder if they might be able to arrange for an abode of their own. He volunteered to trade some of his goods and even one of the packhorses if it might help them secure lodgings of their own. White Quill lit up at the suggestion and exclaimed, *"No! I know!"* Taking off on the run, he left the other two to wonder what he had in mind. When he returned a short while later, they could tell from the grin on his face that he had met with some kind of success. *"Come and see!"* he hollered. *"I got a lodge for us!"*

The others accompanied him to the lodge of the old woman who had doctored him. She was waiting for them, hands on her hips, and after greeting them she turned and cackled, *"Come with me!"* The woman shuffled along, chattering all the way with White Quill, while the other two followed, curious. Stopping occasionally to visit with people she encountered, eventually, they came to a big lodge with many children playing around it. *"Hai, where is your mother?"* she asked one of the older children, who interrupted his play only long enough to nod in the direction of the lodge. Her followers waited outside while she shook the door flap. An attached rattle announced her arrival, but without waiting, she flipped the door aside and stepped inside. In a few moments, she reappeared with another woman, who led them around behind the lodge and stood before a smaller one, adorned with various figures, shapes, and colours.

"This is the little lodge that I made for berry-picking!" the old woman announced. *"Her children have been using it for a place to play. You take it now and show your pretty friend how to set it up,"* she said to White Quill. *"It is for him and the other one."* When she saw their look of delight, she added sternly, *"And, you need to make up with your father!"* Then, with a smile, she said, *"But until you do, it is yours, too,"* tousling his hair as she spoke.

"Thank you!" he responded.

"Thank you, old woman," Badger said politely.

"Yes, thank you!" Andy added. *"I give her something?"* he wondered to Badger.

Hearing him ask, the old woman scoffed, *"Shiaah! You boys just keep bringing me nitapi waksin! I still have teeth!"* she boasted, baring her tobacco-stained teeth.

And so, Andy got his wish. The disappointed children looked on while the trio quickly dismantled their new shelter and dragged it away.

It did not take Andy long to decide on a spot to put it—right beside the river, so they could bathe within a few steps of where they slept, and within sight of Pretty Bird's lodge. Before dusk, they had it set up, their belongings inside, and a fire going. As soon as everything was ready, he went to fetch Pretty Bird. Impressed with the job they had done, she stayed at their fire until her mother came looking for her.

It was unusual for three boys of their age to have a lodge of their own. The care and maintenance of a tipi was something that most young men neither knew nor cared about. Such things were the domain of the women. Boys usually stayed with their family until they had acquired enough horses to take a wife, and even then, the young couple might live with one of their parents. Nevertheless, led by the white boy and his strange way, and with the help of Pretty Bird and her mother, the trio busied themselves learning how to make a comfortable home for themselves.

The men of the camp and most of the older boys were busy every day with the hunt, and Badger was soon anxious to abandon domestic chores to join them. *"We have done too much of this stuff!"* he said disdainfully. *"You need to get Pretty Bird to do all this—you need to get her as your wife! We must be out there, hunting!"* he exclaimed.

White Quill had been intrigued with having a lodge of their own and getting it fixed up, but he was easily distracted by Badger's suggestion. It was Andy who was reluctant; he would have been perfectly content to stay in camp where he could be around Pretty Bird all day. But his friends would not let him; they dragged him along to learn how to hunt.

Andy's companions were persistent and able. Soon they had too much meat for White Quill's mother and her daughters to be able to handle, but that did not stop them from hunting. Others came to know them through their generosity and willingness to provide for those who needed it—and their golden-haired friend was a constant attraction, quickly becoming a favourite to many.

The entire camp was involved in securing and preparing meat for the winter ahead. The women, girls, and young children were busy from dawn until dark. Going out after the hunters to butcher the animals where they had been killed, they would return to camp with the meat and prepare it without help from the men. The men would retire to sit among their friends and smoke their pipes, regaling each other with stories of the hunt and battles fought, while the women toiled. While his companions wanted to be with the men, Andy liked to watch how the women worked on the meat and hides, interested to see how little of it seemed to go to waste.

Seeing his interest, some of the women got him to break open the big bones for them so they could boil the marrow out of them. He also helped them pound the resulting grease into the dried meat, mixing it with berries and packing it away for storage. He wondered why he had never seen his own people preserving meat in such a fashion.

Andy was becoming more and more acquainted with the life and customs of his hosts, making new friends and learning their language and their stories. One day, he was invited to smoke their pipe. He had become quite popular among some of the men because they had learned of his supply of tobacco, something with which he was very generous. One evening, Crane with Many Horses invited Andy and his friends to join his fire, and for the first time, the pipe was passed to him. With the same solemnity he observed in his hosts, he took it and drew a deep breath of smoke and exhaling it between his lips before passing it on. He had learned to overcome the taste of it while smoking with his companions on the boats. But there was so much more to it than what he had experienced among them. Among his Indian hosts, it was ceremony, a rite. He wished he understood it more fully.

Around such fires, he heard the stories. His hosts excelled at storytelling, loving to listen as much as to tell. Nobody ever interrupted someone who was speaking. Everyone listened quietly, and only after the story was finished would others comment, one at a time, until someone else would begin his own story. What Andy came to realize was that these stories had not been made up and were not intended to entertain, though they did that. They were accounts of their past—accomplishments and acts of courage and bravery, which had shaped their lives and defined them as a people. Repeatedly, he heard stories of war and the exploits of warriors. Honour was rarely given to anyone but the one who was outstanding in his endeavours, and it was sought by all. It seemed that a young man's sole purpose in life was to gain honour—and this through warring and raiding. He began to understand his friends' angst at following a different path—his path.

While some of the warriors' actions sounded like defensive measures, most of the valour seemed to stem out of raids of aggression. He heard of small groups of young men who would go out to steal horses from an enemy—capturing horses, they called it. Too often, there would be bloodshed when the raiders were discovered and pursued. He knew that neighbouring tribes would make similar raids upon the *Niitsitapi,* often vengeance raids. But it sounded like his hosts never lost. All he heard was how they won a clash or how they got away with a bunch of horses without being caught. It left him with the impression they were invincible.

When he asked his friends about it, he was told candidly, *"Ha! Nobody talks about that! Sometimes they win, and sometimes they lose, but it would not sound very good if someone talked about how he had been beaten. Nobody does that! It is all about being respected, so they only talk about when they win or when they are successful at capturing horses. And, they do not even talk about that much—the pack horses they capture—just the good buffalo runners."* It was said with a cynical look.

White Quill explained more fully, *"What you want to do is hit an enemy!"* He demonstrated as he spoke, striking Andy on the shoulder. *"It is a great honour to hit him with your hand or your club and take his weapon from him. That is a great honour!"* Badger nodded silently. *"You do not get so much honour if you have to kill him—that does not take as much skill and bravery. You have to show how much skill you have and how brave you are. That is why you have to get up really close—close enough to hit him with your hand. That shows that you are very brave because you have to get very close to your enemy to do it! He could kill you! It is good when you can take his weapon, because not only are you brave, you dishonour him—he is disgraced if you would take his weapon from him."*

When he appeared to be finished, Andy wondered, *"Do they not kill him? It sounded like they killed."*

"Most of the time someone gets killed," White Quill answered him. *"You would not want someone to take your weapon and disgrace you, so you do your best to not let that happen. You want to kill him! Sometimes, someone gets away without killing, but usually, someone gets killed—or really hurt. Did you hear the part about capturing horses?"*

"Yes, what is that?" Andy had wanted to know what that was all about because everything he had heard seemed to indicate that his hosts were great horse thieves.

"Those Crow, who were after our horses when I killed them? They were going to capture our horses. That is what we do—we capture

the horses of our enemies—and it is best if you can do it right under their noses. Anyone can find the herd and run off a bunch of woman horses. I have always wanted to be the one who sneaks into an enemy camp and captures the best horses—the ones where the owner ties them to his lodgepoles at night, rather than letting them out to graze with the herd. You never find good horses in the herd; those are mostly just the pack horses and the horses of the women and children."

There was also much talk about the spirits. Because of the way he had been brought up, Andy paid close attention when his hosts spoke about the spirit world. Spirits were as real to them as the buffalo. Their lives seemed to revolve around trying to live and cope with the spirits who inhabited the world around them. Some were good and brought good things to the people who honoured them, but there were others whose evil could bring misfortune, sickness, suffering, and even death. Spirits surrounded them and interacted with them. They always needed to be praying and making vows and offerings to keep the spirits appeased or at bay. *"Almost every man has a spirit who guides him,"* White Quill told him one day when it came up. *"Even some of the women."*

"You?" Andy wondered.

"No—some say I should go on a quest and seek one. I guess I will someday. But remember me? I am the one who never wants to grow up—I just want to stay a boy!" his friend reminded him.

"You?" Andy asked Badger.

"No." He seemed ashamed to admit it. *"I have never had anyone who would help me."*

"What—how—how you do that?" Andy was curious.

White Quill answered. *"You need to get someone to help you. You need to get someone whose medicine is strong—someone who knows what to do—you really need to know what to do—you could get hurt or even killed! Most boys get their father or an uncle or someone like that."*

Interrupting, Badger lamented, *"That is why I have never done it!"*

But White Quill continued. *"You must sweat and pray first, and then you go off and fast—on some high place—a high hill, or I have heard it is better if you do it on a mountain. You must go without anything—you take your clothes off, and your moccasins and you go without food or even water—well, you might need a little water. Someone will help you—your uncle or whoever it is—they will bring you some water, but you do not take much. You try to go without it. Then, you sit up there like that, and you fast and pray and wait, and sometimes a spirit will come to you. And, if it likes you, it will give you the power it has and give you the songs and the ceremonies you need to have. You need it—this spirit—to be really brave or really good at something."*

"Wow!" Andy exclaimed, fascinated.

"And, sometimes, some wild animal might find you—a real bear or something—or an enemy, and you are all naked and have nothing to defend yourself with, and they kill you," Badger added as if this sort of thing happened all the time.

"What—what are spirits?" the white boy asked.

"You do not know—it could be anything," White Quill responded. *"I think I would like an otter—they are smart—and wise. Some people only want a real bear or something like that, so they will have strength and courage."*

"That is what I want—I want a real bear!" Badger interjected. *"I want to be very powerful!"* Andy listened and let White Quill continue.

"Whatever it is, you need to have it, so you are not a nothing one."

"What do you mean?" the white boy asked.

"If you do not have strong medicine, you will not be very successful at anything—you will not be a good hunter or a good warrior, and you will not get a good wife."

Andy just shook his head. *"Is that—do you—do you want that?"*

Both his companions readily indicated that they did, but White Quill seemed a little less committed to the notion than Badger. Shrugging his shoulders, the younger one admitted, *"I do not know—you know me! Maybe I am just more interested in girls and having fun. None of that other stuff really interests me."* Aware of the spirit world, because of what his parents had taught him and what he had read in his Bible, Andy was cautious.

Coming to understand that warfare and capturing horses were what most boys and young men aspired toward, he also learned that these things were not for every one of them. For a few, like White Quill, these things did not hold such a strong appeal—at least, not yet. These few found Andy's campfire a safer place to be. There, they could talk about other things, and they did—usually hunting and horses—and girls. Sometimes in the company of a friend who had already been there, new boys would show up at their fire. Even a few of the elders, who sometimes spoke against the constant warfare, stopped by occasionally.

There was something else that was different around Andy's fire. Pretty Bird's mother would allow them to be together. If White Quill was around, the girl would usually be there, sitting beside him. Eventually, a few of her friends began showing up. Shadowed by mothers or older sisters, it was about the only place they could experience the mixed company of others their age.

"You need to be careful," Pretty Bird's mother warned Andy. *"Everybody thinks you are different. Not many mothers would let their daughters be with boys like that!"* she told him. *"They trust you—maybe because they see that I trust you—with White Quill around. We do not usually let boys and girls your age do this sort of thing—I have never seen it!"* Indeed, Andy had never seen it around any of the other fires in any other camp, and he considered it an honour to be trusted in that way.

Badger tried to explain it to him. *"It is because they all think we are going to sex them!"* White Quill nodded his head. *"As soon as we get old enough to—you know—when boys start getting horny all the time, they think we are going to go after their daughters or something. Before that, nobody really seems to care—they are together all the time. They are probably right, you know!"*

"It is not just that, you horny dog!" White Quill interjected. *"We are supposed to keep ourselves pure—we are not supposed to be doing that with a girl until we take a wife. It is not like we cannot control it! Just because you are such a horny dog! I could have gone with that Liar girl, but I did not."*

Badger responded. *"Well, why can we not even sit together or be together or talk—without some mother or older sister getting all crazy? We cannot even be together and talk—right in front of her parents—they will not let us! We have to try to meet a girl in the bushes or hide somewhere just to talk to her!"*

"Well, it is not all about sex, you know," his younger friend argued. *"It is supposed to be better if you have never done it until you get a wife. That is what my mother says!"*

Although young people back home had been chaperoned, Andy had never seen them segregated so stringently. *"Me the same,"* he told them. *"My home—a boy and girl, keep themselves pure. Same."* And, although he wished he could be alone with Pretty Bird, he was seldom given the opportunity, so they were almost always in the company of her brother or someone else who her mother trusted.

They did have their moments, though. The first time they managed to be alone, Pretty Bird had been allowed to go along on a hunt—because White Quill and the others were going to be there. But after watching for game from the crest of a ridge, it was White Quill who suggested she remain with Andy, while he and Badger left to scout an adjacent ridge. As soon as they were out of sight, Andy had put his arm around Pretty Bird's shoulder, and she snuggled right into him. He had been looking for a chance to try to kiss her, but now that the opportunity seemed to have arrived, he was not sure what to do. Never having done such a thing, he worried that she might not be receptive to his advance. Hesitant, he first placed his cheek next to hers. Feeling her press herself to him, he decided to make the attempt.

Turning his head carefully, trying to be as casual about it as he could, he lined up on her lips before closing his eyes. Among the boys back home, there had been considerable conjecture on what was involved in such matters. He had heard that he was supposed to have his eyes closed. But following this advice led him to land his lips right on her nose! The promptness with which she moved her lips to his and the warmth with which she responded to his attempt drew him to linger there. When they separated, she gave him a warm smile. Emboldened, he gave it another try. Without saying anything, Pretty Bird leaned into him to let their lips meet. This kiss was longer, and without interrupting it, he pressed his weight against her until she lay back, and they kissed until hearing the others' return.

After that success, Andy began plotting ways to be alone with her. Coached by Badger, and sometimes even her brother, he would arrange to meet Pretty Bird wherever she went alone—to gather wood or fetch water—there to enjoy each other's fleeting affection. He made every effort to be near her, and when they were apart, he missed her.

Summer became autumn, and the west wind seemed to blow constantly. One day it blew cold and hard from the northeast, and heavy grey clouds hid the mountains from view. The next morning, everything was covered in a robe of snow, and a dark sky hung low. Children romped in the first snowfall of the year, while the women went about their chores. Few of the men ventured far from their fires. The snow was only as deep as a man's fist, and when the skies cleared, and the warm sun came out again the next morning, it disappeared rapidly. *"It is time for us to take our trip to the mountains!*" Badger announced to his friends. They had discussed it frequently.

White Quill wanted to take them to his own special place in the mountains. *"You will really like it!"* he promised. *"It is a surprise—I cannot tell you, but I know you, and you will like it!"*

The trip Badger wanted them to take would entail several days' ride and would take much longer. *"Too long—I stay with Pretty Bird,"* Andy protested, not wishing to be away that long.

"Hai! You will like my place! You like to swim, do you not?" White Quill wanted to convince him to go to his place and gave him a little more information. Andy nodded, and his friend continued, *"How would you like to swim in hot water? You come with me, and you will think you are boiled meat!"*

Andy was not sure what he was talking about, but he was intrigued. *"How long?"* was his only question. When he understood that Badger's expedition might be more than several days, it was White Quill's promise of a quick return to Pretty Bird that convinced him. *"But you find a way—me say good-bye to your sister!"* he demanded. *"Alone!"*

White Quill was aware of their clandestine meetings, and since it seemed to be the only way he could get his friend to go along, he came up with a plan. *"If we can go tomorrow, I will see if I can get her to stay with us tonight,"* he suggested. *"We will need to get our things ready, so we can leave. I will ask her to help us. She will—it is my mother I need to convince!*

"You will do?" Andy exclaimed, surprised by his willingness to accommodate them.

"Of course! You are my brother! But remember, I will cut your stones off if you try anything with her!" White Quill warned with a grin, giving him a poke in the crotch.

Pretty Bird's response was not what anyone expected. She was not at all happy to discover that they were planning to leave the next day, and at first, she refused to give her help. It was her brother who finally pleaded with her. She came but spent much of her time trying to talk Andy out of going, while he and his friends worked at gathering a few things together. When they were almost done, White Quill announced, *"We have something we need to do!"* Grabbing Badger by the sleeve, he tugged him toward the door. *"We will return later,"* he said on the way out. *"I will bang on the lodge,"* he added smugly, before letting the door flap drop behind them.

Pretty Bird wore a long face. *"I do not want you to leave!"* she moped as soon as the pair had left.

"Yes, me also. They want me to go," Andy whispered, looking into her eyes and taking her hands in his. Having asked Badger to teach him the words, he whispered, *"I love you!"* His heart was in his mouth; he had been rehearsing it for days. At once, Pretty Bird took his face in her hands and kissed him, slipping her tongue between his lips and deep into his mouth. Startled by it at first, Andy responded in like manner, releasing a passion he had never experienced before. Gently, he pushed her to the ground and laid down beside her on the soft robe.

Left alone with their passion, they kissed and pressed their bodies together as they had never done before. *"I love you!"* the boy gasped, barely separating himself from her lips.

"I love you too!" she breathed in response, hugging him to her. Pressing their bodies together, they kissed long and deeply, until suddenly, pulling her lips away from his, Pretty Bird cautioned, *"We must not do too much!"*

"I know!" Andy replied, kissing her again and wriggling his hips, wanting her to feel his desire for her. But when he felt the girl's hands against his chest, he relented.

"I am sorry!" he gasped and rolled to the side.

"I love you! But I am afraid to do too much!"

"Me, too! I am sorry!"

"Do not be sorry! I want to give you sex, but I am—I am afraid!"

"*We should not!*" Andy agreed, his conscience overtaking his passion. "*I made a vow! To your brother!*"

"*I know! He told me,*" Pretty Bird admitted, with a bit of a grin. "*And, I made the same vow to him.*"

"*But we can do this,*" Andy responded, leaning over to kiss her on the lips. Kissing again, deeply, suddenly, he moved his lips away from hers and blurted, "*You be my wife?*"

Pretty Bird moved her head back. "*Is that what you want?*" she asked.

"*Yes! I love you!*" and he fell once more on her lips, moving a hand and placing it on her shoulder. "*Be my wife?*" he asked again, his heart pounding with anticipation.

Hesitating, she ventured softly, "*That is what my mother wants.*"

"*Is that what you want?*" he repeated her question, looking her in the eye.

Looking into his eyes now, she nodded her head, smiling. "*Yes!*" she whispered, barely audibly, throwing her arms around him.

Andy fell upon her, smothering her with his lips, pressing his hips forcefully into hers. Once again, passion overtook them, checked only by the sound of White Quill's voice and a pounding on the side of the lodge.

When the others stuck their heads in, the lovers were locked in an embrace, with their hips pressed together. Andy wondered how White Quill would react to the sight of such intimacy, but the grin on his face showed no disapproval. Stopping just inside the doorway, with Badger craning to see over his shoulder, he asked, "*Should we wait outside?*"

"*No! Come in!*" Pretty Bird responded brightly and kissed her lover on the cheek. Andy turned his head and kissed her on the lips.

The two boys tumbled into the shelter, and one of them stoked the fire, which the lovers had let die down. "*Shall we tell them?*" Pretty Bird whispered to Andy.

The white boy responded by saying, *"White Quill! I wish to take your sister as my wife!"*

"Hi-yah!" the boy shrieked and bounded to wrap his arms around them. *"I get to have you as my real brother!"* he squealed with excitement.

Badger was a bit less enthusiastic than his friend but came to give them a hug and congratulate them. *"But he still has to come with us!"* he warned the happy girl. Neither lover was pleased about it, but the Indian boys insisted.

"You will have all the rest of your lives to be together!" White Quill told his sister. *"We should get to have him for just a little while longer!"*

Euphoric, Andy's mind raced with a million thoughts. The last thing in the world he wanted to do was to be away from Pretty Bird, but his friends were adamant, and Pretty Bird was resigned to their parting—it would not be that long.

Andy had never seen anything like a marriage ceremony, among the Indians, and asked how it would happen.

"All you have to do is kill my father!" White Quill observed, giving a chuckle.

"What do you mean?" Andy wondered.

The bride's brother replied, *"You will need to give him a suitable gift, to be able to take his daughter as your wife. You will probably need to give him a bunch of good horses, or something he really likes—he really likes horses! I know him!"*

"How will I do that? I do not have a bunch of horses!"

"I will help!" White Quill offered. *"I can give two—no, probably three or four!"*

"I have two!" Badger offered.

The other Indian chided him, *"Hai! We can get more than that!"*

"And I have three. Is that enough?" Andy wondered.

"Seven! Or maybe eight or nine. He will probably want ten and ten. We have many to go," White Quill sighed.

"*Napikawan gifts?*" Andy asked.

"*You could use the fire-sticks you gave us,*" Badger suggested. "*We do not use them!*"

"*And, I give the napikawan gifts!*" exclaimed the white boy, beginning to feel a bit more optimistic. Pretty Bird grinned and kissed his cheek, to which he responded by turning and kissing her deeply.

"*Hai! Look at this!*" Badger exclaimed. "*Are you going to let him breed her right here?*"

"*You dog!*" White Quill scolded, taking a swing at him. "*They are just kissing!*"

"*But you are still coming with us!*" the older one reminded the pair.

"*Yes! You cannot disappoint us!*" the girl's brother agreed.

"*Perhaps we will find some horses to capture!*" Badger suggested.

But Pretty Bird responded adamantly, "*No! I do not want to be a widow before I am a wife!*"

"*Well, with those fire-sticks, and all our horses—what do you think?*" White Quill asked his sister.

With a frown, she said, "*You know our father! He is greedy!*"

"*I will give everything I have!*" Andy said.

"*You may have to!*" Badger added. He was not nearly as enthusiastic as his companions. "*It sounds like we might have to capture a few horses on our trip.*"

"*No!*" Pretty Bird reminded them firmly. "*I will talk to our mother.*"

"*Are you going to tell her?*" her lover asked.

"*Yes!*" the girl squealed excitedly, clasping her hands to her face. "*I want to go and tell her right now!*"

"*Do not go!*" Andy interjected.

"*She has to go soon. Or, our mother will be coming to get her!*" the girl's brother reminded them.

Reluctantly, the two lovers agreed it would be best for her to go. Andy wanted to be able to escort her, alone, but the others said that would not be good, so they all went.

Andy got little sleep that night, and he kept his friends awake for a long time, asking them all kinds of questions about marriage, their way. None of them were confident that the girl's father would view the arrangement favourably. And, that is what kept Andy awake.

15

"Parting is such sweet sorrow!" Andy said to Pretty Bird, recalling his father quoting some English writer to his mother, every time he had left her to go somewhere. He wished he could say it so Pretty Bird would understand. *"I love you!"* he whispered.

"I love you, too!" she whispered back.

Nervous about his next steps in becoming husband and wife, Andy knew that she loved him, and it was the comfort of that knowledge that made him feel a little better about leaving.

And, Pretty Bird knew of his love for her, which made her feel better about letting him go—he would be back before she knew it. And, with tears streaming down her face, she held him, and he held her while his companions waited impatiently on their horses. A few of their friends stood watching them, wishing they could go along. Her mother stood clutching her other daughter's arm as the young couple held onto each other in a final embrace.

"Do you have something for me to remember you by?" Pretty Bird whispered. Unable to think of anything, he stood dumbly before her.

"What?" he stammered, seeing the look on her face. With a confident grin on her face, the girl slipped her hands beneath his shirt. Letting one rest upon his breast, she moved the other to clasp his most cherished possession—the claw he had always worn around his neck.

The girl's mother was about to scold her for her actions but checked herself when Andy blurted, "Oh, his claw!" as if suddenly remembering something long forgotten. He reached for the leather thong by which it hung around his neck and slipped it off, placing it around hers. Gazing into his eyes as she did so, she took the claw and held it to her lips for a moment, then let it drop inside her dress.

Caring not what the girl's mother might say, Andy, kissed her on the lips before turning to hop onto his horse. With her hands clasped over her face, Pretty Bird savoured the smell of him, which lingered on her hands, and he was gone.

Andy experienced a host of emotions as they left the camp, and his friends sensed it—they both recognized that something was different about him that morning, as they rode together. He seemed to have changed, even since the day before. They were used to seeing him dive into anything they undertook with excitement and enthusiasm; that morning, he was pensive and subdued. Never had they seen him so aloof to their adventures.

White Quill led them westward, toward the mountains. The closer they got, the more rugged and wooded the foothills grew, until they found themselves riding beneath towering rock walls. Keeping to a trail near the river, from time to time, they could see *silver swimmers* in its deep pools, the water so clear that they could see all the way to the bottom. Occasionally, the fish would break the surface, some leaping entirely out of the water, making

Andy wonder how he might catch one to eat. His friends scoffed at the idea. *"Nobody eats those things!"* they said with disgust, their noses wrinkled.

With the sun shining brightly and warm, Andy would typically have been the first one into the water, but today, it was White Quill. Taking a break from a long ride, he leapt from the rocks. Coming up with a shout, he called the others to join him. *"Come in, you cowards!"* he hollered, trying to splash them. *"Come on! It is good!"* he beckoned, watching the others get ready. As soon as the white boy had his clothes off, Badger bowled him off his feet, and they tumbled into the chilly water together, both letting out a shriek. It was so cold that Andy could not handle it as long as his friends, soon clambering out onto the rocks to warm up in the sun. When the others finally emerged, they made fun of each other's shrivelled parts and goosebumps, before breaking out the dried meat.

"Where are the little biters?" Andy wondered, drawing attention to the absence of insects that had plagued them for months.

"That is the good thing about Cold Maker!" White Quill exclaimed. *"We will not see them again until after the geese come back."*

"I miss them!" Andy said sarcastically. His companions were glad to see his sense of humour returning.

In late afternoon, they came to a place where the valley broadened, and another trail branched away from the one they had been following. *"This is it, I think! We are almost there!"* their leader announced with excitement. *"You will like it!"* he exclaimed, taking the lesser trail. It was dusk when they encountered pools of steaming water in the dark forest.

Their youthful guide hurried to tie his horse, and gleefully stripping off his clothes, he waded into the hot springs. *"Ahh-h-h,"* he breathed loudly, squatting until he was up to his neck. *"Come in! It is hot!"* he cried. Badger very quickly had his clothes off and stooped to try the water with his hand. Letting out a whoop, he plunged in and jumped on White Quill's head. Still not the Andy they were used to, the white boy came along behind, and it took him a while to enter into their frolicking. There was very little light left when they waded out of the hot water to unload their horses and set up camp.

The cool air had no effect on them. *"Look! You are on fire—you are smoking!"* Badger shrieked, pointing out the steam emanating from their wet bodies.

"It is even better when the jackrabbit whistles at night!" White Quill informed them. *"Sometimes we come here, and when we get too hot, we roll around in the snow! We should come back here when the snow is deep! It is hard to get here, but it is fun!"* His excitement had not waned, though they were all feeling sapped by the water's intense heat.

Without bothering to don clothes, they explored shelters, similar to the war lodge they had made on the prairie. It was apparent that the place had been used by others, something White Quill confirmed. Putting their things into the shelter nearest the water, they returned to the spring, under the stars, until they were exhausted from its heat. Ready for sleep, they tumbled onto their robes and lay atop of them to cool off. There, Andy spoke of Pretty Bird, and his plans to make her his wife.

"Did you sex her?" Badger asked. *"While we were gone?"*

"Shut your mouth, you dog!" White Quill slugged him. *"Is that all you think about?"*

"Is there anything else?" he quipped.

"No! I love her!" sighed the one in love. *"We will not do that... only when we are husband and wife. We have decided that,"* he confided in them.

"We had better start getting horses, then!" Badger observed. Having spoken openly about his love for Pretty Bird, Andy spoke

of it often, continually reminding them that he was anxious to get back to her.

For a couple of days, they used the hot springs as a base for their explorations. On the first day, Badger shot a young deer, which they left for their return. Later in the day, however, when they returned for it, they found that something had taken over the carcass, devouring much of it and leaving it covered with leaves and dirt. Both Indians knew before they even got close to it that something was wrong, from the way the horses spooked. Examining the condition of the carcass, they declared that it must have been a *real bear,* and Badger vowed to return to kill it. The next day, however, in attempting to make good on his vow, there was nothing more than a few scraps of hide and hair left and no sign of the creature that had done it.

The weather changed suddenly. Extreme winds died down in the early evening, and it began snowing heavily. All night it snowed, and they woke up to a dense covering of the stuff—much to White Quill's delight, for they could now roll in it, out of the hot springs.

But as the day wore on, with no let-up in sight, Andy grew anxious. *"Look!"* he said. *"The snow is past our knees!"* He was concerned about getting back to the camp, but the Indians showed no worry. They assured him it would not be so deep, once they got out of the mountains and spent the entire day, in and out of the water, promising their friend they would leave the next morning.

Near dark, knowing their lives together were about to change, the hot water became a place of melancholy as they recalled the times they had spent together. One might have thought that they were never going to see each other again. *"You are the best friend I have ever had!"* White Quill confessed after they had been quiet for a while.

"Yes, me too," Badger added, sounding subdued. In a very soft voice, almost inaudible, he added, *"I do not know what I am going*

to do without you!" It was unlike him to speak like that, and Andy did not know what to say. There was a long silence. He had a lump in his throat when he spoke.

"I love you guys! I really do!" It was only in English that he could so easily express himself; he knew they would not understand, but he said it anyway. "I love you—I love you like I loved my brother!" Ignoring their nakedness, he embraced them, one at a time. *"I love you!"* he said to each of them.

"I love you, too!" White Quill whispered solemnly as they hugged.

Badger had a more difficult time saying it, managing only, *"Me too!"* when it was his turn to receive Andy's embrace. They held onto each other for a long time. *"I love you!"* he managed to whisper awkwardly as they let go. When he heard it, Andy grabbed him and gave him another hug.

"I love you, Míísinsski." he murmured, giving him a bear hug.

Badger wrapped his arms around his friend and hugged him back. Until he giggled, *"I feel your thing!"* And, the moment was gone. With a gleeful shout, he leapt on his friend, and the tussle was on. White Quill was instantly in on it, and there was no more talk of their affection for each other.

By dawn, they were on the trail. They made no stops along the trail until they came in sight of the camp, which had got only a light dusting of snow. Andy kicked his horse and pushed to the front of the line, headed for Pretty Bird's lodge, his heart racing. With his friends lagging, he reached it ahead of them, spotting the girl's mother, toiling outside with some other women. Hearing the clatter of hooves, she looked up, and on seeing the white boy's familiar figure, she spoke something to her comrades and hurried to her lodge. Figuring that she was going to fetch her daughter, Andy pulled his horse up and sprang to the ground, eagerly awaiting her arrival.

At once, a couple of the women gathered their things and hurried off. Those that remained would not look at him and kept working in silence. *"Hai! It is good to be home!"* he said to them, wondering what was going on and why Pretty Bird was taking so long. *"Where is Pretty Bird?"* he asked when she failed to appear. Still, nobody looked at him, until one of the women muttered something he did not understand. Puzzled, he asked again, *"What? Where is she?"* His friends had caught up to him, and they, too, were wondering what was going on.

Finally, one of the women looked up and spoke—a younger woman, one who Pretty Bird had often worked with. *"She is gone! He has taken her away—she had no choice! Bear Rising Up came in here with her father. He had offered him many horses to take her for his wife. She tried to protest, but he would not hear—you should have taken her with you!"* With that, the others all began speaking at once, each saying her piece.

Andy was stunned and could not believe what they were saying. Hoping they were joking, he exclaimed, *"What are you saying?"* The women hung their heads, and he knew it was true. *"Wh-when?"* he asked softly, his throat tight. He felt as if his entire world was caving in again.

"Not long after you left. She prayed...we all prayed that you would return and take her away. Someone even went to try to find you, but the young man was insistent. When he found out that she wished for you, he offered him more horses. His father gave him enough of his own to satisfy the greed of your father. Why did you have to go away? It was you she wanted!"

"Where is she? Who is it?" Andy asked feebly, feeling the blood drain from his face, tears forming in his eyes.

"It is Bear Rising Up," the woman responded. *"He returned with horses from a raid against the Crow—just after you left—he had found her father, and they came together. He has taken her to the lodge of his mother—over there,"* she pointed with her lips and

continued, *"and made her his wife. You must not let her see you lest she die from her sorrow. He is a good man...but she does not love him! It would be best for her to think you died at the hands of an enemy, that she might be content with him,"* the woman tried to console him.

Unable to hold back his tears, Andy turned away and stepped blindly toward his horse. Behind him, he heard the woman say, *"She loves you, Sun Shines on Him!"* Crushed beyond words, Andy burst into tears. Hiding his face in his hands, he leaned on his horse's neck and sobbed. His friends leapt to the ground and rushed to comfort him, standing with their hands on his shoulder. The woman and her companions scattered.

"We should go to our lodge," White Quill whispered. *"Come. My heart has fallen to the ground!"*

"You go," Badger bid them. *"I will bring the horses—go!"*

With White Quill's arm around his shoulder, Andy walked bravely for his lodge, trying to keep his tears in check. People stood and watched, and as soon as he got near, he ran for the door, bursting into tears as he ran.

In the light of the smoke hole, the first thing Andy saw was the willow backrest, which Pretty Bird had made for him. Draped over it was Wolf Tail's claw. Hurrying to it, he clutched it to his chest and fell with his face to the ground, bawling. All the tragedy, all the heartbreak since his mother's death once again consumed him, and he howled with agony. Neither White Quill nor Badger, when he arrived, could console him, and when White Quill too began to sob, the tears started to well up in Badger's eyes.

Suddenly, a lone figure slipped through the doorway. Pretty Bird's mother shuffled toward them and got to her knees, taking Andy into her arms. He looked dolefully into her eyes, and she cupped his face in her hands, kissing him softly on his tear-drenched cheek. *"I could not stop it!"* she began to explain, through tears. *"Nobody could! Once that old dog saw all those horses, he was determined to have them!"* She paused to let her words sink in. *"There is nothing you could have done, my son—had you been here. They would have hurt you if you had tried to interfere—her—you— he would have hurt you both! Oh, how she wanted you!"* She could not contain her own sobbing, and Andy's tears came once more. The woman sobbed for a moment then waited for him to stop before continuing. *"She told me you were to be husband and wife. Oh, she was so excited! All my friends wanted you to have her, too—and I wanted you as my son. But now, we must try to be happy for her."*

"Why? I don't understand!" Andy blurted in frustration and disappointment. "Why are you doing this to me?" he demanded an answer from his god, his voice raised, tears streaming down his face.

"And, now I fear for both of you," the woman continued once he had settled down. *"I fear that she will try to see you...she loves you, boy. And, if she does...he will do something to her...I know it! He will hurt her! He will hurt you both!"* She paused for a moment, to give effect to her words. *"You must go away! I am sorry, my son! You must leave—before she can come to you...because she will! I know it! And, I do not want anything to happen to either of you."*

"I will!" the bereaved boy responded, a sudden look of determination coming over his face. Climbing purposefully to his feet, he looked about his lodge. "I have to go," he uttered, dazed, returning his gaze to Wolf Tail's claw, which he still clenched in his hand. Placing it around his neck and tucking it inside his shirt, he turned to Badger. *"Where is my horse?"* he asked, emotionless, his eyes red from crying.

His friend was sombre, replied, *"Outside."*

Without a word, Andy turned and slipped out. Hurrying to his horse, he untied it and swung up onto its back. It was reluctant to quit the company of its kind. Being uncharacteristically harsh, Andy thrashed its rump. He kicked its sides viciously, to make it carry him away from that horrible place of anguish. Flogging the weary beast as fast as it would go, he could barely see where he was going for his tears. Several times, the animal balked and tried to turn back, but he whipped it and kicked it onward.

The trees, as they slipped past him, seemed barren and stark; the sky was low and grey; the air was cold, and the whole landscape seemed suddenly hostile. There was no place for him now.

His friends managed to catch his horse as it raced back toward the camp, riderless, and the deep impressions made by the animal's hooves now left a trail clear enough for them to follow. Eventually finding the spot where it had turned around on its own track, Badger observed, *"He is on foot."*

Dismounting, he picked up his friend's track and followed it carefully. It led to the top of a high bluff until they lost it on hard ground, where the wind had removed the scant snowfall. Both at the same time, they noticed a rocky outcrop, and White Quill knew that beneath it, there was a steep drop to the river below.

"Do you think he threw his life away?" he wondered out loud, feeling shaken. He had heard of others, jilted in love, doing such a thing. Badger did not care to answer as they moved to the edge of the precipice. There was no sign of their friend. *"Look, you can see the horses,"* White Quill murmured, trying to sound as if he had not been looking for something else, afraid to express his fear. He was beginning to feel desperate. *"What do you think?"*

Badger did not answer him; he just gazed into the distance, not daring to look at the icy water below them. It was too hard for him. He had never been in such a situation before, and he was beginning to feel panic. He turned completely around, trying to see some sign of their friend, but his eyes were unseeing for anguish. Moving to be closer to his troubled companion, he deliberately shuffled closer until their shoulders touched. Together, standing over the steep drop, they did not know what to think.

"Hai!" White Quill cried out suddenly, startling his friend. *"Where are you?"* There was a north wind blowing, which was all they could hear, as it moved through the wind-stunted trees behind them.

"We have to be able to pick up his trail!" Badger exclaimed out of nowhere, new determination in his voice. *"This is silly!"* Grabbing his friend by the sleeve and retracing their steps to where they had lost the track, he started walking in circles. He was relieved when he picked it up again, a little farther along the ridge. It led them to another rocky outcrop, where once again, he lost it on the hard ground. This time, he did not walk over to the edge; he began circling, trying to pick it up again, and that is when he heard Andy's voice.

"I'm over here." He was huddled in the shelter of a scrub pine; his eyes were red. That he had been crying was obvious. Sombrely, his two friends squatted beside him, neither one knowing what to say.

Finally, White Quill took him by the arm and hoisted him up, saying, *"Come! We need to find a place to camp. We are staying out here tonight!"* The white boy gave him a dazed look, and in silence, they made their way back to the horses.

"We might as well stay right here—over there, closer to the river," Badger suggested, leading the way. Shortly, they had a small fire going.

White Quill was the first to speak about Pretty Bird. *"I was in favour of you taking her as your wife,"* he announced sadly, stating the obvious. Andy showed no reaction. *"I wanted to be your brother,"* he continued. *"I am sorry that we made you come with us!"* His eyes were sad. *"I am sorry!"*

Andy took a deep breath and gave a sigh, saying, *"You are my brother!"* Looking too at Badger, he continued, *"Both of you! We are brothers! But there is nothing we could have done! You heard!"* he said bravely.

Feeling awkward but knowing it was something he needed to do, Badger slid over beside Andy and put an arm around his shoulder. *"Brother, I am sorry!"* he apologized. *"We made you leave her! It is our fault!"*

"No," was all Andy said, softly, pursing his lips trying to hold back tears. The three of them sat gazing silently into the fire until Andy broke the silence. *"We must help Míísinsski find his people,"* he said to White Quill.

"Yes! We will travel together—we can spend the winter with his people," White Quill agreed, without emotion.

"What about your family?" Badger wondered.

"You are my family!" he replied without hesitation. *"We must always stay together! Anyway—if I stay here, I will kill my father— or die trying. I hate him!"*

Pausing from time to time to wait for Andy's tears, they made a plan. Badger and White Quill would return to the camp in the morning, gather what they needed for their journey and be back before nightfall.

The next day, however, with both his friends gone, Andy was unbearably lonely. He was glad for the companionship of his faithful horse, which the others had brought back to him. To her, he mourned his loss. "You probably don't even know what I'm talking about, do you, girl?" he whispered to the patient animal, which had long since forgotten the flogging he had given it. "I have lost so many people over the last while that I don't think I can take it—Mum, Matty, Wolf Tail—and now Pretty Bird!" Switching to speak to his god, with deep sadness, he murmured, "God, I don't understand what you're doing! Why is this happening to me?"

Weeping softly, he fell to his knees. "Help me! Please! I don't know what to do! God, O God, please help me! I miss them so much! You gotta help me find my pa! Please, somehow, let Pretty Bird and me be together! I love her so much! Just—you gotta— somehow!" Deep, uncontrollable sobbing choked off his words, and his horse lowered its head toward him. "You know what I'm talking about, don't you, girl?" he whimpered, standing up and rubbing his hand through its mane and scratching its velvet nose. "Yeah, you know! Why don't you take me somewhere?"

Untying it, he hopped onto its back. But instead of fulfilling some mystical bond he had imagined between them, the horse immediately broke for the camp. For a moment, he thought that he might go there—just to the edge of it, or maybe across the river from it—hoping he might be able to catch a glimpse of Pretty Bird. But recalling that angry husbands sometimes cut the nose off an unfaithful wife, he pulled back on the rein. "No, we can't go there!" he said to the horse, turning it around, forcing it to take him in the opposite direction.

By early afternoon, he had reached the top of another ridge; he loved the high country. Overlooking the foothills, he could pick out the valley where Pretty Bird had her new home. He could even see the smoke of the camp, hanging in the air. It was not windy for a change.

Spending the afternoon alone, on his lofty perch, he rehearsed their final parting. His grief was so intense, he felt like it would choke him, and he longed for the chance to hold her in his arms again. How bitterly he regretted leaving her! Despite what her mother had told him, he would rather have died trying to be with her. "Why, oh why?" he cried out to his god repeatedly, punctuated with his sobs.

Finally, when the shadows were long and the air much cooler, he saw two riders leading packhorses in the distance, and he mounted his horse.

His friends had packed everything they could onto the two horses he had been given by Rowand. The only thing they had left behind was their lodge, which they had returned to the old woman, assuring her that they would be back one day to retrieve it. They had brought with them the rest of the goods which the trader had given to Andy and had just begun to unload the pack-horses when Andy arrived. *"Did you see her?"* he asked, as soon as he had dismounted and tethered his horse.

"He went to see her," Badger answered, nodding in White Quill's direction.

Andy asked the younger one, *"What did she say?"*

"She wanted to come with us, but my mother would not let her. She said that Bear Rising Up would come after us with his friends. They would kill you both if they found you together. She said that we should pray to Sun that you might be able to find a way to be together. That is what I have been doing—I have prayed all the way!"

"I have prayed—to my, my uh, medicine. I am not sure it—" Andy lamented, without finishing.

"My mother says she has made a vow to Sun," White Quill continued. *"She will give the Sun dance—a second time—if Pretty Bird would be able to come to you. But for now, you must wait—for a sign and the right medicine."*

"What do you mean?" the white boy blurted, suddenly impatient. *"What is that—the right medicine?"* he asked, feeling like nothing seemed right anymore.

"You need to find your helping spirit!" White Quill informed him. *"You need to seek a vision! We could—"*

"He already has his medicine!" Badger interrupted to remind him. *"Remember? He has told us about it. He already has a spirit helper, what do you call it?"* he asked Andy.

Surprised by his friend's observation, and that he had remembered, the white boy answered, "Jesus." he replied softly.

"You should pray to it, then. Tomorrow we will sweat and burn sweetgrass—and fast," White Quill said with renewed enthusiasm.

"What is that?" Andy asked, not understanding him.

"Fasting? When we do not eat," Badger explained. *"We will burn sweetgrass to cleanse our bodies and purify us—so your helper will be pleased with your prayers and come to you. You have seen*

it before! Remember?" Andy recalled seeing others enter a little shelter covered with buffalo hides, hauling in hot rocks to make them sweat. He knew it to be a prayer ritual, which made him hesitant, never having seen anything like it among his own people. Offering no protest, he would wait and see.

Though they did not understand their friend's medicine, neither of the Indian boys would question it. A spirit helper was a matter of secrecy and utter dependency. *"We will pray with you and ask Sun to have pity upon us,"* White Quill concluded. *"Your medicine should help you!"*

"The sun's got nothing to do with it!" Andy disagreed, shaking his head, not wishing to talk about it further.

A heavy frost covered the ground in the morning, keeping them snuggled beneath their warm buffalo robes. Nobody wanted to be the one to leave their cozy bed to start the fire, but eventually, Badger got up and got a blaze going. After the others were up, the Indians set about building the sweat lodge. With very few words, they gathered a few large rocks and carried them to the fire, dumping them into it. Stoking it well, they appointed Andy to keep it ablaze. Next, they searched the river's edge and gathered a bunch of tall willow boughs. These, they loosely wove into the shape of a dome, sticking the cut ends into the ground, over a small pit they had dug. Covering the sturdy frame with their robes, overlapping them to form a door facing *the place where Sun rises,* soon all they had left to do was to let the rocks heat.

Both Indians had been muttering prayers as they worked, praying over each bit of work they did. Encouraged by their prayerfulness, Andy withdrew to the river's edge to pray to his god by himself.

Soon, they came to get him and take him back to the fire, where they moved hot rocks into the shelter. *"Undress here, by the fire,"* Badger directed, when they were done. Getting themselves naked, he said simply, *"Bathe,"* and led them to the river. Their usual shrieking and antics in the icy water were absent as they quickly and solemnly washed their bodies. Returning to the sweat lodge as soon as they were done, Badger crouched to enter. White Quill nudged Andy to follow, warning him to watch out for the hot stones.

Inside, White Quill adjusted the robes, so no light penetrated, and it was pitch black. Out of the darkness, Badger cautioned, *"Be careful of the hot rocks!"*

Andy could see nothing, but while entering, he had seen the rocks in the centre and now felt their heat. When suddenly the fragrant aroma of burning sweetgrass wafted through the tiny shelter, he asked, *"What are we doing? What do I do?"*

Badger hushed him. *"I am burning sweetgrass on these rocks. Take handfuls of smoke and pull it over you to cleanse yourself. Friend, let in some light so he can see,"* he said to White Quill, who parted the robes a bit, just enough to let Andy see what Badger was doing as he continued. *"When we have done it enough, I will splash water on the rocks to make us sweat...and cleanse us some more. And we pray. When you hear me pray, pray to your medicine!"* He began to sing and tossed more bits of sweetgrass onto the hot rocks, using his cupped hands to draw the fragrant smoke over his body. The other one turned and shut out the light, plunging them once more into darkness.

Andy was sitting closest to White Quill. He could feel him reaching into the smoke, so he tried it himself, just as White Quill began a lilting chant. There was a slight sizzle, as water was splashed onto the hot rocks. The tiny lodge had grown very warm, but the steam made the sweat come.

Badger began to pray. *"O, great Sun, have pity on your children. You give us everything we need to live in this land you have given us. You watch over us and give us health and strength. O, great Sun, continue to watch over us and protect us from our enemies. You make the rain fall, and the grass grow, for our sacred buffalo—that you have given to us. Have pity upon us now and hear our prayers... Have pity on our friend and give him what he asks for. O, great Sun, bring Pretty Bird back to him and keep her safe! When we travel, keep us safe from anyone who would do us harm—our enemies, and anyone else. Keep us safe!"* When he finished, White Quill prayed. Their prayers were punctuated with songs that both seemed to know and sing together.

Andy began to pray very softly, "Jesus, I love thee!" he began, before continuing in his friends' tongue. *"My heart is warm toward you—and I know your heart is warm toward me. It is good you stay with me—and live, inside me—and that you give good things to me. I, uh, I have not prayed—and I am sorry. I know you are with me! I do not understand you sometimes. I follow you—I, uh, I trust you."* He prayed slowly, searching among the Blackfoot words he knew to be able to express himself, wanting his friends to understand his prayer. They had both stopped to listen as soon as he had begun to pray. He had always been amazed at how fervently they had both prayed and wished he understood more of their faith. Their prayers sounded so much like those in his church, only these two were praying to the sun. "God, *I know you made Sun,"* he added, for their benefit, *"and the land...and all. You make Sun—to give us light, and warm. Thank you for the sun! Thank you—all you make... the buffalo, your people...thank you!"* The Indian boys remained silent for a few moments, following Andy's prayer. He continued silently until they began their singing again.

Badger periodically sprinkled the rocks with water, but eventually, it no longer sizzled and sputtered. Although Andy had finished praying, when he found that the others were not done, he began again. Praying aloud, this time, he was not so concerned that the others hear what he was praying. Asking his god for protection, he begged him to make it so that he and Pretty Bird could be together. "Please, I love her so much! In the holy name of thy son, Jesus, I pray. Amen," he concluded. And then, he lifted his arms and sang bits of a hymn he remembered, from church. "Father, I stretch my hands to Thee!" Forgetting what came next, he sang, "—la la la la la-la—Ah! whither shall I go?" Keeping his eyes closed for a moment, he opened them and let his hands rest on his friends' shoulders. "I love you guys!" he blurted, his heart bursting with affection. *"I love you!"* Feeling renewed, he pulled them to him, hugging their sweaty bodies before they all crawled out of the little lodge and made their way again to the river.

Leaving the intense heat of their tiny shelter, they found the freezing water a shock. In it, Andy was reminded of his father baptizing him in the cold Red River, shortly before he had gone west. His fond reminiscence, though, was shattered when White Quill landed on top of him. Solemnity was gone. Shrieking and splashing, they horsed around and rough-housed for a moment, but it was short-lived. Feeling the cold, Andy wanted to get back to the fire. First though, resorting to old times, he grabbed hold of White Quill by his nipples, squeezing them sharply before fleeing for the shore. Both Indians pursued him and knocked him down. With White Quill sitting on his belly and holding his arms to the frosty ground, above his head, Badger pinched and poked him mercilessly.

"Get him! Get him!" the younger boy urged, struggling to hold the bigger white boy down. Badger quit worrying Andy's nipples and hurried to get him elsewhere. But to the younger Indian's surprise, he reached around from behind him and latched onto his nipples. With a shriek, White Quill let go of Andy and thrashed at his betrayer. Immediately, Andy had a hold of him by his most delicate parts.

Squeezing hard enough to make him stop squirming, he demanded, *"Do you say I am the best?"*

"No, No," White Quill protested, squirming, trying to get away, with both still squeezing. Andy squeezed harder, and Badger

twisted. *"Aiyee! Stop! Yes, yes, you are the best!"* the youngest one cried, *"You are the best! I am a dog! I surrender!"*

But the prankster was not faithful to his word. As soon as they let him go, he scrambled to his feet and smacked Badger in the crotch. Fleeing, he was quickly overtaken and tackled to the ground. He tried to curl up to protect himself, while the other two pried on his arms and tugged at him, pinching and poking and gouging until they lay in a knot, giggling and panting. *"Get off me! I cannot breathe! The ground is cold!"* White Quill protested loudly.

Slowly, they separated themselves, reluctant to see an end to their childish behaviour, as if to do so was to give up boyhood itself. Each bragged of besting the others. But Andy stuck his pale chest out and pouted, *"See my red nipples!"*

"See mine!" Badger whined.

"That is nothing!" White Quill lamented, cradling himself gently with his hand.

His companions laughed at him and made their way to the fire, where they had left their clothes.

16

That night, Andy found sleep difficult. Disturbing his companions by tossing and turning and pulling the robe off them, in the morning they were all cranky. On the trail early, Badger led them in a southeasterly direction, staying well clear of the camp where he knew Pretty Bird might be watching for them. Both Indians knew their companion was very sad and took turns trying to get him to talk. White Quill tried joking and telling funny stories, but nothing seemed to cheer him. He seemed to prefer to ride alone, behind the others.

Once they were beyond the camp, though, the white boy seemed to come out of his funk, riding up beside them. *"Where are we going?"* he asked.

Badger answered. *"We are going to Napi-tahta—where my people usually spend the winter. I hope they will be there!"*

"How long?" he was asked.

"It should take us maybe three or four nights, depending on what we do along the way."

"Will there be many people there?" Andy wondered, feeling a little apprehensive about meeting new people.

"Yes, at least as many as were in this camp," he replied. *"There might be a lot more—it depends on where people are spending the winter. Sometimes they are there, sometimes they are closer to the always summer land—we will have to see."* Andy nodded his understanding. *"Why?"* Badger wondered. *"Are you wondering if there are any girls there?"* White Quill whirled around when he heard it and glared at him. The pained look on Andy's face, though, told Badger it had been the wrong thing to say. *"I am sorry—I am a nothing one! I did not mean to say that!"*

Andy shrugged and said it was all right, but his face told a different story. He was silent, and in a few moments, let his horse fall behind the others.

"You nothing one! Why did you say that?" White Quill scolded Badger in a whisper.

"I said I was sorry! I did not mean it!" he responded defensively.

"Well, he thinks you did!"

Andy could hear them and said with a raised voice, *"It is all right!"* But he still did not move up to rejoin them.

"You better say something—he is hurt!" White Quill growled, keeping his voice low. Badger rode on for a while, staring straight ahead. Suddenly, he steered his horse at right angles to the trail and rode a short distance until his horse balked; and there he stopped, with his head hung.

"He did not mean it—he can be such a nothing one sometimes!" White Quill murmured, apologizing for his friend when Andy caught up with him.

"I know," Andy sighed. When Badger made no move to rejoin them, Andy directed his horse toward him, telling White Quill to stay where he was.

Sullen, Badger would not look him in the face. *"I am sorry!"* he muttered when Andy stopped his horse beside him. *"What do you want me to do? I said I was sorry!"*

"Hai, I do not hold it against you," Andy assured him and put a hand on his shoulder. *"I am very sad! Do not hold that against me."* Badger turned to look at him. Both looked sad, and neither one was able to look the other in the eye. After a long moment, the white boy gave a sigh and murmured, *"Come on, let us go."* And, they rejoined White Quill.

All were so tired they stopped early. Andy tried to sleep while Badger went off to see if he could find something to eat. Returning empty-handed, he found both his companions asleep—so soundly that they hardly stirred—until he tried to slither under their robes with them. Feeling the coldness of his bare skin against his warm back, White Quill gave a sleepy protest and moved closer to Andy's sleeping form. It was just getting dark.

In the morning, snow covered the robes, under which they were huddled together for warmth. In the middle, White Quill was the first to awaken. Sandwiched between the other two, still asleep, he could hardly move. Wriggling around to try to get them to give him some room, he got a look outside and saw all the snow, and it gave him an idea.

Trying not to disturb either of his bedmates, he wriggled an arm out and scooped up a handful of snow. Bringing it under the robe, he jammed it right on Badger's crotch. Using both hands, he held it there. His startled friend gave a shriek that must have been heard back at the camp. Sitting upright, he began thrashing about, tearing at the robes and sending snow flying everywhere. When he realized what was happening to him, he hammered on White Quill and tried to push him away. The young prankster kept his head down and clung to his victim with all his might, but he had begun to laugh so hard that he could not hang on and got hurled from their cozy nest. Laying spread-eagled in the snow, he laughed despite the cold. Furious, Badger scrambled to his feet and began kicking snow on him.

Rudely awakened, Andy wondered what was going on, clutching at the robe to stay covered. When Badger turned to face him, Andy saw the snow, still clinging to his patch of curly hair, and figured out what must have happened. He could not help laughing, which incited the angry Indian to turn on him too and begin kicking snow at him.

Badger was still fuming and breathing revenge long after they had settled down and started to brush the snow off everything to find their clothes. It was a chilly start to the morning, but White Quill was remorseless and quite happy that he had got Andy to laugh. After that, things went a little better, though Badger spent a good part of the day plotting how he would get back at White Quill.

Later in the day, the temperature grew mild, and the warm west wind began to pick up. By evening, the ground was wet from melting snow as they searched for a dry spot among the trees. At their fire that night, his friends entertained Andy with more of their stories. He liked to hear them and was intrigued by their spirituality—their stories were often about spirits. Both Indians wondered if perhaps a spirit had beset him, as they tried to understand his misfortune. Badger reminded him of the owls they had heard the night Matthew had died and affirmed his belief that they were the spirits of the dead Cree, there to harass them.

White Quill then related a story about a man said to have been killed by such a spirit. *"He had killed his wife—in a fight or something—and one night, after, he was wakened by the voice of an owl outside his lodge. They say that he went outside to see what it was, and as soon as he stepped outside, he fell down dead. It was that owl—the spirit of his wife—taking her revenge on him."*

"Who knows?" Badger speculated. *"Maybe Bear Rising Up did something—put a curse on you,"* Andy said he did not think that

was possible. *"Hai! I have heard of it,"* retorted Badger. *"Have you not heard of it?"* he asked White Quill, who nodded his head.

"It is a good thing I have that old woman who prays for me!" White Quill informed them. *"The one who healed me. Her medicine is powerful—you saw what she did for me! But I need to seek my own—that should be much better!"*

"I do not know," Badger sighed. *"I have not really seen it work that well. My father was supposed to have had very powerful medicine. And, my mother gave all his horses to those who were supposed to have all this medicine! And, it did not work—I do not know! It did nothing for us!"*

Andy, too, was skeptical and reminded them of what he had said to White Quill's mother: *"My medicine—it made all those things—Sun—buffalo, animals, trees—everything. He made us! He, uh, he takes care of us, he does not hurt us!"*

When he was finished, White Quill responded, *"I know! That is like the medicine of this old woman—it does not let bad spirits hurt people."*

But Badger drew attention to something else. He challenged Andy, *"If your medicine takes care of you, what happened with your brother?"* His younger companion glared at him for being so direct, but Andy just shook his head, wishing he knew their language well enough to tell them more of what he believed. Badger, did not wait for either of them to speak. *"I do not know—I do not think any of that is for me! Let us talk about something else. Have you ever wondered what it will be like when you die and go to the Sand Hills?"*

"What is that?" Andy asked, having heard it mentioned before.

"When you die, you become a ghost and go to live in the Sand Hills. That is where everybody that is dead lives. It is just like here, but everybody is dead—but they cannot die again. It is just their ghosts."

White Quill added to what his friend had said. *"You know that dusty trail we see in the sky at night? That is the wolf trail—that is what you have to follow to go there."*

Andy had heard others speak of following *the wolf trail;* now, he understood what they had meant. *"I heard that,"* he said. *"We call it heaven."* Both his companions tried to say the word, and he continued, *"It is up there, in the sky."*

"No!" Together, the Indians disagreed.

"It is over there—where Sun gets up in the morning!" White Quill asserted. *"And, when you die, someone might kill your best horse and leave all your good things wherever they put you, so you will have them in the Sand Hills."*

"Enough about dead!" Andy interjected. Wishing to change the subject, he said, *"Talk about another thing—girls—we find you a girl!"* Always their favourite topic, the others had been avoiding it, thinking he did not want to talk about it.

"She must have big breasts!" Badger blurted. *"I like big breasts! Did you see that girl that was always singing? I went to the river every time I thought she was going there to bathe!"* Seeking relief from the grief of his loss, Andy joined them in their specious conversation, and eventually, everyone slept soundly.

By morning, the wind had switched again to the north, and the dawn's light was cloaked by heavy cloud. Very quickly, they got their things together and headed south. When they reached a well-used trail, with deep ruts etched in soil, Andy wondered what might have made such marks. *"What is this?"* he asked, thinking it looked like ruts left by wagons. He wondered if they might be near a white settlement, for he knew the Indians had nothing with wheels.

Badger explained. *"It is called the North Trail. It follows Mistakis—all the way to the Always Summer Land, and all the way over to the Big River—that is where the napikawan camp is, remember? Everybody uses it!"*

With excitement, Andy began, *"Do you have, uh—do you—"* and with a sigh, he realized that he had no way to describe a wagon to them. Using his arms, he drew a circle and tried to mimic the wheel of a wagon, but all he got was blank stares. *"At the napi-kawan camp! Remember? A wagon! With wheels!"* Another circle evoked more blank stares. "You guys!" he groaned. *"What made these?"* he asked in frustration, pointing to the ruts in the trail.

"Poles, pulled by horses. You know! You see them all the time!" Badger answered, surprised he had not recognized the familiar track.

"Oh," Andy sighed. Of course, he knew that—travois—but the notion had completely escaped him, thinking there might be others of his kind in the area.

At the south end of the *Porcupine Hills*, the mountains lay before them in a panorama, and Andy stopped for a look. *"This is where I want to live!"* he declared. *"We camp here?"* he wondered. Although it was earlier than they were used to stopping, his companions looked at each other and shrugged.

"I guess we have enough water," Badger observed. So they unloaded their things and tethered the horses on the top of a high butte at the edge of an evergreen forest, with the spectacular view before them. Sitting together, afterward, Badger pointed out the course of a river valley, cut through the rolling plain before them. *"That is called Napi-tahta—it is three rivers—one, two, three,"* he said, pointing out the valleys of the three different forks. *"We have camped there many times...sometimes here, sometimes there—last winter, sometimes over there—three winters ago."* He pointed out each location. *"Sometimes farther down—over there, past that ridge. We live in the best place!"* he exclaimed proudly. White Quill tried to dispute his claim, but Badger kept talking. *"I will show you where we used to run the buffalo over a big cliff—all the way around that ridge over there. We do not do that very much anymore—it is*

more fun to hunt on horses—but you can see all the bones. Nobody seems to camp there anymore. My father took me there once.

"I do not think we will find anyone, though—you would be able to see the smoke. I guess they are camped down at Two Medicine—I do not know—we will have to find them."

When he had finished, White Quill told Andy that, although his people spent most of their winters along *Makhabn*, where they had left his family, they had occasionally travelled through this country on their way to or from the summer hunts. *"I was born right over there,"* he noted, *"along that creek you can see, over there,"* he indicated, pointing out its treed valley. *"It is called the Little High Wood."*

Over the next two days, they searched for any sign of Badger's people, without finding any indication that anyone had recently been there. Disappointed, he led his friends farther out onto the broad prairie where, from the crest of a hill, they searched for anything that might indicate a camp. Still finding nothing, he led them south, thinking that the camp must be on the *Bear River* or *Two Medicine Creek*.

They were headed in that direction when they encountered *Piikáni* scouts. Approaching one another with caution, Badger recognized one of them and announced to his friends, *"It is them!"*

On getting closer, one of the scouts recognized Badger and asked, without greeting him, *"Where are the others?"*

Badger stopped short. *"What others?"*

"Your friend—and the others! Are they not with you?"

A look of surprise came over Badger's face. *"No,"* he answered slowly, just as two more scouts joined them. *"They did not return?"*

"No! You are the first we have seen," the first scout replied. Turning to his companions, he informed them, *"It is Míisinsski — the others are not with him."*

Badger was shaken. *"They left us, back when the berries were ripe!"* he said, quietly. *"They did not come back?"*

"No. Everyone thinks that you were all killed. What happened?" one of the scouts asked.

Badger had a distant look in his eyes. After thinking for a moment, he told them something of the story of the attack on the Cree, and Andy's brother, and finding Andy. "Then, they just left us!" he said, without giving any detail as to how he had been left behind. "And, I thought they would have been back a long time ago...something must have happened," he ventured, letting his voice trail off. Turning in his saddle, he looked at Andy and asked, "Did you hear that? They did not return to our camp!"

"What happened?" Andy wondered.

"They must have run into more than they could handle," one of the other scouts volunteered. "That one was a dog! He probably got them into trouble."

"They were all hot-heads!" the first one exclaimed.

"Except the one who was my friend—the son of Charging in the Water," Badger remarked quietly, with the same distant look about him.

"Yes, he did not deserve what the others got," the first one admitted.

"I wonder what happened to them," Badger said, to nobody in particular.

"Probably the Cutthroats," the second scout suggested.

"Or, Liars," the third one now spoke up. "It was more likely the Liars—they probably went after them."

Badger was suddenly overcome with grief over the loss of one who had once been his best friend. He had never considered that anything might have happened to them, and he began to feel an overwhelming sense of loss. "I must find my mother!" he blurted suddenly and kicked his horse. Andy recognized that something was wrong with him and hurried to catch up. When he got close enough, he spotted his friend's sad face.

"*Stop!*" Andy hollered, and Badger reined in his horse, sitting with his head hung. "*Is it—is it your friend?*" Andy asked him, for Badger had spoken often of Little Dog. The Indian nodded his head without looking up.

"*What is it?*" White Quill asked, catching up to them.

"*His friend,*" Andy replied, honouring the taboo against mentioning the name of the dead.

"*He was my best friend!*" Badger said softly. "*We grew up together.*" White Quill rode over to be beside him. "*He did not deserve what they got!*" Badger continued sadly. "*He was my almost brother!*" The three of them sat on their mounts in silence—until they saw the rest of the camp beginning to emerge from a deep coulee ahead. Badger wiped his eyes and his nose with his sleeve and said with resignation, "*Let us go,*" reining his horse in that direction.

The first riders they encountered also asked Badger about his companions, and he told them what he had said to the others. Word of his return spread quickly, and the whole column soon began to drift in their direction. Several men milled about, on horseback, discussing what they had been told, and then Badger spotted his uncle hurrying in his direction. Others recognized him and parted for him as he slowed his horse and approached his nephew. Stopping a short distance apart, the two looked at each other, neither one showing any emotion. After a long moment, Badger shook his head, almost imperceptibly, and the man just wheeled and rode away. Others turned away as well, and soon the column began to move again.

Shortly, another man approached. "*It is his father!*" Badger gasped, with a look of dread. He pulled up to wait for the man. This man, too, stopped a short distance from them but learned what he wanted to know from the look on Badger's face. This time, Badger could not hold back his tears, which began streaming down his face. The man kicked his horse and came up beside him, holding out his arm to him. Badger leaned over to rest his head against his shoulder, sobbing. The man's face showed his own grief, but he held onto the young man who had been so close to his son. In a moment, Badger sat up and told the man his story.

"*You are my son, now!*" the man said. "*We will talk.*" He then turned his horse to intercept two women who were hurrying optimistically toward them. Speaking to them briefly, they both began wailing as they turned to rejoin the column.

Word of Badger's return had not made its way to the rear, where his mother and sister were riding with some of the other women, pulling a travois and leading packhorses. Spotting him from a distance, his mother leapt from her mount and ran to him afoot. Shrieking for happiness much of the way, she dragged him from his horse, and taking him into her arms, she wept with joy. His little sister was right on her heels and danced about, looking for a way to get her arms around her brother.

In a moment, he stepped back from them to introduce his friends. The excited woman greeted them briefly and returned her attention to her son. Throwing her arms around his neck, she assailed him with questions, while petting his head and stroking his long hair. His friends had never seen such a satisfied look on his face.

Two days later, the camp reached *Napi-tahta* and set up camp on a horseshoe bend on the south fork, near its junction with the main river. Badger had been dismayed to find that his mother and sister were still living in his uncle's lodge. He refused to join them, preferring to sleep as he had—outside with his friends. The morning after they arrived at the winter camp, though, he sought out a group of women. "*I wish to have my own lodge*"— he announced in a loud voice— "*for my mother—you know her— Antelope Woman. Where can I find one? We need a lodge! Does anyone have a lodge for her?*" he asked the women.

Andy saw what he was doing and spoke up, surprising the women by speaking their language. *"We have fire-sticks! We have napikawan robes! And more—come and see!"* He turned and led them to his stock of trade goods, and it did not take long before they had a tipi of their own. He gave up some of the tobacco, two blankets, some coloured cloth and beads, and pots and cooking utensils to get it since Badger really had nothing to trade. The poles, Badger could scrounge, and next, he went for his mother.

He ought to have anticipated trouble from his uncle. As soon as the man learned the purpose of his nephew's visit, he became abusive and refused to permit the woman and her daughter to leave. *"She is my wife! I need them!"* he crowed.

Badger stood right in front of him and snarled, *"She is my mother! She is coming with me!"* Seeing the man's anger mounting, Andy began to wonder where it would end until the man's *sits beside me wife* intervened. She suggested that Badger offer the man a gift, implying that he might feel better about losing one of his wives if he received something to compensate him for his loss. The *fire-stick* Badger had got from Andy, for which he cared little, was just what the man wanted—and the matter was at an end.

Antelope Woman and her daughter erected their new home while her son and his friends removed her scant belongings from her sister's lodge. Andy fetched a couple of metal pots, some big spoons and sharp, metal knives which, at once, elevated the woman's stature above most of her neighbours. They were rich—life was good—and Badger was beginning to feel good about himself. Until one of the leading men summoned him.

"We would like to hear your story," the man said gruffly. He was the war chief; an ugly scar across his face spoke of his qualification for such honour. *"Tomorrow, when the shadows are long. We would like to hear from you."* It was an invitation that was not to be ignored, and Badger grew nervous.

He took Andy aside. Explaining what was expected of him, he asked, *"What shall I say? I am supposed to tell them what happened—what happened on that raid—with your brother and everything."* Andy had never fully understood what had happened that day. Even though Badger had told him some of it, he had always been vague, and there had been differing versions.

"Just tell them," Andy replied. He did not understand why his friend was so nervous.

"But I cannot! I cannot tell them—I will be a nothing one! I will be laughed at—all my friends and everyone will say I am a nothing one—a coward!"

"What do you mean? Just tell them what happened!" Badger just stood with his head hung, confirming something that Andy had long suspected. *"You did not say the truth!"* he groaned. *"You did not say the truth to me?"* When the Indian just kept his head hung and would not look him in the eye, Andy began to feel panic. It had been some time since his friend had said anything about the incident. Afraid of what he might hear, with a lump in his throat, he asked, *"What happened? Tell me what happened!"*

His friend's face was covered with shame. *"I am sorry,"* he whispered. *"I have to leave!"* And, he bolted.

Andy had trouble answering Antelope Woman when she wondered where her son was. *"I think he went out to be by himself—he is worried about talking to those people."*

When everyone was ready for sleep, and Badger had still not returned, he covered for him again, saying, *"He said he might stay away all night."* Neither Antelope Woman or White Quill would believe him. *"I do not know,"* he finally confessed. *"He is afraid of talking to those people—that is the truth! I do not know where he is."* It was too late to go and look for him, and in the morning, his horse was gone.

Worried, Andy and White Quill left to look for him. As soon as they were alone, Andy told his friend all he knew and confided his worst fear: that Badger had had a hand in Matthew's killing. His companion tried to be encouraging. *"He would not have done that—remember what he said at the napikawan camp? Down by the river? He said he was a coward—that he did not kill anyone."* They had both heard him speak of the affair, but they could recall at least three different versions that he had given on various occasions. They both knew that tonight's account, if he showed up, would very likely define his reputation among his people.

They kept their suspicions from his mother and went to the lodge of the war chief when the shadows were long. It did not appear as if they would be given entry since it was crowded inside, and others were waiting outside. Standing near the door, White Quill had a look inside and shook his head to Andy. *"They are wondering where he is,"* he reported. Andy's heart sank. He was pacing nervously when he heard his friend whisper, *"Here he is!"*

Coming from the direction of his lodge, Badger's step was confident. *"Where were you?"* Andy blurted, glad to see that he was all right.

"I had to think—are you coming in?" he asked casually and stooped to look inside, where everyone was waiting for him to appear. Turning to his friends, he said, *"There is not much room in there. Come! I need you with me!"*

Andy responded by putting his hand on Badger's shoulder, saying, *"We are coming with you!"* White Quill followed them closely.

The occupants of the big lodge fell silent as soon as Badger stepped inside. Mostly men, they watched as the host gave a wave of his hand, indicating the newcomers should seat themselves to his right, on the end of the row of guests, nearest the door. It was a place given to those who held little stature. Others shuffled over to make room for them to sit.

The evening began when the host's wife brought out his pipe and helped him prepare it. With reverence, it was lit with a coal from the fire, and after due ceremony, he passed it down the line of guests seated on his left. After making its way to the last man, it was carefully handed back up the line to the host, who started it down the right side. Seated beside his friend, Andy followed the practice he already knew. When he was finished, he passed it to White Quill, and it eventually made its way back to the host. Three more times, the pipe was passed along the lines before it was carefully extinguished by the host and given to be put away.

Shortly, women started serving meat, which had been cooking over the fire at the centre. The host took none but watched with apparent pleasure while his guests feasted. Any who visited did so quietly, with those sitting near them. A few boys were present, sitting close to fathers or uncles, but they were silent, glancing periodically at Badger. They all knew each other.

Finally, when the eating had finished, silence fell over the gathering, and the host cleared his throat. *"Our son—Miísinsski—we still call him by the name of a boy—our son has been gone throughout many moons...returning to us a few days past, without our other sons—those who had left with him on a raid against our enemies, the Liars. We can only guess at the fate of our brave sons. In the time it has taken this one to return to us, they surely would have found their way back to their families...had not some misfortune overtaken them. Indeed, until now, we had believed all had perished.*

"Our hearts were made glad to see this one return to us! We all knew his father—our brother—I miss him still! He was a friend to me—to many of us who remember him. Sun has shown pity on our sister, Antelope Woman, by bringing her son back to her." The man paused for a moment before speaking again. *"Now we know for certain that his companions will not return to those who loved them...we can only hope that they died bravely!"*

With that, the man closed his eyes and began a lengthy prayer, giving thanks to Sun, first for bringing Badger home, followed by rambling gratitude for the many things with which they had been blessed. He implored Sun to have pity upon the spirits of Badger's comrades and asked that he have pity upon the families of the departed ones and bring comfort to them. *"Make them proud of their sons; we hope they died valiant deaths!"* Asking next for favour upon the people in their hunting, he prayed for the buffalo to surround their camp in abundance this winter. Finally, he asked for the health and good fortune of the whole tribe and safety from the depredations of their marauding enemies and any spirits which might bedevil them.

For a long time after, there was silence until finally, the man invited Badger to speak and tell them what had happened. The nervous young man thought for several moments before speaking. His voice was tight and faltered a little as he began.

"My father was a great hunter and a great warrior...you all knew him...maybe even better than me. I knew him for only ten winters, but I was too small to remember very much. He was struck down... by...by our enemy. I was sad for a long time after. I have never really quit being sad! My mother and my sister were sad too. But, he was gone. And, I missed him...I missed him so much I wanted to die, so I could go and be with him. But somehow, I kept going—I lived— but it took a long time! I finally figured out that being sad would never bring him back. I still miss him! I would do anything to have him back!

"I had seen just ten winters when I went to live with my uncle." Pausing, it was evident that he was struggling with what he was about to say, with his uncle present. When he continued, his voice was soft, and those across from him leaned forward to hear.

"My cousin"—people could see he was fighting back the tears— *"was...he was not kind to me! He did things to me that I did not like—but I had to do them—his father, he had taken us into his lodge, and I had to do what he said. I tried to please them, but they would not accept me...they were not very nice...and he was doing all those things, and that made me feel not very good.*

"Some of you have shown kindness to me and my family, and I am glad for that! Some of you men, especially the father of my good friend...gone...showed me how to ride and hunt, because I had no father. I had no uncles, at least not any that would take me—or a brother—not anyone!

"I wanted to be just like my father, but I had no way of proving myself. Other boys my age went with their fathers or their brothers on the hunt...and they took them to war. I had no one to do that with me. I was a nothing one! Finally, I found this thing to do—to go with those ones on their raid...and they somehow let me. I was just going to be a helper, but that was all right—maybe I could do something else, so I went along. When we spotted them—the Liars—your son, the son of Bear Medicine, told us his plan...but...but my...my cousin"— he blurted it out— "and that other, the son of Kills in the Lodge refused to follow him—what he said—and they went ahead of everyone and tried to get glory, all for themselves. It was the son of Bear Medicine and the son of Charging in the Water, that saved us. The Liars had those napikawan fire-sticks. They might have killed us...but those others went and got them." Looking intently at the ground in front of him, reliving the account vividly in his mind, he murmured, "And, they killed the brother of my friend—this napikawan here." So soft were his words that those sitting at a distance had to ask others what he had just said.

It took him a long time to continue. "I did not release my arrow! I was there, ready to shoot—my hands were too weak!" A murmur went through the crowd when he made his admission, ceasing as soon as he began to speak again. "My hands were weak, because—" he wiped tears from his eyes with his sleeve— "because when I saw that Liar fall...when I saw him fall, it was my father! I saw my father fall! And I saw me! As a little boy! I was kneeling over him! I know it was not real, but that is what I saw, and I wanted to run up to him and be with him and help him because it was my father!" he said, sounding stronger. "And when I kept looking, I knew it was not him, and I was not there anymore...but I was very sad for the little son of that fellow!

"And, when it was over, and they were celebrating and everything, my cousin humiliated me—he would not even give me a chance to say anything. I tried to tell them what I had seen, and he mocked me!"

The boy's voice was much stronger now. "Who was it that I saw? Was it my father, coming back to see me—to tell me something? I have never told this to anyone because I did not want them to think I was a nothing one. I have never had a vision or anything like that—I do not even know what it is—I have only heard from others. And, when I was just standing there, and they were celebrating, I was just standing there and not knowing what to do...and I was very sad because of my father—" his voice faltered— "and he just ridiculed me. And after, what they did is...they...they"—he stammered— "they got me and...they, they—" He could not get the words out of his mouth, for it was too humiliating. Instead, he just said, "And then, they tied me...and they left me there with those dead ones, all tied up to them! On top of me!" Seeking strength in his friends beside him, he made brief eye contact with Andy, who was sitting beside him, next to White Quill. "My friend—we call him Sun Shines on Him—it was his brother that they killed—with the Liars—he was a napikawan, just like this one. They should not have hurt him, but they did—so, this one came along and found me—after it all happened. And, if it had not been for him, I would have died there, because I had been trying to get away—because they had tied me—but I could not.

"So, this one saved me, and we are friends now." Having gotten the worst of it out, he was feeling much stronger as he continued. "I have taken him as my brother—and White Quill, here, is our brother. And, what happened to those others, I do not know!

"And, you probably think that I am a nothing one, but I do not care! I know that people say...about how good it is for us to die in battle...and be brave...and I know that is what we say, it is better to

*die bravely, in battle...or something like that...rather than become
an old man who is feeble. But when my father died, I did not understand all that. All I knew was that—"* He paused and swallowed
hard before trying again. *"All I knew was that, uh, my uh...my
father was never going to come home to our lodge again."* He made
another long pause, trying to keep his composure. No one spoke;
everyone waited for him to continue. *"I had no father...to teach me
to ride or hunt...he would not teach me...to be a warrior or anything
like that. Without my father, how could I...how could I learn to be
brave? My uncles lived in another camp and...where were...where
were—"* His voice trailed off, and he did not finish. He moved on
to say something different.

*"My father was well-respected because he was brave—and he
was! But that did not help me! I had seen just ten winters! For me, he
was gone. I did not care about honour and things like that...I did not
care that he died bravely! I would rather he would not have died at
all!"* The tears were now streaming down his face. Trying not to be
seen doing it, Andy slid his hand to his friend's leg. Strengthened
by his touch, Badger continued, speaking more confidently. *"I
have thought many times about telling my story. For a long time,
I did not even want to return here. I was certain that those others
would have humiliated me...they had left me behind—left me to
die! And, they said I was a nothing one...alone...and with nothing...
they left me with those dead ones...in the place of the Liars...where I
would have died...but for my friend."* He put a hand on Andy's knee,
and their eyes met. Until that point, his gaze had been fixed on the
ground in front of him.

"My friend has different medicine from yours," he continued.
*"He says that I saved his life, but I think he—it is his medicine that
saved my life. I think I would be dead right now, disgraced—at least
I would have been able to go to my father. But I know it was his
medicine that prevented me from returning with my companions.*

And if I had, I would certainly have got whatever they got. And I would not be here now!

"They had even killed his brother—not much older than us. But instead of seeking revenge...against me, or anyone—I know anyone else would have gone out for revenge! But he treated me as his brother!" Taking a deep breath, he looked into each one of the stern faces opposite him.

"I do not know what I saw that day—whether it was really my father trying to come back and say something to me, or what it was. I have had to do a lot of thinking! And, I do not know what has become of those others. I think they must have got killed...I am glad they had no children to mourn for them...like me."

Nodding in the direction of a small boy he had spotted earlier, he asked, pointing with his lips, *"See that boy?"* Everyone turned to look in the direction he had indicated. *"He is happy! There is no sadness in his face—he has not lost his father—his eyes are not dead."* Addressing the lad, he said, *"I hope you do not get left all alone...as I was!"* Waiting for a long moment, Badger now did the hardest thing yet. He got to his feet and paused, looking around slowly at the men watching him. Giving it enough time for them to know that he was not afraid of them, he stepped for the door and ducked out underneath the flap without a backward glance.

Andy looked at White Quill as if to ask what they should do next. Some of the younger men looked indignantly after the departed speaker. But before they could say anything, one of those sitting to the left of the host spoke out, *"Son!"* gesturing for the lad Badger had spoken to, to come to him. The little boy scrambled to his father's side, sitting on his lap and draping an arm around his neck. Everybody watched to see what the man would do next, or if he had something to say, but he only stared thoughtfully into the fire.

Still, nobody spoke. Some looked at Badger's companions, wondering if one of them might have something to say. The host's wife looked to her husband. So did many others, and finally, he spoke. "*This young man—his heart is good! We all know what he is speaking about! Many times, I have gone to war against our enemies.*" Shaking his head slowly, he thought for a moment before continuing, "*Many times! As a young man, I sought honour—by leaving our camp to capture the horses of our enemies. I struck my first enemy when I was about his age. And, it was my father who was with me—and he honoured me for it! He had given me his finest buffalo runner when I killed my first buffalo, and now, I had killed my first enemy. He spoke my name in front of the others, and honoured me for what I had done! Some of the others did, too.*" There had not been a lot of emotion in the man's voice; now, he became more animated. "*I killed many more of our enemies after that. I have captured many of their horses. Many of those times as a young man, with my father.*" He paused for a long time. "*But I have left too many of my friends behind, dead at the hands of our enemies. I have returned home, singing my victory song, but you could not hear my songs for the wailing of those whose sons...and husbands and fathers and brothers...had failed to return with me. I have seen too many of them—our young men—go off, never to return again... to their mothers and their sweethearts. Indeed, now four more of our sons have gone to the Sand Hills, rather than come home. Did they die valiantly? We can only hope so! We have listened to their mothers mourn since the season when the berries were ripe. All our hearts are grieved! Every time one of our sons fails to return from battle, we grieve.*

"*Surely, the mothers and wives of our enemies cut themselves in their sorrow, as ours do, when sons perish. Surely their little boys cry when their fathers fail to come home from a raid...as did our son... Miisinsski! I say his name again, Miisinsski! Miisinsski!*" The man paused, and a couple of the older men repeated the boy's name.

To everyone's surprise, the man who had so many times led them to war, simply reached over and put his hand on the shoulder of the little boy, seated on his father's lap, near him, and said to the man, *"Take care, for your son!"* and in standing up, signalled that the meeting was over.

"Yes," some of the men muttered, getting to their feet, but nobody said anything more, while they filed out.

Andy and White Quill stepped aside, permitting others to leave the lodge first. When it was their turn, Andy went first. *"Wait,"* whispered White Quill, grabbing him by the sleeve and pulling him to the side, once they were out. *"Let us listen to hear what they say."*

Standing in the darkness, they heard some of the talk around them. Some of the older ones seemed to have received Badger's remarks with favour, but most of the younger ones judged him harshly. The man with his young son was among the last to depart. He scooped the boy up and held him tightly, disappearing silently into the darkness.

When his friends reached Badger's lodge, he was busy telling his mother, and some of her friends, some of the things that had happened since he had left them. Ending his story, he answered many questions until they turned to White Quill to ask him about himself. Antelope Woman recalled meeting his mother and others of his camp, on previous occasions. They next questioned Andy and were amazed at how well he spoke their language. Talking long into the night, finally, someone suggested sleep. Nobody mentioned what Badger had told the men.

17

The next morning, while on their way to the river, White Quill mentioned that some of the men had repeated Badger's name after he had left the meeting. *"I heard that! What does that mean?"* Andy wondered.

"It is an honour! When they say your name out loud—it is an honour!" the young Indian replied, grinning at their friend.

"Did they? Who was it?" Badger asked. His friends tried to describe the men who had done so, but apart from the man who had been their host, he was unable to recognize who it had been. It was comforting to know that at least a few of the men had seemed sympathetic, but it worried him that some had spoken derisively.

Afterward, Badger wanted to go hunting, as his mother had no food at all, and he went to see the hunting chief to find out if it was all right to hunt on their own. He was a little nervous about approaching the man because of what had occurred the night before. But he was greeted warmly. Sensing the boy's nervousness, the man placed a hand on his shoulder and praised him, *"It is good that you go hunting! I saw into your heart last night, and I could tell that it is good—better to hunt and look after our families than go off to make war!"* Relieved, Badger hurried to join the others and tell them what he had said.

It was fall. The buffalo had not yet become plentiful in the area; they would be expected in greater numbers once the snows came. Snow out on the prairie usually drove the animals up against the mountains in winter, where they sought shelter in the treed valleys, grazing on the wind-blown ridges. Throughout the winter, the *black wind* often swept the grassy foothills completely clear of snow and warmed the temperature above freezing.

White Quill suggested that they head in the direction of the *Little High Wood*, where he claimed to have been born. The creek was barely a trickle when they reached it, and it was frozen along the edges. Crossing back and forth across the stream as it meandered, the Indians pointed out old campsites, littered with bones and remnants of earlier tipi rings near groves of cottonwood. When they reached a spot where the valley broadened and all but disappeared, they spotted another hunting party.

Recognizing one another only as *Piikáni,* the two groups approached. The others were out from a camp that had just arrived where the *Little High Wood* flowed into *Napi-tahta,* and they agreed that they would hunt together.

Five in number, one of them appeared to be the eldest and took charge. He led the others in a southeasterly direction to the crest of a ridge where they could get a look at a broad, open plain beyond. Almost at once, they spotted buffalo. It would be difficult to approach them without being seen, so they planned to separate. One would remain behind, while the others rode along the ridge top, out of sight of the herd, descending along a distant draw that would take them to the very edge of the broad plain. After waiting the indicated time, the one would charge out into the valley, in plain view, and simply chase the animals in the others' direction, where they would be concealed.

The plan was frighteningly similar to the one in which Matthew and the Cree had encountered Badger's comrades, and it played heavily on Andy's mind. Badger, thinking the same thing, offered to be the one to stay behind. But they both knew that it did not make sense. *"I will do it! I will be fine,"* Andy assured him. *"You go. Get nitapi waksin for your mother!"* Punching him affectionately on the shoulder, he sent him with the others.

This time, things proceeded precisely as planned. When he broke cover, Andy was quickly able to position his horse so that the stampeding herd veered in the direction of the others' hiding spot. When the buffalo were almost upon them, the hunters burst from their cover, flogging their excited mounts toward their startled quarry. Racing out among the rushing beasts, the hunters approached within an arm's length of their targets before releasing their arrows. Andy saw the surging, dark mass yield the forms of collapsed animals as he followed.

In no time at all, the hunt was over. Twelve animals lay strewn across the prairie. Some of the hunters sang as they returned to their kills on frothing ponies. Among them, it was conceded that Badger had dropped four animals. One of the other hunters had dropped three. White Quill was happy to pull his own arrows from one of the carcasses, but there was a dispute among the others when one claimed to have downed two. Proven right, that hunter sang while the other tried to make the best of his poor showing.

Badger announced that he and his friends needed only one animal, besides which he would take the tongues of all they had killed. The rest of the meat was left to the others, and they soon had all the tongues and the meat of a choice cow butchered and loaded onto packhorses.

The two Indians had been singing their *wolf songs* on the way home, and they started up again as they neared their lodge, announcing their arrival. Badger's mother and sister emerged to greet them, making a fuss over them and giving them hugs, as soon as they dismounted. Once most of the meat was unloaded, Badger went calling with the rest. Taking one of the tongues and a huge chunk of choice meat, he went to find an old couple who had been his friends—the man who had once given him his treasured pony.

Finding their lodge, he had to pound on its side before he could get any response, shouting to announce his arrival. On recognizing him, the old woman set his gift aside and threw her arms around him. After demonstrating her affection for him, she led him to the old man and hollered in his ear, telling him who was there. The ancient medicine man used his hands to feel the visitor's face, the muscles on his chest and on his arms, and patting his flat belly, he grinned with delight, muttering his joy at the visit. Giving them an abbreviated description of his adventures, the young hunter left them with the meat and promised to return for a lengthier visit.

In the following days, the three boys continued to hunt together, always sharing their abundance around the camp. When Andy saw how few of the young men their age seemed to want to have anything to do with Badger, he realized how lonely his friend's existence in this camp had been. But the three of them stuck together and soon gained the respect of most by keeping the elderly and the widows supplied with fresh meat. And eventually, because of their hunting success and the reputation it was bringing them, others began to ask to accompany them on their hunts. By the time the bitter cold arrived, they always hunted in the company of others.

The days were short, and the campfires long. Every night the men gathered to talk of deeds done and honours gained. Young men were frequently heard boasting of their accomplishments, seeking honour and respect from those older. Badger's speech had gained him a certain amount of respect among some of the elders who, after a lifetime of warring, now recognized folly in their endeavours. The women, always the bearers of the tribe's grief, when they had heard of his speech, had begun to encourage their boys and young men against warring and raiding. These pastimes were the primary aspiration and pursuit of most of them, and many discounted his speech as cowardice. Some were very loud in proclaiming their scorn for him. Others pondered the things Badger had said, silently. The camp was divided over the issue, but since war parties rarely departed in the dead of winter, it remained to be seen whether any of the young warriors would entertain a change of heart.

One day, a mid-winter delegation arrived at the camp to invite the leading men to a council at the camp downstream, where the *Little High Wood* met *Napi-tahta*. Such events were also a social time, and when Andy's friends heard about it, they insisted on taking him.

Since *the time of the first frost,* other camps had established themselves along the three forks of *Napi-tahta,* and people had been visiting back and forth ever since. This would be the first time, though, that they would be attending en masse. Not all families were attending, but many of those who did took down their lodges and brought them along. With no need for scouts, due to the short distance and time of year, the entourage was strung out over a wide area.

At the host camp, lodges were scattered among the giant cottonwoods, which flourished in the broad valley bottom. Badger's people camped more or less together along the *Little High Wood,* up from *Napi-tahta.* By sundown, the camp had more than doubled in size, and there was much activity, with people mingling and visiting. Most of the young men and older boys spent time brushing their long hair, painting their faces, and putting on their best clothes, to strut about and display themselves before the girls of the other camps. Many girls turned out in their finest dress, hoping to impress while trying not to be seen to do so. Mothers and aunts were vigilant, making sure that none under their charge were unsupervised, though occasionally, young couples would arrange clandestine meetings. Some of the young men conspired with sisters and friends to arrange to be left alone with the girl of their desire. And, Andy's friends kept a lookout and pointed out many of the young beauties, even though he professed to have no eyes for any of them.

On the first night, men from the different camps invited others to their lodges to feast. All the leading men did so at the lodge of the host, a man called Running Wolf—an outstanding warrior and hunter, brave and well-respected by all. Some met inside lodges, but with the weather remaining mild, many people were gathering outside, around huge fires. The drumming and dancing lasted well into the night, and everyone was filled with goodwill and laughter. Men gambled and smoked, women visited, the young courted, and children played.

Buffalo were nearby, and the celebrations went on, with new-comers arriving each day. On the third day, a party from White Quill's camp showed up. The farther people had to travel, the fewer they were in number. In this case, it was a small group that came on horseback and had already been put up in others' lodges by the time White Quill learned of their arrival.

Upon receiving word of their attendance, he searched the camp inquiring after them, finally tracking down a man and his wife. Eager to hear news of his family, he waited until the man had gone to feast before speaking with the woman.

His father, she told him, had left sometime before, to travel again to the *napikawan camp*. It was presumed the object of the trip was *napiohke*, and this time, his mother had refused to accompany him. Pretty Bird was now married, which of course, he knew, and the woman said the couple seemed happy. The young man was utterly devoted to his wife. He loved her dearly, continually showering her with his affection and boasting what a fine wife he had. *"Is she happy?"* he asked. The woman assured him that she seemed to be content.

Visitors from nearby *Káínaa* camps also showed up. Among them was a young man who was reputed to be an outstanding dancer. When he learned it, recalling Wolf Tail's dance, Andy persuaded the others to see if they might be able to watch him. When they found him, White Quill walked right up to the fellow and introduced himself, beckoning the others to join him. The young dancer was called Many Hands. His father was *Káínaa*, and his mother was *Piikáni*. He invited them to a feast that night at his parents' lodge, where there would be dancing.

When the trio arrived, it was not yet dark, and many people were already in attendance around the fire. The drumming began when the last light of day faded from a crimson sunset into the dim gray of dusk. Children were always the first to dance, joined shortly by those a little older. While people visited and watched, various young men began taking their turn.

"I do that!" White Quill exclaimed to his friends.

"Hai! You do not!" Andy quipped. *"Let us see you!"*

Badger agreed, thinking that White Quill was kidding, but without further persuasion, White Quill started dancing on the spot and then made his way out by the fire, where he joined the other dancers. Surprised, Andy elbowed Badger, cracking a grin as they watched.

Shortly, White Quill cried out to Andy, *"Sun Shines on Him! Come! You can do it!"* His friend shook his head and hung back, but Badger pushed him forward. Having become a favourite around the camp, with his long, blonde locks, he received encouragement from others.

Suddenly, Many Hands appeared from among those who had been standing nearby. Taking Andy by the elbow, he said, *"Come! I will show you."* With the encouragement of others, he stepped forward, red-faced, with his teacher. *"Watch!"* the young man said, beginning to move his feet and his body in time to the drum. The step seemed simple enough, and as soon as Andy got it, the people cheered. Following Many Hands' example, he began to get the hang of it, and momentarily White Quill joined them. His face glistening, he paused to toss his jacket to Badger. Andy followed White Quill and Many Hands around the fire a couple of times, before bowing out.

"You make a good dancer!" Badger exclaimed. *"I have never done that,"* he told his friend, silently adding it to the list of things he had missed because of the loss of his father.

During a break, they heard that there was soon to be a special dance, and Andy's friends showed their excitement. The *assinahpeska,* they explained, was a dance in which only those who were unattached were expected to participate. Quickly checking each other's appearance, they hurried forward, dragging a reluctant Andy with them. *"Just watch us and do as we do,"* they told him excitedly.

Watching the others jostle for position, he joined the young men and boys in lining up opposite their female counterparts, some distance apart. Singing as they danced, the two lines made their way toward one another, and coming near, retreated to the side from which they had begun. It soon became apparent that each participant was trying to position themselves to line up with someone from the other side, to whom they were attracted. Andy just went along with his friends.

The dance proceeded for some time, the two lines closing, then separating several times. Some of the vainer young men had stripped to the waist and removed their leggings from their breechclouts. Their lithe bodies glistened in the firelight. Finally, the tempo of the drums varied, and from the rush of participants, who had been taking a break at the sidelines, Andy figured something special must be in store.

This time, when the two lines advanced together, a girl came right up in front of him. She was one of many who had been admiring him and jostling one another to approach him. Before he knew what she was doing, she swirled the blanket, which all the girls held over their shoulders, over his head and groping with her hand, clutched his face and kissed him. As quickly as she had done so, she drew the blanket off them and retreated, her face aglow. Not expecting it, Andy was left standing, surprised, and dead still, and a little embarrassed. Looking around him, though, he discovered that many of the other boys had been similarly favoured by other girls. The onlookers all roared and cheered. Turning around, he saw that he was the one many were watching, so he bowed his head a little, before dancing toward the anonymity of the crowd.

After the dance was over, Andy learned that both his friends had received similar gestures from girls who had been making eyes at them. Still a little out of breath, they joked about what this might mean and tried to catch sight of them.

"Now we must give gifts to those girls," Badger warned his white friend.

"What?" Andy wondered, *"Gifts? Why?"*

White Quill explained the tradition. *"They kiss you! And, they expect that you will give them something—it is a way to be able to meet them. Some are lovers already—did you see how some of them seemed really interested? They are probably going to be husband and wife. Some fellow who really likes a girl will have something very special to give her—like a bunch of horses or something like that.*

"Did this dog tell you what he did?" he interrupted himself, giving a look at Badger. *"He grabbed her breasts!"*

"Lots of guys do that!" his friend countered. *"Nobody can see because you are under that blanket."* Andy grinned and shook his head. *"I will tell you what!"* the excited Indian continued. *"If she comes to get me to give her a gift after that, there is no telling what she might do!"*

"Yes, but what if she shows up with her brothers?" the other Indian warned.

"Ha! She will not know me! I have never seen her before—she is from another camp."

Their minds on girls, Andy's friends wanted to stroll around the camp, looking at them. Drumming and singing came from many directions, and they wanted to check them all out. Andy chose to remain behind to see if he could find Many Hands. While the other two headed off, he mingled with those around him.

His blonde hair always drew people's attention, and before long, admirers, many of them children and girls, surrounded him. Most wanted to know where he had come from and why he was there. Even some of the older people, always friendly and engaging, took the time to talk with him. Many made good-natured jokes about the colour of his skin, and he was complimented on his dancing.

Before long, the drums began again, and Many Hands showed up. The young *Káínaa* had changed and was now sporting much more elegant garb. A shirt and leggings of pale antelope skin were worn beneath an apron-like garment, predominantly white with black designs, hanging to his knees, from the bottom edge, long black fringe hung to his ankles. A vest was white, with black designs, and from his neck hung a necklace and a mail-like breast-plate of white eagle bones. On his head, he wore a headdress of upright eagle feathers, and in his hand, he held a similar feather adornment. Other young men, also in their best attire, joined him, and Andy admired them all.

When he was done, Many Hands invited Andy to accompany him around the camp with some of his friends. He introduced him to his best friend, Little Man, a young *Káínaa* about Andy's age, and together they headed off to see what they could find.

Walking around and looking at all the activity, they visited with many of the young people they encountered. Everyone was friendly toward Andy, a few inviting him to go hunting or to visit in the coming days. Many Hands went out of his way to introduce him to girls he recognized, looking for an opportunity to wink at him from behind their backs, unaware that the white boy was nursing a broken heart.

Late in the night, Badger caught up with them; they had found a fire, around which almost all those present were their own age. Bringing along Many Hands and Little Man, they joined White Quill and other youthful revellers under the watchful eye of mothers. A few members of the Brave Dog society were also present to curtail the ambitions of those who aspired toward more romantic endeavours.

Finally, a dim light in the east heralded the coming of day, and with the mild, west wind having given way to a chill breeze from the north, people began disappearing to their lodges. Finding White Quill's mother and sister already asleep, the boys quietly clambered under their robes.

The next afternoon, a couple of girls came to Andy and White Quill, hinting at their desire to be rewarded for their affection. Feeling awkward, Andy was anxious to send them on their way and quickly resorted to Rowand's dwindling supply. A brief time later, two more appeared, both having favoured White Quill at other dances. Andy's bounty was again called upon to answer the need. *"You should not dance,"* he chided his friend. *"I have few gifts."*

"What is this?" Badger queried, feeling jealous. *"Why are they all after you?"*

"Maybe it is because I do not go around grabbing them like you did!" White Quill retorted.

For two more nights, the people feasted and celebrated together. A few sweat lodges appeared and were periodically occupied by those seeking communion with the spirits. During the day, there were hunting parties going out and returning laden with meat for the feasts. All the people were in high spirits, and good-will prevailed.

On the last morning, the lodges of the visitors were packed up, and the camp began to disperse. The *black wind* had licked up the snow, leaving the prairie mostly bare, but where it was in drifts, it was so hard-packed that a horse did not break through the crust. Having a relatively short distance to travel, Badger's group left later in the morning, arriving at their familiar campsite in the afternoon.

Shortly after that, it snowed heavily, followed by a period of intensely cold weather. The cold seemed to last forever, and nobody was willing to leave the warmth of their cozy lodges to hunt. The women always had lots of work to do, but the young men and the boys soon became restless.

By a stroke of good fortune, Badger had gathered a bunch of saskatoon and chokecherry branches, intending to make them into arrows. Now, confined by the weather, that was about all they had to do. Chipping away at some rock he had found, he tried to fashion arrowheads. Dissatisfied with the result, he tried pounding away at one of the metal spoons Andy still had in his treasure. Managing to fashion an excellent point, soon they were all at it, converting his few remaining utensils into arrowheads. *"We can trade these!"* Badger muttered optimistically, as he toiled.

The air outside was still and very cold during the days, and the nights were clear and even colder. During the daytime, the sun shone brightly but failed to warm the air. The horses had taken refuge in the cottonwoods that grew along the river, and after several days, resorted to eating the bark. Each morning, the boys who tended them returned with news of their starving and a few dying. From one smiling moon to the next, the relentless cold took its toll upon the people and the horses. The dogs thrived, able to feed on the frozen carcasses of those horses which had succumbed to the cold. The presence of wolves and coyotes, venturing into the tree cover after the same bounty, drove the horses out onto the prairie, where they had no shelter and perished in even higher numbers.

The buffalo had been so plentiful before the freezing weather that nobody had bothered to stockpile much meat. Now, the harsh cold had begun to take such a toll upon the horses that they were soon in no condition to run the buffalo, and the hunters could no longer hunt on horseback. Some of the people were beginning to have to ration their food supplies. The dried meat, saved from the fall hunt, began running out, and some families had none. When food had first started to be scarce, Badger's family had been well-stocked, and seeing the distress of their neighbours, they had shared what they had.

As the situation worsened, groups of hunters ventured out against the cold, looking for game. In most cases, they were not gone long before returning empty-handed and discouraged. One desperate man, whose family had resorted to eating their dogs, went out alone. When he failed to return by nightfall, the wailing of his wife and children only added to the gloom which had fallen over the camp.

When rations started to run low in his mother's lodge, Badger determined to set out on foot, in search of fresh meat. Ignoring his mother's fearful warnings, he said he would leave the next morning. Andy and White Quill wanted to join him, trying to convince him that together they would be more successful than if he went alone. His concern was that, if by some misfortune they should fail to return, nobody would be left to provide for his family. He insisted that one of them stay back to look after them. With some reluctance, Andy had to admit that he was the least familiar with what would be required for the hunt and consented to stay. Everyone in the leather home prayed for success.

At first light, the two young Indians set out. Wearing their warmest clothing, they shouldered their bows and arrows and headed toward *Mistakis*. Crossing the river on thick ice, they made their way up the valley, seeing where the horses had been all through the trees. A few stragglers stood watching them. They had not seen their own horses for several days and wondered if they would survive the cold.

Continuing up the river valley, they came to a ravine with good cover in it. There, they spotted fresh deer tracks, with no sign of other hunters. *"You go up there,"* Badger told his friend, pointing to the top of the ridge. White Quill knew immediately what he had in mind, and without anything more being said, he trudged up the steep slope. Deer always tended to move to uphill when alarmed.

As his companion was nearing the top, Badger moved to the opposite side of the ravine and began moving cautiously through the bush growing along that side. His idea was that any game would flee to the higher ground, out of the valley, where he hoped his companion might get a shot.

On top, White Quill tried to stay low, seeking cover in the stark wolf willows, when he could. He had gone some distance when he heard Badger's shout, his voice clear in the frigid air. Scrambling for cover, he swept out his bow and arrows, and very shortly, three deer bounded from the ravine. Not far from the top, they halted and turned to look back, watching for the source of their alarm. Nervous, their big ears searching for some hint of danger, they looked behind them, with their breath forming clouds of vapour. The young hunter, concealed not far away, dared not move until, one at a time, the animals began to recover from their alarm and nose and nibble at bunches of grass, occasionally turning to look back.

They were between him and the ravine and began moving toward him, completely unaware of his presence. The wind was right. With two arrows in his mouth and one already on his bow, he made ready to draw it as the deer moved closer and closer, stopping now and then to forage and look around cautiously. A few more steps and the first would be in range. *"Sun,"* he prayed, *"have pity on us and let me take these for food! Give me success. Have pity upon me and my friends. Help me!"*

He was hoping that Badger would not now come tramping out of the ravine, as the deer edged ever closer. Shivering from the excitement as well as the cold, he waited breathlessly until all three were within range. Slowly, quietly, he drew back his bow, his cold fingers barely able to hold the arrow to the bowstring.

Thwat! The first arrow was gone. Not even watching to see if it found its mark, he immediately focussed upon his next target, which was already wheeling to take flight. Swiftly, he had the next arrow in the bow and drew back as the deer bolted. He had fired at the most distant animal first, recognizing that by the time he drew a second arrow, the others would be in flight. *Thwat!* He released the second arrow and snatched the last from his mouth. He almost dropped it, his cold fingers, clumsy. All three of his targets were now racing away from him, as he concentrated on his final shot, desperate to kill something. Firing over the rump of the last animal, he shouted for joy when the arrow struck it in the back of the neck, and it somersaulted to the ground.

Grabbing a fourth arrow from his quiver, White Quill clambered to his feet, stiff from the cold, looking around to see how well he had done. Just as the first animal bounded out of sight, over the top of the ravine, he thought he might have seen it falter. Right behind it, the second had obviously been hit and struggled to follow its mate. After a few more faltering steps, the wounded animal stopped and turned to look in White Quill's direction, and as it did, it slowly sank to the ground. The third animal was already on the ground. Before anything else, he snatched up his mitts and drove his freezing hands into their warmth.

"Hai-ya!" he cried with excitement and began to sing a *wolf song*, bounding up to the nearest animal. His arrow had hit it right in the centre of its neck, apparently striking the spine and severing the spinal cord. Its eyes were still wide-open, and appeared

very much alive, though it did not move. The second animal lay dead with the point of an arrow protruding from the opposite side from which it had been hit. *"Good shot!"* he breathed proudly to himself. Wanting to see if maybe he had hit the first animal, he hurried to the edge of the ravine, where he saw it near the bottom, breathing heavily and spraying blood from its nostrils. Knowing it would not last long, the elated young hunter gave a shout of joy. As he worked at getting the fourth arrow to his bow, beginning his descent down the hill, the wounded creature saw him and took flight, but shortly collapsed to the ground. Once again, the boy shrieked for joy, knowing it was finished. He turned back to await his companion.

When Badger topped the ravine, White Quill was standing over one of the fallen deer, warming his hands on it. Seeing only one other down, Badger chided his friend, *"Why did you let one get away?"*

"Ha! You know so little!" White Quill retorted jubilantly. *"It is in the ravine—three of them! Three arrows, three deer!"* he shouted and began to sing once again and dance.

"We have meat! Even if it is just deer!" Badger exclaimed when they came together, throwing his arm around his excited friend's shoulder. *"We should take the hindquarters of these two and send others back for the rest,"* he said, reaching for his knife.

Great was the relief and celebration in Badger's lodge when they returned so soon and deposited their bounty beside the fire, in the center of the cozy lodge. Making a fuss over the cold but happy hunters, his mother lopped off the first piece of meat, to be put on the fire to roast.

While White Quill told their story, Badger left to inform others about the location of the kills. Keeping two hindquarters for themselves, he shouldered the other two and took them to the lodge of the old couple, stopping at the chief's lodge to tell him of their success and where the remainder of their kill would be found. The old woman thanked him heartily, and when she hollered into the old man's ear, he beamed and nodded with delight. By the time the proud hunter made his way back to his lodge, a group of hungry women were hurrying out to get the remainder of the kill.

Another group of hunters, who had ventured out that same day, matched the boys' good fortune. They, too, shared their bounty and the next night, a *black wind* hit the sides of the lodge so hard that Andy thought it would collapse. Immediately, the people knew what was happening and began to rejoice.

In good spirits once again, the people ventured from their lodges to celebrate the return of milder weather. Two days later, melting snow lay in puddles, and the children were covered in mud, playing outside for the first time since it had turned cold.

With the milder weather, the remaining horses fared better, but they would not fully regain their strength until the grass turned green. The hunters could not run them hard, and hunting continued to be difficult. Food remained scarce throughout all the camps, with most of the men restricted to hunting on foot. Soon there was little game left in the immediate area, so the hunters with the strongest horses were chosen to go further afield in search of buffalo. Fortunately, the herds were not too far off, and they were able to bring down enough that the women were kept busy hauling it back to camp.

Andy had never quit thinking about his father's return. He was anxious to get back to Edmonton House to meet him but knew it was far too soon to be thinking of that. Rowand had told him that it would be summer before his father might return, and so, Andy forced himself to be patient. Every day he spoke with anticipation of seeing his father.

But something else was also on his mind. *"I want to find the father of Wolf Tail,"* he announced one day when he and his friends were alone.

"What are you talking about?" Badger exclaimed. "Do you want to die?"

"No! We should do this," Andy replied, "I think it is the right thing to do. He is not our enemy! We did nothing to his sons." White Quill looked at him quizzically.

"The cold winter must have done something to your thinking!" Badger observed. "All he knows is that we left with his sons and his horses, and the next thing he knew, his sons were dead, and his horses were gone. Are you crazy?"

"But we did not do anything! I wish to tell him what happened! I wish him to know the truth!"

"You are crazy!" Badger snorted and stood up from where they had been resting, slouching off.

After that, Andy tried to explain the concept of forgiveness and reconciliation to Badger, but it was a hard sell, and Badger's mother wished him to have no part in the idea. Having lost her husband to war and seeing other young men struck down the same way, she could not bear the thought of losing her precious son, so recently returned to her. White Quill, though, was more willing. To his ears, it was an adventure, and soon they were both hounding Badger.

At night, away from his friends' influence, Badger let his mind play with the idea and began to imagine being free of the burden he carried—they all carried. It was difficult for them to live with the knowledge that Wolf Tail's father considered them the vilest of enemies.

Andy spoke of setting out as soon as the worst of the winter had passed, and after finding Wolf Tail's family, carrying on to Edmonton House. The allure of such a daring adventure eventually gripped both his friends. Badger's only reservation was his mother and his sister. Without him, there would be nobody to provide for them, and they would again be thrown into dependence upon others. He felt torn—part of him wanted to be on the trail with his friends, but the burden of his responsibility to his family prevented him from doing so.

One day, though, when the first crocuses were beginning to show their furry buds, Antelope Woman took him aside. *"My son, I know that your friends are leaving soon,"* she began. *"I want you to go with them! I have been waiting for the right time to tell you this, but your sister and I are going to live in the lodge of your uncle—the brother of your father."* Unaware that she had received an invitation from his uncle, Badger was taken aback by the idea.

"Am I not capable of providing for you?" he asked, his brow furrowed.

"Certainly, you are capable of providing for us!" his mother encouraged him. *"But you are a young man. You must find yourself a wife and raise your own family!"*

"Mother, I have only seen ten and six winters! Barely! I am too young to take a wife!"

"Not so! But anyway, you must ready yourself for that! If you spend all your time looking after us and the old people in this camp, as you do, you will never acquire what you need to take a wife."

"Of course, I will!" he disagreed.

"My son, you and your friends are young! You should be with them—enjoying yourself! You are too young to be tied to a family. Someday, that will be your life. When you do take a wife, you will have many babies, and you will have to look after them." Pausing and looking wistfully into the distance, she continued, recalling how tragedy had intervened in her own life. *"I knew before they even brought him back that our life together was over. The spirits told me...as soon as he was injured, I knew I was going to lose him... even before they brought him to me."* Speaking softly, her voice faltered. Tears rimmed her eyes while Badger sat quietly, listening to her words.

She had seldom spoken of his father; her voice was thick with the love she still bore for him. The boy did not say anything and let his mother continue. *"I never wanted him to go to war...but it was so important for him! He wanted to be able to sit with the others—with the great warriors. He wanted to be able to tell of his own brave deeds. He was always so proud when he brought his war trophies home to me. I did the scalp dance for him—I did not know any better then. But I was always afraid that one day some woman would be dancing, waving his scalp over her head...and then it happened."* Tears now streamed down her face. Sobbing quietly, she was telling her son things he had never heard.

"When they brought him to our lodge, he could hardly speak... but he did recognize me—I know he did, even though he was so weak! As I knelt over him, crying, he reached up and touched my face and told me not to cry...he was going to be all right. I just smiled and nodded, but I knew he would leave us to travel the Sand Hills. Soon, he fell into the sleep of death." Tears coursed down her face as she pressed on with her painful story.

"He was so proud of you, my son! He loved you as much as he loved me! He always dreamed of taking you hunting with him. He looked forward to being with you when you killed your first buffalo—" Her voice trailed off, and her hands dropped limply to her lap. She gazed silently at the ground in front of her while Badger sat pensively and waited for her to go on.

"My little sinopah!" she finally continued, with a sigh, reaching out to put her hand around his neck and pull him to her shoulder. He let her hold him like that while he listened. She put her head beside his and drew in a strong breath, savouring the man-smell of his body, and she kissed his neck. *"I am so proud of the man you have become! Your father would be so proud of you! This is why you must go. You must not be tied to your mother and your little sister! I will not let you! I am honoured that you are so devoted to us, but you must be free. You must let us go!"*

When he heard her say it, the boy drew a deep breath, and his body shuddered. Antelope Woman squeezed him tightly to her.

"Before you go, there is something I must say!" Her voice faltered, but she took a breath before uttering, *"I have done you a great wrong, my son.*

"After your father died, I did not know how to go on. You will remember, we had to go to live with my sister and her husband. I made my eyes blind to the suffering that you and your sister faced when we moved there. I neglected you! Both of you, and for this, I am sorry! You grew up without me! I could not be there for you, and you were all alone!"

Releasing her grip on her son's shoulder, the woman fell forward with her face in her hands and sobbed. It was the son who now reached out to his mother and put his arm around her shoulder.

"Sinopah!" she sobbed, letting him pull her to his chest, *"I am so sorry that I let that boy hurt you!"* Her body heaved from her deep sobbing. Badger patted her shoulder with his hand, and with his other hand, he pressed her face to his chest and listened. *"I am so sorry because I knew what he was doing to you, then. I know he tormented you and hurt you and humiliated you!"*

Badger remembered those years so well and all the cruel things his cousin had said and done to him, shaming him and bullying him relentlessly.

Antelope Woman struggled to regain her composure. *"I am sorry,"* she wept. *"I knew he was cruel to you! Yet, I could do nothing to stop it! I am so ashamed of myself. I am sorry I let him hurt you,"* she gasped, as she sobbed. *"Your uncle was so mean to us! He was even mean to my sister! And, his son was just as bad. He was wicked! I am glad he is dead!"* She spat out the words.

"It is all right, mother—I am all right." The boy spoke softly, trying to reassure his mother. *"I do not hold that against you, mother,"* he said, using Andy's expression. *"You did not hurt me— he did,"* he assured her, speaking softly. *"I love you! You are my mother, and I love you!"*

Seeing his words were having a calming effect, and wishing to help her past her bitter guilt, Badger took her face in his hands and looked directly into her eyes. *"Look at me! I am all right! I have made it! I am a man—well, almost—but soon, I am a man. He cannot hurt me anymore. Is it not him who walks the Sand Hills? You and my father gave me the strength to survive, to be me. That little boy was not me!*

"I have strong medicine now! It has made me strong! Sun Shines on Him shared it with me. It is not like ours. His medicine tells him to show kindness to those who are his enemies. He does not hate that one for killing his brother! He has never spoken of seeking revenge! I do not really understand it, but when I think of living at peace with other people around me, it makes me feel better than having everyone at war with us and hating us! Maybe, if my father was still alive, I would have been killed by now, gone to war."

"Oh, my son!" his mother murmured, looking into the eyes of the man her son had become. *"I am proud of you! I am so, so proud of you!"* She was able to sit up straight and look him fully in the eye. Taking his face in both her hands, she smiled at him. *"You are so handsome! You are so strong and kind! And generous! You are exactly what I had always prayed for! And, you do not talk of war! I hate war and claiming war honours and all that boasting!"* Beginning to regain her composure, her voice became stronger. *"My son, you have turned out so well! Your medicine, whatever it is, is strong and good."* She looked down for a moment, but when she looked up into his eyes, she wore a glimmer of a smile.

"You are a man, like your father, yet you are gentle and kind. You are strong and courageous, yet you hold your mother in your arms." After a pause, touching her son's face, she continued softly, her voice firm, with a soft determination. *"It is time! It is time for you to leave behind your childhood. When you left us, you were still a boy. You tried to act like a man and talk like a man, but you were still a boy. Now, you have returned a man—a good man—"* she

paused and drew a ragged breath. Sitting up straight and letting her hand fall to her son's shoulders, she continued, *"—as good a man as your father!"* Hearing this, Badger was unable to hold her gaze and looked down. Placing the stub of her index finger under his chin, Antelope Woman lifted it until he looked into her eyes. *"You are as good a man as your father, my son."* She smiled at him. *"And I love you for it!"*

Badger let her words sink in and felt his heart swell with pride as she compared him to the man he still loved, and so many others admired and respected. A sheepish smile crept across his face, shortly breaking into a broad, proud grin. *"I love you too, mother,"* he whispered.

"I love you, my son. And I let you go. Your sister and I are moving to live with your uncle. She is excited about the move to the home of her cousins—they will love her. And they are the same age—and they are girls! I do not need to worry about raising a boy any longer—my boy has become a man!" she teased, pinching Badger's cheek.

Badger grinned at the maternal gesture, allowing her to mother him one more time.

18

Once Antelope Woman had brought her intentions out into the open, preparations were made quickly for her and her daughter to move. The woman's sister was disappointed to see her leave, but since moving out of her lodge, they had spoken little; her husband had discouraged it. It made for an easier departure, and within a few days, Antelope Woman and her daughter had gathered their things and made ready their packs, while Badger and his friends fetched their horses. The boys planned to escort them to their new home before departing on their quest.

The horse that had once been Wolf Tail's was one of the sturdier horses and had survived the harsh winter. Badger suggested they take it along and return it to his father—a gesture of peace. The others agreed. Andy's favourite, the one given him by Wolf Tail's father, must have perished during the freezing weather, for they had not seen it since. One of Rowand's horses had also disappeared over the winter. From those they had left, they each chose a horse to ride and left leading Wolf Tail's animal. Badger's mother and sister rode double, leading a packhorse.

On the fourth day, they encountered a hunting party that knew of Antelope Woman's brother-in-law and the location of his camp. A couple of the hunters agreed to take them there after stopping at their own camp with the spoils of their hunt, and in the late afternoon, they arrived at the hunters' camp near the shore of the *South Inside Big Water*.

Andy was always amazed to discover that his companions seemed to know people in any camp they visited, and he admired the richness of their relationships. Antelope Woman was quickly recognized and welcomed by old friends, including a cousin. Badger knew some of the young men his own age, and even White Quill found a distant relation who was part of the camp. The evening, therefore, was spent feasting and visiting.

The next morning, Sun had not yet begun his journey across the blue when Antelope Woman rousted the young travellers, eager to get underway. Teasing the boys for being so sleepy, she heaved their warm buffalo robes aside, leaving only the crisp morning air to accompany them on their way to their morning bath in the icy waters of the big lake. Without taking time for a morning meal, they left and followed the *North Trail* in the direction of the *Always Summer Land*.

The night before, it had been agreed that the hunters would catch up to them later in the day. It was an easy route, with generations of travois and horse traffic having etched a clear road through the foothills. In the middle of the afternoon, a couple of the hunters caught up to them, and it was late afternoon when they reached their destination.

Badger's sister received a warm and enthusiastic reception from her cousins, and it was apparent that he would be leaving her in good company. His uncle treated his mother with great respect and offered to have her live in her own lodge until she was fully ready to move in with his family. He made it clear that he had his own *sits beside him wife* and was bringing his late brother's wife into his family out of respect for him. He promised to provide for her and her daughter as bountifully as he provided for his own wives and children. Seeing them so well-received and promised such good care brought Badger great comfort, and he gave up the dread of leaving them behind.

Although sad to be parting after what seemed such a short reunion, Badger and his family promised to see each other at the Sun dance. After one last round of hugs and whispered reminders of affection, he mounted his horse and headed north with his friends. His mother and sister watched him until he disappeared over a distant hill before turning themselves to their new lives.

Wolf Tail's people, the *Atsíína,* generally lived to the east of the Blackfoot. They, too, were buffalo hunters who lived much like their neighbours, their lives bound to the movement of the vast herds. Badger had inquired among his uncle's people, where he might expect to find them, so he had an idea where to lead the others.

His uncle had cautioned him to watch out for the *Cutthroats* and the *Parted Hairs,* who also lived to the east and southeast. An encounter with either of them could be fatal. So, following his uncle's advice, Badger decided to stay within sight of *Mistakis* until after they had crossed *Makhabn.*

Journeying north, they crossed the flat prairie, keeping the mountains to their left, with the *Place of the Sweet Pine* to their right. The flatness was interrupted periodically by broad river valleys, coulees, and rugged badlands, and it was while they were in the badlands that squabbling crows and magpies drew their attention to a grisly sight. Strewn across a flat meadow were the bodies of four Indians and the carcass of a horse. All young men, they could not have been dead for more than a few days. They had been scalped and their bodies stripped. By their dress, or by their hair and ornamentation, one Indian could usually identify another, but with no clothing or other identifying features, Andy's companions were not sure who the unfortunate souls might have been. They were reasonably sure they were not Blackfoot, but they could have been *Atsíína* or *Cutthroat*— either friend or foe. From what they could tell, the unfortunate souls had been taken by surprise. The whole scene gave them an eerie feeling, and their immediate reaction was to make for the nearest cover, hiding there until after dark. Thereafter, travel would be at night.

Smoking a pipe while they rested for the remainder of the afternoon, they speculated on what could have happened and wondered whether they should continue. *"That could have been us!"* Andy observed, keeping his voice quiet, *"Perhaps this is not a good idea."*

"Not so!" Badger responded, *"Only if it was Cutthroats—or Parted Hairs! Or Spotted Horses People. And who knows? If they had seen your skin and your hair, they might have left us alone."*

"Hai!" White Quill's eyes grew wide in agreement, looking at Andy he added, *"If we travel by day, you must be in the lead...and take your shirt off! And, do not braid hair as you do. Let it hang down, so they can see that you are a napikawan!"*

"Yes,"—Badger agreed solemnly— *"we will follow behind you if we see someone, but if we yell for you, turn and ride as fast as you can!"*

Alarmed, Andy asked. *"Why, what do you mean?"*

"If we see someone we think will attack, we had better try to run for it!" White Quill informed him casually.

"I do not know!" Andy had a worried look on his face. *"Perhaps this is not such a good idea!"*

"Let us go on just a little farther and see what it is like," Badger suggested. *"We should be fairly close by now."*

"*Listen to us!*" White Quill exclaimed, looking disgusted, "*We sound like a bunch of women!*" They finally convinced themselves it was safe to continue and tried to rest.

At dusk, they moved on. Travelling by night on horseback was so much easier than it had been for Badger and Andy when they had been travelling on foot. Cloaked by the darkness, they rode together, passing the time by talking and joking while their mounts plodded, on seemingly tireless feet, across the prairie.

On their third night's ride, they encountered horses grazing on the open prairie. Moon was starting to show her whole face and painted them with her pale light, letting White Quill spot them from a distance. Horses were easy to distinguish from buffalo, at night, because many bore white markings, making them stand out under the light of the night sky. "*There must be a camp nearby!*" Badger surmised in an excited whisper. "*We must find some place to hide our horses, where we can tether them, so they do not try to join these ones. Then we will scout on foot.*"

Finding an island of dense brush on the barren plain, some distance away, they led their horses into the thickest part and tethered them securely. Returning to the herd afoot, they split up to see if they could find the camp. Andy was the first to find it—set in a shallow depression. The pale lodges, their tops darkly stained by smoke, stood out in the brilliant moonlight. His heart leapt to his throat when he realized its occupants might well kill them if they were discovered. He had no idea how to identify them; all he could see were the lodges, many of which had horses tied near them. No fires glowed, and nobody moved about. He counted twenty-two lodges before retreating to the place where they had agreed to meet. Badger was already there, and White Quill arrived a few moments afterward. Both had found the camp, too, and guessed it was likely an *Atsíína* camp, but neither had enough confidence in his decision to let themselves be seen.

"*We have to go back and find a better place for our horses!*" Badger whispered though they were already some distance from the camp. "*We will leave Sun Shines on Him there and—*"

"*No!*" Andy cut him off in a whisper. "*I am not staying alone! I am coming with you!*"

Nodding his concession, Badger continued. "*We will all come back, then. And find a place to hide. We have to watch and see who they are. They could be Cutthroats!*"

"*And if they are, we will have to stay hidden until it is dark again—all day!*" White Quill added, a warning evident in his voice.

It was a *Cutthroat* camp. They had returned to their horses to move them into better cover, even further away, before jogging most of the way back to observe the camp. Dawn broke too soon for them to get as close as Badger would have preferred, and with the flat prairie offering so little cover, their only place of concealment was a low patch of wolf willow, within sight of the camp. They could not risk being seen, trying to get any closer, so flat on their bellies, the trio waited.

The sun had just begun to warm their skin when they spotted a group of boys, coming out to gather the horse herd, moving it off to water. Though some distance from their vantage point, Andy's friends quickly agreed upon their identity.

"*Cutthroats!*" The way Badger whispered it sent a chill down Andy's spine.

"*We are dead!*" White Quill remarked as if their fate was inevitable.

"*What do we do?*" Andy asked, fear clouding his face. "*We should run—now! Maybe they will not see!*"

"*No! There is nothing we can do—we must wait,*" Badger said conclusively.

"*Can we not run?*" Andy wondered.

Both Indians shook their heads. *"We would be seen!"* White Quill assured him, his eyes following the *Cutthroat* boys through the bushes. *"If they see us, they would chase us down on their horses."*

"So we wait until they return to their camp,"—Andy queried— *"then run?"*

"No! We must wait!" Badger said firmly. *"They will probably bring the horses back where we saw them and spend the day watching them. I just hope they do not move them over here and find us!"*

"Maybe I should stand up and let them find me! You said that because I am napikawan, nobody will bother me."

"No!" his companions cut down his idea in unison.

"I do not like this!" Andy confessed.

"None of us do! Pray!" Badger urged, and soon all of them were whispering prayers, watchfully.

At mid-morning, they spotted hunting parties leaving the camp. To their very great relief, all headed out in the opposite direction. Sometime later, a large group of women and children on horseback, pulling empty travois and leading empty pack animals, left in the same direction. *"They are following the hunters,"* Badger breathed. At the same time as the women were leaving the camp, the *Cutthroat* boys brought the rest of the herd back out, moving them just a little farther away from where they had found them.

Throughout the day, Andy's companions took turns keeping watch, neither one willing to trust their white friend to know what he should be watching for. Occasionally the sound of children at play, muffled by the distance, could be heard coming from the camp. All day, the five young *Cutthroats* sat in the shade of a sarvis berry patch near the camp, glancing up occasionally at the horse herd. They spent most of their time talking, wrestling, and in turn, sleeping, completely unaware they were being watched by their enemy.

From time to time, others would come out to the herd and catch horses, leading or riding them back toward the camp. In time, they would be seen riding out. When one group of three young riders headed directly toward their hiding spot, White Quill put his companions on alert. It soon became evident that the riders had other things on their mind though, for suddenly they burst forth in a horse race, tearing past, just wide of the bushes, paying not the least bit of attention to anything but winning their race.

Shortly after that, the horse-watchers all got to their feet. It looked like they were discussing something among them, and in a moment, three of them left. By mid-afternoon, the first of the hunters reappeared. While they were still some distance away, the three missing horse-watchers were seen hurrying back, naked, carrying their breechclouts and their long hair wet. They had obviously been to the water and did not wish to be caught neglecting their duties. Eventually, the other hunters returned and were followed sometime later by the women and children, their animals loaded with meat.

As Sun was about to return to his home, the horse-watchers once again drove the animals to water. *"We are going to be all right,"* Badger announced. *"They are going to water them, and then they will go back to their camp when they are done."* Sure enough, it was dusk when they brought the horses back and retired to the camp. Andy wanted to leave right away, but Badger made them wait until it was completely dark. Finally, to the sound of drumming and singing from the camp, and with Moon not yet having begun her journey, the boys scurried from their cover. They hurried back to their horses, relieved to find them as they had been left. That night they rode hard, wishing to put the most distance between them and the *Cutthroats* as possible.

For the next few nights, they stopped early, more interested in finding good cover than making distance. One day, however, Andy was keeping watch during the daylight and shook his companions awake when he saw riders approaching. Instantly alert, his companions agreed they were *Atsíina*. Directing Andy to remove his shirt and tousle his hair, they gathered their horses and broke their cover, with him in the lead. Immediately, the riders spotted them and became visibly wary, reaching for their bows and adjusting their course to meet them. Andy led his friends, who made no move for their weapons, showing their peaceful intent.

The white boy hollered a nervous hello, as the two parties neared. Stopping to let the *Atsíína* approach, the trio sat with their hands folded in front of them. Badger gave a greeting, first in Blackfoot, then in sign, indicating who they were. In the same manner, the others confirmed they were *Atsíína*, a scouting party. There was one young man of perhaps twenty winters and four others, all in their teens. The scouts were already aware that the *Cutthroats* were in the area and wanted to know every detail of the newcomers' encounter. Badger signed what they knew about the camp, the number of lodges and horses, and its whereabouts.

After, they all got off their horses to smoke together. The *Atsíína* examined Andy's pale skin and golden hair thoroughly and had many questions for him, which his companions translated into sign. After smoking, the trio was invited to accompany them for the rest of the day and return with them to their camp in the evening.

When they eventually reached the top of a butte, offering a commanding view of the surrounding prairie, they dismounted and spent the rest of the afternoon sitting in the shadows cast by their horses, smoking their pipes and watching for any movement on the prairie. The young scouts were eager to talk about the horse-capturing raids they had been a part of, proudly showing off wounds acquired and bragging about the number and quality of horses they had stolen. The eldest had struck an enemy on a couple of prior occasions and took immense pleasure in telling the strangers all the details.

When asked about the purpose of their trek, Badger told them about Wolf Tail and what had happened. The *Atsíína* signed that they knew the man and had heard that he had lost his sons to horse thieves, identified as a party of *Káínaa*. They recounted how he had given chase but lost the trail when heavy rain had washed away any tracks. No mention was made of anyone other than the *Káínaa*. They said Wolf Tail's people would likely be found a few days' ride farther north.

In late afternoon, the scouts led the way to their camp, where they told the leading men what they had learned from their guests. In much the same manner as Wolf Tail's father had welcomed Badger and Andy into his lodge, one of the men invited them to be his guests for the night, feeding them amply. The next morning, getting instructions on where to find Wolf Tail's father, the seekers departed with youthful optimism.

Late the next day, they were intercepted by more *Atsíína* scouts, who approached them with usual caution. When they were close enough, Badger hollered a hearty greeting and signed to identify themselves as *Piikáni*. The fierce-looking scouts looked them over suspiciously, as Badger signed who they were and what they were doing there. "*They are suspicious,*" Badger whispered to his comrades when he had finished signing. "*I think they recognize his horse!*"

"*Tell them why we are here!*" White Quill suggested.

"*Yes!*" Andy agreed nervously. "*Tell them!*"

"*I did!*" their friend responded impatiently, as one of the scouts directed his horse toward them, shouting something none of them understood. Riding straight up to Badger, his face set in a stern glare, he gestured forcefully for them to dismount. The other scouts had encircled the boys with their bows at the ready.

"*Do as they say!*" Badger warned his friends sharply, seeing there was no opportunity for flight. "*Leave your weapons!*" he commanded, alarmed, swinging off his horse. "*I think we are in trouble!*" His startled companions did as he had instructed and stood submissively before the aggressive *Atsíína*.

The scouts' leader shouted a command, and two of his companions leapt from their mounts. The three boys were shoved to the ground and their weapons taken from them.

"Tell them we are friends!" Andy urged, panic rising in his throat, afraid they were about to be butchered. White Quill attempted to sign but was struck with a bow and given a kick in the ribs. When his companions tried to intervene, they were given the same treatment. Another attempt on Badger's part to sign was rebuffed with an angry boot. Roughly, one of them pulled at White Quill's shirt and ordered them to remove their shirts.

"Do it!" Badger ordered, sitting up and whipping off his shirt, hoping it was some strange way to get a better look at Andy. *"Maybe they wish to see Sun Shines on Him!"* he uttered nervously. As soon as they had cast off their shirts, they were ordered to remove the remainder of their clothing. Their belts were then used to tie their hands behind their backs. While that was being done, their captors bantered excitedly, with one of them gathering up the reins of the boys' horses.

Once bound, the captive boys were driven ahead of their captors. They were forced to run, hounded by those on horseback who lashed them with harsh leather reins and whips.

"What are they going to do with us?" Andy gasped as he ran, cringing as a well-directed leather strap sang through the air, threateningly close.

"I am not sure. They are not going to kill us!" Badger replied hoarsely.

"Not yet, anyway!" White Quill puffed.

Trying to encourage one another, they were periodically allowed to stop and rest, while the *Atsíína* drank from bladders they were carrying. Offering nothing to their captives, they taunted their exhausted captives by spitting mouthfuls of water onto the dry ground.

It was a long time after the last such stop that they reached the camp. Its inhabitants had somehow learned of the party's return and came out to meet them to see what was happening. First, boys on horseback raced out to see who the scouts were bringing in and shouted insults at the captives, some daring to try and whip them with their ropes. A few women and younger children, and finally a group of men, stood at the edge of the camp, where the boys were made to stop, while their captors sang.

Badger and Andy scanned the crowd for any sign of Wolf Tail's father, recognizing him instantly when he strode into view. His big frame was hard to miss as he stepped out from behind one of the lodges, pausing to look over the grim procession.

Andy stepped up to the man, and when he saw what he was doing, Badger joined him. The pair stopped in front of the man's imposing frame while White Quill stood back, watching, feeling very vulnerable.

Taking in the situation with just a glance, their friend's father locked his eyes sternly upon Badger and hollered something over his shoulder. Continuing to glare coldly at the captives, he was joined shortly by the man who spoke Blackfoot. The big man said a few words to him before the interpreter turned to address the boys. *"Why have you come here?"* he asked.

Words poured from both boys' mouths at once as they clamoured to explain. Andy turned to his friend and said firmly, *"Let me speak!"* Badger fell silent, and the white boy turned back to the big man. *"We come to tell you of your sons—the Káínaa killed them—not us. They are dogs! I wish—I wish they had killed me, not your sons!"* Andy paused while the man relayed his words. The big man's face remained expressionless, so Andy continued. *"The Káínaa came to us—they said they have a message from you. Suddenly, they—"* He could not hold the man's gaze, looking away for a moment.

When he turned back to face the man once again, tears rimmed his eyes. *"They—they came after your sons."* Andy's voice began to crack, and a tear ran down his cheek. Again, he paused while the interpretation was made, glad for the opportunity to try to contain his emotions. *"The Káínaa said"*—he continued— *"if we did not flee, you would kill us—they said you would think we, uh, betrayed you—we did not—they did. I am sorry! We fled with them.*

"Our hearts were heavy—we did not know what to do! We are sorry! Our hearts were warm toward your sons—toward your son, the older one, much!" he said to the man, remembering not to speak the names of the dead. *"We did not know what to do. Our shame...we fled with those dogs...the Káínaa. But we did not go with them. We left them as soon as we could."* Pausing for a moment, he continued before the interpreter could speak. *"My friend and I ask...you not hold this against us."*

Pausing briefly to see if he had anything more to say, the interpreter spoke again to the big man, who still showed no expression on his face. Stoically, he looked at Badger, pointing to him with his lips to indicate he should speak.

"His words are good!" Badger began. *"Your son was our friend! We were friends with all of them! We have much sorrow—great sorrow! Our hearts are heavy! My friend said we should come—that you might know what happened, and not hold it against us."* Lacking Andy's conviction, he was parroting the reasons Andy had given him for coming on such a quest in the first place.

Once the interpreter had conveyed Badger's words, Andy interjected with calm resignation, *"Our lives are in your hands."* With that, he looked at the ground, a habit he had picked up from his friends when they had nothing to say.

"Yes! Our lives are in your hands," Badger echoed respectfully before the interpreter could speak again.

After hearing what they had said, the big man uttered something to the interpreter who, pointing with his lips at White Quill, asked, *"Who is he?"*

"He is our friend." Andy stammered nervously, not sure the man was buying their story. *"He is...uh, he is called White Quill. He is Piikáni, like us, er, like, uh...like, um...him. He comes because he is our friend. He...um, he hears us. He hears us speak of your sons and...he wished to come with us."*

The big man listened to the interpretation and stood silently, looking coldly from one boy to the other, weighing their words. A long moment passed, and the boys grew increasingly fearful. At last, the big man addressed the interpreter, who turned to Badger and said, *"He says, you say the Káínaa stole his horses, yet it is you who rides the horse of his son!"*

Badger cast a glance sideways at Andy, hoping for inspiration, but Andy's face was blank. Nervously, the Indian stammered, *"I do not know!"* unable to think of a satisfactory answer.

Fearing what the man's conclusion might be, Andy spoke up and admitted, *"We did not know what to do! We, uh, we brought it to you!"* The man remained stone-faced, causing Andy to drop his eyes to the ground, his confidence in the success of their mission faltering. There was a long silence. White Quill was the only one to see the man's expression soften.

The pair were fearing the worst when the big man stepped toward them. They were startled when he stepped behind them to untie Badger's hands. As he did so, the interpreter joined him in loosening Andy's bonds while one of the scouts hopped down to remove those on White Quill's wrists. When they had finished, the big man stepped back. He spoke harshly to the scouts, whose previously boastful demeanour turned sullen before the big man's admonishment. Rubbing their wrists, the trio watched with relief as one of the scouts retrieved their clothing, which had been stuffed into a leather bag.

After covering themselves, Andy returned to his horse, where he retrieved Wolf Tail's bear claw necklace. He had placed it on his saddle two days prior, not knowing when they might encounter the *Atsíina*. Solemnly, he approached the boy's father and handed it to him.

Letting it rest in his palm for a moment, its familiar shape evoked painful memories for them both, and the man carefully closed his fingers around it, his face creased with renewed pain. As if sharing one mind, Badger walked over and retrieved Wolf Tail's horse, returning to stand beside Andy and hand the reins over to the grieving father. Without a word, the big man took them in hand. Giving Badger an embrace, holding him close to his chest, he reached out and pulled Andy to him as well. Holding them close for a moment, he let go of his embrace and stepped back to speak through the interpreter.

"He says your hearts are good!" the man proclaimed after listening to what was said. *"You have strong courage to come to him like this! Your courage gives honour to his sons. Go with him!"* With a nod to the boys, the big man gestured for them to accompany him. All three boys breathed a sigh of relief, realizing how bad things might have gone for them.

Following the big man, Badger and Andy recognized some of the suspicious faces around them. They tried to smile, while the scouts hung back, glowering. At the man's lodge, his wife and daughter stood with the other two wives watching. Wordlessly, the lesser wives took charge of the horses, while Wolf Tail's mother met them with an icy glare, shooing her daughter into the lodge.

She listened to what her husband had to say, glancing periodically at the boys. When he had finished speaking, he answered her questions, and she gave them a long, sombre look before turning to talk to the interpreter. *"Go with her for something to eat!"* he said, ushering them into the lodge.

The boys dove hungrily into the offering of dried meat, trying to ignore the uncomfortable silence that filled the lodge. They were relieved when the interpreter stepped in with the father. There was a discussion between the two before the interpreter turned to address the boys. *"My friend wishes me to tell you that he hopes you will stay. He wishes to give a feast and celebrate your return. His heart feels warm toward you, since your hearts were warm toward his sons, and you were brave enough to bring your message to him. He says that back when—before—when you were here—his son had asked if you could stay and live with them as his brothers. He would have permitted it, had—"* He let his voice trail off, knowing the boys would understand.

The boys were surprised by the man's kind gesture, never having imagined that they would be received so warmly. Taking a moment to ponder what had been said, Andy spoke up. *"Say to him...his son was like a brother."*

The interpreter spoke to the big man who smiled fondly.

"Me too!" Badger echoed his friend's sentiment. The man smiled at Badger and gave something else to be translated, getting to his feet as he finished.

The man who spoke Blackfoot also climbed to his feet, addressing the boys as he rose, *"He needs to speak to the others; there are some who do not feel the same way as he does. Best you wait here until he comes back."* With that, the two of them turned to leave.

"Wait!" Badger cried as the men were about to step through the doorway, *"Will we get our weapons back?"* The two men departed without giving any reply.

19

That evening, the interpreter spent some time with the three relieved boys. They learned from him that on the day of the slaughter, when the horse watchers failed to return by midday, their mother had asked a couple of their friends to ride out and find them. The friends returned with their grim report, and the boys' father raced out. But by the time he and others had pieced together what had happened, heavy rain had all but obliterated the trail. Finding only the odd sign of any track, they had soon lost any hope of tracking the killers and returned to their camp, grieving such great loss. *"There was mourning throughout our camp,"* he told them. *"After, their mother cut off three fingers and slashed her arms and legs—to show her grief. Even he cut his hair short, and their sister cut herself. It was a very sad time!"* Immediately, the camp had moved away to another site. The family had never stopped grieving.

Wolf Tail's father had been unwilling to accept that those who had befriended his sons could have had any part in the killing. *"But nobody could understand why you disappeared with those other ones."* The grief-stricken father had reluctantly reached the conclusion that Andy and Badger had been somehow complicit. Nobody, however, had any difficulty attributing blameworthiness to the *Káínaa*. And so, the younger men of the camp had readied themselves to mount a war party, to wreak revenge upon the perpetrators. Nobody knew from which camp the killers had come, but such detail was never necessary; what the vengeance seekers were after was simply the blood of their enemy. It mattered not whether it was the blood of the actual perpetrators. The older men, however, including the boys' father, thought differently. They had recounted their long-standing peace with their Blackfoot neighbours and how they had always been strong allies. After heated discussions in the lodges of the leading men, it had finally been determined that no vengeance party would go forth. It had been agreed that in the next *season of ripe berries*, when the *Káínaa* held their Sun dance, a delegation would make its way to meet with their heretofore allies to discuss compensation for the atrocity. Now, yet another round of discussion had begun. *"Tomorrow, there will be a council. We will see, then, what will become of you,"* the man concluded ominously.

The supporters of those who had captured the pair were the most outspoken in favour of some type of vengeance. They had been advocating that the boys should be put to death and regretted not having done so when they had had the opportunity. Since their return, there had been discussion throughout the camp regarding the matter. Now, the council would decide. The following night, the boys sat with the interpreter, who kept them apprised of the discussion.

Only three men spoke. The first was a young warrior who decried any solution which did not involve the shedding of

Blackfoot blood. He glowered openly at the Blackfoot boys and gestured animatedly toward them while making his case. Next, an older man, well-respected as a warrior, spoke quietly and eloquently of keeping the peace. He argued that all Blackfoot ought not to be held responsible, and sombrely reminded listeners that their value as allies easily outweighed the need for retaliation. When he had finished, he took his seat, and those in attendance waited to see if anyone else would speak. At last, Wolf Tail's father cleared his throat. In measured fashion, he gazed at his three guests as he spoke, pausing periodically to allow the interpreter to make his words known to them.

At the first such pause, the interpreter turned and spoke quietly to the boys. *"He speaks in favour of sparing you young ones. He says his heart feels warm toward you. He has taken you into his lodge, so you will be under his protection. Nobody can harm you so long as you are his guests. He does not wish revenge to be taken against you."* When he had finished, he looked at the big man who continued. As soon as he was done, the interpreter spoke again. *"He says that he has lost three fine sons. You, his sons admired. Indeed, many of the young ones of this camp admired you. His son had begged him to take you into his lodge and treat you as his brothers. The younger ones also."* Again, he looked to the big man, and after he had spoken a third time, a murmur went through those assembled. The interpreter had to raise his voice to relay the big man's words, *"Our brother admires the bravery and courage you have shown in coming to him. It is this which speaks to him and says that your hearts are good. Had he encountered you at the Sun dance, riding upon that horse, he might well have held a different view...but since you have been brave enough to come to him—and placed your lives in his hands—he is certain that your words are good. He would like to take you as his own sons. He will not allow anyone to harm you!"*

Before the translator had finished, the advocate of vengeance was on his feet, followed by others who shared his appetite for revenge. They started for the door.

Called up short by the elder, the hot-tempered young men turned and glared as the man spoke sharply to them. The words of the old man seemed to settle them, for they resentfully returned to their seats. Pausing for a moment, as the room submitted to his quiet authority, the elder turned and looked to the interpreter.

"*What do you wish to say?*" the interpreter asked Badger, who was now more nervous than ever.

"*What do I say?*" the boy whispered anxiously to his comrades. "*I do not want to say the wrong thing!*"

"*I do not know!*" Andy whispered.

Looking to the interpreter, Badger asked, "*What should we say? Are we expected to become Atsíína?*"

Before the man could respond, White Quill straightened up and addressed the elder. "*You might think it strange that I should speak. I was not there, but my friends cannot find their tongues.*" Looking into the eyes of the one who had lost his sons, he continued. "*I did not know your sons, except through the words of my friends. I would be happy if someone would speak of me as they have spoken of your sons. My friend,*" —he said, placing his hand on Andy's shoulder— "*this one, who I called Sun Shines on Him—he liked your son. He would never have allowed any harm to come to them—had he been able to prevent it. I know him well! I know them both well! You are right to believe them. Their words are good. Their hearts are good!*"

The interpreter looked at Badger, who nodded his assent. The man then conveyed White Quill's words to the audience. When he was finished, Andy spoke up, also addressing himself to Wolf Tail's father. "*Do you remember what brought us to your camp—last berries ripe season? My brother was killed by his friends,*" he said softly, putting his hand on Badger's shoulder, who looked at the ground in front of him. "*I do not know what happened—to my*

320

brother. But I know this one did not harm my brother—it was the others. He took me as his friend. He looked after me when I did not know what to do. I now love him...as I loved my brother. I know his heart is good. I know he did not kill my brother. So, I say to you, our hearts are good. Our hearts feel warm toward you. We came here so that your heart also might feel warm toward us." Looking around at the others, he added, raising his voice, *"All of you—we do not wish to be enemies!"* When he had finished speaking, the group listened while his words were repeated to them.

In response, Wolf Tail's father addressed the assembly. As he spoke, the interpreter leaned toward the boys and told them that he was announcing a feast, the next night, in honour of his new sons, and that their weapons would be returned to them as soon as the council was over. With that, the elder stood, and everyone rose to file out, leaving the suspenseful trio breathing another sigh of relief.

Afterward, the boys went with Wolf Tail's father, and while they listened to him tell the rest of his family what had transpired, their weapons were brought to them. The man's wife and daughter, already under their robes, were solemn but nodded their understanding.

That night, before going to sleep, the boys talked about what had taken place and agreed that it felt good to have done what they did. *"I have never made peace with anyone before,"* Badger said. *"It feels good!"*

Sleep came to them quickly, that night, only to be jolted awake by the frantic screaming of Wolf Tail's mother. Unsure what was going on, they could see the light of early dawn in the smoke hole, and rain was drumming the sides of the tipi. They were alarmed by shouts outside the lodge. Wolf Tail's father was not present. Dressing as quickly as they could while the women huddled on the other side of the lodge moaning desperate prayers, the boys hurried to see what the commotion was about.

Outside, in a steady rain, they spotted a gathering a few lodges away. *"I will wager that they have been raided!"* Badger surmised, leading them toward the activity. There, they learned that a couple of the boys, checking on the horses at first light, had returned to report many of them missing. Immediately, a group of young men had rallied to see if they could find any sign before the rain washed it away. The others stood and watched, while the excited warriors hurried about, making ready to give chase. Racing to their lodges, they returned clutching weapons, medicine bags, and clothing. Younger brothers and some of the fathers anxiously readied what horses had been tethered inside the camp, uttering prayers of well-being and success, as the hopefuls flung themselves onto their mounts. Another group hurried to retrieve what horses were left, and soon it was just the older men, women, and youngsters who stood in the rain, wondering what would be the outcome.

The mood in the camp was tense as everyone waited for word, and when the warriors did not return shortly, it was concluded that there must have been a track for them to follow. By the middle of the afternoon, still, no one had returned. The rain had stopped, but dark clouds hung low over the sodden prairie. Nevertheless, hopes were high that the pursuers would return in victory, with the missing horses.

When none of the warriors had returned by nightfall, some of the women began to talk in fearful tones, many struggling to restrain anxious tears. Although the remaining men tried to be optimistic, dark countenances betrayed their true feelings. The celebration feast for Badger and Andy forgotten, nobody drummed, and no one sang that night. A woman's wail drifted woefully through the night, wordlessly conveying her fear that her young husband would never return. The older men cautioned everyone to be vigilant. With the excitement of the day wearing off, the boys joined others to sit around the inside fires, where conversation was subdued. Once again, the rain drummed against the lodges as a wakeful sleep descended on the camp.

Before first light, Andy was obliged to step out of the lodge to relieve himself, before anyone else had stirred. Slipping out under the door flap, he was startled to step into heavy, wet snow. Hesitating for a second, he took only a few steps toward the back of the lodge, where he did his business, with the snow falling on his bare skin. He wondered how the warriors would fare in it, as he made his way back to his warm bed.

The commotion made by the women when they discovered the snow disturbed everyone. As they stoked the fire, they chattered among themselves, waiting for it to warm up, making it difficult for the boys to sleep. It would be a day spent inside.

By mid-morning, the snow was halfway up to Andy's knees, when he trudged outside to help the girl bring in firewood. It was as they were struggling back to the lodge, loaded down with dead branches, that the jubilant warriors made a triumphal return.

At first, all he heard was their singing, eerily muffled by the falling snow. The snow was coming down so heavily that he could see little. As he stood and watched, others who had heard the singing stepped out to see what was happening. His friends had heard it and joined him at the front of the lodge.

Suddenly, through the curtain of snow, there emerged the first of the returning warriors, singing their victory songs. Parading themselves noisily among the lodges, their women hurried through the snow, rejoicing at their safe return. One of the warriors, when he passed nearby, tossed something to his woman, and Badger announced that there had been bloodshed. *"Did you see that?"* he asked Andy. Without waiting for an answer, he continued, *"It is a scalp! Someone paid with his life."* No sooner had he said it, than a woman's ghostly wailing pierced the heavy snow. *"Eeyii! One of them did not make it back!"* he announced sombrely.

Despite the death of one of their own, the camp entered into rejoicing. Their young men had overtaken the horse thieves, *Cutthroats*, in the middle of the previous day. Abandoning the stolen horses, the thieves had fled, only to be chased down by their determined pursuers. With two of five having been killed in the initial clash, the rest of the thieves took shelter in a patch of bush, atop a hillock. Occupying the higher ground, and armed with guns, they had faced their pursuers in a standoff. Severely outnumbered, they may have hoped to be able to hold out until dark and then sneak away. The *Atsíína* though, seeing that dusk would soon give their foe that opportunity, overran their position on horseback, routing them, but in doing so, one of their own had been lost. In the end, all five of the raiders had been slaughtered. Scalping them and taking their clothes and weapons, the victors backtracked to gather their horses and return to the camp.

Victorious warriors would never forsake an opportunity to flaunt their success. Wishing to make a glorious entry by the light of day, they had held up overnight, not far from the camp. Heedless of the anxiety faced by those left behind, they had endured the discomfort of the snow, timing their return so that everyone would see their triumphal return. The heavy snow could not dampen their spirits.

The boys' adoption took place quietly now, overshadowed by the victory celebration going on elsewhere in the camp. Most people were celebrating the return of loved ones, with the wives of those who had struck an enemy proudly performing scalp dances. But to one family, consoling themselves away from the celebration, the jubilation was without meaning.

The morning after the wintry celebration, the day dawned bright and sunny. The snow lingered for a few more days, and each day grew successively warmer. By the fourth day, the ground was saturated; the pools of muddy water staining the landscape were the only evidence snow had fallen just days earlier. The stream that was their water source was a torrent, and within a week, new grass was beginning to show. Spring had fully arrived.

One morning, in early spring, a group of excited boys came to call, inviting the three newcomers to a celebration. Their leader spoke animatedly, telling them that they wished to perform a ceremony, whereby the newcomers would be taken into their society. The trio was happy that the attitude toward them had changed entirely.

That evening, they followed their hosts on a long hike down the much-receded stream, where the ceremony was to take place. A sweat lodge stood close to the stream. Buffalo robes, spread out around a fire, spoke of their intention of spending the night.

At first, three of their hosts drummed and sang, while most of them danced, to conjure up the proper spirit. When the dancing finished, the boys all sat together and passed a pipe, until, at last, the leader indicated they would sweat. It was dusk.

Two of the youngest *Atsíína* boys were to be their attendants and used sticks to move hot rocks from the fire into a pit in the centre of the sweat lodge. As they did so, the two eldest stripped, directing their guests to do likewise, before making for the stream. After a bracing dunk in the chilly water, they all crowded inside the small structure. The attendants each held a firebrand outside the door, allowing the boys to see and get themselves seated. Inside, the structure was so small that the participants sat with shoulders touching and their crossed legs resting against each other. Eventually, the leader called for his things—a pouch of water and a buffalo tail, with a small leather pouch. When the items had been passed to him, he signalled the attendant to cover the opening, bringing complete darkness over the occupants.

In the sticky blackness, the leader uttered a prayer before drawing sweetgrass out of the pouch to place it onto the hot rocks, sending its sweet smoke wafting through the tiny enclosure. At once, all the Indians began drawing the smoke over their bodies, with cupped hands. Feeling their movements, Andy did likewise. All whispered prayers into the darkness, and when they fell quiet, water sizzling on hot rocks could be heard as the leader dipped the end of the buffalo tail into the pouch of water to splash it onto the hot stones. Instantly, steam filled the little lodge, and they felt the heat intensify as they returned to their prayers.

The ceremony was similar to the one Badger and White Quill had performed for Andy, the previous autumn. He could not understand what the *Atsíina* were praying but caught a few of his friends' words. *"...thank you that you have taken pity upon us and spared us from death,"* he heard White Quill say before his voice trailed off into a murmur. He heard much mention of Sun, their deity, and thanksgiving. Andy had never seen boys his age, back home, so diligent in their faith and in their prayers. In silence, he listened to them while they communed with their gods. They sounded at least as earnest as Reverend Jameson.

The leader periodically interrupted his prayers to splash water onto the rocks, sending a new wave of sweltering heat among them, and they all drew in deep breaths of the hot, moist air. Sweat ran down each boy's body, mingling with that of their neighbours where their bodies touched.

Finally, after all had been silent for some time, the leader called for his assistants to throw aside the opening. Suddenly, the small chamber was filled with light from the campfire and a blast of night air. Everyone tumbled out and made their way to the stream, long hair clinging to sweaty foreheads and necks. Hastening to the water to rinse off, they returned to stand solemnly around the fire to dry off.

The three inductees were directed to remain naked while the others dressed. *"They are going to paint us,"* White Quill whispered to Andy.

Two of the celebrants began laying out and mixing their painting materials. Sombrely, and with all the seriousness of the most devout parson, the eldest of them prayed, and the painting began. He started on Andy, beginning with his face. While Andy stood patiently, Badger described what he was doing. *"He is painting you just like our friend who is dead!"* he said, being worked upon himself, by another.

"Do I look like him?" Andy asked, excited to hear it.

"Looks the same to me!" His friend replied in a whisper, not wishing to distract the solemn painters from their concentration.

Finishing Andy's face, the artist made his markings on the white boy's chest and stomach and continued down his legs. Turning him around, the design was brought around onto his buttocks and down the back of each leg to his feet. Directed that he must not sit down, he stood and watched while Badger was finished, and White Quill received his markings. When they were done, each wore a unique design on his face, but from the neck down, they were almost identical.

Next, the drumming began again, and the three boys were directed in the dance they should perform. It was not entertainment, as Andy had once thought; he knew it was ritual—a carefully choreographed and meaningful ceremony. The dance and everything surrounding it were parts of a sacred rite, intended to invoke the spiritual power afforded members of the society by its spiritual protector. Every move had meaning, and it was carefully explained. When at last, the neophytes had mastered the dance and were able to perform it without instruction, there were no accolades from the *Atsíína* boys, only solemn preparation for their own participation.

As the rest joined in, the drummers began to sing. It sounded to Andy like all the songs he had ever heard the Indians sing—a chant, words indistinguishable to him. Any tune there was to it was lilting and went in time with the drums. He danced as he had been shown, though suspicious that he might be allying himself with a different god. Silently, as he moved in time to the drums, he affirmed his allegiance to his own god.

After it ended, the boys could wash off to sit around the fire, where the two groups communicated mostly through sign. At first, the leaders spoke about the spirit of the horse, which guided and protected the members of the society. The *Piikáni* boys glanced at their pale friend to see how he might react, but his face showed nothing. The *Atsíína* spoke of the attributes of the horse, its intelligence, its strength, and its stamina, which were now imbued upon its newest members, provided they kept the tenets being laid out for them. Their hosts informed them that only boys their age were permitted in the society. During this period of their lives, they would begin going to war against the enemies of their tribe. In doing so, they could now call upon the spirit of the horse to give them success in such endeavours. But they had to be careful to observe all the practices and ceremonies they had now been given. To ignore them could even be fatal.

All were solemn when the two officiants finished speaking, and Andy was particularly quiet. Aware that he was uncomfortable, his two companions tried to move the conversation on, and most of the interaction after that was light-hearted.

The *Atsíína* loved to joke and laugh; laughter was the universal language of the Indians, intermingled with cheers of encouragement as they challenged one another to feats of strength and ability. Imagining that his pale skin meant he would be unable to best them, the *Atsíína* were intent on testing Andy, more than the others. His ability and strength impressed them, and they soon treated him as one of their own.

When finally, they dragged the robes out around the fire and crawled underneath them, the interaction between the two groups largely ceased. Lying on their backs, looking up at the dark sky, with the fire little more than embers, they were unable to see well enough to sign. Each group spoke quietly among themselves. *The seven persons* had not shown themselves at all that night, for cloud, and nobody knew how late it was when the talking ceased.

The trio of newcomers had been wholly accepted by the entire *Atsíína* camp. Even the haughty scouts, who had initially been in favour of their harsh treatment, eventually gave them the hand of fellowship. It did not hurt their relationship when Badger offered their leader his knife.

Badger was a much more capable hunter and rider than most and became something of a hero, in that regard, to others their age. He was regularly invited to accompany others hunting. White Quill was admired for his sense of humour and Andy for his good nature. Wolf Tail's family continued to show their affection and generosity. The man had given each of them two horses as a gift, upon taking them into his family. His mother and his sister lavished them with newly made clothes, and they were always welcome around any fire.

Moving about with their adopted family, the trio continued in their generous ways, keeping the old people and the widows supplied with meat. They stayed back, though, when some of their friends accompanied a group of young men on a raid.

The grass was fully green and the vast prairie was carpeted with wildflowers when Andy learned that some of their hosts intended to make a trip to the *napikawan* camp. The purpose of the trip was to trade furs and meat for goods and ammunition, and he saw it as his opportunity to perhaps receive word of his father. Andy had been intending to return to the fort in early summer, hoping his father might arrive with the first boats. This would give him the chance to get there early.

But the burly factor was a worry to him. He had promised the man that he would use the trade goods that had been given to him to induce the Indians to come to the fort; however, he had not kept up his side of the bargain. Having witnessed the brutal effect of the *napiohke* on the Indians, he had instead been encouraging them to stay away. Even so, beginning to feel a desperate optimism about being reunited with his father, he decided to go along, if he could, and face the man.

Not all were intending to travel to the *napikawan camp;* most would journey south, following the buffalo. Fortunately, Wolf Tail's family was among those journeying to the north, and they welcomed their three new sons along.

After just a few days of riding north, the flat prairie began to give way to rolling parkland, and Badger and Andy agreed that it looked like the country in which they had first met. It seemed to the Indian, though, that they should be travelling in a more westerly direction, to reach the *napikawan camp.* The *Atsiína,* however, insisted they were moving in the right direction.

Eventually, cresting a broad river valley, they spotted the fort below them. Andy and Badger recognized instantly that it was not the fort they had visited the year before. The valley here was much broader and not as deep; the tree cover was not as dense, and this fort was smaller. It was not set upon a hill; clearly, it was not Edmonton House. But it was the destination of the *Atsiína,* who made camp across the river from the fort. While the women set up, the men sat and smoked, discussing how the trading would be conducted.

Andy was left wondering where in the world they could possibly be, since he was sure he had never seen this fort before, even on his journey up the river. When he learned that the trading would not take place until the next morning and that the Indians would not cross the river until then, he could not wait. *"I am going across the river,"* he told his friends. *"I must know where we are!"*

"You are not going without us!" White Quill exclaimed, and they headed off to get their horses.

Andy led them to the edge of the wide river, but he was happy to let Badger lead the way across it. They entered at a ford. The current was strong and in places came well up on the horse's sides, giving Andy concern, but it did not seem to faze his companions in the least. Reaching the north shore, the leader held back and directed Andy, bare-chested, to take the lead. *"Make certain they can see your hair!"* Badger hollered to Andy, nervous about the reception the *napikawan* might give them.

The fort was clearly smaller than Edmonton House. There were no Indians camped around it, and only a solitary figure stood guard on the stockade to perceive their approach. Soon joined by another, they stood together watching.

"Hello!" Andy shouted when he thought they could hear him. "Where are we?"

"Yuh's in hell! Yuh's crossed the river an' now yuh's in hell!" came the reply from a man on the stockade, who snickered at his own humour. When the boys got a little closer, the man hollered again, "Who are yuh and who's yuh got with yuh?"

"My name is Andrew Preston! These are my friends!" Andy replied, waving his hand in his companions' direction. "This is not Edmonton House, is it? Where are we?"

"Reckon it's still a ways up," came the reply from the other man, who was now joined by a third. "Sounds like yer lost!"

"I'm with the Indians across the river! Where are we? What is this place?"

"I reckon we knows that, but what's yer business here?" the first man interrupted.

"They've come to trade, but I'm looking for Edmonton House," Andy replied, reining in beneath the walls of the fort.

All the men guffawed. "Yer a bit off—this's Fort Pitt! Reckon yuh got a ways to go. C'mon 'round t' the front. Yuh might's well c'mon in. Ain't much hap'nin' 'round here these days! Gate's on t'other side—I'll let the boss know yuh's here!"

Around the other side of the fort, the gate stood open. One of the men remained on the stockade, while the one who had done most of the talking climbed down and approached the gate. Inside, there were a few people who seemed busy and paid little attention to the new arrivals.

"C'mon in. Yuh kin tie yer critters over here," the man said, leading them to a rail.

"Can my friends come in?" Andy asked, remembering how poorly Badger had been treated at Edmonton House.

"Reckon they can," the man turned to reply. "They's only two o' them. There ain't a bunch hidin' in the bush, huh?"

"Nope," Andy replied.

"I reckon not—we'da seed 'em cross the river with yuh. They Big Bellies?"

"What?"

"They Big Bellies?"

"What do you mean?

"Are they Big Bellies? You know—what kinda injuns they are— Big Bellies?"

"No, they're *Gut People*."

"*Gut People?* How come you callin' 'em that? That's Blackfoot calls 'em that!"

"'cause I'm Blackfoot, er, I mean, I'm with them—I speak their language, I guess. These guys are Blackfoot. They're with me." The man scrutinized the others more carefully.

"Guess they do look a bit that way. 'Em ain't Blackfoot duds, though! Look more like Big Belly stuff," the man observed. Andy was not sure what he was getting at and made no response.

They were busily tethering their horses when they heard a voice behind them say, "Howdy!" It sounded eerily familiar to Andy, and whirling around, he immediately recognized the man who had abandoned him on the river, a year before. His mind flashing back to the incident, he was too startled to reply. "Well, I'll be! Never thought I'd see you again! Injuns didn't getcha?" the man exclaimed, equally surprised.

"No, sir," Andy replied coldly, recovering from his shock, not too sure what to make of the fellow. "Still got my same friend you wouldn't pick up, too!" he said, nodding at Badger.

"I thought you said there was just one of 'em!"

"There was. I've been with a whole bunch of 'em—all winter—this is another one of 'em."

"Blackfoot?"

"Un-huh, but the ones we came with, across the river, they're not."

"What are they?"

"Gut People," Andy replied, knowing only their Blackfoot name.

"Big Bellies!" the first man said.

"That's all right! Nothin' to worry about there," McConnell replied. "What brings you here?"

"I'm looking for my father, William Preston. He was supposed to—"

"Of course! I know!" McConnell interrupted, grabbing his chin and rubbing it thoughtfully. "Ya know, I met your old man! He came through here last fall, yes he did! Just a bit after you threw your fit down there on the river. Heard you and your brother were both dead, so he went on down the river."

"He what? Both of us?" Andy exclaimed. "Where'd he get that from? Who told him that?"

"Don't know! Someone, I reckon! Word gets 'round these parts pretty good, but it ain't always right. Pretty choked up, he was!"

"Is he coming back? Where is he? Did he say he was coming back?" Andy peppered the man with questions, eager to extract something useful.

"Don't reckon so! Reckon he'd heard your ma'd died, then you boys and all—he wasn't in too gooda shape."

"When did you see him? How long ago?" Andy pried further.

"Come on over to the kitchen," McConnell said, turning to lead the way. "Told you!" he continued as he walked. "Wasn't that long after we saw you, a week or so. Last August, maybe?"

"What is it now? What month?"

"May—end o' May."

"Where did he go? Did he go downriver?" Andy continued to question the man.

"Un-huh—carried right on. The boats don't wait for no one! I got no idea where he was goin' after that."

"My father was here!" Andy exclaimed to his friends. *"Just a short time after this dog left us on the river! This is the dog who would not pick us up. Do you remember?"*

"Yes! I remember the voices of their fire-sticks! Is he the one who shot at me?" Badger asked, eyeing the man suspiciously.

"No, that was another," Andy assured him, remembering the scene vividly. *"This man met my father! My father came here not many days after this one left us!"*

"Where is he? Is he here?" his friend asked.

"No, I do not know! I must try to find out!" Andy said, turning back to McConnell. "Why didn't he stay—and come looking for me? Didn't you tell him where I was? Why didn't he stay? Why'd he go back?"

"He figured you for dead, just like he'd heard. The Blackfoot don't usually go around leavin' strange folks wandering 'round their territory. That's why I was for you coming along with us— remember? I wanted you to come on with us! I dunno! For all I knew, they'd taken two o' yer fair-haired scalps into Edmonton House. How am I to know? I didn't ask him! He was pretty touchy!"

Suspicious, Andy continued pressing the man for information. "What did he say to you? Did he say how he knew we were both supposed to be...both supposed to be killed?"

The man had to think for a moment before replying. "I reckon that was it," he said. "I reckon he'd heard that a bunch of Blackfoot was wavin' a couple of fair-haired scalps 'round. Upset him real good! That's why I didn't ask him a whole bunch of questions. Didn't want to upset him more."

Something did not seem right—the man was being evasive. Andy figured him to be hiding something, but he could not understand why. Turning to the other man, he asked, "Did you see him? My father, Will Preston?"

The man looked at McConnell before answering. "Yep. Just like boss sez. Broke all up cuz his boys wuz dun in by them injuns. 'Dirty injuns,' he sez. 'I's gonna shoot the buggers,' he sez."

"He said that?" Andy asked frostily. "Is that what he said?"

"Yep!" the man replied confidently. "'Shoot the buggers,' he sez!"

McConnell interrupted him, hedging. "Well, no, not really like that!" A little wiser than the other, he explained, "He was pretty upset, but I don't think he would have used that kind of language! He's a preacher, remember?" he prompted the man.

"Yeah! No!" the man corrected himself, now flustered. "That ain't just 'xackly whut he sed. Just sumthin' like it. Maybe didn't say it like that, just 'shoot 'em,' maybe. I dunno—don't 'member!"

Knowing without a doubt that his father would never have used that kind of language, Andy was certain they were both lying to him and continued his interrogation. "I met Mr. Roland at Edmonton House. He said my father was coming back here, or there, I mean Edmonton House, this summer." He, too, was getting flustered.

"Roland? Who's he?"

"You know! The guy from Edmonton House!"

"Rowand, you mean?" The man looked at his companion and gave a smirk.

"Yeah, Rowand! I even work for him, you know! I—"

"One Pound One! The king!" the man jeered to the other, interrupting and not seeming to care what Andy was trying to tell him.

"I work for him," Andy repeated. "He paid me to spend the winter with the Blackfoot," he said defiantly, trying to intimidate the man, using his relationship with Rowand, even though he felt foolish for having forgotten his name. "He sent a letter to my father. I wrote it when I was there, and he was...last year, I mean, I wrote it right there...and he was going to send it with the next boat!" he challenged. "You shoulda got it! Didn't you get it?"

Grabbing his chin again, acting surprised, the man blurted, "Say! You know, I totally forgot about that! Yep, he did! He sure did! I got that letter right with the next batch of mail going down the river."

"You still have it?" the boy exclaimed, his voice shrill. "Why didn't it go last fall? He said it would be on the next boat...and that my father would have it last fall!" Andy was growing agitated, struggling to understand what seemed purposely vague.

"Hey, look, son!" McConnell responded, getting angry. "When there's furs to go out, mail waits. I got it right there at my place, waitin' for the next boat!"

"That won't be 'til this summer! Can I see it? It's my letter! Let me see it!" the feisty boy demanded.

"Sure, you can! You better write him a new one an' tell 'im we'd heard wrong—you're not dead! Fancy that!" he exclaimed, calming down and snickering to his colleagues. "C'mon over to my place." They had reached the door to the kitchen and had been standing outside it. Now, the man led them to a building that stood across the yard.

Reaching the door of the small building, McConnell strode inside and went straight to a table. Sitting down and fumbling through a few papers, he stood up and said, "Nope, it's not here! It'll be at the trading house. We'll have to go over there." He seemed nervous and was getting agitated again.

Back out to the yard, the trading house was at the other end of the row of buildings, which formed the back of the fort. Andy began doubting the man as they traipsed across the yard. In the trading house, McConnell again rummaged around for the letter. After a few minutes, he flopped a leather pouch onto the counter. "It'll be in here," he declared. Reaching into it and feeling around, with a look of surprise, he exclaimed, "There's nothing here! It's supposed to be in here! This is the mailbag! But there's nothing in it! Musta been stolen! There's always injuns coming and going in here. They've stolen it! I'll be damned!"

"I don't believe you!" Andy reacted angrily. "You said none of the mail went because there was no room for it! You said they had to leave the mail, so they could take furs. There had to be room for one little letter! Where's the rest of the mail? You're lyin'!" he accused the man, his voice raised.

"You little shit!" McConnell snapped, instantly furious. Red in the face, he shouted, "You come in here accusin' me of lying? Who the hell do you think you are? I own this place! You're in my post! What I say goes! The letter's been stolen! You hear! Don't you come marchin' in here, you self-righteous little Bible-thumper, accusing me of things I didn't do! Get to hell outta here! An' take your dam' injuns with you. Get to hell outta here!" he roared.

Badger and White Quill were startled by the man's sudden outburst. Neither understood what was being said, but the tone of the man's voice told them enough. Seeing Andy's face flush with anger, they knew something was wrong, and both instinctively placed their hands on their knives.

"Oh, no you don't!" McConnell yelled. Seeing what they were doing, he swept a gun up from behind the counter and waved it in their faces.

"What are you doing?" Andy shrieked, once again finding himself face to face with a firearm. At the same time, he saw his friends' hands upon their knives. "No! *No! Leave your weapons! We must go!*" he commanded them, worried about how they might react. Returning his attention to McConnell, he stepped between him and the two startled Indians. "Don't shoot us, okay? We're leavin'! We're leavin'!" he assured the fuming man, turning to crowd his friends toward the door. A man who had followed them inside had also grabbed a gun and was pointing it at them. *"Get out of here! Go!"* Andy ordered his friends and ushered them out the door. Hurrying toward their horses, they were followed into the yard by the irate men watching them depart.

The Indians asked Andy anxiously what was happening. He replied, *"That dog face gives us trouble! He lies to us! Something is wrong! We must leave here. Do not take up your weapons! We leave now!"* he ordered them.

"What was he saying? Why is he so angry?" White Quill wanted to know, looking nervously at the men, who stood watching them, guns in hand.

"Come!" Andy said, untying his horse, *"I will tell you when we are out of this place. Come! Hurry!"*

Alarmed and nervous, the Indians did as their friend had instructed, but as soon as they were clear of the gate, they persisted with their questions. *"What is happening?"* Badger demanded to know.

"That man does not speak the truth! He is the man who was the chief of the napikawan...who brought me to the place where you found me. He does not speak the truth about my father! He says that my father came through this camp less than...less than a moon after he left us on the river. The chief of the other napikawan camp says the same—and I believe him! Their story is the same...My father came last falling leaves season. But when I spoke to the other chief, I gave him a message. I made...my marks. You know the marks I make on rocks with pieces of burned wood? I made those marks on"—Andy was flustered and struggled to find the right word to explain himself— *"on a skin! It was a message to my father. I made my marks on a skin...and gave it to the other chief napikawan...to send it to my father, but this man took it...and now it is gone!"*

"What did he do with them?" Badger asked as they made their way in the direction of the river.

"I do not know! All I know is that he is not saying the truth. He is hiding something!" Andy replied, still mulling over what had just happened.

Suddenly, a plan popped into his head, and pulling up his horse, he told the others, *"Hai! I have an idea! You two wait here! Wait here!"* he commanded without telling them what he was thinking.

Turning his horse, he urged it back to the fort. The two Indians looked at each other and followed at a distance, stopping to watch once Andy got close enough to the fort to holler at those on the walls. Once again, only one figure stood on the top of the stockade, but as he approached, this man was soon joined by others, until, by the time Andy had stopped and looked up at them, there were four men above him. McConnell was among them. Two rested guns on the top of the stockade.

"Hey, Mister McConnell!" Andy hollered. "You wanna trade with those Indians across the river?"

"I thought I told you to get the hell outta here!" shouted McConnell angrily.

"Do you want to trade with 'em?" Andy repeated himself, defiant.

"What's your point?" McConnell roared. "You're wasting my time!"

"They're with me!" he hollered. Trying to bluff the man, he announced boldly, "And I can tell them not to come over here if I want! All I gotta do is tell 'em! So, I want to know what's goin' on! You're lyin' to me about my father! What're you hiding?"

"You little shit! Who in hell do you think you are? Shoot 'im! Shoot 'im!" he ordered the others. The two men with muskets gave him a look of shock. Surprised by the order they had been given, they hesitated. "Shoot 'im, dammit! Shoot 'im, I said!" the man screamed. In an instant, his underlings snatched their weapons to their shoulders.

Startled by the response he was being given, Andy could not believe they would actually shoot him! He had never dreamed his bluff might turn out like this! But both men were cocking their weapons and appeared intent on following the man's order.

Andy responded immediately, jerking his rein viciously. Steering his horse around, he was unable to tear his eyes off the guns that were pointed at him. The smoke from one of them instantly preceded a tearing blow to his left shoulder, which almost ripped him from his mount. Even the weapon's deadly roar escaped him as he clutched for anything to hold onto. Conscious of the sound of another shot, almost on top of the first, he heard only the whizzing of its ball past him and knew the stakes could get no higher.

The horse under him leapt to full flight, almost unseating him before he managed to get a grasp on the saddle with his good arm. Terrified, the injured boy tried desperately to cling to his perch. His left arm was useless as the animal, spooked by the shots, sped away.

Frantic, Andy struggled to stay atop his horse, but every movement of the galloping animal challenged his grip. The panicked beast, sensing the rider's weight shifting, shied from it, causing the boy to slip from the saddle and tumble to the ground, limbs flying.

Stunned and winded from the fall, in extreme pain, Andy gasped for breath. Another projectile kicked up dirt beside his head, followed by the sound of its shot, and brought him to his senses.

Aware of the clamour of galloping horses and more dirt flying, a familiar voice called to him. *"Here! Get up!"* Looking up, he recognized Badger's anxious face and outstretched arm. *"Grab my hand!"* the boy cried urgently, reaching with one hand while trying to control his mount with the other. Knowing it was now a matter of life or death, Andy reached out desperately with his good arm.

His rescuer clasped it with all his strength and giving the mightiest effort of his life, dragged his friend up.

Hanging precariously across Badger's horse in front of him, Andy was vaguely aware of White Quill's presence beside them and knew he was shielding him from the awful gun. A couple of other shots never made it to them.

Their frenzied flight took them to the merciful cover of the bush, beside the tranquil river. Aware of the bush tearing at them and the horse's abrupt stop, Andy heard a frantic voice, *"Get off! Get off! Wait here!"* before being dropped to the ground. His legs crumpled beneath him, and he fell in a heap, confused and in tremendous pain.

Horse and rider gone, he wondered, where is he? Something is wrong! O, God! O, God, help me! There is so much blood! Where is it all coming from? Help me, Jesus!

Blackness—

20

"There is something about it I just couldn't get rid of!" Will Preston told his friend, the Reverend Gideon Jameson, relaxing together in the parsonage at the Red River settlement. "I got as far as Rainy Lake and could go no further. There was just something in my spirit that kept telling me that I needed to go back!"

"Well, if it is the Lord, then you must obey it," his friend responded sombrely. "You had asked me to pray, and we have been, Miriam and I both. She told me a while ago that she believed you would be back, so I think there was something to it!"

"Oh, I know there is something to it! I felt, after I had lost my whole family—my whole family! —that this must all have been a big mistake. I doubted the Lord, Gideon! I even cursed him! I spat, and I cursed him! I was not a very good Christian! I thought, how could he do this to me! I had been out there serving him! I had given up so much to serve him, and this is what I get?" He paused, thoughtfully, while his friend remained silent, patient.

"But then,"—Will continued— "in some quiet place in my heart, I knew I had to trust him.

"I felt like Job! My whole family, gone! Stripped of everything!" Pensively tugging at his beard, he paused, then continued quietly. "We don't know why these things happen, but we know he causeth all things to work together for good to them that loveth God. 'Trust in the Lord with all thine heart and lean not on thine own understanding; in all thy ways acknowledge him, and he wilt make thy paths straight.' I must trust him! He has turned me around, half-way to the east...and who knows where I would have ended up? And I believe he is sending me right back there...right back to where I was!"

He was trying to convince himself, as much as his friend, that this was the right thing to do. Looking into the fire, he kept pulling idly at his beard and continued, "I sure miss them, you know, Elizabeth, and the boys. I have beaten myself up so many times...for having left them for so long! They were just boys when I left, you know...though Matthew, I guess, was a young man. I had hoped he would teach here for a while and then join me in the Lord's work. Andrew was the rascal! He was a match for anyone! Bright as could be! Loved his brother. O, God, I hope they didn't suffer! I hope it was quick!" The man's voice trembled, and he paused, lost in the memory of his sons' lives. With unseeing eyes, he stared into the fire, but the images he saw were of his family.

In a moment, he spoke again. "I haven't told you—I haven't told anyone yet—they were scalped!" Will's chin quivered again, and he fought back tears.

His friend reached a hand and rested it warmly on his friend's shoulder. "You don't need to say anymore," he said gently, his own heart heavy with the burden of his friend's loss.

Will appeared not to have heard him, and with an absent look in his eyes, he uttered, "They can be so savage! I've heard of them cutting the bodies to pieces!" He winced as he spoke, imagining for the thousandth time what might have happened to his dear boys. "That man at the fort, though! It was hard on him too! But he was still so good to me! He's the one who took them up and...I'm going to look him up when I go through there. Anyway, McConnell, I think, this fellow told me what happened. I could tell it upset him to have to tell me." He stared into the fire with eyes that were looking into the past. They glistened with tears. For a long time, neither spoke.

"It will be so hard to go back to them—" he continued with a sigh— "knowing what they did to my boys! I can't believe it! They treated me so well! One of them, Buffalo Child—I'll always remember him—he promised he would teach them to hunt and shoot buffalo from a running horse—with a bow and arrow, no less! —when I brought 'em out. They'd have loved that! Matthew might have...but Andrew would have tackled it, whole hog!"

Reverend Jameson just listened. He had done a lot of listening. When his friend had first shown up, the fall before, he had been on the brink. The first thing he had asked was whether his boys had gone looking for him after their mother had died. Hanging his head, Jameson had admitted they had. "I'm sorry, Will! They didn't tell a soul! They were just gone!" he had said remorsefully. "We didn't even know until they were gone!" At that, Will Preston had broken down and sobbed, telling his friend what he had been told—slain by the Blackfoot. Not wanting to believe it, he had hoped beyond hope that he had been misinformed. But this McConnell fellow had apparently seen it. What were the odds, he had asked? In mourning, he had begun to question his calling—his missionary effort in the west. Finally, in despair and brokenness, he had set out for Montreal, intending to return to his home in the north of England.

And now, he was on his way back, drawn by some power greater than himself and greater than his circumstances. Crediting that power with giving him the determination, he was returning alone to the mission he had begun with such hope and optimism three years earlier. It would be a difficult journey. Gideon Jameson prayed quietly while he sat with his colleague. And, in his prayer, he asked that the bereaved man might somehow be able to meet up with that kind man at a fort, somewhere along a big river in the west.

* * *

At that very moment, somewhere along that big river in the west, Reverend William Preston's son was clinging to life, by the grace of his god and the faith of an Indian medicine man.

As Badger had pulled his gravely wounded friend up in front of him and raced to safety, White Quill's horse had been shot out from under him. Struck in the hindquarters by a ball intended for its rider, the animal had gone down while pulling abreast of Badger's horse, its young rider knocked unconscious in the fall. After depositing Andy in the cover of the bush, Badger had returned for his other fallen friend, who he found lying on the ground near his crippled mount. Without regard for the danger, he dismounted and muscled the lifeless form onto his shoulders. Carrying him to safety, he used his own horse as a shield from the gunfire punctuating his flight.

Letting the young Indian's body slump to the ground beside the other, Badger was horrified by the sight of them, falling to his knees beside them, in shock. Andy's face was paler than he had ever seen it, and he was covered in blood—breathing, but barely. Certain White Quill was dead, Badger gasped in relief when he saw his chest rising and falling. Sitting on his heels beside them, he begged the gods for their lives, until *Atsíína* warriors came charging from the river to investigate the shooting.

White Quill began to stir as they were loading Andy awkwardly onto a horse, in front of one of the *Atsíína*. Once they were on their way, White Quill was hefted on behind another rider, dazed, but able to hold on. Having discovered that his own horse had also been struck, Badger, too, doubled with another rider, leading his limping mount.

Taken immediately to the lodge of Wolf Tail's mother, Andy was laid on the ground, inside. His friends watched silently as the women stripped off his blood-soaked shirt to reveal a vicious wound below his left shoulder with blood still oozing. A man with healing power was summoned, and after striking a bargain with Wolf Tail's father, began his ministrations.

Sending one of the women for what he needed, and chasing the others from the lodge, he instructed Badger to help strip the rest of the white boy's clothing off. When the woman returned carrying a bundle, the medicine man took the items and dismissed her distractedly, turning his full attention to his patient, lying prone before him. By sign, he instructed Badger to help him spread out a colossal wolf hide and move Andy onto it. The coolness of his friend's skin startled the young Indian, but before he could comment on it, the medicine man nodded that he should wait outside.

For three days, the family was not allowed to return to their lodge. The medicine man, during that period, did not leave Andy's side except for brief periods during which he would go to the top of the ridge above the river to rest and pray. When he returned, he would sing songs and perform his ceremonies, shaking a rattle and making incantations and burning sweetgrass over the young man's body. Nobody was allowed inside. From the outside, they could hear him blowing his eagle bone whistle and chanting.

Badger and White Quill also prayed. They fasted, as they had always understood was necessary for effective prayer, and they prayed to Andy's god, asking him to spare their friend's life. They did not return to the fort when the *Atsíina* crossed for trade. Frightened and despairing, they went by themselves to a spot where they could keep an eye on the lodge in which their friend fought death. On the fourth day, they saw the old medicine man come out and beckon one of the women. When they saw her return with food, they rejoiced and hurried to the lodge.

Andy had regained consciousness. He was terribly weak, and the man had him trying to chew on raw buffalo meat. When he saw his patient's friends, he instructed them to go and get a fresh buffalo liver, assuring them that their friend would recover if they could get one for him—he needed what blood he had left to be strengthened, and the organ would do that. They raced to get their things and hurried off on their quest.

Raw buffalo liver brought a little colour into Andy's pallid face, but he had difficulty taking it. Still dazed and confused, he said nothing, responding to questions most of the time with a vacant stare.

The *Atsíína* were finished trading at the fort, having begun the day after Andy was shot. Nowhere near as unruly as their Blackfoot neighbours, a few of the men had returned with cups full of liquor, but none had become disorderly. Most of what they had for trade was exchanged for women's goods and ammunition. The alcohol had been given only as a gift from the trader to some of the men.

When it was announced that the camp would be moving, the medicine man insisted that his patient stay put. As the rest pulled out, it was only Wolf Tail's family and his two best friends who stayed behind.

Still very weak, Andy had no recollection of what had happened. He was too weak to walk, and he was too feeble even to ride on a travois. It took another three days for him to be able to move about at all. On that day, his friends were able to help him up and walk shakily, and the medicine man consented to let him ride on a travois. Flanked by his worried companions, Andy was moved in the same manner as the very old and infirm, and the very young and helpless.

His friends told him repeatedly what had occurred. Piecing together what they knew with what Andy could recall of the incident, they began to understand the true character of the man named

McConnell. With abject disappointment, Andy was able to conclude that there would be no reason to return to Edmonton House. His hope of reuniting with his father crushed, he resigned himself to live with the Blackfoot, holding no hope of his father's return.

After joining up with the rest of the camp, Badger and White Quill accompanied their hosts in the hunt, while their friend recovered. Wolf Tail's sister once again became Andy's companion, always under the watchful eye of her mother, who had no more sons to watch out for her. Both waited on his needs and helped him shuffle about the camp. The girl warmed up to him. On friendly terms, they attempted each other's language and smiled together, but Andy kept her at a distance. When his friends teased him about being in love with her, he denied it fiercely.

One day though, alone for a few moments, she gazed into his eyes and surprised him by leaning forward, kissing him on the lips. He told his friends about it later and asked if they could move to a lodge of their own, as they had among Badger's people. Both his friends understood, without being told, the real reason Andy wanted distance from Wolf Tail's sister. So, they suggested that they soon head for the *Place of the Sweet Pine*, far to the south, where they might meet up with their families. Since it was customary for a significant number of *Piikáni* camps to meet for the Sun dance, it seemed likely that both their families might be there. When Andy understood this, he became single-minded at the notion of seeing Pretty Bird again, even though it could only be from afar. As soon as he was capable of riding on his own, they planned to head south.

When they told Wolf Tail's father of their plans, he was visibly disappointed; his wife was stoically accepting. After their daughter heard of Andy's impending departure, she actively avoided him. When she did see him, she was ambivalent, even cold toward him. As if out of spite, she let him see her flirting with some of the other young men. It was time to leave.

Parting was difficult for everyone. Wolf Tail's father embraced each of the boys as he had his own sons. The man's wife cried softly, and his daughter was nowhere to be seen. There was some mention of the *Atsíina* attending the Sun dance, but no commitment was given. Before their departure, however, Wolf Tail's father asked Badger to go out to the herd and bring Wolf Tail's horse to him. Andy sat with the big man, while they waited, speaking little. White Quill tried to soften the awkwardness by joking with them.

When Badger returned, leading the beautiful, spotted buffalo runner, the man got up and strode toward them, taking the rein. As they made ready to leave, he called Badger over and placed the reins in his hand. Speaking slowly and signing at the same time, he said that he was the most like his son, a good rider and an excellent hunter; it was right for him to have the animal. Next, he stepped over to where Andy was already mounted, handing him Wolf Tail's bear claw. Hesitantly, Andy reached out and took hold of it. Acknowledging that his son had loved him as a brother, the man turned away and disappeared inside his lodge.

Somberly, the trio departed the camp they had entered so uncertainly weeks before, but with so much more than when they had arrived—horses, clothing, and friends. They had been greatly favoured, and all were grateful. As they left the camp, Andy had a sense that the Blackfoot were his people now. He was going home.

Having ridden little since being shot, Andy was unable to ride for very long. By the middle of the day, he called a halt, and after eating some buffalo meat, fell asleep until the middle of the afternoon. After another short ride, he had to stop again to rest, well before evening. This went on for several more days. While he rested, his friends hunted, leaving him in some shady spot. If near water, they would frolic while he slept. In this fashion, they travelled until Badger decided that, once again, they would have to travel under cover of darkness. The parkland behind them, they were venturing onto the wide, flat expanse of the prairie, where any but the smallest living creature could be seen from a great distance.

Night travel was more comfortable for Andy. It helped him regain his strength by allowing him to rest during the heat of the day, travelling only in the cool of the night. Each day, his friends killed a buffalo, often taking only the tongue and liver. By the time they crossed the *Red Deer River,* which told them that they were in their home territory, Andy could ride most of the day without stopping to rest. During this time, the boys grew ever closer to each other. White Quill and Badger cared affectionately for their friend, and Andy's admiration for them grew even stronger. Each of the boys privately wished their kinship would last forever.

Keeping watch for any sign of their own kind, they eventually tracked a camp of *Siksika,* who welcomed them. It was some days later that they discovered a camp of their own people, who were also making their way to the Sun dance. As always, Badger and White Quill were acquainted with some, and as usual, Andy became an attraction.

Around the fires in the evenings, and often well into the nights, the talk was of war and courageous acts of bravery. Andy found out that his having been blooded made him somewhat special, and the angry scar of his healing gunshot wound made him into an even greater celebrity. It set him together with some of the others, who had also been wounded, though none by a *napikawan.* He tried to downplay the incident, and only in response to Badger's bragging on his behalf, did he tell the story. People found it strange, though, when they learned he had no plan for retribution.

Badger limited his own bragging to his skill in the hunt, his stories soon verified by those who accompanied him. White Quill made no mention of the scalps that he had taken. Instead, he made his usual mark as a jokester, who could also hunt. They were well-received and welcomed around the fires of any of their hosts.

Those they were travelling with were eventually joined by others, who accompanied them on their journey. Visiting carried on late into the night, reminding Andy of the previous winter's gathering at Running Wolf's camp, and the starts came later and later each morning. His friends always recognized people they knew, and in visiting, found others they knew in common with their fellow travellers. Each day, anticipation was building for the great gathering to come.

Once they arrived at the Sun dance camp, the sojourners joined a group of over three hundred lodges that were already in attendance. When Andy asked his friends how many more people might show up, they could not give a number but indicated a great many. Having learned that it was not uncommon for eight or more to live together in a lodge, he quickly realized that it was going to be a greater gathering than anything he had seen since leaving England with his family several years before. It struck him that he would be the only white person present.

Andy's companions seldom left his side and included him in everything they did. Able to speak their language quite proficiently, and identical to them in his dress, the people treated him as one of their own. Having been so well-accepted among the people, he began striking out on his own, wandering around the big camp, making new friends—always with one eye out for one friend in particular. He did not find her, but one day, someone else found him.

Andy was lost in thought one day, watching the intriguing activities of members of the *Mosquito Society* when someone startled him from behind. Two women had been standing behind him. One of them recognized him and gave a shriek, suddenly embracing him. Turning to see who was accosting him, he was surprised to find that it was a close friend of White Quill's mother. *"He is dead! He is dead!"* she cried as she clutched at him. *"You can go to her now!"* she exclaimed, hugely excited.

Struggling to understand the woman's excitement, Andy stepped back a little, his eyes widening as the pieces fell into place. *"Pretty Bird? Do you mean Pretty Bird?"* he asked her, his heart suddenly in his throat.

"Yes! Yes! She is a widow! You should go to her!" The woman seemed so excited that she could not stand still.

"Where? Is she here? Where is she?" Andy asked, filled with excitement himself.

"She is not here! She waits to give birth! She will be so happy! You must go to her!"

"Where? Where is she?" Andy cried urgently.

"She is not here! She could not travel any longer because her time had come! She is with her mother!"

"Where is she? What happened?"

"He was killed by the Liars! You must go to her! Do not wait! You must go now!"

Andy was grinning from ear to ear, overcome with a tremendous sense of relief and excitement. *"Where is she? Where can I find her?"*

"She is with her mother. They are camped with her aunt! She is there, along Napi-tahta!" The woman gave a nod of her head to indicate the direction.

"When did this happen? When was he, uh, killed?" the white boy asked excitedly.

"Not long ago! It happened when the grass comes green! We were not expecting a raid," the woman replied, her face darkening briefly as she recalled the memory.

"I shall find her!" Andy shouted, interrupting her, taking the woman by the shoulders. *"Stay here!"* he told her. *"Do not go anywhere! I need to find my friends. No!"* he said, changing his mind. *"Come with me! I will never find you again! I must find my friends! They will take me there. Come with me!"*

"I am coming! You go! I will come with you!" the woman cried excitedly. Their exchange had caused quite a commotion, and people were now staring at them, amused.

"Come!" Andy cried, grabbing her arm and heading off to find his friends.

"Wait!" the woman hollered. She turned and reached out to take the hand of the woman who had been accompanying her. *"Come on, hurry! Come with us!"* Holding each other by the hand, they followed Andy as he dragged them through the great camp.

Much to Andy's relief, Badger and White Quill were right where he had left them, watching a group of young men playing hand games. *"Hai!"* he cried as soon as he saw them. *"Hai! Come! Come!"* he hollered when they looked up and saw him. *"I have something to tell you!"* Seeing his excitement, they hurried toward him. With the two women in tow, he cried, *"It is Pretty Bird! They know where she is!"*

White Quill suddenly became almost as excited as Andy. *"What? Where?"* he exclaimed.

"What are you talking about?" Badger asked his breathless friend when they came together.

"It is Pretty Bird! Her husband was killed! We need to find her!" Andy informed them.

"Yes! You need to take him there!" the woman interjected, winded from Andy dragging them. *"She will want to be with him!"*

"My sister!" White Quill turned to face the woman, *"Where is she? What happened?"*

Andy and the woman both started to answer at the same time. *"Her husband was killed by the Liars!"* the woman replied. *"Now, she gives birth to his baby! You need to go to her...and take your friend to her!"*

"Wait! What are you saying? What happened?" White Quill insisted on knowing more.

"The Liars! They raided our camp! He went out against them and

was struck down! The poor girl! She had few tears for him!" By now, the woman was beginning to settle down.

"Where are they? Where is my mother?" White Quill asked anxiously.

"They are along Napi-tahta. Where that boy was taken by the underwater people. Do you remember the place?"

White Quill recalled the incident and nodded, *"Yes! When did you leave them there?"*

"We have been, uh...four nights coming here. You could be there in less than that! It would not take you that long!"

"Do you know this place?" Andy asked his friend.

"Yes! I know it!" White Quill assured him. *"Do you want to go there?"*

"Yes! Right now! Can we?"

"So, you wish to be tied to a woman then?" Badger interjected, sounding gruff.

"Wait!" Andy cried suddenly, his friend's interruption reminding him of their initial goal. *"What about your mother and your sister?"* He had missed the sour note in Badger's voice.

"They are not here!" Badger replied. *"I have not been able to find them,"* he said glumly, trying to allay a looming sense of loss, which had begun to stir inside him.

"We go now?" Andy asked the younger one excitedly.

"Yes! I am ready! Let us go!" White Quill agreed and turned with Andy to retrieve their horses.

Badger, swallowing the lump that had suddenly found its way into his throat, called after his friends. *"Maybe I will stay here. You go with him,"* he said with mounting gloom.

Ignorant of his friend's angst, the excited white boy exclaimed, *"No! You have to come with us! Come on!"*

"Yes! Come!" the younger one urged. Badger gave a shrug of indifference and followed, keeping his eyes down. His friends were too excited to notice his lack of enthusiasm.

As soon as they could retrieve their animals and get their things together, they were on their way. Taking only their favourite mounts, White Quill gave instructions to a friend, who agreed to keep an eye on the rest. The two Indian boys conferred briefly on the route they should take, and the trio set off to find the one Andy loved. Relying entirely upon his Indian guides, he had no idea how far they would have to travel. It did not matter to him.

That night, just before dark, they stopped to have something to eat and rest the horses. *"How far?"* Andy asked, munching blissfully on dried buffalo.

"How far have we come, or how far until we get there?" White Quill asked.

"How far until we get there."

"Unh," the younger one's face contorted as he thought about the answer. *"The way you ride, maybe when the geese fly south!"* Snickering at his own joke and giving his friend a slug on the arm, he continued more seriously, *"Maybe we travel the distance we have come, two more times, maybe three."*

"Are we going to ride through the night?" Andy wondered, wishing they would and hoping the others would agree.

Their guide just shrugged and said, *"I do not care! What about you?"* he asked Badger.

Badger had been unusually quiet, and he too shrugged. When he avoided making eye contact with Andy, the other two finally perceived something amiss with their good friend.

"What is wrong?" the white boy asked, paying more careful attention to him.

"Nothing!" his friend responded sulkily and got to his feet. *"I am going to check on the horses,"* he said.

"What is wrong with him?" White Quill whispered, watching him go.

Concerned, Andy scrambled to his feet. *"I do not know. Wait here!"* he told the younger one, who heedlessly followed at his heels as he trotted to catch up.

"Hai! What is wrong?" Andy called out to Badger, who just quickened his pace. Hurrying to catch up, Andy grabbed him by the shoulder. *"What is wrong?"* he asked again, his voice rising. Badger stopped and stood with his back to them, trying to shake Andy's grip.

"Nothing! I just have to pee."

"No, you do not," Andy responded, recognizing something in his friend's voice. *"Something is wrong!"* he asserted, trying to step in front of him to see his face in the failing light. But the Indian kept turning away from him.

Feeling Andy grip him more firmly and try to pull him around, the sullen one relented and faced his friend. Andy did not need to say anything. When he got a look at his friend's face, he saw everything he needed to know—his fear, his anxiety, his kinship, his loss—all at once. He just embraced him and held onto him, not saying anything, with White Quill standing beside them. Watching quietly, he also sensed what was going on.

Guessing at the problem, Andy whispered, *"It is Pretty Bird—is that it?"* as he let go and stepped back. His friend hung his head, and Andy knew his inkling was correct. *"You think I am going to leave you—like you thought I would leave you at the napikawan camp—is that it?"*

"Maybe."

"Míisinsski! You are my brother! You and White Quill! I do not have anyone else—you are my only family!" Andy tried to reassure him. *"I do not know what is going to happen, but I need to see her! I need to talk to her—I do not know—"*

"I am such a woman!" Badger berated himself through gritted teeth, looking at the ground. *"A nothing one!"*

"No, you are not!" Andy tried to assure him.

"You do not want a friend who behaves like a woman!"

"You are not a woman! What is wrong?"

Badger pulled away and sat down on the ground, pulling his knees up in front of him and resting his chin on his knees. Andy squatted in front of him and put a hand on his shoulder. White Quill sat down quietly on the other side of him.

"*I should be happy for you,*" Badger sulked, fearful of losing the white boy's friendship. "*I am not a very good friend...to behave this way!*"

"*I do not think that,*" Andy told him, speaking softly.

"*I do not know—I guess I am jealous of her! She will have you all to herself...and we will never see you!*"

"*I thought that might be it!*" Andy sighed. "*You will live with us! Both of you! We will all live together!*" Badger did not reply. Staring straight ahead, he rubbed his chin on his knee. "*I do not want us to not be friends,*" Andy said softly.

"*You will spend all your time with her! When will we hunt? When will we travel about...as we have been doing? You will have to stay with her! I guess that is only right, but then you will never want to be with us,*" his sad friend lamented.

For the first time in the conversation, White Quill piped up, "*It will be you and me, I guess,*" sounding compassionate.

"*But we can do things together—all of us,*" Andy tried to reassure them.

"*That is what you say, but it will not be the same,*" Badger countered.

Andy was quiet for a long time. "*You are right,*" he conceded at last. "*I know you are right—maybe I should not be doing this! We are too young!*"

"*She is not so young! She has already had a husband...and has his child. She is no longer a virgin!*" Badger observed, testing his friend's resolve.

Andy was quiet again, before saying, "*I have not stopped thinking about that...ever since we left...I think about it all the time! I do not like it, but it is not what she wanted—I know it is not! She wanted to be with me, not him! Remember?"* Without waiting for a response, he continued. *"I do not know if we are too young! I think I—no, I do! I love her! I know I love her! You know how I liked that other girl? Remember how I used to talk about her?"* Badger shrugged, and White Quill listened quietly. *"When I saw her—that other girl—when we were in that camp, last moon? It only made me want to be with Pretty Bird...And, when she tried to kiss me? It felt like I should not!"* he told them.

"Has she not been unfaithful to you? She has taken a husband!" Badger goaded him, receiving a sharp glare from White Quill.

"No!" Andy disagreed abruptly. *"She did not take him! He took her! She did not want to go with him—we all know that! She was going to be my wife! She said she would go with me!"*

White Quill nodded his agreement, but there was another long silence before Badger spoke. *"Yes, you speak the truth,"* he sighed with resignation. *"White Quill and I have spoken much...about the two of you, ever since we started out for the Sun dance. Should I tell him?"* He looked at the other Indian with a hint of a grin. It brought a smile to White Quill's face, and he shrugged in a way that said he wanted the story told. Badger's grin widened as he continued. *"Pretty Bird wanted us to help you steal her from her husband!"*

"What? When? When did you see her?" Andy asked, visibly pleased that she would have considered such measures. *"How do you know that?"*

"When we saw her—as we were leaving—last falling leaves time. She told us to make you wait for her," Badger admitted, looking up at him with a smirk on his face. White Quill, too, wore a sheepish grin. *"We had a plan!"*

"What plan? Tell me!" Andy beamed with anticipation.

"I guess we can tell you now. During the Sun dance! That is why we had to be there. He"—Badger said, nodding at White Quill—*"was going to hide her someplace...He was going to have his mother tell the husband that she saw her ride out alone. His mother was*

going to be concerned, saying that she saw two young men of another tribe—Káínaa!"—he said with some contempt in his voice— *"She was going to say they followed after her. White Quill would then lead the searchers away—to look for her. But she would not be anywhere—we would not find her…Her husband would not suspect you, because we would all be right there with him—looking for her! We would all take part in the search. We would pretend to be upset and look all over for her."* Badger's wide grin showed how pleased he was with their plan, and he looked for his friend's response.

"It would have worked!" White Quill asserted. *"We would have made it work!"*

"So, you want us to be husband and wife?" Andy asked, more focussed on Pretty Bird than whether their plan might have succeeded.

"Yes!" Badger admitted, nodding his head. *"We both do! But you will not be able to be a boy and behave foolishly anymore. You will have to be responsible—like a man—and look after your wife. You will not be able to do things as we do any longer!"*

"I can!" Andy protested indignantly. *"I want to keep doing those things—like we do! I do not want to be like those older ones! I do not want it to be any different—I want to keep doing what we do! But we can—we do not have to strut around bragging to everyone—about what a great warrior you are and how many horses you have captured! I do not want to be like those who do that—like his father,"* he said, nodding in White Quill's direction. *"The old dog! I am sorry, friend,"* he interrupted himself, looking at the younger Indian.

"You are kind to call him an old dog!" White Quill responded. *"He is a…what? Uh,* a bugger!*"*

"No…a shit!" Badger added, pleased with himself for remembering something Andy had taught them.

Andy just smiled at them, continuing, *"Or like your friend, Elk Back Side, or whatever he is called. I do not want to have to be always proving myself, like Sits in the Middle and his friends—trying* to make a name for themselves. Do you know how they were always trying to show everyone how brave they are?"

"I told you! They are dogs!" White Quill reminded them.

"Hear me!" Badger interrupted. "My mother told me, just before we left, that my father did not like going to war. He never liked it! He would rather have stayed home with her, with us. He was always worried that he would not come home to us. She thinks that I have more courage than him—because I have said I will not go to war!"

"Yes! That is what I mean!" Andy exclaimed. "Your people are strange that way! They have enough land and enough buffalo to live at peace and not bother anyone. But they are always going out to make war—looking for trouble. I do not understand that! The women do not want it! If your father had not gone to war, he would still be alive. You would still have a father! And my brother! He would still be alive! We would be with my father...but for your friends going out to make war—to get honour for themselves! It is not good!"

Badger did not disagree. "I am fortunate to be a good hunter! If it were not for that, I would be a real nothing one. Someone who cannot brag about something—hunting or warring—or capturing horses—is a real nothing one!"

"What about me, then?" the younger one interjected again. "At least you can hunt! What can I do?"

"Listen to what you are saying!" Andy scoffed. "Everyone likes you! Anyway, you can hunt—as well as anyone! What about those three deer? One, two, three!"

But Badger would not be interrupted. "Do you remember how difficult it was for me to return to my people? Do you remember when I made my talk to the old ones? And many our age would have nothing to do with me—with us—because of what I said?"

"Yes, I know," Andy replied, recalling how many of Badger's peers had avoided them after that.

"How then"—Badger continued making his point— "do we not

be nothing ones, if we do not go to war and capture horses? How will we get rich? If—"

"*What do you mean rich?*" Andy interrupted, "*We are rich! Look at all we have! We have all the food we want! We have horses! We have a lodge! We have everything we need! Life is good for us!*" he asserted, amazed that the others did not see it.

"*Careful! You are starting to sound like one of us!*" Badger chided him. "*But no!*" he continued. "*That is not rich! Rich is having many horses...a big lodge...and many wives. And being respected!*"

"*But I do not want many wives,*" Andy continued to disagree with his friend. "*I only want one! And you know who that is!*"

"*That is what we mean,*" White Quill spoke up. "*You are respected and important if you own many horses...and a big lodge, and many wives—like he said! A man who has only one wife will wear her out. If he is good a hunter—like our friend—he needs many wives...to tan all the hides and look after all the meat!*"

"*But why do you need so much?*" Andy continued to protest. "*You can just go out and kill a buffalo, and you have all you need!*"

"*Do you not remember how hungry we were when Cold Maker was angry with us—when the buffalo calves were black?*" Badger reminded him. "*Do you remember what we ate? Nothing!*"

"*Some people ate their dogs!*" White Quill pointed out.

"*Anyway!*" Andy pressed his point. "*Maybe we should just make our camp in one place and not move around.*"

"*What do you do when the buffalo move away?*" White Quill, this time, challenged him. "*Look at your napikawan friends!*"

"*Friends?*" Andy retorted sarcastically.

"*Look at those dog faces,*" the younger one began again, laughing.

"Buggers!" Badger interjected.

"*They need us to bring meat to them because they cannot move about and follow the buffalo,*" the younger one finished saying.

Andy pondered that thought for a moment. "*All the more reason for us to stay together then. Just us—we will live together! We will all* share—like we do. We just need to find wives for you!"

"I agree with that!" Badger piped up. "With big breasts! What does he call them?" he asked White Quill. "Tits! Big tits!" he exclaimed, groping an imaginary pair with his hands. "When can we start?"

"Just as soon as I find mine!" Andy replied enthusiastically. "And we will all live together!"

"I hope I can do as well in finding a wife! Do you have any more sisters?" Badger asked White Quill enviously, getting up and making for the horses.

They took a couple of breaks, sometime in the middle of the night, resting only a short time at their horses' feet. At first light, they were riding hard. In the afternoon, they came to *Napi-tahta,* farther out onto the prairie from where they had camped along its banks previously. Pausing at the edge of the coulee, overlooking the slow-moving river, White Quill had to think for a moment and decide which way to go before heading upstream. It was early evening when they spotted three lodges in the valley below them.

Andy hardly heard his friends' banter as they made their descent into the valley. His heart threatening to jump out of his chest, he was filled with anxiety. What if she was different from what he remembered? What would he say to her? Would she still feel the same way about him as she had the year before? What if her husband's brother wanted to take her as his wife? It was apparently his right to do so. He was uneasy and filled with doubt as they neared the camp.

Someone in the camp had already perceived their approach, and a handful of men gathered to watch them, while the women and children disappeared. But the watchers must have recognized them as *Piikáni* because the women and children soon reappeared and watched with interest the trio's approach.

White Quill kicked his horse ahead of the others and was already speaking to the men when his companions arrived.

Turning at once to Andy, he grinned and said, *"This is it! She is in the lodge of my uncle, over there,"* pointing with his lips toward one of the lodges. *"This is my uncle,"* he announced, indicating a middle-aged man standing among the others. *"He is called Painted Wing. Uncle,"*—he addressed the man— *"this is my brother. We say he is Sun Shines on Him."*

"We can see why you call him that," the man responded quietly, looking the white boy over. *"We have heard much about this fellow!"* Stepping up to Andy, he extended his hand warmly. *"Welcome!"*

"It is good," Andy replied, gripping the man's hand.

"And, this is my friend, Miisinsski," White Quill introduced Badger, who also was greeted heartily by the man.

"Come! These boys will look after your horses," the man said, beckoning three youngsters who had been scrutinizing Andy's appearance with curiosity. They all stared with wide-eyed wonder as he dropped to the ground and held out his rein to them. Two of them shrank back, but the smallest stepped up boldly, and examining every inch of the strange-looking newcomer's body with inquisitive, black eyes, he took the rein from him. As he did, Andy squatted down, eye-to-eye with the little fellow and reached out his hand to him. Grinning happily, the lad checked over his shoulder to see that his friends were observing his bravery.

"Oki! Tsa niitapi," Andy said to the brave one, reckoning him to be no more than five or six. The boy seemed startled to hear him speak and smiled bashfully, backing toward his friends, holding dutifully onto the rein. He wore a proud grin on his face as he turned away and joined his friends with the horses.

All were smiling at the little boy's behaviour when Painted Wing invited his visitors to his lodge. A scorching day, the sides of the abode had been hitched up on the poles to allow a breeze through. Once everyone was seated, a pipe was lit and passed around. There was no talk during the passing of the pipe, but when that was finished, the boys were asked about their journey and who they had seen at the Sun dance. Andy's gunshot wound was still very red and visible, and Badger gave a lengthy and detailed description of the event. Surprised to hear that there had been no reprisal, the men were astonished by White Quill's assertion that his friend's medicine did not permit him to seek vengeance. They were even more astonished when he suggested that Andy would, some time, be pleased to tell them of this medicine. Painted Wing cautioned that it was not right to speak of one's medicine openly, as it might thereby lose its power. *"No, it is not like that,"* White Quill assured them confidently.

Painted Wing turned to his nephew and changed the subject. *"My son,"* he began, *"I am afraid I have some bad news for you—about your father."* White Quill looked impassively at his uncle. *"I think he has left...He has not been back, but we hear he is among the Stoneys—he has a wife there—I am sorry!"*

"This is no surprise to me," the young man responded frostily. *"He is a dog!"*

"Ke-yah!" Painted Wing seemed to agree with him. *"I have never liked the way he treated my sister! However—it is now up to me to look after Pretty Bird—and I guess you should have a say as well."* It was the first time since they had arrived that Andy had heard Pretty Bird's name.

There was a prolonged period of silence during which the nervous white boy fidgeted, unsure what was going to happen next. Finally, Painted Wing broke his own silence. Addressing Andy, he said, *"And, I suppose you are here, hoping to take Pretty Bird as your wife,"* he said, looking sternly at the white boy.

"I am," Andy replied nervously, taken off guard by the directness of his question.

"Do you understand that she has already been the wife of another man...and that she now carries his child?" When he heard those words, Andy's heart sank; he was uncertain what the man was getting at. Was he saying that her deceased husband's brother

would be taking Pretty Bird as his wife, which he knew to be the custom?

Not sure what to say, Andy responded, *"Pretty Bird was given by her father to that fellow. She did not want to go with him. I have heard he is dead. Is that not so?"*

"Yes," the man replied, admiring the boy's own directness. *"You have heard correctly. But she now carries his child."*

Still, Andy did not understand his point. *"I have heard that,"* he replied.

"Will you still have her as your wife...even though she has been with another man?"

"I—" Andy started to answer.

"And carries his child?"

"I will!" he answered emphatically.

"Such a woman does not command a very high price! The other gave her father many horses for her," said Painted Wing, pausing to see what his reaction might be.

"I do not know what you mean," the young suitor responded, not totally familiar with the marriage customs and blinded by the dread of being so close to Pretty Bird and losing her.

"Did you bring something—that her mother may have something for the loss of her daughter?" the man asked.

Andy thought for a moment before replying. *"I did not think—"*

Before he could finish getting the words out of his mouth, Badger interrupted. *"He has horses! Good horses!"*

Surprised, Andy looked at him, not sure what to say. He knew that sometimes a young man had to pay compensation for a wife, but his friends had made it sound like he would not likely have to do such a thing. *"I have, uh, horses—three horses,"* he responded, not knowing how something like this was supposed to proceed. *"And I have a lodge. I mean—"* Turning to Badger, to whom the little lodge had also been given, he asked, *"Do I have a lodge?"*

Badger nodded emphatically. *"I have my own lodge,"* the suitor turned and told the man, his confidence returning slowly.

"That is not very much!" Painted Wing chided, melting what little confidence Andy had just gained. *"The other one gave her father much more than that!"*

"Well, that is all I have," the rattled boy said forlornly, unable to hold the man's gaze.

"No! He has more than that!" White Quill piped up. *"My friend and I have horses. He can have those! Uh, there are three, so that is six!"*

"Her brother! White Quill, you are a good young man!" Looking toward the other men, the uncle reminded them, *"This young fellow was just a boy when he saved the life of his best friend. He killed two of the Crow...They were about to slay his friend...he then took part in a raid upon the Liars! He will be a fine warrior! His medicine is strong, this young man! And, he has not yet sought his vision!"* Turning back to his nephew, he asked him, *"Do you want this fellow to take your sister as his wife?"*

"Yes, I do!" the boy responded enthusiastically.

Painted Wing glanced at each of the Indian boys, before studying their pale friend. Andy felt sweat begin to form on his forehead and the back of his neck. He stared at the ground.

"My heart feels warm toward this young man," the man announced finally. *"We will sweat...and perhaps we shall know what the answer will be."* And, calling to the woman who had been busily working around the lodge, he ordered, *"Make ready for us to sweat!"* She acknowledged him only by turning for the door to begin his bidding. Turning to White Quill, he queried, *"Does he know what to do?"* His nephew assured him that he did. *"Help him prepare himself then and bring him to me by the river."* And with that, the meeting was finished.

Seeing his confusion, Andy's friends explained what was happening. Painted Wing would stand in the place of the girl's father and would consider Andy's offer of horses as compensation for taking her away from her mother. The invitation to sweat with the man looked promising, they assured him. At least the answer had not been no.

Excited by what they had to say, Andy was nonetheless beset with doubt. He was just 16. He had heard of boys back at the settlement who had married that young, and a few Indian boys seemed to marry that young too, but it did not seem common in either culture. Most of the *Piikáni* were in their twenties before taking a wife. But his friends assured him that they knew of lots of others who married at his age, or even younger.

Wondering what his father might think, Andy's heart still tugged him toward Pretty Bird. Ever since hearing of her husband's death, he had prayed and prayed to his god to know if it was right for him to take her as his wife. He had been begging for some kind of a sign, that he might know for sure, but he had not recognized any. Finally, in a last-ditch bargain with his god, Andy agreed to abide by the uncle's decision as if it were the answer to his prayer. If the uncle said no, Andy would consider it his answer from his god. If the uncle said yes, he would know that it was the will of his god. "Well, I guess I'm gonna find out," he sighed to himself, wishing for something more direct.

When White Quill and Badger brought their friend to the sweat lodge, they found Painted Wing in the company of another man. As soon as Andy arrived, he followed them in stripping and walking in silence toward the river to bathe. The women had just finished putting hot rocks inside the structure.

Andy found the heat in the dark place next to unbearable, his breathing seemed to do nothing, and he longed for a gasp of cold, fresh air from outside. The other man, who Painted Wing had introduced as a holy man, had begun murmuring prayers immediately and placing bits of sweetgrass upon the hot rocks. Its sweet smoke filled the small shelter.

Pleased to be able to demonstrate his knowledge of the ritual, Andy was quick to draw the smoke over his body, demonstrating his competence at it. Closing his eyes, he prayed softly to his god. "God, I don't know if this is the right thing for me to be doing. I wish I knew—I wish my father was here to help me. But I come to thee, as my father in heaven, to give me guidance. I love her so much! Please make it right, dear Lord. Please close the door if it is not thy will...but please make it thy will.

"I love thee, Lord, and want to do the right thing. Do not allow me to stray from thy will, thy good and pleasing and perfect will. O, Jesus, Jesus! Thou hast helped me in the past. Thou hast spared my life. Guide my steps aright. In thy holy and blessed name, I pray to thee. I love her! O Lord, please let me be with her! I love her so much!" Hearing that the two men were whispering their own prayers, he continued to murmur the name of Jesus.

A quiet peace came over Andy as he sat sweating into the darkness. He had noticed that the words he spoke in prayer were different than his everyday conversation—similar to how his father had prayed—and made him feel nearer to his god.

He was interrupted from his meditation when one of the men splashed more water on the hot rocks. The steam was oppressive, and the sweat poured from his body. He could feel that the men were cupping smoke in their hands and passing it over their bodies. "Jesus, may this be a sweet incense unto thee," he prayed, doing the same. "I know thou hearest my voice, truly one calling from the wilderness—really, the wilderness. Cleanse me, thy servant." Andy began to find himself able to focus his thoughts and his mind. "Jesus, Jesus," he murmured. Deep in his meditations, he felt a little light-headed, and his head seemed to be spinning.

Abandoning himself to whatever was happening to him in the steam and the darkness, he completely lost track of time, finally at peace, feeling near to his father and near to God. He sat there, sometimes praying, sometimes thinking, and sometimes listening to the others, when suddenly the covering was thrown back, and the other man grunted that they should step outside. The sweat was over.

The warm evening air now felt cool against Andy's skin. He was feeling exhilarated as they made their way solemnly toward the river. Slowly wading out into the refreshing water, he wanted to shriek for joy, but he made himself conform to the men's solemnity. Reaching the deeper water, he wished he could dive and frolic with his friends, as they were in the habit of doing. Instead, following the others' lead, he quietly slipped his head under the water, drifting with the current and running his hands across his skin and through his hair.

All too soon, the men headed for shore and Andy trudged along with them, disappointed to leave the water he loved, but anxious to know the outcome of the sweat. Stopping only to pick up their garments, they made their way to Painted Wing's lodge before dressing. As they dressed, others began to file in.

Not wishing to be presumptuous, Andy at first sat down at the edge of the proceeding, beside Badger and White Quill. But Painted Wing asked him to come and sit beside him. Once all were seated, the men in the lodge began recounting their war honours, speaking slowly and without interruption. After the retelling of the fortunes of the tribe and stories of daring and bravery, all eyes came to rest on the white boy. Knowing it was his turn to share his story and convince them that he was honourable enough to take one of their own, Andy thought for a moment before he spoke, choosing his words carefully. *"I like to take care of the old people"*— he began— *"and the ones who cannot get food. I can hunt and bring them food. I love Pretty Bird and will look after her well. But—"* Afraid that what he had to say might end his chances, he paused. Finally, uncomfortable with the silence, he took a deep breath and sighed, *"I do not like killing and war. I will not kill someone!"* With that, he looked at the ground in front of him. Nobody spoke.

Andy's heart sank further and further with each passing moment, fearing that he had thrown away his chance to be with

Pretty Bird. It was awkward! Cruel, even, he thought. Then, Painted Wing broke the silence.

"*My son, you speak with few words! I admire that!*" Andy turned and looked the man in the eye. "*You have shown yourself a good young man of courage. War has robbed us of many of our young men. It leaves us with too many widows...I have lost a son, myself. When we get older, we see the wisdom of making peace with our neighbours. Yet you—little more than a boy—possess such wisdom already! Your words are good! We see that your medicine is strong because your heart is strong! My heart feels warm toward you.*

"*I may lose my other sons in war. Even now, as they visit their friends at the great Sun dance, they make plans to go, after...to make war upon our enemies, and capture their horses—so they can claim honour. Their mother never knows if they will return! Will she be happy if they die bravely? Would she not be happier if they lived to give her grandchildren? Yes! Do you think she likes them going to war? No!*

"*You, my son, follow your own trail...one that is strange to us. We do not know it.*

"*I have heard many things spoken about you! I know that you will be welcome in any of our camps. Many of our people hold you in great wonder. I myself, wonder about your medicine, and what takes you along that trail of yours! It is not wrong!*" For a long time, he looked at the hopeful boy beside him. Finally, he concluded, saying, "*It is my hope that you will remain with my people...You and your wife.*" Despite the solemnity with which the message had been delivered, Andy could not keep the grin from his face.

21

Andy left Painted Wing's lodge feeling as if he was walking among the clouds. His steps were light, and his heart was bursting with anticipation until White Quill informed him that he had visited Pretty Bird during the sweat. *"Is she—does she—is she all right?"* he asked, trying to read the look of concern in his friend's eyes.

"My mother is with her; I do not know. Girls have babies all the time, but she looks—she doesn't look very well!" He was very evidently worried about her.

"Is she going to be all right?" Andy responded nervously, his excitement from the day's events evaporating in the night air. *"Did she say anything? Did she say anything about me?"*

Her brother hesitated before responding, *"She is weak. All the time—as they travelled to the Sun dance—she became weaker, and finally, my mother insisted that they must stay here...until her time comes."* White Quill paused, *"She is afraid! She wants to be your wife, but she is afraid you will not want her,"* White Quill told him guardedly. *"She is most of all afraid that you will not want her since she will have a little one."*

"That does not matter!" Andy exclaimed earnestly.

"I know why she is afraid!" Badger interjected, *"Sometimes a woman whose husband dies, if she has children she is not taken as a sits beside me wife. She is taken as a helper wife...and she and her children are always poor. She is afraid that will happen to her if you do not want her!"*

"That will not happen!" the white boy responded indignantly. *"I want her as my wife—my sits beside me wife! My only wife! Do you think I can see her?"* he asked the girl's brother. *"I do not care if she has a baby!"*

"She wishes to see you!" White Quill assured him, heartened by his friend's certainty. *"But she is afraid that if you see her, you will not want her."*

"What do you mean? Can I see her?" he wondered.

White Quill thought for a moment. *"I will see—come!"* he replied, heading for one of the lodges. At the door, he told Andy to wait and ducked inside. They could hear muffled voices, and then White Quill popped his head out. *"Come!"*

Inside, Pretty Bird's mother and two other women were just getting to their feet. As soon as she saw Andy, Pretty Bird struggled to get up. *"No! Do not get up!"* her mother ordered firmly.

Ignoring her, the girl winced and said to her brother, *"Help me!"* holding out her hand to him. Both White Quill and Andy hurried to help her, but the women intercepted them and helped her up, seeing she was determined. Andy was alarmed when he saw the size of her belly. He had seen pregnant women before, but Pretty Bird's belly seemed to protrude far more than any he had ever seen. Her face glistened; her sharp, pleasant features were swollen and obscured, but her beautiful eyes were as he had remembered. Nobody said anything, and the girl looked at the ground while her mother steadied her.

Reaching for the hand of the one he thought he loved, Andy brought it to his lips and kissed it gently, in the manner he had seen his father do with his mother. She looked up at him and started to say something, but her words died in her throat as her face became taut with excruciating pain. With a sharp cry, she grimaced and doubled over, awkwardly off-balance. *"What?"* Andy blurted with alarm, as the women helped her to the ground. *"What is wrong?"* he asked anxiously. Pretty Bird seemed not to hear and clutched her abdomen, rolling desperately onto her side with the women doing their best to comfort her. *"What do I do?"* he pleaded helplessly.

"Take him away!" Pretty Bird's mother told her son sharply.

"Come!" White Quill urged his friend, taking him by the arm. He, too, was alarmed by his sister's sudden condition. *"We must leave!"*

"No! What is wrong?" Andy protested with a whisper.

"You must leave!" said one of the other women, more gently. *"We are taking care of her!"*

Reluctantly following White Quill outside, Andy's heart was pounding. "O, Jesus, help her!" he wept. "Jesus! Help her!" Suddenly the air was cut by a primal scream from inside the tent—it was like no sound any of the three boys had heard before. Looking back anxiously, Andy cried desperately, *"What should I do? Something is wrong!"*

Before he could say anymore, White Quill grabbed him forcefully by the arm and pulled him away. With near terror on his face, he ordered Badger to accompany them, dragging Andy in the direction of the river.

"No! I do not want to leave her!" Andy protested anxiously and tried to pull away. His friends forced him along.

"We should leave!" Badger assured them, also alarmed. *"It is probably her time! She is having her baby! It is nothing! They do it all the time! Come!"* Badger hoped his confident assertion would

comfort his friends, but inside felt no confidence she would be all right.

Taking over the lead from White Quill, Badger led his friends to a spot near the river, where they had spread their robes and planned to spend the night. Andy could not sit down and paced fretfully. White Quill, unable to forget the scream they had heard, cast about for some way to distract himself and his friend.

"Come!" he said, whipping off his breechclout and moccasins. *"Let us swim!"*

"Yes! Good idea!" Badger agreed, beginning to shed his garment. Seeing that Andy was not inclined to join them, he hollered to White Quill. Grabbing the front flap of Andy's breechclout, he shrieked, *"Grab him!"* Seeing what he intended, White Quill grabbed the back flap, and they both tugged, bouncing him on the taut leather.

"No! Stop! Let go! You dogs! Let go!" Andy protested angrily, swinging at them while they jostled him.

"You have to come!" White Quill insisted, finding it difficult to be his jovial and light-hearted self. Letting up, he started pulling at the knot in Andy's belt.

"I will do it! Let me go!" Andy snapped and swatted at him, in no mood for their fun. They relented and waited for him to untie his belt. Grudgingly flinging his garment onto their robes, he accompanied his friends to the water.

He was much too distracted to enter into their well-intentioned fun. Badger recognized it and made a suggestion. *"Come!"* he urged. *"We will just float down the river—like we do. Come!"* he repeated, lying back in the water and letting the current carry him.

"Yes! Good idea! Let us float!" White Quill agreed, joining him. It was something he knew Andy enjoyed. With reluctance, the white boy followed.

He would have enjoyed it more under any other circumstance. Once, under a full moon, they had drifted for what seemed half the night. Now, laying his head back in the water and looking up at the dark sky, he tried not to let worry overtake him while his friends did their best to distract him.

Talking as they gently floated downriver, Andy's friends heard him speak of his wonder at the notion of becoming a husband—and his fear. *"I have been thinking about what you said,"* he said to Badger. *"I do not want to lose your friendship—neither of you!"*

This time, Badger was more encouraging. *"It is too late now—you are going to do it!"* he responded.

"I don't know," Andy sighed to himself. Inside, he feared for Pretty Bird's life. He had never seen anyone in her condition, but he tried to be brave.

It was the middle of the night when they returned to the quiet camp. After a short and fitful sleep, Andy was up at first light, prowling around Pretty Bird's lodge when he spied her mother step outside. She looked haggard, and her face was drawn; her eyes looked sad. Hurrying over to her, he asked, *"How is she?"*

The woman would not look at him, heartbreak crackled in her voice as she answered him softly. *"It was twins—a boy and a girl. The little boy had no life in him...and I am afraid the little girl will soon follow him."*

"O, God!" Andy started, tears suddenly welling up in his eyes. "What...*Can I see her?"* he asked.

"No!" the woman rasped. *"You must not see her! You should ride away and let her mourn! That would be better!"* The woman's words cut like a knife. Andy could not understand why she was suddenly so short with him. Stunned by her unexpected rejection, and not knowing what else to do, he turned away and fought back tears until he could not hold them any longer. As they spilled down his cheeks, he ran, bewildered and distraught, chased by an intense sense of rejection.

It was later in the morning that his sleepy companions discovered him missing. Upon learning what had happened with Pretty

Bird, they hurried to their horses and set out in search of Andy, picking up his track where he had left the camp.

Andy's anguish had driven him out onto the prairie. Climbing out of the coulees along the river, he had run. Until at last, he collapsed among some wolf willows, growing on the lee side of a hillock. There, he sat despondently, finally sobbing himself into a half-sleep.

His friends found him staring forlornly into the dirt. Seeing that he had been crying, they stood over him, waiting for him to speak. *"Is she all right?"* he finally whispered, looking up at them with his lower lip trembling. When White Quill assured him that she was, fresh tears flooded his face, and he buried his face in his hands. His mind had spun out of control through the night, shaping more and more painful ways Pretty Bird might be ripped from him again.

When the sobbing subsided, Badger softly recounted what Pretty Bird's mother had already said, *"She had two babies. One was dead."*

"I know," Andy grunted, looking down and wiping his eyes and nose.

"It was a little boy that died," White Quill added sadly. *"The other is a little girl—she is probably going to die,"* he said with apparent resignation.

"How is Pretty Bird? Did you see her?" Andy asked, without looking up.

"She was asleep when we left," her brother told him.

"Why did she tell me to leave—your mother—why did she say that? Why could I not see her?" Andy blurted, his voice thick with emotion, looking up at White Quill.

"I do not know," his friend whispered.

"Why can I not be there? She needs me!" the sorrowful one complained, his eyes rimmed with tears. *"I need her! Did you speak to her?"*

"*No. She was resting. She is very weak...Apparently, she had a lot of blood!*"

"*I wish we had never come here!*" Andy murmured bitterly. "*It was a bad idea!*" He wrapped his arms around his knees and pulled them up in front of him. Placing his chin on them, he was silent for a while. Finally, he looked up and growled at the others, "*Why are you here? Are you supposed to keep me from seeing her?*" His friends did not respond. Badger gave the younger one a nod, and they moved away a short distance and sat down together.

Feeling bad for taking his frustration out on his two closest friends, after a few minutes, Andy got to his feet and stepped over to where they had begun to play a hand game. "*I am sorry! I am worried about her! Do you think I would be able to see her? Can we go back and ask if I can see her?*"

The Indian boys looked at each other, and White Quill responded, "*I do not know! Nobody said anything about that—we just came to find you. I could go and see—but I think you should wait here,*" he cautioned.

"*Tell her that I want to see her!*" Andy urged as his friend made for his horse. "*Please hurry!*"

"*We might be over at the river when you come back!*" Badger hollered after White Quill. Turning to Andy, he urged him, "*Come! Let us go to the river.*"

Lacking the will to object, the white boy followed him. Leading Badger's horse, they walked to the edge of the coulee and made their way down to the river's edge. There, they horsed around, wrestling in the water, doing the things they had become so accustomed to doing during their days of idleness. But Andy's heart was not in it. Done with play, he became pensive and sat on a rock, keeping watch for White Quill's return. Turning to his friend, he said, "*Míísinsski, I love you! You are my family now. You and White Quill are all I have. If Pretty Bird and I get together, I want you to be part of our family. Will you come and live with us?*"

Badger's response was immediate. *"My heart feels the same way toward you! I was hoping that you really meant it when you said that before, because I am—I mean, we are going to live with you...whether you want us to or not—White Quill and me. We have already decided that!"*

"Really? Have you talked about it?"

"Yes," Badger grinned playfully. *"We are too used to living all together."*

"Do you think that I am too young?" Andy asked him directly, his eyes seeking an honest answer.

"No! Sometimes people become husband and wife very young. Usually, it is the girl who is younger than the boy, but it happens."

"Will we get into trouble? Will people—?"

"No!" Badger cut him off, anticipating his question. *"Everybody likes you! And Painted Wing likes you."*

"How do you know that?"

"He sent us to make sure that you do not leave. Our friend will go to him and ask if you can see her. —You will! He will let you!"

"I hope so. I sure hope so!" Andy sighed, just as Badger gave him the shoulder and nearly knocked him into the water before leaping on top of him.

They were still wrestling on the muddy bank when they heard White Quill holler. Badger had managed to get on top of Andy and was pinning his arms to the mud above his head. As he turned to look, his opponent gave a great heave, and they were back to wrestling. Struggling and giggling, they squirmed around in the mud, until White Quill's horse stood over them.

"So, you prefer Badger to my sister?" the young Indian teased wryly, seeing that Andy was lying atop Badger, holding him spread-eagled.

"Yes!" Badger responded, puffing, *"I am the girl this time. Last time, he was the girl!"*

"Get him!" Andy whispered in his friend's ear. *"Now!"* he blurted, and the two of them scrambled to their feet. They grabbed White Quill by the leg as his horse lurched away, startled by the sudden movement. Taking their friend by surprise, they hauled him to the mud, where they both sat on him.

"Fill his breechclout with mud!" Andy shouted gleefully, momentarily distracted from his gloom. White Quill struggled to get away, uttering threats while Badger sat on him, trying to stuff his garment full of mud. Andy was plastering him everywhere else, but their young friend fought back hard, grabbing handfuls of sticky mud, slopping it on his attackers.

"Hai! Look!" Andy exclaimed after they had finally relented and got to their feet. *"We are all the same colour!"*

There was a muddy plume in the river, where they went to wash off, and Andy maintained a better disposition as they headed for the camp.

When they reached Painted Wing's lodge, he greeted Andy gruffly, *"So, you decided to return!"*

"Yes, I have come to see Pretty Bird!" Andy replied, trying to sound confident. *"We are going to be husband and wife!"* he said, getting right to the point.

"You are a determined young man!" Painted Wing observed, eyeing the boy carefully. *"I was waiting to see how you would respond, and it is a good thing that you returned—the girl has a child that needs a father. Have they told you? She will need a husband to care for them!"*

"Yes, a little girl. I wish to take them both. I will be her father! You may have everything I own!" Andy informed him, anxious to give a good impression.

The man looked at him for a moment longer before saying, *"You can keep everything you own! You will need it, so you can provide for your family."*

Until that moment, Andy had been uncertain as to what might happen in that regard. At last, flooded with relief, he broke into a grin and extended his hand to the man. *"Thank you! I will take good care of them!"*

"I believe you will," the man replied, taking his hand, returning the smile. *"You should go and see her!"* he said, thrusting his jaw in the direction of her lodge.

Taking a few steps in that direction, Andy stopped suddenly. Turning to Painted Wing, he asked, *"Do you know why her mother told me to leave?"*

"Maybe she just wanted to see if you would!"

Relieved, and feeling good about himself, Andy trotted to the lodge where he found Pretty Bird reclining against a backrest, cradling a tiny bundle. Her mother and a friend stepped away, and Andy hurried to the girl's side and knelt before her. She glanced at him briefly before returning her gaze to her infant. Shuffling closer to sit beside her, he snuggled her and leaned over to get a better look at the baby girl.

She was tiny—too tiny. Alarmed, but trying not to show it, Andy whispered, *"She is pretty,"* and rubbed the tiny, blotchy cheek with his fingertip. *"Like her mother,"* he breathed, looking into Pretty Bird's eyes. She tipped her chin upward and met his gaze. Her face was still puffy, and the playful sparkle was absent from her eyes as she smiled at him sadly. *"What are you going to call her?"* Andy asked.

"It has not been decided," the girl replied, returning her gaze to her child. *"My brother has something to call her,"* she volunteered quietly. Looking around, Andy noticed that his friends had not followed him inside.

"White Quill?" he asked, still looking at the tiny infant. She had a shock of black hair. *"What is it?"* he asked her when she did not respond.

The girl did not answer for a long moment. He glanced up at her face, and she spoke at last. *"He should tell you. Do you like her?"* she asked timidly. Her voice was weak, and she was very subdued.

Andy thought for a moment before answering. *"Yes...I love her!"* he whispered. *"I love her, and I love you! I love you both!"* he said quietly, fully aware that the women were straining to hear his every word. A glimmer of joy crossed the young girl's face but was quickly overcome by a dark shadow of concern as she continued to gaze lovingly at her baby. Perplexed, Andy repeated himself, *"I love you."* He gave the girl a long time to respond, but she showed no emotion. The same feelings of rejection he had felt that morning were beginning to mount within him, until finally, she spoke, her voice very soft.

"How can you love me? I have been with another man. Mine is the child of another!" She did not look up at him but gazed at her daughter, tears trickling down her cheeks.

There was no hesitation in Andy's response. *"That does not matter!"* he responded, *"I love you! And he took you...you did not take him!"* Seeing no reaction, he added, *"Did you?"* He thought the women must be able to hear his heart pounding.

"No! I never wanted him! I always wanted you!" she responded, her voice a little stronger as she turned and looked him fully in the face. *"I never stopped wanting you! I longed to be with you, not him."* The tears were now streaming down her face as she poured out her heart to him. *"I prayed to Sun that you would return for me. I tried to remember about your medicine...so I could pray to it, too...But I had given up hope...And then, when I became pregnant, I believed there was no hope.*

"When he died, I wanted to die also. I did not want to be a widow! A widow with a child can only become a slave...to the wife of some man who does not love her! I thought to—I thought to throw my life away—"

"*No!*" Andy interjected. "*Do not speak like that! I am here! I have never stopped loving you! We are young, but I want to be your husband! I can look after you!*" he said. "*I want you to be my wife!*" He heard the women stir, but he did not bother to look at them.

"*Are you sure that is what you want? I have been with another man,*" Pretty Bird whispered weakly, sadness and fear weighing her down.

"*I know! That does not matter! I want you to be my wife! I want us to be together—always,*" Andy affirmed, looking up to see her mother's stone face. Intimidated by her expressionless stare, he looked back at Pretty Bird and took her awkwardly in his arms, trying not to disturb the infant. He was comforted when she placed her hand on the back of his head and pulled him to her. Pulling away, just enough to be able to do so, he kissed her. "*Will you be my wife?*" he whispered softly. He knew from her smile what her answer would be, and as soon as she assented, her mother and the other women were upon them, showering them with their approval. Pretty Bird's mother tugged him to his feet and embraced him enthusiastically.

Andy did not understand what she meant when she whispered, "*I will not be able to do this again. You are a good son! You will take good care of my daughter!*" With that, she gathered her things and left the lodge, giving orders to the others.

Puzzled by her behaviour, Andy looked at the others for meaning. "*If you are to take her daughter as your wife*"—one of the other women answered, seeing his bewilderment— "*she must not speak to you. She must not even let you see her!*"

"*What?*" Andy asked, incredulous, never having realized this was their custom.

"*When a woman takes a husband, her mother is not allowed to speak to him, and she must avoid meeting him,*" the woman informed him.

"Why is that? Is that true?" Andy looked at Pretty Bird, who nodded. *"Who will look after you with the baby?"* he asked.

"His family, or her sisters, if she had any, would help her—but we will help her," the woman explained.

"We will take care of her," the other woman agreed. Andy had not noticed her before. She had apparently been resting on the other side of the lodge when he entered. *"And now, you should let her rest,"* the woman urged him.

Andy frowned. *"I just got here!"*

"She is tired," the woman reminded him.

"When can I come back?"

"When Sun returns from his rest," the woman replied.

Andy had sat down as soon as the mother had left. Now he turned to Pretty Bird and gently leaned to kiss the baby; next, he leaned over and kissed its mother. *"I love you,"* he whispered. *"I do not want to go!"*

"I love you, too," the girl whispered, giving him a warm smile. *"I wish you would stay."*

"Can I?" Andy turned quickly to see what the women would say.

"Go! She will be stronger tomorrow," came the firm reply.

Andy looked into Pretty Bird's eyes. They were filled with emotion, and she wore a tired smile. *"Yes—I will be back tomorrow. I love you,"* he whispered and kissed her again.

"Please hurry," she replied softly. *"I love you!"* Andy climbed to his feet and had just turned away when he heard her say, *"Little Lark!"*

"What?" He turned toward her.

"Little Lark—that is what I want to call her," she repeated, her voice soft.

"Little Lark?" Andy repeated. *"You love larks!"* Andy's face lit up with excitement as the meaning became clear to him. *"I understand! I like it! I like it!"* he said, returning to kneel again at her side. *"How are you, Little Lark?"* he whispered, rubbing the tiny cheek

with his fingertip. *"It is perfect!"* he said proudly, giving Pretty Bird another kiss before standing up.

"I will miss you!" she said as he turned and stepped toward the door.

"I miss you already! Get better soon!" Andy replied, slipping out the door.

His comrades had a small fire going, over which they had *nitapi waksin* roasting. Looking at him expectantly, Badger asked, *"How did it go?"*

"I am not sure," he replied.

"Why? What happened?" White Quill wondered.

"I am not sure. I asked her if she would be my wife. I think she said she would, but I am not sure. Your mother hugged me and then left," Andy informed them. The Indian boys looked at each other and gave a whoop, slapping hands and congratulating each other. *"What?"* Andy asked, not understanding.

"You are husband and wife!" Badger exclaimed.

"It means that my mother has become your mother!" White Quill announced. *"And I am your brother!"* he shrieked, and both Indians pounced on their friend.

After that, the marriage seemed complete. Andy had never seen anything in a Blackfoot camp like the marriage ceremonies he had witnessed back at the settlement, where the whole community would come together in a church. Here, it seemed that the young couple simply took up residence together.

Such was the case when he returned to his wife the following morning. A bed had been prepared for him, right beside her, and one of the women informed him that it was for him. He should sleep beside her from now on, she told him. *"You must not do sex until she has healed,"* she told him, embarrassing him with her directness. *"She is very sore, and she still has blood,"* she continued. *"She will not be able to do sex until after the next moon. You leave her alone until then,"* she cautioned, sounding as if she was scolding him.

The women provided him with a willow backrest, and after saying they would come back periodically to check on Pretty Bird, they left.

Following an awkward silence, Pretty Bird spoke. *"She will not eat,"* she announced softly.

Andy gazed into his wife's eyes. Her face was not so puffy this morning, and her voice was stronger. *"What does she eat?"* Andy asked.

"Silly!" the girl rolled her eyes, teasing him. *"She drinks my milk."* But her face quickly darkened as she continued, *"or she is supposed to drink my milk."*

"Oh," Andy nodded his head, embarrassed about being so naive. Since living among the Blackfoot, he had seen women nursing their babies openly, something he had never witnessed at the settlement.

"Perhaps with you here, she will nurse," Pretty Bird wondered, pulling her dress down over her shoulder to expose her breast. Andy was wide-eyed while she lifted the tiny form to her nipple and rubbed it to the baby's lip. He watched carefully and saw the tiny baby wriggle her head and latch onto it. *"She has taken it!"* the young mother exclaimed in a whisper. *"She likes you!"* Andy leaned forward to get a closer look, but almost as soon as he did, the infant quit sucking and released the nipple. *"No!"* the mother whimpered. *"Here, baby, here you go,"* she whispered, trying to tempt the babe back to the nipple. Once again, the tiny lips took it and suckled weakly, but persistently. Andy looked into the girl's face and saw it glow with satisfaction and contentment. Returning his gaze to the suckling infant, he saw her let go. Its mother could not entice her to nurse again.

"Why do you not eat, my little one?" she whispered, glancing up at Andy. *"You must eat and grow strong."*

"Let me hold her!" the boy offered. Wishing to impress his new wife, he summoned his courage and squirmed to get into a position to take the child. Gingerly, he took the tiny life into his hands and held her close, cradling her awkwardly.

They took turns holding the baby, talking quietly until Pretty Bird was too exhausted to stay awake. Lying together, she placed the baby upon Andy's bare chest, covering her with a very soft, winter rabbit skin. With a deep sigh, the anxious mother leaned into her new husband's shoulder. He remained motionless, letting them both sleep upon him.

The quiet rest of the little family was interrupted by the baby's whimper. Pretty Bird awoke in an instant and tried to get the babe to nurse, saddened when she would not take her milk. *"If she does not eat,"*—she told Andy in dread— *"she will die."*

Lying close, they talked quietly. Andy learned how much Pretty Bird had missed him. She had wanted to leave her husband to try to find Andy, but she had abandoned the idea for fear that she would be pursued, and they might both be put to death if found together. Eventually, giving up any hope of ever seeing him again, she had resigned herself to her husband.

He had been kind to her, she told him. He had loved her deeply, and it had pained him that she was so distant. When she informed him that she was going to bear him a child, he had been over-joyed and proudly made the announcement to the whole camp. A brave warrior, he had been on raids against their enemies and was well on his way to becoming a leading man. And so, he had been among the first to rush out in defence of their camp, the night he was struck down.

Others, she told Andy, had mourned more than her. Her tears had come from facing the prospect of life as a widow with a child, not from losing her husband. Convinced that she would never see Andy again, and even if she did, that he would not want her in her circumstances, it was in despair that she had faced the birth.

When she had begun to feel so ill, she had prayed that Sun would let her and the baby die together. Then, when she became the reason that some had to stay behind and miss the Sun dance, her despair had grown into blackness. Until hearing of her brother's return, along with the boy with the shining hair. *"Do you really love me? Even with my baby?"* she asked Andy.

She hardly dared to believe he could be telling the truth when he answered gently, *"She is our baby!"* Pretty Bird responded with a kiss.

But later that day, while Sun stood over their camp on the river, Little Lark left them. Lying together, watching her shallow breaths grow weaker and weaker as she lay on Andy's bare chest, Pretty Bird finally whispered softly, *"She is gone."*

Even at her young age, Pretty Bird was no stranger to death and had known the end was near, never giving up the hope that each new breath brought—to the very last one. New life was never a certainty among her people. Her eyes closed with resignation, and a silent tear rolled onto Andy's chest, beside her daughter's still form. Andy clutched the lifeless baby girl to his chest and wept with his wife. More death.

Andy asked that they not place their infant child on a high branch—he had concerns about her being carried off by a predator. Instead, he wanted to bury her.

They went alone and buried their daughter at the foot of a sapling, just above the high-water mark along the river. He wrestled a slab of sandstone over the grave and scraped upon it the sign of a cross and other of his markings, promising his wife that she would be able to see her again when they would be joined in death. Afterwards, seeking their own solitude, he gathered their robes and hauled them through the trees, until he found a secluded spot. There, exhausted, Pretty Bird's sorrow took her into a deep sleep, in the solace of her new husband's arms.

When Andy awoke, Pretty Bird was looking up pensively at the sky through the trees. *"Have you ever noticed that the larks do not sing in the valley?"* she whispered. *"I miss them down here! They give me so much joy!"* The few clouds in the sky were being painted with the soft, pastel colours of the early morning sun, still beyond the horizon.

"How are you?" Andy whispered.

Tears rimmed Pretty Bird's her eyes. *"I do not want to leave them here!"*

Andy had not even thought about the other twin! *"What did they... Where did they?"*

Pretty Bird responded quietly, *"I do not know! I suppose...I do not know! I do not want to leave this place where they are!"* She began weeping softly.

"We do not need to leave right now. We can leave when we are ready," the young husband assured his new wife softly, pulling her closer.

"Last night, I heard an owl! It is not a good sign!" she murmured. Andy's heart sank, recalling what his friends had told him about the spirits of the dead haunting the living as owls.

"That was not them!" he told her gently. *"Their spirit has gone to be with, um, my medicine, who loves them...even more than you or I love them."*

"I do not know!" the girl sighed. *"I do not know your medicine. I want to believe what you say, but I am afraid."* With that, she sobbed fully, and the tears streamed down her face.

"Please trust me!" her husband pleaded. *"My medicine is strong! It is good!"* Pretty Bird's only response was to cling more tightly to him. They stayed that way until they began to hear activity in the camp.

Going to investigate, Andy found that the lodges were down, and everyone was getting ready to move. White Quill and Badger were helping Pretty Bird's mother pack her things, but as soon as she noticed Andy, she turned and walked in the opposite direction. Feeling disappointed by a custom he could not understand, he retreated so she could resume her duties. He admired her, wishing things did not have to be that way.

Badger came over when he saw the exchange, and awkwardly expressed his sadness at the baby's death. After staring silently at the ground for a moment, he moved on to inform Andy that the camp would be moving soon, headed to the Sun dance. He and White Quill had gathered all their things and were ready to go.

Andy's thoughts then turned back to his new bride, and he wondered aloud whether she would be able to travel. White Quill had joined them and, after expressing his sorrow over the death, assured him that his mother said that she would be fine.

Andy and Pretty Bird paid a final visit to her daughter's grave and hurried to get ready to leave.

The young couple rode with the women, whose horses were pulling the travois. Badger and White Quill rode off to the side, keeping them in sight. Pretty Bird's mother rode well-behind Andy, so she was out of his sight, a custom which still confounded Andy.

By mid-afternoon, when they would normally have stopped for the day, Pretty Bird was haggard. Determined not to be a burden, she refused to say anything when it was decided they would press on. Since the others were anxious to make it to the Sun dance, Painted Wing wanted to travel as long as they could. When they finally stopped to make camp at sunset, Pretty Bird could scarcely stand as she dismounted. Andy refused to allow her to do anything, and as soon as he had laid out a robe for her, she was asleep.

For two more days, the routine was the same; starting early, they travelled until evening. With the long, hard days, Pretty Bird gained little strength and remained quiet and withdrawn. She did not want Andy to leave her side and clung to him at night, and at times he would wake to her body trembling, wracked by silent sobs.

They saw the sprawl of the Sun dance camp from a great distance. The final day of ceremony was to begin the next morning. Badger left immediately, in search of his mother and sister, and when he found them, he was delighted to discover that she had brought his lodge along with her. He had already decided what he wanted to do with it, and in the evening, he led Andy and Pretty Bird to their new home.

22

At the Sun dance, seeing others his age move on in life, Badger wondered if the time had come for him to take a new name and enter the realm of manhood. His name was that of a boy, and he wanted one which was better suited to him, as a young man. Others his age were already making arrangements to leave in search of a vision from some spirit helper, which would guide them into their adulthood. From such a vision, a young man might derive the spirit power necessary to become successful in the pursuits of manhood, and a proud father or a respected elder might present him with a new name, a man's name, one which represented the giver's vision for his life.

Having no wish to go to war or raid the camps of the enemy, he could see no point in seeking the aid of a spirit helper. He was intrigued, however, with the spirit which seemed to be Andy's helper, and which attended his endeavours. If his friend was to be believed, it was his medicine which had given its power to Sun and the creatures from which others claimed to derive their spiritual power. He had decided it would have to do. At least for the time being, he would wait and see where it would take him. His only wish was that it attracted more of the flair and mystique of others' spirit helpers—he had always been envious of such things.

When they were all together at Pretty Bird's lodge that night, he told them what he had been thinking. Andy thought about it for a moment and asked the others, *"What is a good name for our friend? We need to give him the name of a man!"*

White Quill responded with one of his wisecracks, but Andy chided him. *"You dog! I am serious!"* he exclaimed. *"Why do we not choose a name for him? He has no father to give him one, so should we not be the ones to do it? We are his best friends!"*

"Yes! We will do that!" White Quill said, becoming more serious. *"Hai! You have to leave now!"* he told Badger, giving him a friendly shove. *"We must decide on your new name!"*

"No," Badger protested weakly. *"You do not have to. I could get that old man or the old woman who gave me my first horse to do it."*

"No, we are going to!" proclaimed Andy authoritatively. *"We must think about it. We will think about it, and we will have a ceremony—give you a new name—soon!"*

"Yes! We will do that!" White Quill agreed. *"But later! Now we need to get ourselves ready to be seen by some girls!"* he urged, nodding to where they kept their things, for they had already moved in with Andy and Pretty Bird. Shuffling on his knees to his pile of belongings, he was joined by his friend, and they combed and braided their hair and painted their faces and bodies. Andy ribbed them, but Pretty Bird pressed through her discomfort to give them her advice for attracting girls' attention. Amid good-natured joking and teasing, they soon disappeared and left the young husband alone with his new wife.

Each day, with rest, Pretty Bird was gaining more strength. The puffiness left her face, and her bleeding stopped, but most of the time, she remained quiet and subdued. She always wanted to be close to Andy but showed little sign of responding to his affection. This puzzled him, for he remembered the bright and outgoing personality she had once possessed and how she had responded to his passion. He longed to experience her body and to know her touch, but instead, he indulged her need for long hours, lying in each other's arms and talking quietly.

Once, on the last day of the Sun dance, they took a walk through the camp, after Pretty Bird had spent time combing and braiding his golden hair, which now hung past his shoulders. Her face showed her immense pride while she walked confidently beside him.

At the end of the great celebration, families started pulling out of the big encampment for their summer buffalo hunts. White Quill had only been able to visit with his family for a few days before they departed, heading northwest. Choosing to remain with his friends, he and his sister bid farewell to their loved ones, and the next day they too moved out onto the prairies. Pretty Bird was gloomy and White Quill rode away from the others, alone, both missing their family as their camp made its way toward the southwest.

That evening, they all sat quietly beside an outside fire and let Pretty Bird prepare a meal—her first since she and Andy had been together. Andy tasted what she had made, and smiled his approval, encouraging the others to try it. At once, the girl's dour disposition left her, and after that, she delighted herself in waiting upon him. Her sudden cheerfulness lifted everyone's spirits, and they began considering Badger's new name.

"I have been thinking," White Quill announced with uncharacteristic seriousness. *"Why do we not call him Good Friend?"* Andy and Pretty Bird considered it while he continued, *"His friendship is important to me, and he is a good friend to all of us, is he not?"*

"Yes!" Andy exclaimed, *"What a good name—Good Friend!"*

"*Yes! I agree.*" Pretty Bird assented. "*He saved my husband! He is indeed my good friend!*" she said, snuggling and holding Andy by the arm.

"*How do you like it?*" Andy asked Badger.

Looking thoughtfully toward the evening sky as he considered it, Badger nodded, "*It will do.*" The others sensed some reticence and suggested a few more names, but the conversation kept circling back to Good Friend. The more he thought about it, the more he began to like it. "*I think I like it!*" he announced finally, interrupting their brainstorming.

"*What? After Buffalo?*" White Quill asked a name that had just been suggested.

"*No, Good Friend! I like it! I want a name that says who I am, not what I have done!*"

"*Good Friend!*" Andy repeated. "*I do not think you really have a choice. We decide, do we not?*"

"*Yes!*" White Quill responded, "*It is up to us, not up to you!*"

"*I know,*" Badger agreed. "*But I still like it. You can stop trying to think of other names, now.*"

"*Good Friend!*" announced Andy. "*Stand up!*" he ordered, climbing to his feet. When Badger stood up, his friends all scrambled to their feet. Andy embraced him first, proclaiming, "*You are Good Friend!*"

"*Yes!*" White Quill agreed, trying to pry them apart and give a hug of his own. "*Give him to me!*" he muttered, and wrapping his arms around him, he hugged him too. Pretty Bird was too shy about embracing him but smiled her affection for him. White Quill asked Andy to say a prayer to his medicine, asking their friend to be blessed and successful in his life, something in which Andy was glad to oblige.

By the time dusk fell over the camp, the four of them were laughing heartily, happy to be in one another's company. White Quill was filled with entertaining stories and jokes and kept everyone entertained until long after dark. But when Pretty Bird began to ready herself for sleep, her brother knowingly tugged on Good Friend's arm and nodded toward the door. *"My sister says we are sleeping outside tonight!"* he said wryly, winking at his friend. Shortly, they left the young couple alone inside their lodge.

In the quiet darkness of their lodge that night, Pretty Bird returned Andy's affection for the first time since giving birth. When she sat up from where she had been lying in his arms, Andy realized with nervous excitement that she was lifting off her dress. He felt her hands tugging at his belt, and in a moment, she brushed his garment out of the way. Still unable to allow him to know her fully, they revelled in the intimacy of their nakedness, and she delighted herself in finding ways to please him.

After that, they took every opportunity to be alone. Andy hunted little, preferring to remain near his wife in camp, helping her dry and preserve the meat the others brought back—just to be close to her. But one day, she suggested he accompany the others to the river while she picked berries with some of the other women, and he agreed. He had missed the horsing around with his friends.

Spending the day with Badger and White Quill and a few of their friends, though, something seemed to have changed. Quite sure that it was not him, Andy assumed it must have been the others who now acted differently toward him. They seemed distant and were awkward about allowing him to join them in their play. It seemed they were more comfortable when he sat at the edge of the water and watched. On the way back to camp, he asked his two friends if they had noticed the same thing.

"They think it strange that you should want to behave as they do," Good Friend suggested. *"They say that they are not used to having a man playing with them."*

Andy protested. *"I am not a man! I am still a boy! I am just like them!"*

"Yes," White Quill agreed. "But to them, you are not. They think that having a wife means you are no longer a boy and no longer do the things that boys do."

"Why should that make a difference?" Andy wondered.

"I think it has to do with sex!" Good Friend opined. "They all wonder what it would be like, and they think that you have it all the time."

"No!" White Quill disagreed. "That might have a little bit to do with it, but I think it is more about seeing you as better than them."

"What? I am not!" Andy protested, "Why do they have that idea?"

"They see you as a man, now," the younger one agreed with his friend. "Boys can hardly wait to be a man—except me!"

"And me!" Good Friend piped up.

"Anyway, they say you now get to do what men do. Men are either hunting or warring or bragging."

"I do not do any of those things!" Andy reminded them.

Both shook their heads, and White Quill continued. "No, but men take no time to be foolish and play as we do! Men do not have time for boy things!"

"But I am not like that, am I?" the white boy persisted. "Is that what you think?"

"We know you too well to think that way!" White Quill grinned.

"Yes," Good Friend agreed with a chuckle. "You are still the first one in the water!"

"It felt strange!" Andy concluded. "I hope they get over it! I am still just like them!" Hoping he was right, his friends said nothing more about it.

For many days, the camp moved from place to place, always toward *Mistakis*. Buffalo were in abundance, and they had to travel little. The camp moved only when the buffalo had been pushed too far away for the women to carry the spoils back to camp.

One day, Pretty Bird declared that she had dried enough meat and pounded enough of it into pemmican. "We do not need more!"

she told them. Instead, she suggested that Andy accompany her to a beautiful spot she had discovered while out berry-picking with the rest of the women. *"Maybe we will stay out all night,"* she suggested. *"Perhaps I will bring our robes, just in case."*

Andy was puzzled. *"Why are we leaving so late in the day? And why do we have to bring all that stuff?"* he wondered aloud. But she simply arched her eyebrows playfully and handed him things to be loaded onto their horses.

Passing the berry-pickers returning from their chore, the young lovers arrived at the spot near the end of a hot afternoon. It was an idyllic location. The saskatoon and chokecherry bushes were plentiful, though most had been stripped of their fruit. At a bend in the creek, the trees grew tall and leaned out over glassy water, creating a green canopy over the lazy river. From where he stood, Andy thought the water would hardly cover a child's knees, but in the shady spot, Pretty Bird pointed out the dark water—a deep pool. The sandy beach was covered with the footprints from all the children who had played there throughout the days of berry-picking. But now, the place was deserted.

Pointing out a spot among the bushes, near the beach, Pretty Bird directed her husband to lay out their robes. As he bent to his task, she commanded him, *"Do not turn around! You must not look!"*

Keeping his back to her, Andy grinned and asked, *"Why? What are you going to do?"* expecting some mischief.

"I have a surprise for you! Do not turn around until I tell you!" The sound of her voice told him she was moving toward the water.

"All right! But you must hurry!" He waited for a moment and turned around as soon as he heard her call. Her smiling face and bare shoulders were all that was out of the water. Her clothing lay abandoned at the shore.

"Come!" she called out to him with an excited voice. *"The water is warm!"*

Andy started to grin as he strode for the beach. As he neared the water's edge, she urged him to remove his garment. *"But you will see me!"*

"Yes! I know! I want to see you in the light!"

"What if I do not want you to see me?" Andy teased, standing watching her, a grin of anticipation on his face.

"Oh, but you will!" Pretty Bird responded, lifting herself out of the water until the tops of her breasts were exposed.

Guessing that she had planned it all, he teased, *"You must not look!"* In response, she placed her hand in front of her eyes but spread her fingers apart so that he could see that she was watching him. *"You are looking!"* he protested.

"No! I have my hand over my face! Come! The water is nice!"

Andy was just a little nervous. Although they had explored and caressed each other's bodies in the dim light of their lodge, they had never really seen each other in the light of day. Looking around to ensure they were alone, he slipped out of his moccasins and untied his breechclout, letting it drop at his feet. His wife let her hand fall and admired him openly as he eagerly made his way toward her. His excitement was obvious.

With the water at his knees, he paused, holding out his hands to her. Setting her chin toward him, she looked him in the eye and rose out of the water, stepping toward him. Andy broke her gaze and examined her slender figure as she emerged from the water's cloak. His eager eyes took in every detail of her body as they closed the distance between them. Embracing her, he pressed his lips to hers.

For several moments they kissed deeply, embracing, until the girl pulled away. Taking him by the hand, she led him into the deeper water. There, starting from his broad, young shoulders and working her way down his body, she used the river water to cleanse each part of his body with her hands. When she had finished, she stood before him and allowed him to do the same for her.

Finally, she whispered into his ear, and in response, he swept her into his arms, carrying her from the water to their robes. There, locked in each other's embrace, tenderly and lovingly, they fully became husband and wife.

The next day, when they returned to their lodge, Andy's friends immediately recognized that something was different. The lovers arrived, riding double on Pretty Bird's horse, Andy's mount trailing behind on a rope. Pretty Bird emanated a joy and a zeal they had not seen before, and Andy's affection for her was immense. Their faces shone like the sun!

She was still unable to accommodate Andy's passion as frequently as they desired, but not knowing that, Good Friend and White Quill found reasons to stay away, taking extended hunting trips or visiting other camps.

Once the lovers found themselves well within the home range of the *Piikáni*, they left the camp to ride alone among the rolling foothills. Caught up in their young love, they wandered and camped along the clear streams which rushed from the mountain canyons, wholly absorbed with each other.

One morning, when it dawned cold and grey, and the mountains were not visible for cloud, they knew their happy, rambling days would soon be over. Good Friend and White Quill had tracked them down from time to time to check on them. The last time they had been together, they had agreed to meet on the shores of the *North Inside Big Water* when the first snow appeared on the peaks of the mountains. The leaves had already burst into brilliant colour, when one morning, the clouds cleared away to show the rugged peaks agleam with fresh snow against a dark blue sky, telling them it was time to head for their rendezvous.

Within a day, they stood together on a high hill overlooking the length of the big lake and explored the beautiful area together. Waiting for the others to show up, the lovers made their camp where generations of Indians had camped before them, along the shore of the sheltered bay at the end of the great lake. The mornings were cooler, but the days remained warm. Andy swam in the chilly water beneath the nearby waterfall, while Pretty Bird sat on the big rocks and watched. Afterward, she delighted in making love to him at the water's edge.

They were lucky not to have been interrupted one afternoon when they heard the clatter of hooves on the rocks. Startled at first, they looked to find Good Friend and White Quill in the company of Many Hands and Little Man, on the other side of the chattering creek.

Returning cheerfully together to the lovers' camp, Pretty Bird prepared a meal using a chunk of buffalo meat brought by their guests. As she worked, the others smoked together, while Good Friend and White Quill spoke about a recent visit from their *Káínaa* friends. During their stay, a band of *Kotonáá'wa* had also been visiting—a hunting party. The *Kotonáá'wa* would be leaving for their homeland, and always looking for an adventure, the four boys had asked if they could go along. *"We want you to come with us!"* Good Friend said hopefully. Pretty Bird was every bit as eager as her youthful husband.

After their meal, they moved camp to meet the *Kotonáá'wa* hunting party. The *Kotonáá'wa* would be returning to their mountain home any day, so the youthful adventurers waited for them in sight of their generations-old route. Keeping out of sight, just in case someone unexpected came along, Little Man was musing and observed, *"This would be a good place to ambush them!"* Andy was horrified by the comment but kept it to himself when nothing else was said about it.

When the *Kotonáá'wa* arrived, some of the older boys came over to smoke with them and size up their pale friend and his young wife, trading stories by sign.

Stopping not much later for the night, the *Kotonáá'wa* travelled with few lodges and most slept outside. Early the next morning, the camp was on the move, pressing for their home across the mountains. Andy and Pretty Bird stuck with their friends who visited with others around their age as the slow procession, laden with meat, made its way into the mountains. They stopped for the night at the foot of a mountain pass.

The next day, the riders crossed over the continental divide, where their horses trudged through the remnants of an earlier snowfall. Seeming to pay no heed to the breathtaking view, the Kotonáá'wa did not linger at the top and proceeded straight down the other side. Andy was particularly taken by the sight of the snow-capped peaks surrounding them in every direction. He and Pretty Bird stopped to enjoy the view, while their four companions lingered impatiently, unaccustomed to the closeness of the mountains and eager to re-join the hunting party.

Not long after they resumed their journey, dropping down a steep slope and continuing down the valley bottom, they came upon a deep, narrow gorge, carved into solid rock. The river ran deep and slowly through it. Moss lined the rock on both sides of the gorge, and without exchanging a word, both Andy and Pretty Bird knew they had found a place they wanted to stay. Their companions could not be persuaded to stay there with them and pressed on to catch up with the Kotonáá'wa, making a loose arrangement to pick up the lovers on the way back—whenever that might be.

Their friends had barely disappeared into the trees before Andy tore off his clothes and took a flying leap into the blue waters at the bottom of the deep gorge. He surfaced with a gasp, expecting to see his bride watching him with concern, but instead, he looked up just in time to see her fling herself from the rocks to join him, having doffed her garment.

The four young Blackfoot boys followed the trail of the Kotonáá'wa further into the mountains. All were growing increasingly edgy, uncomfortable with the closeness of the mountains and forests that seemed to crowd them more with each bend in the trail. Before long, they overtook the *Kotonáá'wa*. After another gruelling day, they entered a broad, open valley—the home of the *Kotonáá'wa*.

Feeling more comfortable, now that they were out of the forest, the boys basked in the attention that was paid to them as they paraded with the triumphant hunters through the camp. Their arrival was too late in the day for a formal celebration, but they were told that the following night, a feast would be held to honour the returned hunters. But that did not stop anyone from impromptu celebrations long into the night.

The Blackfoot boys were welcomed with open arms and invited to sit around the fires of several young men. Despite the limits of language, they all shared stories of conquest and honour, both at war and with women—it was a familiar scene for young Blackfoot.

The next day began late and was spent in pursuit of girls and gambling and horse racing. The *Kotonáá'wa* boys were eager to pit their sure-footed mountain horses against the newcomers' mounts.

A stocky boy, about 15, challenged Little Man to a horserace. They agreed to race to a lone sapling hardly visible across the valley, and the first one back after rounding it would win the others' bow. Little Man agreed. He was not much attached to his bow and was confident his horse was up to the task. The stocky boy called his sister over to start the race, and as she neared the pair, Little Man's mouth fell open—she was the prettiest girl he had ever seen. She smiled and made eye contact with him as she walked between the two mounted boys. Suddenly motivated, Little Man focussed his attention on the race, and at her signal, he was off at full speed.

He could hear the other boy a short distance behind him, and as he rounded the tree, he could see that he had the race won already. Congratulating himself, he flew toward the finish and toward the lovely girl. He arrived well ahead of the stocky boy and crowed victoriously to the crowd that had gathered as he leapt to the ground, flushed with pride.

The defeated boy walked sheepishly over to congratulate Little Man, handing over his bow. But to the Blackfoot boys' surprise, he gestured that they should race again. Little Man looked at him with incredulous eyes—why would he want to run again when he had been so soundly beaten? The boy indicated that this time, the winner would get the loser's horse. Little Man could hardly believe his luck. He saw that the boy's sister had her eyes on him and agreed to the stakes, climbing back onto his mount, which seemed barely winded from the first race.

At the starting signal, Little Man once again took the lead. But he was soon surprised to find that the *Kotonáá'wa* boy was keeping right up to him. He urged his horse onward. As they neared the tree, both horses were neck and neck, but the stocky boy seemed completely relaxed. As if he had done it a hundred times before, he expertly guided his horse forward just enough to take the inside of the turn around the tree, leaving Little Man to fall in behind. After that, there was no contest.

Little Man knew he had been duped as he watched the stocky boy keep pulling away, all the way to the finish line. With his head hanging low, Little Man ceded his mount to the cocky victor and disappeared from the rowdy group, with Many Hands following close on his heels. The girl was nowhere to be seen.

Hardly noticing the dejected pair's departure, the stocky boy turned to Good Friend and grinning wryly, offered to race for the same stakes. Not willing to lose the horse that had belonged to Wolf Tail, Good Friend declined, ignoring the teasing of their hosts. Only White Quill understood his unwillingness to agree to this wager.

Instead, the Blackfoot boys gave themselves to trying to attract the attention of the *Kotonáá'wa* girls. They brushed their hair and painted their faces, doing their best to win the attention of the opposite sex, hardly noticing that the celebration in honour of the successful hunt was beginning. The parents and other adults were used to such antics and kept a careful watch on their charges so that none of the young *Kotonáá'wa* girls would find themselves alone with the visitors.

To the surprise of their kinsmen, Little Man and Many Hands rejoined the celebrations, announcing loudly that they would like to stay for several more days and throwing themselves into the celebrations. They danced and made light of the races earlier in the day, appearing to have forgotten the loss altogether. But as the night wore on, Little Man pulled White Quill and Good Friend aside and informed them of their plan.

"We have been watching how these fools keep their horses." His voice was spitting with anger. *"They will be easy to take, but we will have to do it tonight!"* he whispered in a sinister voice. *"We will come and get you when it is time to go!"* White Quill and Good Friend stood in stunned silence as their friend outlined his plan. When they objected, they were silenced with a hiss. *"That female dog cheated my best horse away from me! I will have it back! And when we get back with these horses, we will be honoured!"* the surly boy proclaimed. Although Good Friend and White Quill were both reluctant, they felt they had no choice other than to aid in its execution.

Slipping into the darkness in the middle of the celebration, their goal was to gather their own horses, as well as whatever *Kotonáá'wa* horses they could round up, and disappear into the dark forest. It seemed simple enough, White Quill and Good Friend both had to admit as they went about the task with their *Káínaa* friends. The risk seemed minimal. If they were perceived in their efforts, they would simply abandon the *Kotonáá'wa* horses and fly away on their own.

Their plan worked better than they could have imagined! The nights had been cloudy and dark, and the treacherous boys had been counting on having a dark night, but while they moved quietly among the horses, Moon shone her light through a sudden opening in the clouds. Unlike the Blackfoot, the *Kotonáá'wa* often posted a guard to look after their horses at night. But because of the celebration, the horses had been left unguarded. The boys easily got their own animals together and silently worked several other animals away from the herd. By the time the clouds closed over the night's soft light, they were well clear of the camp.

All night, they drove the horses as quickly as they could on a dark and unfamiliar trail. At first light, after making sure they were still on the right trail, they urged the animals into a gallop. Late in the day, they came to the big river, beyond which they would begin their journey up the valley where they had left Andy and Pretty Bird. Shortly after that, they would be over the pass.

Hearing shouts and the sound of many horses' hooves on the rocks, Andy leapt to his feet, and he and Pretty Bird dove for cover just as the herd burst into the grassy meadow above their quiet gorge. Not seeing the startled pair of lovers, the boys continued to urge the stolen animals onward, except for White Quill, who broke off to search for his sister and her husband. When the white boy recognized his friend, he emerged from their hiding place, amazement and confusion written on his face. "*What is going on?*" he cried.

"*Come quickly!*" White Quill cried in a shrill, worried voice. "*They have captured the Kotonáá'wa horses! They are right behind us! We must hurry!*"

"*No! You dogs!*" Andy cried, instantly grasping the deadly seriousness of the situation. He stepped closer to his friend's frothing horse, which was anxious to be with the others.

"*We had to! They were going to do it anyway!*" White Quill told him breathlessly, as Pretty Bird joined them to stand with her husband, concern etched on her young face. "*We did not want to, but we had to! Hurry! Where are your horses?*"

"Over here!" Andy indicated distractedly. *"Where are the Kotonáá'wa?"* he asked nervously, as his friend dismounted and strode purposefully to help retrieve their mounts.

"We do not know!" White Quill called over his shoulder anxiously, as if expecting to see their pursuers appear at any moment. *"We have not seen them, but they are certain to be right behind us. Hurry! We need to leave!"*

Andy grumbled about the predicament his friends had cast upon them, while he and Pretty Bird raced to gather their things together and climb onto their mounts. Placing his wife in the lead, Andy fell in behind, and White Quill brought up the rear as they rode to catch up with their friends and their booty.

The ride was too frantic for talk. Racing along the narrow trail, the trio were kept too busy dodging branches and trees. In the absence of conversation, their minds were free to imagine the multitude of ways the vengeful *Kotonáá'wa* warriors might retaliate. Betrayal by those they had taken in would not sit well!

The fleeing Indians knew this would surely mean the end of the peace, which was never more than tenuous between the two peoples. Andy shuddered at the chilling similarity between this and the heinous acts perpetrated by the *Káínaa* against Wolf Tail and his brothers. He breathed a silent prayer, hoping there had been no bloodshed.

It was dusk when their exhausted horses reached the top of the pass. There, Good Friend was waiting for them, appearing relaxed and even grinning. *"I could see you ride through that clearing down there,"* he said, pointing to a meadow in the valley behind them. *"I have not seen the Kotonáá'wa. They must not be that close!"* he said excitedly.

"Where?" Andy wanted to know, turning to look behind him.

"Down there!" Good Friend replied, pointing out a grassy clearing in the forest below them.

"Where are the others?" White Quill asked.

"*They did not stop!*" Good Friend replied, keeping an eye on the meadow below. "*I told them I was going to wait here for you. They are not a long time ahead of us. We will be able to catch up to them.*"

"*What did you nothing ones do?*" Andy asked impatiently, taking advantage of his first opportunity to question his friends.

"*It was their idea!*" Good Friend responded defensively.

"*Little Man lost his horse in a race and decided to take it back,*" White Quill explained, also sounding defensive. "*Then, they wanted to take a bunch of their horses as well. We had to go along with them!*"

"*You did not try to stop them?*" Andy queried.

"*They would not be stopped!*" Good Friend explained. "*They were going to do it with us or without us. What could we do? Tell the Kotonáá'wa? Then, we would all be in trouble!*"

"*I am afraid to ask—did anyone get hurt?*" Andy inquired, cringing.

"*No! I think we are going to get away with it!*" White Quill responded, venturing a grin.

"*Sure! Get away with it!*" Andy growled, "*And start a war over it! How many horses?*"

"*Not sure!*"

"*Quite a bunch!*" came the other's reply.

"*And Little Man got his horse back!*" White Quill confirmed, trying to hide a smirk.

"*Let us get going!*" Andy urged. "*I do not want them to catch us!*"

They found the jubilant *Káínaa* at the bottom of the pass, where they had stopped to get fresh mounts from the herd. It was almost dark.

"*Is it not a fine bunch we have captured?*" Many Hands asked Andy exultantly.

"*No!*" Andy responded angrily. "*How could you do that, after they had made you their friends?*" he asked, thinking of Wolf Tail and his father.

"*The nothing ones! They took his horse!*" Many Hands replied smugly. "*It was too easy!*" he continued, gloating now. "*We could not just go and get his horse and leave these behind!*" he said, gesturing toward the herd. "*They are so foolish!*"

"*They are not foolish!*" Andy griped. "*They trusted you! I thought you lost the horse in a race!*"

"*The Kotonáá'wa always betray our friendship!*" Little Man interjected, changing the subject. "*They are always the ones to break the peace! They come into our land, and they take our buffalo...They are thieves! It is good that we did this to them before they had a chance to do the same to us! It will teach them a lesson!*"

"*We will have much to tell our friends!*" Many Hands cried, with a whoop, kicking his horse in the ribs, to end the conversation.

The rest of their ride was in the dark. Upon reaching the mouth of the valley and the open foothills, Many Hands instructed Little Man to stay behind and keep watch from a vantage point. If the *Kotonáá'wa* were indeed following them, he would be able to see them from a good distance and be able to get away to warn the others. In the meantime, the rest would carry on and make a cold camp at the river.

After locating a suitable place to spend the remainder of the night, the Indian boys still took time to recount their adventure, before trying to sleep. Good Friend and White Quill were both excited to have made their first horse raid, and Andy found himself caught up in the excitement of it, despite his misgivings. He found the sense of relief and satisfaction which came from evading the pursuing danger exhilarating, though now he was fraught with feelings of anxiety and guilt.

As exhaustion set it, the bragging was abbreviated, and the young raiders, having had no rest in two nights, went to sleep as soon as they laid down. Sometime in the night, Little Man rode into the camp, bringing the Indian boys to their feet, weapons in hand while Pretty Bird and Andy ducked quickly into the bushes.

"It is me! We are not followed!" the *Káínaa* boy announced when he was challenged by the others. Ignoring them, he slid off his horse and tethered it. Dragging his robe off his saddle, he flopped it down and was asleep before the rest were settled again.

It was just starting to get light when Many Hands roused them. *"Come! It is time to leave!"* he urged, kicking at the others with his foot. Still sleepy, everyone fumbled around to collect their things, before retrieving their horses. When the sun came up, and they began to feel its warmth, they were well within the safety of their homeland. Stopping to rest in a place where they could keep an eye on their back trail, the *Káínaa* were ready to divide the horses, before splitting off to return to their own camp.

"It is not right!" Andy objected. *"It is not my medicine! It is not right to take something that belongs to another!"* Neither of his friends said anything, and Many Hands and Little Man watched them stare at the ground.

"Yes! I agree!" White Quill said finally, looking up and making eye contact with the *Káínaa*.

"Yes, it is not our medicine!" Good Friend followed his friends' lead. *"We do not wish to have any of those horses,"* he said, turning for his horse.

The *Káínaa* boys looked at them incredulously. *"Why not? Are you certain?"* Many Hands asked.

"Yes," Good Friend assured them, standing beside his mount. *"You should not have done that! You betrayed them!"*

"What are you saying? We did not betray them!" Little Man retorted haughtily. *"This is why the Káínaa are braver than you Piikáni!"* he asserted, but recognizing his own arrogance, he caught himself and added, *"Are you sure you do not want any?"*

"No, you take them," Good Friend replied and turned to hop onto his horse. White Quill had already gotten onto his. Andy and Pretty Bird, too, turned and headed for their mounts.

"Fine by us!" Many Hands responded with a shrug. Turning to Little Man, he said, *"Let us go!"* and hopped onto his mount.

The *Piikáni* boys sat on their horses, and the four Indian boys stared at one another for a moment before Little Man wheeled his horse. Without a word, Many Hands followed, and very shortly, they had rounded up the herd and were gone.

Andy and his friends rode on in silence. Finally, Good Friend turned to Andy and spoke. *"What would you have done if we had taken some of those horses?"* White Quill heard his question and kicked his horse ahead, so he could listen to Andy's reply.

"Would you have taken any?" Andy responded, turning to look at White Quill, letting him know that he expected an answer from him, too.

"I wanted to, but I knew you would not like it," the younger one admitted readily. Both looked at Good Friend.

"Yes, probably I would have taken some," he admitted, staring at his horse's bobbing head as it plodded along.

For another long period, they rode in silence before Andy dropped back to ride beside his wife. Eventually, Good Friend reined in his horse to let them catch up. White Quill saw what he was doing and waited until they all came together.

Good Friend nodded his head slowly and said, *"I know what you mean. It would not be right."* White Quill was eager to agree, and the look on his face said he was disappointed with himself. They did not speak again of the incident, and nobody ever heard anything of their raid on the *Kotonáá'wa*.

23

Will Preston was looking forward to reaching Fort Pitt, hoping to see the man who had been so kind to him once before. Arriving at the fort in late summer on one of the boats, he was disappointed to learn that the man was away on an annual trip to York Factory. Sorry to have missed him, as soon as the goods for that post were unloaded from the boats, they carried on. Nobody at the fort had claimed to know anything of his sons, so he made his way still further west, arriving at Edmonton House near the end of September.

It was there, speaking with Samuel Hathaway, that he learned of a fair-haired boy living among the Blackfoot. It did not take much inquiry to find out who the man was speaking about.

"Is his name Andrew Preston?" the boy's father cried, at once hopeful and fearful.

"Yep, that's him, awright!" Hathaway confirmed, not realizing who the man was. "Andy, he called himself. He was s'posed to bring his injuns back here to trade—but he never showed! The little beggar!"

"Andrew?" the anxious father inquired. "I'm his father!" he uttered. "He's alive? What about Matthew? Matthew's my other son! Do you know anything about him?" he asked urgently. "Someone said they had both been killed by Blackfoot!"

Taken aback to learn who he was speaking with, Hathaway became flustered. "Nope, not Andy," he responded. Subdued, he said, "I didn't know, sorry! Yeah, we saw him 'round here. I guess the other one got killed 'way last year. Didn't git Andy, though. Lotsa life in that one! We saw 'im 'round here last summer," the man explained and dodged Will's further questioning, claiming nobody really knew what had happened. "The boy's the only one that really knows that!" he concluded.

"Where did he go?" Will inquired urgently, relieved to hear the good news of his youngest son. "Someone said they had both been killed by Indians!" he blurted. Hathaway assured him that Andy had been very much alive the last time they had seen him. But that had been the previous autumn.

The shock of his eldest son's death fresher in his mind than it had been for a long time, Will was elated to hear that Andy had apparently survived the attack.

Armed with such good news, Will waited no longer. Figuring he knew the Blackfoot around Rocky Mountain House well enough to enlist their help in finding Andy, he hurried on to the next fort.

* * *

Andy and his comrades had returned to Good Friend's camp for the fall hunt, and by the time the first heavy snow arrived, they had settled in and gathered the necessary supplies for the coming season.

The winter was mild. Had it been harsh, the Indians may have stayed closer to their camp. As it was, when word arrived that the

Americans were trading whiskey some days' ride to the east, some of the men began making regular trips there. The whiskey seldom made its way back to the camp, but its effects became darkly familiar. The boys knew of two men who had died at the whiskey fort where fights and arguments had become a regular report.

It was during this time that Pretty Bird discovered her monthly bleeding had stopped, and in the season *when the buffalo calves are black*, she made her announcement to Andy. Good Friend and White Quill were away, visiting one of the other camps, and she and Andy had the lodge to themselves. After spending the afternoon making love in their cozy dwelling, Pretty Bird traced her finger across her husband's chest while they lay beside the fire, bathed in its warmth and soft light. *"Your seed has given me something,"* she whispered to him.

"Yes, I know," he sighed with a grin of contentment upon his face. *"It was good! I like it when we do not have to worry about our friends being around."* She rolled her eyes playfully as her meaning escaped his understanding.

"Yes, that, too." she purred. *"But that is not what I am speaking about. Do you know what I am speaking about?"* she whispered, kissing Andy on the neck.

Andy had his eyes closed and was paying no attention to what she was saying. *"Uh-huh."*

"Your seed! It has grown into something!"

"Uh-huh," Andy grunted.

Pretty Bird gently but firmly placed her finger on his chin and turned his face toward her. *"You need to pay attention to me! I am telling you something important!"*

"Later," he protested, turning toward her and attempting to slide his body atop her.

"I am carrying your baby!" she whispered, resisting his effort to wriggle himself between her legs.

He froze, suddenly very attentive to what she was trying to tell him. *"You what?"* he exclaimed, jerking his head back to search her eyes for meaning.

"I am carrying your baby!" she squealed with delight, a wide grin spreading across her face.

"My baby? What do you mean?"

"Your baby!"

"You mean...How?"

"Silly! I am pregnant! You made me pregnant!" She beamed.

"How did I do that? How do you know?" Andy asked, incredulous. He had little understanding of such things.

"I have not bled since the time of the falling leaves!"

"What do you mean? How?" Andy now lifted himself off her and looked down at her belly.

"You are silly! Your seed! It has made me pregnant!"

"Yes, but how do you know? Are you certain?"

"Yes! My bleeding has stopped. When I get just the right amount of your seed, it grows into a baby!"

"You are going to have a baby?"

"Yes! Your baby!" Pretty Bird continued, glowing with joy.

"When? Do you know when it is coming?" A torrent of questions poured from Andy as he tried to process her news.

"Probably before the leaves turn yellow!"

"How do you know? Are you all right?" Andy was suddenly concerned, getting to his knees. *"Did I hurt you? When we—"*

"No! That is fine!"

"Does my...does...does it hurt the baby?" He knew nothing about his wife's anatomy or the development of a baby.

"No! You are silly! People do sex right up until the day the baby is born. It grows right up here," she told him, showing him.

Andy was bewildered.

"You are silly!" Pretty Bird teased, grabbing him by the shoulders and pulling him to her. *"Do not worry about that! I love you!"* she moaned, pressing her mouth to his.

Over the winter, Andy watched in wonder as his wife's belly grew. Pampering her, he tried to keep her from her work, but she would only smile with amusement at his efforts and push past him, on her way to gather wood or bring water to their lodge. Good Friend and White Quill behaved like proud uncles and indulged both parents. Pretty Bird was anxious to send word to her mother, and as soon as the warmer weather arrived, she dispatched them to take the news back to the soon-to-be grandmother.

Good Friend's people had been camping between the *North Inside Big Water* and *Napi-tahta* since the early spring. As the spring wore on, rumblings of concern began to steal into the camp. Visitors brought word of a strange disease ravaging some of the camps to the south. Several people were said to have perished, but it did not reach the camps farther north.

To no one's surprise, hostilities with the *Kotonáá'wa* had resumed, and parties of young men were once again venturing across *Mistakis*. The first brought back several horses, but the second returned with horses as well as a teenaged girl and two small boys.

On seeing her hands bound and bowed head as she was paraded through the camp, Andy struggled to accept that the girl would be used as the Cree girl had. Her captors and their friends would use her, and she would eventually be traded off to someone who could not afford the gifts that were necessary to take a wife from among his own people.

The two small boys, wide-eyed with fear, were very young and were given to two families who would raise them among their own children. If they could overcome their fear and any lingering animosity they might harbour toward their new people, they could eventually become *Piikáni;* if not, they would probably leave or be killed.

There were other war parties—south, against the *Crow* and the *Snakes*, east against the *Cutthroats* and the *Spotted Horses People* and north, against the *Liars*. Good Friend's camp had remained deep in the heart of their established territory, where it was thought they would be relatively safe from attack. But one morning, the camp awoke to alarm. Constantly wary of raids, most of the men tethered their best horses inside the camp, some even going so far as to tether them to their lodge poles. But overnight two horses— both good buffalo runners—had gone missing, seemingly stolen from the heart of the camp. The owners were suspicious, but since no other horses were missing, and the herd had not been disturbed, they believed that the animals must have come loose and wandered off. An enemy might be expected to sneak into the camp, seeking the buffalo runners, but they usually left by way of the herd, stealing any horses they could make off with.

The owners of the missing animals scoured the area, but could find no sign of them, so, when Will Preston showed up, the first to greet him were highly suspicious.

He had reached Rocky Mountain House the previous fall, where his intention had been to call upon his *Piikáni* friends and imme- diately set off in search of his son. In his fervour to find his son, however, he had forgotten that the *Piikáni* would be off hunting buffalo at that time of year, getting ready for the winter ahead and that they would not likely be at the fort until spring. The Cree, who were in more frequent attendance at the fort, refused to guide him, wary of their enemies to the south.

The factor discouraged him from heading out on his own, warning that he would not be safe travelling alone. So, many days' ride north of where his son was wintering, Will Preston had waited for the *Piikáni*. But the *Piikáni* did not return to the fort until the worst of the winter weather had passed.

As the snows diminished, he formed a daily ritual. Each morning he peered over the walls to see if the *Piikáni* might have arrived overnight. And each evening, he checked with the watchman on duty to see if there had been any sign.

The first *Piikáni* to arrive were unknown to him. They had been wintering with the *Siksika*, north of their usual territory and had no intention of returning to their homeland until the time of the Sun dance. But as he described his boy, pale-skinned and hair the colour of the sunshine, those listening smiled and knew of him immediately. The presence of a golden-haired young man among the *Piikáni* had become known to many. Some said they had seen him at the Sun dance, but none knew exactly where he was spending the winter. At their words, a tiny shoot of hope formed in the distraught father's heart as he dared to imagine his son alive somewhere.

After that camp left, no other *Piikáni* appeared until the weather had begun to show signs of warming and the snow had started to melt. The next to arrive, though, had also heard of the white boy. Some even thought they knew where he was wintering.

Will had no trouble finding someone willing to guide him. But first, they wanted to trade with the whites, hoping to get a taste of the *napiohke*. They were given only small amounts, as a gift, and all the anxious parson could do was watch with disappointment while they debauched themselves with what they got. When at last they were ready to leave, he was their anxious yet welcome guest.

Only a few days from the fort, however, several of the Indians with him began to complain of sore throats and choking. At first, it was thought they were suffering from the effects of the *napiohke,* but when children began to develop the symptoms, great alarm arose in the camp.

Six days out from the fort, the camp came to a standstill. Too many of the people were afflicted for them to continue. Will had seen the disease before but could do nothing for them; he had to watch helplessly while it ravaged his hosts. Some had developed a membrane-like obstruction in their throats and airways, and when some died, others began to think that it was an evil spirit, brought among them by the *dog face*. Only through the intervention of some of the leading men were a few of the young hotheads prevented from killing Will.

For the period from one smiling moon to the next, the camp stayed where it was, with Will doing what he could to aid them in their distress. When the worst had passed, the camp journeyed on. But their steps were heavier than before, burdened by the loss of their loved ones.

Upon reaching this group's main winter camp, it was assumed the sickness had been left on the trail, but not long after they had arrived, it broke out again. The people were piteous in the jaws of the strange disease, and fear swept through the camp. Will again did what he could to help them. Day and night, the people saw him caring for those who were sick, bringing water and firewood, stoking fires and watching out for children, but whispering and suspicion followed him everywhere. It was only when they began to receive word of similar suffering in other camps, where Will had never been, that their animosity toward him relented.

When the disease finally left them, Will was exhausted but had so ingratiated himself to the people that some begged him to stay. He had heard so much, however, about the young man he was certain must be his son, that he did not wish to linger. Taking no time to rest, he set out with two young men to find Andy.

They spent four nights on the trail before they were intercepted by a scouting party, searching for horse thieves. Letting his guides return home, the scouts, all of whom knew Andy, were happy to escort Will to their camp where they assured him the golden-hair would be found.

Andy was working with Pretty Bird, tanning a buffalo hide, while Good Friend and White Quill watched, smoking their pipe.

They heard that scouts were returning with a stranger—perhaps the horse thief—and they all stood to see if they could catch a glimpse of the group that was just then descending into the river valley. Unable to see much, because of the bush, Andy and Pretty Bird returned to their work, disinterested. Good Friend and White Quill, though, put down their pipe and headed off to see what was happening.

A short time later, while Andy was on his knees, scraping the hide, he heard a familiar voice behind him. "Andrew?"

Instantly recognizing the voice, he whirled about, not believing his ears. Immediately recognizing his father's familiar form, he scrambled to his feet and raced to him, crying, "Daddy!" his voice breaking as he fell into the man's outstretched arms.

"Andrew!" Will gasped, wrapping his arms tightly around his cherished son. "My boy, my boy!" Hugging his son to his heart, tears streaming down into his beard, he rocked him from side to side.

"Daddy," Andy murmured, holding onto him in a bear hug. "I'm so glad to see you! I love you! I've missed you so much!"

"I love you, too, son," his father sobbed, overcome with emotion. Neither one was paying any attention to those around them, watching. "And I've missed you, too! I was told you were dead!" Will managed to say finally. "It's been a long time—such a long time!"

"I know," Andy replied, a sad smile melting onto his face. "So much has changed..."—he whispered, almost whimpering—"there's been so much that—"

"I know, son, I know. But I've found you! We're together now!" The pair remained oblivious to the crowd they were attracting.

"Do you know about Mum?" Andy asked softly, pulling himself away and looking into his father's face. Will closed his eyes slowly, the heartbreak washing over him afresh. He nodded slowly. "And... Matty?" Andy choked as he said his name. "Do you know about

Matty?" His father continued to nod in silence, his face sad, trying to hold back the emotion that the devastation of the last couple of years had wrought.

Opening his eyes, at last, the man gazed at his son, recognizing deep regret written on his son's face. "It's not your fault, son." Andy broke into sobs and buried his face in his father's shoulder. Will was gentle. "It's all right, son! We know where he is!" he assured him. "I'm sure there is nothing you could have done."

"I don't know," Andy whimpered. "I've felt so badly about Matty. We should never have gone!"

Seeing his son's downcast spirit, Will interrupted, "I'm so proud of you, son!" in an effort to distract him from his remorse. "You've done so well! Let me have a look at you!" he exclaimed, stepping back and holding his son at arm's length, looking him up and down. "You've sure grown! You're almost as tall as I am!"

"I reckon so," Andy said, wiping his eyes. "Almost as tall as you!"

"I almost didn't recognize you," his father said. "But the blonde hair was a dead give-away."

"Yeah, I sort of stand out, don't I?" Andy replied, grinning. "They get quite a kick out of my hair around here," he said, nodding in the direction of those watching.

Still reeling from the shock of his father's sudden arrival, he wanted to introduce his father to his bride. "But hey, you need to meet someone!" Turning to search for Pretty Bird among those gathered, he saw no sign her. So, he pushed his way through the curious faces to where he had left her, calling her name. The hide upon which they had been working was abandoned, and turning back to his father, who had followed him, he said, "Just wait! I'll be right back!"

He ran toward his lodge. Alarmed when he did not find his wife there, he emerged from the doorway and spotted her brother, pointing with his lips toward the back of the lodge. Looking in that direction, he saw his wife standing beside her horse. *"Hai! Wait!"*

he cried and ran to her. *"What are you doing?"* She cast her eyes to the ground as he approached and took her by the hand. *"What is the matter?"* He had never seen her so worried. Her brow was furrowed, and her eyes fearful. Alarmed, he whispered, *"What is the matter?"* taking her into his embrace. She was trembling. *"What is the matter? You are shaking!"* he observed gently, leaning back to have a look at her.

"You are going to leave me now!" she said in a low, accusing voice.

"No! Never! I will never leave you!" Andy assured her, holding her in his arms. *"I love you! I love you!"* he whispered, squeezing her tightly.

"That is your father?" Pretty Bird whispered.

"Yes! It is my father! I want you to meet him!"

"You will go away with him!"

"No! No, I will never go away! I will stay here, with you...He will be with us! I will never leave you!" he tried to reassure her.

Drawing a deep breath, she looked into his face and said softly, *"Make a vow that you will not leave me?"*

"Sinopah! I will never leave you, I vow. I love you! I love you! You are going to have our baby!" he said, holding her in his embrace.

When she suddenly stiffened and tried to pull away from him, her young husband saw her looking past his shoulder and turned quickly to see his father, a broad smile covering his face.

Facing him, and hugging Pretty Bird to his side, the young man announced, "Daddy, I have, um...I guess I am sort of...I am...This is my wife! I am, kind of, married to her. *Pretty Bird.*"

Will's warm smile surprised Pretty Bird, and she felt some of her fear and apprehension about his intrusion in their life together lift. He strode up to her, and gently taking her hand in his, he bent over and kissed it. This was something she had only ever seen her husband do, and it eased her fear a little further.

"Oki, my daughter," he said to her gently.

"He looks like he is glad to see you!" White Quill whispered to Andy, standing beside them.

"Yes, our hearts are glad," Andy grinned.

"Yes, my heart is glad!" his father repeated, having heard the comment. He was still holding Pretty Bird's hand and smiling at her. *"My heart is also glad that you have such a lovely wife!"*

Andy was surprised to hear his father speak Blackfoot and exclaimed, "You speak their language!"

"Yes. Remember, I have been with them too!" Will now stepped away from Pretty Bird, but still held her hand.

"Yes. I should have known that! It's all I speak, now. I have hardly spoken any English since Edmonton House," Andy observed. "How much do you know?"

"Not near enough! But it's coming back pretty well," his father replied.

Wishing to impress his father with his knowledge of the language, Andy turned and addressed Pretty Bird. *"This is my father! He is called, in my tongue,* Will." Turning back to his father, he added, *"This is Pretty Bird, my wife!"* Will opened his arms and took a step toward the shy girl. With just a little nudge from Andy, she stepped forward to receive another embrace. *"And, this is her brother,"* Andy interrupted.

White Quill was uncertain how to greet the stranger. Sharing Pretty Bird's concern that Andy might now abandon them, he cast his eyes to the ground. When Will reached out his hand, the boy looked up timidly. Offering his hand to the man, he broke out in a grin when Andy's father grasped it and shook it heartily. *"He is called White Quill. He is my brother now!"* the white boy said with obvious affection.

"Your brother, my son, then!" Will said. The boy startled when Andy's father pulled him to him and gave him a hug.

Beckoning Good Friend, who had been watching from a distance, Andy said to his father, *"This is my other brother, Good*

Friend." Andy said. *"Good Friend, this is my father. He is called* Will." Good Friend nodded his head and looked at the ground. Will released the younger Indian and stepped toward the other, reaching out his hand. Shuffling hesitantly up to the bearded man, Good Friend looked up and reached out his hand to him. Andy was not used to seeing either of his friends behave so shyly. Among their own, they were both self-confident and outgoing.

"Son!" Will said to him too, reaching to take the boy's hand and clasp it in both his own, before pulling him into an affection- ate hug.

"He helped me after Matty was killed," Andy told him sombrely. "We have been together ever since. I—er, we gave him his name," he announced, with pride in his voice.

"Good Friend!" Will repeated. *"Be my son, too! My heart is warm toward you. I am thankful you helped my son! Thank you!"* Good Friend returned his gaze to the ground but felt a swell of pride and affinity for this man forming in his heart.

Suddenly, Andy shouted to the crowd, *"My friends! This dog face is my father!"* There was a murmur among them, and some gave a cheer. *"Hai, Comes Last!"* he called to a young boy who stood nearby, watching. *"Please look after the horse of this dog face. He is my father!"* At once, the boy darted to take the rein, his proud smile showing his delight at having been asked. *"Thank you, little friend. Put it with my horses!"*

"You seem to rule the roost!" Will observed.

"Not really. Come to my, uh, *come to her lodge,"* Andy said and watched his father put his arm around Pretty Bird's waist. She looked up at him as she walked beside him and put an arm around him affectionately.

"You have your own?" Will asked.

"Yup," Andy replied with pride. "Well, actually, it belongs to *Pretty Bird.* They—the women—own 'em."

Tired of watching the conversation without understanding, Good Friend elbowed his white friend, *"Hai! Speak so we can understand!"*

Once inside Pretty Bird's lodge, they sat around the fire. Andy took the place of the husband, at the rear, opposite the door, giving his father the seat to his left.

"The place of honour! Thank you!" Will said as Good Friend and White Quill sat to his left. Andy tried to make Pretty Bird join them, but she persisted in preparing a meal, refusing to let him help, insisting he remain seated with his father.

"Daddy," Andy began, a little nervous, looking at Pretty Bird as he spoke. "There is something more I need to tell you. Um... Pretty Bird is...uh...she's gonna have, um, a baby...and I'm, sort of, the father." He looked at his father nervously, trying to read his expression, uncertain how he would react to their news. "But she's my wife!" he added, hoping to assure him that it was all proper. "We're, um, married...sort of. They don't seem to do it like we do, but we are."

"I see that!" Will smiled and winked at her, bringing a happy smile to her face. "But what do you mean that you are sort of the father?"

"Well, I am! We've...you know. We...uh—"

Seeing him blush, his father interjected with a grin, "I think I know! Let's just say she's your wife," relieving him of an explanation.

"Yeah! You know! It's just—" He was interrupted by Comes Last, who came in noisily, having put the horse away. Lugging Will's things, he dropped them inside the door and flopped himself down beside White Quill, who draped his arm over the boy's shoulder.

"Thank you, little friend!" Andy said.

Will started again. "I know! Congratulations son! I'm proud of you and don't worry, I approve!" He put his arm around Andy's neck and pulled him over and kissed him on the top of his head.

"And I very much approve of your wife!" Releasing him, Will got to his feet and stepped over to give the young mother another, loving embrace. *"Daughter, I am happy about your baby! My heart is full of joy! I will be a grandfather!"* he said, smiling at her. *"When?"* he asked her.

Pretty Bird's hands proudly moved to stroke her belly as she looked at the ground. *"At the time when the leaves are yellow, I think,"* she informed him shyly.

"Hai! I am so happy!" Will said with enthusiasm, *"I am very happy for you!"* Releasing the girl, he returned to sit beside his son, smiling proudly. Then, turning to him, he gazed at him lovingly and said with fondness, "My little man!" The young couple basked in the man's obvious affection for them.

Over the rest of the day, aided eagerly by his friends, who very quickly warmed up to the bushy-faced man, Andy filled his father in on all that had transpired since Matthew's death those many months prior. Andy listened solemnly as Good Friend recounted in greater detail than ever before, exactly what had happened on that day and how it had affected him. His heart went out to his friend, who laid himself bare before the others, speaking of his own shame and embarrassment, and how without Andy, he would have died that day.

When he finished, no one knew what to say, and a heavy silence fell upon the lodge. Until at last, stirred by compassion, Will thoughtfully pushed himself to his feet and stepped over to kneel in front of the Indian boy, embracing him. *"I can see your heart...It is good!"* Will whispered earnestly, hugging him to his chest. *"My heart is warm toward you, my son!"* He felt Good Friend sink into his embrace, and a bond formed between the two.

In another moment, he reached out an arm to White Quill. *"Come!"* he beckoned him. The boy shuffled closer. *"I want to take you both as my sons! I want you to know that I love you!"* And he embraced the two of them. Both boys, fatherless in their own way, cherished the love they felt from him and were delighted by the great honour he was showing them.

Andy watched with pride as his father won over his friends and his bride. He cast his eyes around the lodge, watching the firelight flicker on their faces as they listened to his father, and asked him questions and answered his. His eye lingered on his young wife, who would bear their first child in a few months. She was now at ease in his father's presence.

The proud young man watched with amusement as Good Friend and White Quill tried to outdo each other in impressing Will with their stories. He could not imagine anything more perfect than this day!

Before long, the Indians were behaving as if Will had been with them forever. Food followed the conversation, and after they had eaten Pretty Bird's meal, they all settled down around the fire and Andy invited his father to tell them of his travels.

Will had already mentioned that he had set out to cross *the big water*, believing both his sons to have been killed. Speaking in Blackfoot, he told them all that had happened. But when he spoke affectionately of the man, at Fort Pitt, who had been so kind to him, Andy could hardly believe his ears as his friends looked at one another in amazement. "McConnell?" he interjected, spitting the man's name.

"Yes—McConnell! That's it!"

"That dog!" his son cursed. *"He shot me! Look!"* he exclaimed, lifting his shirt to show the wound, still very visible.

"What? What happened?" Will exclaimed with shock, examining the scar.

Pretty Bird pressed herself closer to Andy while he told his story, clutching his arm as he recounted the painful experience.

"And I thought he was the nicest fellow!" Will said in disbelief when he had finished.

"He says the white man is a dog!" Andy told the others in response to their puzzled looks.

"Yes! My son is right!" Will conceded. *"He is a dog!"*

After the shock of this discovery wore off, he continued with his story, telling all that had happened to bring him back to the west. Late into the night, the conversation wore on, each listening with rapt attention to the speaker. The drumming, which had been heard earlier in the evening, had long since stopped, and the camp had fallen silent as they talked around the small fire in Pretty Bird's lodge.

During a lull in the conversation, White Quill scrambled to his feet. *"I need to pee!"* he uttered and hurried for the door. *"I have a joke, I must tell you! On Sun Shines on Him! I will be right back!"* Slipping out, he let the flap fall behind him. Andy told his father how White Quill was always telling jokes and playing pranks on people, and that they called him the Joker.

In a few moments, impatient to hear more, Good Friend said, *"He only said he was taking a pee. I wonder what he—"* His words were cut short by the sudden clatter of horses' hooves outside and taunting shouts.

Everyone looked at one another, puzzled, but Pretty Bird knew instantly what was happening. *"My brother! Something is wrong!"* she shrieked, her voice shrill with alarm. Suddenly hysterical, she leapt to her feet, screaming, *"No! No! Brother!"*

Andy raced to her side and caught her at the door. *"What is wrong?"* he uttered, grabbing her by the shoulder.

"The horse takers!" Good Friend exclaimed, already on his feet and grabbing for his weapon.

"My brother! My brother!" Pretty Bird wailed, trying to get past Andy, who held her back, his heart cold with fright.

"What is it?" Will asked urgently.

"Horse takers! Stay with her!" Andy burst out sharply, standing in front of his wife to prevent her from going outside in search of her brother. *"Stay with my father!"* he ordered her firmly, holding onto her until his father could take her into his arms.

Good Friend, his bow and quiver in hand, raced out the door with Comes Last, at the same time as a shot tore through the still night. There was more shouting and shooting. The sound of horses could be heard racing up, out of the valley they were in. Will held onto Pretty Bird, who screamed frantically for her brother, as Andy headed out the door. In a moment, they both heard his high-pitched scream pierce the confusion. "Aaaaaagh! No-oo! No-ooo!"

"Wait here!" Will cautioned Pretty Bird. Suddenly both were desperate to get to Andy, recognizing his cry. *"Wait!"* he repeated and raced for the doorway. "Andrew, where are you!" he cried, his voice thick with panic. Stepping outside into the darkness, he tried to make sense of the mayhem that had arisen so suddenly. Pretty Bird scrambled out after him and grabbed onto his arm.

The sound of sobbing from the side of the lodge drew them in that direction, where they found Andy, on his knees, cradling a form in his arms. They knew in an instant that it had to be White Quill, and both feared the worst. Pretty Bird threw herself down beside her brother's motionless body and began to wail along with her husband, clutching at the figure he was cradling.

Taking in the sudden horror, Will recognized what must have happened and uttered, "Let's get him inside!" scooping the fallen boy into his arms. Pretty Bird clung to him, and Andy raced ahead to hold the door flap. His friend's head hung grotesquely as his father carried him to the fire.

White Quill's upper body was covered with blood. His neck and chest had been gashed open, and it was evident that there could be no life in him. His skull showed a vulgar white wound, where his scalp had been sliced, and his braid ripped from his head. Pretty Bird and Andy both fell at his side and wept hysterically. Will knelt over them and hugged them both as he stared at the young man they loved, the boy who moments earlier had been alive and joking—suddenly gone. Pretty Bird's wailing subsided into deep, uncontrollable sobs, while Andy held onto her tightly, weeping.

Suddenly, Good Friend burst through the doorway. *"Did White Quill come ba—"* His words were cut short when he saw, and he stopped cold in his tracks, gaping in shock at what he saw. Staring in silent disbelief for a moment, slowly, softly, he advanced and gazed down at his friends, his chin quivering and his eyes flooding with tears.

Just as suddenly as he had arrived, he whirled and bolted for the doorway, vanishing into the night and the shouting and confusion that now filled the darkness outside. Having no idea where he had gone, Will stayed with Andy and Pretty Bird, who held onto each other and wept over the one they had loved.

An eerie silence settled over the camp; only occasionally were quiet voices heard outside. Eventually, Andy looked up at his father, mournfully, and held out his arm to him. Will moved and embraced them both, to weep with them.

Good Friend and the warriors who had rallied in the darkness did not return that night. When light finally came, Will coaxed his son and his wife to allow him to remove the body and prepare it for burial. While he went about his grim task, they left to be by themselves. With their arms around each other and a robe over their shoulders, they disappeared. Will was grateful when Comes Last came to the lodge to inform him that the pair were at the crest of the river valley, mourning. Occasionally, after that, Will could hear them wailing.

Throughout the morning, Comes Last brought Will news of what had happened the night before. Raiders had gotten away with two more buffalo runners from inside the camp, but this time several other horses had also been run off from the main herd as well. The older men were speculating that at least two enemies had snuck into the camp, as they had on the previous night, and cut the two horses loose. They may have been attracted to Andy's lodge, being the only one in which there was a dim light and quiet voices. Whatever had happened, White Quill, stepping out of the lodge to relieve himself, had become their unfortunate victim. It would have all happened so fast he probably had no idea what was happening when he was grabbed from behind and his throat slashed. Fearing detection, it was surmised that the murderers had quickly taken his scalp and leapt upon the stolen mounts, racing to where they had already separated several horses from the herd, shouting their arrogant insults to the slumbering camp.

At midday, the camp was alerted that there were riders at the top of the ridge, and it was quickly ascertained that it was their returning warriors—waiting for the camp to assemble below. Andy and Pretty Bird saw what was happening and hurried back to the camp to stand anxiously among the others. They knew the warriors had met with victory—that is why they were waiting for the camp to assemble—but the people were left wondering, at what cost? Andy's family grew frantic when they could not pick out Good Friend among the warriors.

All at once, one of the warriors separated from the others and bolted down the hill, holding his bow aloft, singing his victory song. It was Good Friend's horse, but not recognizing its rider, Andy's heart sank, and his face contorted in anguish. He fell to his knees and began to sob uncontrollably. While Will and Pretty Bird tried to console him, the other warriors followed the first, racing down the ravine toward the camp, singing their songs.

Once they had made their way into the camp, their women ran along behind them, joining them in song, celebrating their return. Two of the warriors had their faces painted entirely black with red stripes, and those who understood what it meant, knew that they had each killed an enemy.

The one riding Good Friend's horse, leading the rest, came directly for Andy, and it was not until he stopped and called to him that Andy recognized his beloved friend behind the paint, his long hair cut short. Lifting his leg over the horse's neck and dropping to the ground, Good Friend strode up to Andy, looking him squarely in the eye. Taking his shocked friend into his arms, he held him close for a long time, both of them sobbing. When they separated, their faces were streaked with tears. Silently, Good Friend lifted his hand and displayed a thick, black braid of hair.

"I came alongside him and pulled him from his horse." His voice was empty of emotion. *"He swung his weapon at me, and I was able to grab it and pull him off. I then pursued the other... caught up to him, and he jumped from his horse to fight me. I was so angry, I jumped off mine and ran toward him...All I could think of was to swing my bow at him...But he had an arrow in his and shot it—missed, luckily. I just hit him. I hit him with my bow, but it did not do anything...We struggled a bit, and he got me down. I think that if it had not been for the others, he would have killed me,"* he announced, his voice beginning to show his relief at having survived the ordeal. *"They struck him...the others...and they killed the other one...but they let me—this one—kill him. He was almost dead. They gave me a club, and I killed him!"*

The two young men looked deep into each other's eyes, before Good Friend asked softly, *"He is gone?"* Andy could give no answer, but when he broke down, Good Friend knew. Ignoring everything else that was going on around them and the warriors who were still parading about, noisily proclaiming their victory, he took his friend in his arms, and they sobbed. Hearing his wife grieving nearby, Andy reached out and took her from his father's arms and the three of them embraced, crying.

When they finished, Good Friend handed the scalp he had taken to Pretty Bird. She snatched it and threw it in the dirt in front of her, spitting on it and stomping it with her foot, raging through her tears.

"They were Cutthroats," Good Friend announced dispassionately when she had worn herself out. *"Just two of them. And"*—he

continued, a glimmer of an uncertain smile upon his face— *"I struck one of them, or both, really. And I killed the one!"* Then, his eyes filled with sorrow, he admitted, *"I did not follow our medicine...All my eyes could see was our friend...and what they had done to him. Will your medicine hold that against me?"* he asked Andy.

"I do not know. We will have to talk to my father—but later— come with us." He took his wife by the waist and put his arm around Good Friend's shoulder, who tossed his rein to Comes Last, and they walked away sadly.

The trio made their way to the hilltop, where Andy and Pretty Bird had spent the morning. Returning to the camp in the afternoon, the couple had cut their hair cut short. The two Indians had wanted to cut their arms and legs as a sign of their grief, but Andy had stopped them. Instead, he and his wife had joined Good Friend in cutting their hair short as a sign of their mourning.

Will laboured through the day digging a suitable grave for the one who, just the day before, he had taken as his son. The ground was rocky, and there was no implement resembling a shovel. Using his bare hands and a stick, he and Comes Last had made a shallow grave, and while the rest of the camp celebrated the return of their warriors, Will helped bury a son.

None of them slept much that night, and the next morning, the camp moved.

24

Before White Quill's death, Badger and Good Friend had been trying to follow a path different from that of their peers. Without him, Badger found himself very much alone again. Some of the other young men had attempted to goad him into joining them on a retaliatory raid against the *Cutthroats,* but he ignored their urging, spending much of his time by himself. Many evenings, he spent talking to Andy and his father about the revenge he had taken against White Quill's killers. Blinded by rage, he had felt driven to exact vengeance upon those who had taken his friend's life; but now, it weighed heavily on him.

Both Will and Andy tried to explain the teachings of their god. They spoke of turning the other cheek and forgiving one's enemies, but Good Friend showed no response. Inside, he felt deeply conflicted, at once justified in the actions he had taken against his friend's killers yet burdened by the guilt of it. Other than Andy and Will, nobody in the camp understood his turmoil.

One day, he took Andy aside and asked for his help. *"I intend to seek a vision!"* he declared. *"I must find my own spirit helper...I hope it is your medicine which comes to me. If it does not come to me, then some other spirit—whatever comes to me—will be my helper,"* he announced with determination. *"I must know that there is something there! I must know! For me!"* The young Indian would not be deterred and stoically informed Andy that if he was not prepared to assist him, he would go alone.

Good Friend's decision concerned Andy; it was totally uncharacteristic of him and seemed impulsive. But since White Quill's death or since he had struck down the *Cutthroat*—Andy was not sure which—Good Friend seemed to have changed. Always brooding and showing a quickening temper, he had been struggling greatly.

Andy agreed to help him, and the plan was made to depart the next day. Going immediately to his father, Andy asked him what he should do. "Go with him!" Will told his son, after thinking about it for a moment. "If he is really seeking an encounter with God, he will have it! You need to be praying for him. And fasting—you fast with him, while he is out there! I will do the same. Go with him and encourage him to seek the God that is above all others. And tell him that he will find him if he seeks him with all his heart and all his soul and all his might. That is what the Bible says: with all our heart and all our soul and all our might! I know he will find him—because he is seeking!" Surprised, by the summary way his father advised him, Andy went to tell Pretty Bird of their mission and have her make arrangements for a sweat.

The next day, Andy and Good Friend entered the sweat lodge together. Will prayed silently, sitting near the tiny shelter, listening to the muffled petitions of its occupants. When they were finished, the pair walked solemnly to the river, before mounting their horses and heading for Good Friend's chosen site.

It was a high butte, which rose above the prairie, some distance from the river valley in which the camp stood. *"Someone has already sought his vision here,"* Good Friend observed, pointing out a shallow depression, which had been scraped out and surrounded with rocks. Grass was growing in it, so it had been some time since it had been used. Being the most prominent point on the plain for a considerable distance, it was not surprising that others would have chosen it for the same purpose. Now, laying his buffalo robe in the depression, Good Friend stripped himself and handed his clothes to his friend.

Andy reached out and hugged him tightly. *"I love you!"* he whispered to him, holding on to him until he stepped away.

"I love you too, brother!" the Indian sighed and turned away to stand at the end of his robe. Staring toward the eastern horizon, he did not look again at his friend. Andy tied the seeker's things onto his horse and rode away, leading his friend's horse.

Good Friend had pointed out a thicket, some distance away, where he wanted Andy to wait. There, Andy made a cold camp, and after tethering the horses, he began to pray. When darkness came, he laid down to try to sleep. He was not used to spending the night alone. The yelping of coyotes and the howling of wolves usually did not bother him, but thinking of his friend alone on the hilltop, he fretted and dozed fitfully. In the morning, although anxious to check on Good Friend, he forced himself to stay put and trust that his friend was safe. He had brought no food along, only water, determined that he too would fast.

Good Friend took no water when Andy went to check on him in the evening. *"I have heard nothing,"* he told his white friend glumly.

The second day, the Indian again took no drink, and while his friend sat with him in the sun's final rays, he asked, *"Does your medicine speak my tongue?"* Andy assured him that he did.

On the third day, Good Friend was sullen and despondent, having seen or heard nothing. He wondered if he should give up his quest. Remembering his father's admonition, Andy encouraged him to stick with it. He said he would and took a short drink.

On the fourth day, the sun was unusually warm, so Andy set out at midday to take water to his charge. As soon as he emerged from the thicket, he saw his friend making his way toward him. As they approached each other, he saw Good Friend's proud grin.

"Well, what happened?" he asked with great interest.

"I cannot tell you, but I know what I must do!" Good Friend announced confidently.

Andy was grinning. *"What? Tell me what happened!"*

"I cannot—you know we cannot say!" Nothing Andy could say would make him divulge what had happened on that hill, but he knew that something had changed. His friend was no longer moody and sullen and seemed to have returned to his former self, never speaking of whatever it was he had encountered upon his quest.

That fall, Andy became a father. Their camp was in a pleasant river valley, and the leaves had just begun to show the first bits of yellow when Pretty Bird's time came. On a warm fall day, attended by Good Friend's mother and his sister, she gave birth to a son. Nothing in his appearance gave away the fact that his father was a blonde-haired, white boy. His skin was brown, and his hair was black, but when he was hungry, Will informed them that his shrill cry sounded just like Andy when he was a baby. Andy loved his son and gave him the name, Matthew William Preston, but insisted he be called by the name of White Quill.

Devoted to his wife and his infant son, Andy was a much-admired presence in his camp, where some were very curious about the spirit power he seemed to possess that allowed him to maintain his countenance of peace. Having nothing to do with the warring of most his age, he did not seem to need to accomplish their heroic deeds. An enigma to them in that regard, he was loved by all.

As time wore on, Will and Good Friend spent less and less time camped with Andy and his family, and more time travelling together among the other camps of the Blackfoot. The following year, they met up along *Little High Wood Creek*, not far from the horseshoe canyon where Andy had spent his first winter among the *Piikáni,* and it was there that Pretty Bird announced that her bleeding had stopped, once again. Will and Good Friend were pleased to be there to celebrate the joyous news. Friends, when they heard it, came to call, bringing well-wishes. Sacrificially generous, some brought gifts, and one woman graciously laid a *napikawan* robe over the expectant mother's shoulders, an item her man had just brought her from the *napikawan* camp on the Big River. It was 1837.

AUTHOR'S AFTERWORD

In 1837, smallpox devastated the Indigenous peoples of the western plains of North America. The disease wiped out half or more of their population, killing or sparing at random. It shattered the dominance of some of the most powerful tribes, among them the Blackfoot, who were particularly hard hit. Some camps, some families were wiped out entirely by the capricious disease; some individuals were left horribly scarred and disfigured, yet many were left untouched. It is believed that the deadly disease was introduced among them from contaminated blankets, distributed as trade items from Fort Benton.

GLOSSARY

BLACKFOOT WORDS

ah - yes

Asinaa - the Cree, also referred to by the Blackfoot as the "Liars"

Atsíína - the Gros Ventre, periodic allies of the Blackfoot, who called them the "Gut People"

iiníí - buffalo

iksokapi - good; it is good

Káínaa - one of the three tribes of the Blackfoot confederacy, living mostly to the east of the range occupied by the *Piikáni;* referred to by Europeans as the Bloods

Kotonáá'wa - the *Ktunaxa* of southeastern British Columbia; referred to by the Europeans as the Kootanai; periodic allies of the Blackfoot

míísinsski - badger

Makhabn - the Bow River of Southern Alberta, flowing through modern-day Calgary. The word means the river where the bow reeds are found.

Mistakis - the Backbone (of the world) - the Rocky Mountains

Napi - Old Man, the one who the Blackfoot believe created the world *napikawan* - white man

napiohke - white man's water—liquor

Napi-tahta - Old Man's River, the Oldman River in southern Alberta

Ninastako - Chief Mountain (literally, the chief of the mountains) located in northern Montana just south of the Canadian border

nitapi waksin - real food, referring to buffalo meat

Niitsitapi - the real people - the Blackfoot name for themselves

Oki, tsa niitapi? - hello, how are you?

Piikáni - one of the three tribes of the Blackfoot confederacy, living along the Rocky Mountains in an area extending from the North Saskatchewan River in Alberta to the Musselshell River in Montana. Originally referred to by the Europeans as peecunie, they are now referred to as the Peigan in Canada and the Blackfeet in the United States.

saa—no

Siksika - literally, black foot - one of the three tribes of the Blackfoot confederacy, living to the northeast of the Piikáni

sinopah - a small fox - sometimes used as a term of endearment for small children

BLACKFOOT TERMS AND EXPRESSIONS

Almost mother, or almost brother, or other relative — someone who stands in the position of a blood relative, often a man's second or subsequent wives.

Always summer land — the hot, arid land of the southern United States

Bear River — the Marias River of northern Montana

Blackfoot — a federation of three tribes, the Siksika (Blackfoot), the Piikáni (the Peigan), and the Káínaa (the Bloods), all sharing a common language

Black wind — warm, westerly "Chinook" winds of southern Alberta and northern Montana

Big mouth fire-stick — cannon

Big River — a term which could mean either the North Saskatchewan River in northern Alberta or the Missouri River of Montana, depending upon the context

Place of the Sweet Pine — one of the names for the Sweetgrass Hills in northern Montana. Also known to the Blackfoot as the Blood Clot Hills.

Brave Dog Society — A society of young men whose responsibility it was to police the camp and maintain order

Buffalo runner — an especially fast and well-trained horse used for hunting buffalo

Cold Maker — the spirit which brings cold weather and rules the winter

Crow — the Crow

Cutthroats — the Assiniboine

Dog face — someone with a beard, a white man.

Elk River — the Yellowstone River in Montana

Fire-stick — the long-barrelled musket of the Europeans

Gut People — or Entrails People, the Gros Ventre

Home days — summer

Liars — the Cree

Little High Wood Creek — Pincher Creek in southern Alberta

Long tail — magpie or cougar, depending on context

Medicine — the term used by most of the plains Indians to describe supernatural or spiritual power. One's spirit helper, the spirit of some creature that had committed to assist the individual, was also called his "medicine"

Medicine bundle — a bundle of items, such as animal skins, feathers, rocks, and artefacts which the holder believed gave him supernatural power

Medicine man — a man believed to be the possessor of great spiritual power, which he could wield and command at will for the good, or ill, of anyone he chose

North Inside Big Water — Waterton Lake, Alberta

Parted Hairs — the Lakota

Real bear — grizzly bear

Sand Hills — the place of the Blackfoot afterlife, situated in southeastern Saskatchewan

Silver swimmers — fish

Sits beside me wife — the main wife of a Blackfoot man. A man often had many wives who came under his protection and provision and aided his sits beside me wife in household chores, mainly, handling and processing the buffalo and hides

Snakes — the Shoshone

Society of Mosquitoes — one of the Blackfoot societies, open to young boys only.

South Inside Big Water — St. Mary's Lake, Montana

Spotted Horses People — the Cheyenne

Sticky mouth — black bear

Stoneys — the Nakota, of central Alberta

The big water — the ocean

The North Trail — an ancient trail along the foot of the mountains, running from the North Saskatchewan River on the north, to the Yellowstone River on the south, and beyond

The season of ripe berries — summer

The seven persons — *Ursa major*, the big dipper

The time of the first frost — late fall

Thunder — the spirit which rules the summer

Two Medicine River — the Two Medicine River in north-central Montana

Underwater person — spirit beings who the Blackfoot believed to inhabit the waters

War lodge – a makeshift shelter made from sticks and branches

When the buffalo calves are black — mid-winter

When the buffalo calves are yellow — early spring

When the buffalo plant is in flower — spring

When the geese fly south — late fall

When the geese come back — early spring

When the grass becomes green — spring

When the jackrabbits whistle at night — mid-winter

When the leaves are yellow — fall

Wolf Trail — the Milky Way, the path taken by departed spirits to reach the Sand Hills

Wolf song — a song of good luck

EUROPEAN EXPRESSIONS

'baccy - tobacco

Big Bellies - European expression used to describe the Gros Ventre

Bug's Boys - from a biblical reference to the devil, a phrase used by trappers and Early Europeans referring to the Blackfoot

Coup stick - from the French term, to hit or to strike. It refers to the practice of claiming honour in war by striking an enemy

Pecunnies - name used by some of the Europeans for the Piikáni, a mispronunciation

Upper house - Rocky Mountain House, so referred to because it was above Edmonton House on the North Saskatchewan River

Printed in Canada